# COLOUR ME
# WHITE

**A novel**

# Ed Bonner

bonner.edwin@gmail.com

2024

*This book is dedicated to my wife, Adrianne, for her patience, tolerance and critical skills and above all her unflagging encouragement.*

*The book is dedicated to the memory of my parents Riva and Orka, Sabina and Seftel for their stories and their values.*

ISBN: 9798339524021
Imprint: Independently published

bonner.edwin@gmail.com

2024

# Table of Contents

Chapter 1: *Department for Racial Reclassification, Wynberg, Cape Town  1976* .............................................................. 1

Chapter 2: *Groote Schuur  1976* ...................................... 10

Chapter 3: *District Six / Manenberg / Mitchell's Plain  1958 - 1976* ................................................................... 18

Chapter 4: *Sea Point  1958 -1976* ................................... 27

Chapter 5: *Groote Schuur  1976* ...................................... 40

Chapter 6: *Taken by the Music Manenberg  1977* .............. 48

Chapter 7: *Fresnaye, Sea Point  1976* ............................. 54

Chapter 8: *Toilet duty  1977* ............................................ 60

Chapter 9: *The English patient* ........................................ 64

Chapter 10: *The Newlands Hotel  1977* ............................. 70

Chapter 11: *Cruel Death of a Courageous Man  1977* ........... 79

Chapter 12: *The Good Doctor  1953 -1977* ........................ 82

Chapter 13: *Protest  1978 -1982* ..................................... 88

Chapter 14: *London  1982* ............................................... 95

Chapter 15: *Richard Simpson  1984* ................................. 107

Chapter 16: *Obz  1985* .................................................. 117

Chapter 17: *Sophie goes to Berlin  1985* .......................... 124

Chapter 18: *The Defence and Aid Fund  1985 - 1990* ......... 128

Chapter 19: *Karen  1982 - 1999* .................................... 133

Chapter 20: *The end of Thatcher  1990* ........................... 137

Chapter 21: *Simon  1996 - 2001* .................................... 141

Chapter 22: *Philip  2001 - 2005* ..................................... 147

Chapter 23: *Sophie's return  1996 - 2005* ........................ 157

Chapter 24: *The Prisoner  2005* ...................................... 169

Chapter 25: *Simon Loses It  2005* ................................... 174

Chapter 26: *The TV Debate  2005* ................................. 177

Chapter 27: *The Darkside Doctor  2005* ......................... 180

Chapter 28: *Mr John Jameson  1979 - 2005*..................... 188

Chapter 29: *Old Friends Meet Again  2005*...................... 192

Chapter 30: *Names Become Faces  2005*........................ 196

Chapter 31: *A Lesson in Star Wars  2005* ....................... 203

Chapter 32: *The cat is unbagged  2006*.......................... 208

Chapter 33: *The Press Club Luncheon  2006* ................... 214

Chapter 34: *Nervous Expectations  2006*........................ 219

Chapter 35: *A Night to Remember  2007*........................ 223

Chapter 36: *The Reunion* ............................................. 228

Chapter 37: *The Aftermath*............................................ 236

Chapter 38: *Politics  2008 - 2010*................................... 239

Chapter 39: *Skoppensboer  2010* ................................... 244

Chapter 40: *Unfinished Business  2010* .......................... 250

Chapter 41: *Further Unfinished Business  2010* ................ 253

Chapter 42: *Mr X  2015* ............................................... 262

Chapter 43: *State Capture  2017* ................................... 265

Chapter 44: *Sophie's Choice  2018*................................. 269

Chapter 45: *Bali  2019* ................................................ 272

Chapter 46: *Salt River – the Shelter  2019* ...................... 275

Chapter 47: *Farewell  2020* .......................................... 278

Chapter 48: *The Plague  2020* ...................................... 281

Chapter 49: *Paying the Piper  2024* ............................... 288

Chapter 50: *Colour Me White*........................................ 290

*Acknowledgements* ..................................................... 292

*About the Author* ........................................................ 293

*"Overcoming poverty is not a gesture of charity. It is an act of justice.*

*It is the protection of a human right, the right to dignity and a decent life."*

**Nelson Mandela 2012**

*"Let them live but let them be woodcutters and water carriers in the service of the whole assembly." So the leaders' promise to them was kept.*

**Joshua 9:21**

## SKOPPENSBOER

'n Druppel gal is in die soetste wyn;   *A drop of gall is in the sweetest wine;*

'n traan is op elk' vrolik' snaar,   *a tear's on every happy chord,*

in elke lag 'n sug van pyn,   *in every laugh a sigh of pain,*

in elke roos 'n dowwe blaar.   *in every rose a dead petal.*

Die een wat deur die nag ons pret beloer   *The one who through the night observes our fun*

en laaste lag, is Skoppensboer.   *and laughs last, is the Jack of Spades.*

**Afrikaans poem by EUGENE MARAIS**

# Glossary

Dagga – cannabis

Skunk – Industrial strength cannabis

Tik – methamphetamine, meth

Skoppensboer - The Angel of Death

Afrikaner – white South African of Dutch origin

Afrikaans – Afrikaners' language of Dutch origin

Kleurling - Afrikaans term for person of mixed race (pleural: Kleurlinge)

Coloured, Cape Coloured, Cape Malay – official classification of mixed-race people in South Africa

Kapie – colloquial term for Cape Coloured people

ANC – African National Congress

'Bleddy' – mispronunciation of 'bloody', meaning 'very', as in 'bleddy nice'

AND THEY SAID IT WAS OK

And they said it was ok
It said so in the bible
And if it said so in the bible
It must be ok and it was.

They were hewers of wood
And drawers of water
And their skins were dark
And their hair was short

and curly and the pencil
Would stick and not fall out
So they were natives
But could not be owners.

Their places were behind. Sparse,
They could only live there
By special permit
called *Dompas* - dumb passes

That had to be shown
On demand or else
Although the land was theirs
And they were ten to one

And the others one to ten
But *they* made the laws
Because their hair was straight
And their skins light

And those in between
Were not one to ten nor ten to one
But little to anyone
Except themselves.

And they said it was ok.

## *Apartheid*

*Legal discrimination along racial lines in South Africa ended with the demise of apartheid but racial categorisation is still being used by the government for monitoring economic changes and continues to cause controversy.*

**Mohammed Allie**

*The apartheid-era Population Registration Act of 1950 classified the population of South Africa on the basis of their race. Nearly 80% were classified as 'Native' (Black), 9% Coloured, 9% White, 2% Indian.*

*Coloureds (Afrikaans: Kleurlinge) are a multi-racial ethnic group native to Southern Africa who have ancestry from more than one of the various populations inhabiting the region. In the Western Cape, a distinctive Cape Coloured and affiliated Cape Malay culture developed. They form nearly half of the total population of the Western Cape. Genetic studies suggest the group has the highest levels of mixed ancestry in the world. The maternal lines of the Coloured population are descended mostly from ethnic African Khoisan women. Western European lineages contributed 37% to paternal components and South Asian lineages 18%.*

*Although 'apartheid' no longer officially exists, the population of South Africa continues to be classified on the basis of their race.*

*White South Africans are South Africans of European descent. In linguistic, cultural and historical terms, they are generally divided into the Afrikaans-speaking descendants of the Dutch East India Company's original settlers and known as Afrikaners, and the Anglophone descendants of predominantly British colonists. 60% speak Afrikaans, while 40% are native English speakers.*

# Chapter 1:

## *Department for Racial Reclassification, Wynberg, Cape Town 1976*

The journey from Mitchell's Plain on the windswept Cape Flats to Wynberg in the leafy suburbs of Cape Town was only about fifteen kilometres, but they were worlds apart. She sat on the crowded and uncomfortable bus seeing but not seeing the corrugated houses of the black townships and then the poorer white suburbs flashing by. Then there were trees, everywhere; gardens, manicured pavements, parks. You didn't get that in Mitchell's or Manenberg, she thought, although she could vaguely remember the greenery on Table Mountain lording it above District Six before they were relocated.

Karen Willemse was filled with trepidation. She was en route to meet the person whom she hoped would be the bridge from her world to the other, and she reflected that of course the person would be a man and of course he would be white, because that was the way of things in 1976 apartheid South Africa.

The world she hoped to leave behind was one of unemployment, grinding poverty, alcohol, drugs and crime; a world where aspiration was in very short supply. This was a time of student political upheaval and brutal police suppression in the black townships, but for the people who were neither white nor black - the inhabitants of the Cape Flats, the mixed-race Kleurlinge - political rights were less of a problem than poverty and crime, drugs and drink. Karen Willemse wanted out.

Karen knew that certain official tests had been set up to determine the race of individuals who wanted to appeal against their birth classification. The most infamous of

## CHAPTER 1: DEPARTMENT FOR RACIAL RECLASSIFICATION, WYNBERG, CAPE TOWN 1976

these was the *krill* test - if a pencil placed in one's hair fell out, they were white. If it fell out with shaking, *Kleurling,* and if it stayed put, black. That simple. Imagine that, she thought, a simple pencil could determine the cards that life would deal for you. Insane! Regrettably, Karen was well aware that other tests might also take place. Individuals could also be subjected to humiliating examinations of the colour of their genitalia or any other body part that the determining official felt was a clear marker of race.

One of her older cousins, Katrina, had 'passed' this test. The pencil had fallen, but her examining officer was a vile white man who still had made her drop her *broekies* and then fiddled with that part of her body where he was in no way welcome to go. It was rumoured that others had suffered worse. Kat had gone on to get a well-paid job in Johannesburg and married her white manager. She had only ever been back twice to visit her mother and that was without her husband. They had seen photos of him. No-one admired Kat, but many envied her.

Karen hoped that by making a good impression on the white man, he would exert his power by signing a piece of paper that would be her passport to a world of employment and high earnings, a world where she could live in her own apartment, where the buses had seats and not wooden planks; a world where she could sip cocktails in an air-conditioned hotel lounge and not have to drink the excuse for brandy that was wrecking her father's liver.

She understood that if that document could be gotten, it would mean estranging herself from her parents, family and her many friends. Yes, she could visit them whenever she wished, but they would have difficulty in visiting her. A wedge would be created that would drive them increasingly apart until eventually there would be little left of her old world - a world obsessed with race, and because of this, beset by poverty.

What of the man she was about to meet, Mr Kobus van den Berg? He would certainly be a descendant of the Dutch settlers who had sailed 300 years before from Holland into Table Bay Cape Town on the *Goede Hoop.* As a member of the ruling white Nationalist party, he would consider himself apart from and significantly superior to her. He would be confident, disdainful. He would be in control. They always were.

She wondered how Mr van den Berg would see her, this young woman from Mitchell's Plain, a large and growing Kleurling township on the outskirts of Cape Town about which he would have heard much but seen nothing because not many whites went there. Would he assume that her family, like so many others after centuries without hope, respect, or aspiration, had succumbed to drink or meth? Certainly her father was going that way.

What would Mr van den Berg want of Karen for him to sign those papers? Would he settle for just the pencil test? Unlikely. She was certain he would not hesitate to transgress the rigorously enforced racial laws created by his own people to prevent people of different colour from crossing the ethnic line they called the colour bar. She could picture him looking her up and down, deciding whether fucking her would be the price she would have to pay. Was she happy to pay that price?

Karen checked in at the reception of an unprepossessing three-storey building that was home to the Department of Racial Reclassification, walked to the first floor and sat in a dull, cream-coloured waiting room, where the only picture was one of his President – their President.

It is part of South African folklore that the nation of mixed-race people who later carried the inglorious racial classification of 'Coloureds' began nine months after the arrival of the first Dutch settlers in the Cape in 1652. This of course was another white arrogance. The uncomfortable truth was that the indigenous dusk-skinned hunter-gatherer San people had been there for thousands of years before the Dutch ships arrived. Those Dutch Protestants were to form the Afrikaans people into which Jacobus (Kobus) Willem van den Bergh would be born nearly three hundred years later, by which time the Boer War had already been fought and lost against the intensely disliked British.

Kobus had been named for his two grandfathers who had both been farmers, as had their Dutch forebears. Fortune had not smiled on Kobus's grandfathers. Having lost their farms under English rule in the early nineteen-hundreds, they had struggled to find work in the neighbouring towns of Stellenbosch and Paarl. It got worse until the white Afrikaner Nationalist Party that came to power in 1948 formed *die Broederbond* – the Brotherhood – and created posts in the civil service especially for unemployed or displaced Afrikaners. Kobus would have earned his position as Director of the Race Reclassification Board not by his education but by membership of that brotherhood.

Kobus van den Berg looked at his list. Next was a girl aged 18, from one of those nearby Coloured towns (one should really say 'residential suburbs for Coloureds only'), where the people were of more hues than the drab houses. By and large, the Cape Coloureds were an unfortunate people, accepted neither by the indigenous blacks nor the colonial whites. Indeed, they were regarded as a separate nation, which was the reason that, to distinguish them from whites or blacks, 'Coloureds' was spelt with a capital 'C'. Many of them drank heavily, and for the most part had ceased the struggle to raise themselves from the madness that was apartheid.

No wonder this pretty girl wanted out, he thought as he studied her photograph and neatly written application form. He called her name: Miss Karen Willemse. An Afrikaans name.

She knocked and entered. She saw the man in whose hands the cards of her future were sitting and about to be dealt. His large office was entirely unremarkable, its only redeeming feature being the large window affording a view of the huge umbrella pines lining the slopes of majestic Table Mountain, to which his desk faced. To his left were several huge khaki-coloured filing cabinets. Three were filled with reclassification applications, four with files of those already rejected this year, and only half of one with those of applicants who had passed the *'krill'* test.

Kobus was fortyish, quite short, quite wide, and had more hair above his lip than on his head. He was by no means what you would call handsome but was an easy-going man whose bass voice would roar with laughter especially when jokes with a racial slant were repeated. He was liked and respected by his white staff, and his family adored him. Karen looked at the family photograph on his desk – wife, four children, all shiny white – no need for gang culture there, none of the humiliation of serving a race to whom you meant nothing, to whom you were just cheap labour, as her parents had done and been all their lives.

Kobus was immediately struck by her appearance: tall, slim, elegant. Good-looking. Not a big backside like some of them, but nice enough. Light-skinned and hair that would make the *krill* test unnecessary, but he would do it anyway. No good letting these people get ideas beyond their station. As he looked at her standing nervously in front of him, he felt that powerful throb in his trousers just south of the border; all the more thrilling because he was well aware that sex between whites and the other racial groups was strictly prohibited in law by the Immorality Act. Therefore, she was forbidden fruit; and as Kobus well knew, forbidden fruit tasted sweetest.

## CHAPTER 1: DEPARTMENT FOR RACIAL RECLASSIFICATION, WYNBERG, CAPE TOWN 1976

Now he spoke:

*'Goeie more, Juffrou Willemse – jy kan sit.'*

'Good morning, Meneer van den Berg, but I prefer to stand.'

'I see you also prefer to speak English, Miss Willemse...Why? Most of you Kleurlinge speak Afrikaans, what I think is a much better language than English. Whatever; my English is OK also. What I can do for you, Miss Willemse?'

'You can colour me white.'

Kobus chuckled at the perceived absurdity of her request. 'You think I'm a magician? What, just wave a magic wand?'

'Your pen is your wand, Meneer; you can sign the form that will change my life.'

'You think a piece of paper can make you white? It doesn't work that way. You is white, or you isn't. Simple. In any case, why you want to be white? Not that I'm blaming you, of course.'

'*Meneer,* you don't understand. I don't want to **be** white. I want to be **classified** white. My people don't have equality. We are treated like shit. The only jobs we can get, if we're lucky, is in factories or as maids. I want a better chance with *you* people. I want to be a nurse. If you classify me white, I can get into the white nursing college at Groote Schuur.'

'We need Kleurling nurses too, you know.'

'I'll get paid more if I'm white, a lot more. You know that. It's the only way I can improve my earnings, take care of my parents.'

'I'm not interested in how much you can earn, Willemse, I'm interested in keeping wiffa rules.'

'The rules are fokken stupid, Meneer.'

'*I* don't make the rules. *They* do,' said Kobus, motioning to the photo of the President on the wall.

'Why such stupid ones, Meneer?'

'They keeps us whites pure. We doesn't want to be mixed like you.'

'So why you Afrikaners like fucking us Kleurling girls so much?'

'Careful, Willemse. I could throw you out just for that. Personally, such activities is not my preference.'

With a sardonic grin, Karen sneered, 'There isn't an Afrikaner man born who wouldn't *naai* me if he got the chance.'

'Don't push your luck, Willemse, ok?'

She wondered if she should have called him *Baas.* That was how they liked to be addressed – it showed respect. Boss.

'Well, what about it, Meneer van den Berg? Will you colour me white?'

'Very unlikely, Willemse. How much white blood have you got?'

'My grandfather on my mother's side, and my great-grandfather on my father's side.'

'That's enough to make you a Kleurling, which you already is, but nowhere near enough to make you white.'

'Maybe there's more, how do I know? My mother was a beautiful woman when she was young. Maybe my father's not my father, maybe he was the director of the hotel where she works...... how do I know what she did to keep her job? In any case, *my* people think I am quite white.'

'That's just compared wif them.'

'There's plenty Afrikaners more dark than me.'

'I told you lady, don't be cheeky..... but OK let's talk. Your skin is quite light and your hair is not so *krilly*. If I wanted to - which at the minute I doesn't - I could do things for you.'

'How much will it cost, Meneer? I don't have much cash.'

'You can pay in other ways too you know, Willemse.'

*There. It had been said. They understood each other. Now just the price to be settled.*

## CHAPTER 1: DEPARTMENT FOR RACIAL RECLASSIFICATION, WYNBERG, CAPE TOWN 1976

Karen winced - she knew it would come down to this. It always did.

'You've got a bleddy good body, Willemse. How many of us Afrikaners you fucked? Lots?'

'That's none of your business! Your business is, if I let you enjoy yourself, will you give me the papers?'

'I could try, maybe.'

'Trying is no good. Just give me what I need and then I will give you what you want.'

'I'm not stupid, Willemse. You think I'm going to give you papers and then you say *tot-siens* and tra-la-la off you go? No, lady, it's your call. You go first.'

'OK, you give me the papers, and same time I will give you what your *piel* is banging under the table for.'

'It's you who is bleddy cocky, Wllemse - I ekshly don't like fucking Kleurling women, but I do like white women what is sexy, so ok I will make you white. And when you are white, then it's not illegal to give you some good Afrikaans *piel*, Miss bleddy lucky Willemse....'

'I want you also to change my name to Williams.'

'You want to be English too? Maybe you want to eat *piel* also.'

'I'll do whatever you say, *Baas* - just give me the papers.........'

Kobus van den Berg got up to lock his door - not that the receptionist downstairs didn't know what would be happening - and when he returned to his seat, Karen could hardly miss observing the bulge in his khaki trousers. This randy *oke* means business, she thought. She grimaced as her mouth tasted the bile. She mustn't retch, not now.

He motioned for her to come and stand next to him. He reached for a pile of forms on his right, took one and placed it in front of him. As he started writing, he began to stroke that not very big but nice-enough backside with his left hand. His lips went dry. He licked them. Karen Willemse stared straight ahead at the portrait of the white President of the Republic of South Africa on the wall opposite the desk and wondered whether he too had a predilection for women of a darker hue. Quickly, she redirected her attention to Kobus, whose hand was now moving vigorously on her arse. She was taller than this panting seated man. She could see the beads of sweat on Kobus van den Burg's head and wanted to add her spit but controlled herself. It was all she could do not to throw up.

He signed the document. Stood, walked round behind her. She turned her head to look at him and saw the spreading stain. It was her good fortune, that like most men in such a situation, his desire was well ahead of his performance, and all Kobus van den Burg managed to do was to soil the front of the khaki trousers that had been pressed so neatly by Anna, his black maid. Anna, whom he loved to *naai* whenever his wife and kids were out, salving his conscience by paying her a few extra rands; nothing that would make him poor or her well-off, but enough for her to buy a new toy for her little boy back home in the townships.

As he stood there gasping and clutching his crotch, Karen Williams, nee Willemse, grabbed her new passport to freedom and headed for the door, slamming it as she heard him curse her nation: *'Fokken bleddy Kleurlinge!'*

Karen wanted to vomit when she left the office, and very nearly did in the bus on the way back to her home. One would have expected her to feel traumatised by the experience, but Karen was nothing if not resilient. Once the nausea of Kobus passed, she felt elated. The price thus far had proved relatively modest, and the prize would be life-changing, because Karen was now officially white and had papers to prove it. She was certain of one thing though – the way ahead would not be straightforward. The colour of her skin, not the papers she now carried, would always be the way by which she would be judged. That was what apartheid was all about.

# Chapter 2:

## *Groote Schuur 1976*

Cape Town on a sunny summer's day is the most beautiful of cities. On one such January afternoon, the sky was cloudless. The sun scorched down on imperious Table Mountain and the suburbs that rested below. In the courtyard of the famous Cape Town hospital that was Groote Schuur (pronounced *Skeer,* meaning *Big Barn*), a nervous group of thirty newly enrolled nursing trainees had been milling round for the last twenty minutes. Filled with trepidation, waiting to hear the inaugural address by the small, severe, middle-aged Matron Gray. Amongst this group of innocents were two eighteen-year-olds, Karen Williams and Sophie Levine, as different from each other as they were from the rest of the group, but for very different reasons. Sophie was Jewish, but she was white. Being white granted her a status far higher than Karen's. They had one thing in common though - both were *buiterstaanders,* outsiders.

Groote Schuur is one of the most respected and easily the most beautiful of the large rambling Cape hospitals that had first seen the light of day in the late nineteen-thirties. Matron Gray's corn-coloured, close-shorn hair seemed to blend imperceptibly with the amber walls reflecting the rays of sunshine peering over the side of Table Mountain and Devil's Peak. Unlike those walls, however, she was not splattered with bird shit, although many of those who had been in her charge for a while thought it would be no less than she deserved.

Matron Gray had spent her entire adult life at this august institution in the forefront of healthcare for the white residents of Cape Town. The venerable spinster, who began her every speech by saying 'My name is Matron Gray and kindly address me as such' pursed her thin lips and peered over her gold-rimmed spectacles at the crowd assembled before her. They always looked the same: nervous, unsure. She knew that in two years' time, they would be proud, confident and eager. They were her putty, and she would mould them; and heaven help those who would not be shaped.

She reminded the group of student nurses of the importance of maintaining the highest of ethical standards. They were only the latest recipients, she said, of the moral baton that thousands had carried before them, and, one hoped, thousands would after. She ran a very tight ship, and she wasn't about to let any novice with misplaced attitudes about sexual freedom or disrespectful conduct lower her standards, nor those of the famous hospital. They were informed in a quiet but unmistakably warning-laden tone that the excesses of the swinging sixties and seventies had no role to play at Groote Schuur. Political activities (covert for anti-government agitation) would not be tolerated. Anyone who dared to as much as think otherwise would receive the shortest of shrift, be handed a letter of excommunication and be unceremoniously cast out.

She emphasised to the rather nervous group, most of whom were barely out of school, 'The motto of this hospital is *Servamus - we serve.* Never forget that, and never forget that ten years ago at this very hospital, Professor Christian Barnard carried out the world's first heart transplant on Mr Louis Washkansky even though he was a Jew. We are proud to uphold that tradition of excellence, and no one here will bring that down. Do I make myself clear?'

The throng was silent.

'*Do I make myself clear?!*'

'Ja, Matron Gray', they chorused.

'Now, go and pick a roommate, find rooms, get a good night's sleep and be in Ward 4 at exactly 7a.m. Be warned

## CHAPTER 2: GROOTE SCHUUR 1976

- I do not tolerate lateness. Ten seconds past seven is the same as ten minutes past seven. BOTH ARE LATE.'

Some had already picked their mates. For others that was a task still to be done. Sophie was one who had not yet been invited to share. This was probably not because of her appearance. Unusually for a Jewish girl, Sophie was blond. Like most women in the group, she looked to be of standard Afrikaans or English–speaking Christian background and did not stand out in any way whatsoever. She assumed therefore that it must be because of the surname she bore on her nameplate - Levine, not one commonly found in such a group. Her background ensured she would forever be on the edges of South African society, so it was up to her to make the first move.

Sophie's eyes scanned the group, settled on the tall figure pushing a strand of black hair from her perfect face as she stood on her own at the edge of the group. The olive-skinned young woman seemed strangely out of place, far more than she. Sophie approached her, eyed her nametag. Karen Williams. Sophie was small, attractive and feisty with short blond hair and deep blue eyes, but in the prettiness stakes she ran second to the slim and statuesque Karen.

'Hey, howzit Karen, have you got a roommate yet?'

Karen, quite nervous, replied wistfully, '*Nee, man*, it seems I'm not very popular at this moment.' The moment Karen spoke, her accent told everything one needed to know. The beautiful woman with whom Sophie now shook hands was obviously of mixed-race stock that in apartheid South Africa was a race apart. Their backgrounds were as different as two women's could be. To say that Karen's heritage was much less salubrious than that of Sophie was not an exaggeration, but from the moment Sophie spoke with Karen, they felt the instant connection of the outsider.

'Well, Miss Karen Williams, I'd be very pleased if you'd share with me.'

Karen's look of delight left Sophie in no doubt that she had chosen well.

As they unpacked their small suitcases, Sophie asked the question Karen had been dreading. 'Where you from?'

'There, near Observatory.'

'Don't bullshit me, Karen, ok? If we're going to be mates, and I hope we will, there's no room for telling porkies. So, where you from?'

'Mitchell's Plain.'

'Thought so.'

'And you?'

'Sea Point.'

'I didn't think Jewish girls from Sea Point did nursing.'

'They don't. They go to university to get an MRS degree. They study psychology or get married to rich *okes*, preferably both.'

'So what you doing here?'

'In Sea Point everyone thinks alike. That can be very limiting. The lady in number 57 will have exactly the same values as the woman in number 56 or number 58. Whatever anyone says echoes what's in everyone else's mind. It's like hearing the same news on the radio all day long. That can be stifling. I had to break out of that zone of comfort, find a real challenge. Does that make sense to you?"

'No, not at all. We just *soek* to do what's the easiest.'

'This place doesn't look so easy to me.'

'Listen, I seen what was coming if I stuck around there in Mitchell's. It's Povertyville. Drugs. Babies, lots of. Husbands who beat you and then fuck off, never to be seen again. This is my chance to earn a decent living, to get away from a life without hope. My big chance.'

'Well, babe, seems like we're in this together so let's not bugger it up.....'

'Sophie?'

'Ja?'

## CHAPTER 2: GROOTE SCHUUR 1976

'Thanks.'

A few minutes later, a knock on the door was followed by a note slipped under it. *"Matron Gray wishes to see trainees Williams and Levine in her office in fifteen minutes."*

Immediate panic. Where was the Matron's office? What would happen if they couldn't find it and were late? But find it they did with five minutes to spare. They stood nervously in the corridor outside.

'Why do you think she wants to speak to us, Sophie? Are we in shit already? Surely that isn't possible.'

'We're about to find out. Here she comes.'

The Matron stormed into her office summoning the two nervous novices to follow.

She turned to face them. 'Listen very carefully. Hear what I am about to say. I do not like trouble. I repeat, I - DO - NOT - LIKE - TROUBLE. I have singled you two out because you are different, and I sense potential problems from both of you. Levine, we don't get many Jewgirls doing nursing, in fact I can count on the fingers of one finger how many we've had, and that's you. You people', she sneered, 'too posh to clean bedpans, hey?'

Sophie was not sure whether to respond. She muttered: 'Well, I'm here, Matron Gray.'

'When I want your opinion, I'll ask for it!'

'I thought you had, Matron Gray, you said -'

Mistake.

'Shut up, Levine!!! I can see that you will not last long here....'

'Yes, Matron Gray, sorry Matron Gray.'

'And as for you, Williams, you can fool some of the people ... I don't know how you got in here...' She peered at her notes. 'Oh I see, Kobus van den Bergh ... we know all about him! Now listen very carefully, it will take just one false move to make me send you back to you know very well where. Do I make myself clear? DO I MAKE MYSELF CLEAR, WILLIAMS?!'

14

Karen couldn't get the words out quickly enough: 'Ja, Matron Gray.'

'Now get out, the pair of you, and stay out of trouble!'

Like a duet in an opera, soprano Karen and mezzo Sophie responded in one voice, 'Ja, Matron Gray.'

They couldn't exit quickly enough.

As they lay on their rather hard mattresses in their plain and not very large room, they began to talk.

'You know, Karen, when I was a girl at school, the teachers treated me like an adult. Now that I'm supposedly grown up, they treat us like bloody children. My father wasn't thrilled when I chose to do nursing.' The thought ran through her mind that perhaps her father had been right, perhaps this suffocating environment was not for a person used to expressing herself freely. Nevertheless, she was determined not to allow herself to be cowed.

Over the next days, Karen would describe to Sophie what growing up in the townships was like. It was not a world she, Sophie, had experienced. It was not a world any white girl knew.

'I've never been out that way, except to the airport,' Sophie mused shamefully.

'Tell me something I don't know. Very few white people do come to the townships. Except doctors.'

'Actually, my dad's a doctor, and he goes to a clinic in that area every month for a whole day. I think it's in Manenberg. He's told us a lot about it, so I'm not entirely clueless.'

Karen smiled wryly. 'I used to live in Manenberg. When I was younger, I thought that all whites were doctors because doctors were the only whites who came there. Maybe I even saw your dad. Then we moved to Mitchell's Plain.'

'Tell me about Mitchell's.'

'I was only there in my teens. I was born in District Six - we could see Table Mountain from our window. You know

CHAPTER 2: GROOTE SCHUUR 1976

what, Sophie, we were bleddy happy there. The first ten years of my life were such lekker fun you wouldn't believe. I used to play silly games with the dozens of other kids in the streets and in the little park. There were lots of flowers and lots of trees in that park, it was really nice.'

'District Six doesn't exist anymore, does it?'

'No, the bleddy government didn't want mixed-race people in white areas contaminating them, so they flattened it and moved us out to Manenberg. Now that was the bleddy pits, I can tell you. I didn't *smaak* Manenberg, not at all, but then we moved to Mitchell's Plain. I was very happy in Mitchell's.'

'What was your school like?'

'Crowded, but it wasn't so bad. I was probably the only one in the class who did any homework, always got top marks, but I was more interested in sport, especially netball. Captain, if you don't mind!'

Sophie laughed. 'Ja, I can just see you bossing the smaller ones around!'

'The boys at my school used to come and watch us play, not because they liked netball but because they could catch lots of sights of our white *broekies* as our little skirts flew up. We *smaaked* teasing them so we made sure we did a lot of jumping. Then those *okes* would discuss which of us girls would likely have the best *doos.* One of our girls got into a stack of trouble because she played one match when she wasn't wearing *broekies*. She went commando, completely *kaalgat*. You could see her *doos,* hair and all! Phew, our coach was *woes,* really angry, and suspended her from the team for a month. Nobody tried that stunt again!'

'And out of school?'

'That's for you to guess. Lots of peer pressure. The boys were heavy into smoking dagga. The girls, we had to help in our homes. More often than not our mothers were out working, the dads many out of work and getting heavy drunk so the older children had to care for the kids. In some

16

ways I was lucky I was an only child, but I used to go and help my best friend Sarie, she had five to look after. I think that's where I got the feeling to do nursing. We didn't have luxury, but the community made up for it, warm and friendly. We cared for each other, a lot, you know, but then the drug dealers fucked up everything good an' proper.'

How the two came to be such close friends is not easily explained, but they gravitated to each other like opposite poles of a magnet. Despite, or more likely because of their differences, they were to become inseparable until events that had everything to do with the prevailing policy of apartheid were to drive their lives in very different directions.

# Chapter 3:

## *District Six / Manenberg / Mitchell's Plain 1958 -1976*

A short distance from the beautiful city centre of Cape Town, District Six had been in existence for over a century. The suburb was old and colourful, colourful in every sense of the word. During the earlier part of the apartheid era, District Six was relatively cosmopolitan. The community consisted largely of mixed-race residents known as Cape Coloureds, or simply as 'Kleurlinge.' Some were Christian, most were Muslim. At one time there had even been a sizeable Jewish Community in District Six, but as they became more affluent, they gravitated to more well-to-do suburbs. Affluence and mobility were luxuries not available to those with darker skins. They spoke a patois of English and predominantly Afrikaans called *kombuis taal,* kitchen language, with an accent that the patronising whites in the city found endearing.

In 1958, eighteen years before she stood in that hospital courtyard, Karen Willemse entered the world in an overcrowded hospital in District Six. Karen was an only child. Her parents had lost a little boy to illness four years before, and Magda had several miscarriages after that before they were blessed with the sweetest little girl.

At the beginning of 1967, the tightly pigtailed nine-year-old ran into the little shop in District Six bearing the Afrikaans name *"Tante Zena se Kombuis"*, and in smaller letters underneath, *"Auntie Zena's Kitchen".* The sweet-sour smell of pickled fish was redolent - a smell that Karen *smaaked,* really liked, but a taste she was not yet mature enough to enjoy. Auntie made and sold various Cape Malay recipes like mincemeat *bobotie* served with *blatjang* chutney that was more to Karen's taste. It was her favourite food.

Zena, whose daughter Eva was Karen's best friend, would always give her a few sweeties. Karen gave Auntie Zena (who was not really her aunt) a warm hug, and Zena responded with a gentle kiss.

School was ok, but Saturdays were what they waited for. Karen, Eva and their friends (some, not including Karen, in traditional Muslim dress) used to take the bus safely unaccompanied every Saturday morning to the Labia bioscope to see the forever-ongoing Lone Ranger serial and whatever *fillim* was showing. Then they would all return to Auntie Zena's to spend their sixpence spending-money on ice-creams or ice lollies.

What Karen enjoyed most of all was the *Kaapse Klopse* Carnival (the whites called it the Coon Carnival) which had been enjoyed for decades by mixed race and whites alike. The outbreak of joy that traditionally took place on the second day of January was a minstrel festival where thousands of celebrants from District Six and Bo-Kaap dressed in colourful silk garb, grabbed their banjos, horns and pennywhistles and took to the streets. The music was cheerful and sing-along rousing. The musical march took them through the crowds of thousands lining the streets of Cape Town. Some of the minstrels would wear weird masks and replicas of a devil's face – they were called *Achas*, and little Karen and her friends were terrified of them. When a group of Achas approached, the kids would flee to the nearest bedroom to hide under the beds. But the Achas would come looking for them and they would be exposed by the resident adult who would take great delight in hearing their screams. It was all such lekker fun! For the Cape mixed race community, it was the biggest event of the year. Karen would stand with her ma and pa and watch the parade and love the upbeat folksy tunes.

But then the shit hit the fan for Karen and the other children and their families. In 1966, the Nationalist government decided that it was unwise to have people of mixed race living so close to the city. Ignoring that thousands of families of all hues and religious beliefs had co-existed there amicably for nearly two centuries, the white government stated that interracial interaction bred conflict, necessitating the separation of the races. They deemed District Six a slum, crime-ridden and dangerous; they claimed that the suburb was a vice den, full of immoral activities like gambling, drinking, and prostitution. Though these were the official reasons, most residents believed that the government sought the land because of its proximity to the city centre, Table Mountain and the harbour and would be better served by housing low-income whites only. So, by order of the Group Areas Act, they rezoned the suburb, appropriated the land and renamed it *Zonnenbloem* as it had been in its earliest incarnation – Zonnenbloem, the sunflower. Ironic, really; the most vibrantly colourful flower, to be occupied by whites only.

In February 1967, the government announced that relocation was about to commence. Everything that Karen loved - Cape Town city, Table Mountain, the Klopse Carnival, Tante Zena se Kombuis, Eskimo pies, the Labia cinema - were all about to become distant memories.

'Whatchumean we hev to move from Distrik Ses, Pa?'

'Demmit, Keren, the bleddy gummint they say there's too much crime here and everyone's smoking *dagga,* and we're too close to the white suburbs and because of us the crime is bad there also, so they say we mus move to Manenberg in the bleddy *gramadoelas...*'

'Where's that, Pa?'

'It's bleddy far, my *skattie*, that's where!'

'But then I can't go to Auntie Zena after the fillims.'

'Auntie Zena's also got to move to this place, we's all got to move, the whole bleddy lot of us. You not going to be going nowhere for Eskimo Pies, my girlie, because there's not going to be no bioscope and no bleddy fillims there by Manenberg and not too many shops also.'

'Why, Pa, isn't it a nice place?'

'No, my sweetie, it's a real shit-hole; there's bugger-all there' – and then, thinking there was no need to make his daughter feel any more unhappy than was absolutely necessary, he said, '*Nee, man*, I mean Manenberg's a very nice place ekshly, en I'm sure we going to be very heppy there.'

'I don't want to go, Pa, I want to stay here. Who will I play with there by Manenberg? I'll lose all my friends, Pa.'

'*Nee,* don't worry, my Karentjie, they's all got to move too.'

Karen rushed off to tell Auntie Zena and Eva the bad news that their homes were to be exported, and Zena, who was well aware of what was to come, had to explain what 'expropriated' meant.

Tragically, Kallie's words were prescient. The people moved out, the bulldozers moved in. The existing colourful old homes in District Six were razed and replaced by small characterless bungalows. Despite the heartfelt and pathetic protests of the local people, the large community of 60,000 was uprooted and forcibly moved to new townships.

In midwinter on the windswept Cape Flats 20 kilometres further inland, the Willemses found themselves in Manenberg. No one quite knew why the new township was called Manenberg - there wasn't a hill or berg in sight, let alone a mountain. As colourful and verdant as District Six had been, Manenberg was drab and flat. Just row upon row of new but bleak semi-detached one- or two-bedroom houses and project-style apartment blocks, all with monotone dull red roofs.

The streets were mostly untarred, the kerbs unpaved. Worst of all, there were no trees. There was no street lighting. Hundreds of houses that all looked exactly the same. If you came home a little drunk, as Karen's dad did frequently, it was not easy to spot which house was yours. The most characteristic thing about the Cape Flats was the ever-present wind blowing sand and dust from the rough beaches a few kilometres away. After a while, the red roofs looked the same colour as the walls.

Her parents, like everyone else there, hated it and bemoaned what had been lost. What they missed most of all was the spontaneous excitement of the annual carnival, never the same after the participants and spectators were relocated. 'We can't even walk to see the Kaap Klopse Carnival no more,' said Magda. The minstrels were eventually banned. It was a sad end to a Cape tradition enjoyed by all races.

Unemployment was very high. By contrast, Karen's parents Kallie and Magda were decent people and both in work, often not the case with many other residents. Kallie was employed as a janitor in a large residential apartment block in luxurious white-residents-only Sea Point, and her ma as a maid in that fancy Southern Sun hotel in the city centre, of course solely for white holiday-makers. Magda spoke for the entire community when she said to her husband, '*Ag man,* we's now got to be bussed in to work from the bleddy Cape Flats. Ninety minutes each way with all the *skollies* smoking dagga and drinking on the bus. Those young guys is plain rude.'

Kallie agreed. 'Thet's three bleddy hours wasted every day, down the fokken pan. Those *bliksems* really buggered us!' They would have to leave their home at six every morning to catch the bus into the CBD, although it might have been quicker (but much less safe) to walk into town, so congested was the highway with buses and minibus-taxis.

Another big change was that those living in Manenberg never saw white people unless they were employed by the wealthier whites on the other side of De Waal Drive. In District Six, a small percentage of the residents had been white or Indian, even some black. Nobody seemed to care much about what colour you were, you just got on with the daily business of living. But here in Manenberg, aside from a few black families, almost everyone was of mixed race, and for the younger people the only perception they had of white folk came from the overworked doctors at the small clinic, and the stories brought back by their parents, those that worked. The two lessons they learned from these stories were that the whites were either rich or very rich, and that they, the Kleurlinge, could never be.

Manenberg with its seven shops and two liquor stores wasn't the only new district, although it wasn't easy to tell one from another. It did not take long before the gangs and dealers took over all the new townships. They preyed on old and young alike, and kids as young as ten were enticed or bribed into becoming runners. The police were either not interested, or working in collusion with the gangs, so vigilante groups sprung up that engaged in armed conflict with the gangs. It was not unusual to read headlines like *"Boy, 12, Slain in Crossfire."*

Kallie worried for his daughter. 'Karentjie, you mustn't go out on your own anymore. Those bleddie skollies are fokken dangerous. They's going to say they will give you all sorts of lekker stuff if you take their peckages to someone and collect money for them. Those peckages are full of dangerous *kak,* so you mus jus say for them *nee*, no way. They's also going to offer you lollies but those are not lekker lollies, these are lollies that you smoke and they will make you bleddy sick. Leave those *okes* alone my baby, they's very bad people.'

Karen was one of very few who took heed.

The re-zoned families on the Cape Flats gradually lost their sense of belonging. When the opportunity arose for Karen's family to move to nearby Mitchell's Plain, a newer rehousing project and a 'proper' town ten times the size of Manenberg, they were only too happy to relocate once more. Mitchell's Plain had paved streets, some street lighting, shops and a medical centre.

CHAPTER 3: DISTRICT SIX / MANENBERG / MITCHELL'S PLAIN 1958 -1976

Schooling in Mitchell's was overcrowded but fun, sport on the grassless fields more fun, and after school most fun. The parks, such as there were and the streets were where most activities took place after school, but the activities were not unenjoyable. Karen was very popular with boys and girls alike, and because of her height and lissom body excelled at netball.

Unfortunately but predictably, dark clouds were gathering.

It didn't take long before the gangs of indolent thugs took control of Mitchell's Plain too. They terrorised the citizens as they fought for control of the turf. They had easy access to guns that had been stolen from army stores, and those that couldn't get their hands on guns used knives, pangas and machetes. Dealing drugs offered the best source of income short of robbing banks, and there weren't too many of those in Mitchell's. Gangs such as The Americans, The JFKs and The Hard had sprung up in the suburbs, and recruitment of dealers was rife amongst teenagers who moved about on their Chopper cycles. By the time the kids were fourteen, many belonged to a gang called The Hard Livings. The name would be tattooed on their arms, and gang fights involved guns and pangas. Most feared and coveted was membership of one of the 'Numbers'. There was '26' and '28', and the rivalry was fierce.

Never a day passed when a young guy somewhere in Mitchell's was not shot dead on the street, sometimes with innocent bystanders alongside them as the bullets flew across the streets. They were a big worry to the Cape police, not to mention to the local people, and Pollsmoor Prison was already overcrowded with the worst of them. Even while in Pollsmoor they continued their gang affiliation, all inmates being forced to join 'Number 27'. This did not of course completely override earlier affiliations, and infighting was fierce between '26' and '28' prisoners.

This was the culture that surrounded the young teenager. Nevertheless, Karen had settled well in her newer environment, made friends, and enjoyed the company and occasional hand of the brash teenage boys. She would arrive at a 'social' with lipstick on, and some lucky *jolla* boy would leave with lipstick on. Although she did not mind occasionally being touched up by a local guy, she could by no means have been described as sex-wild or undiscriminating. Nevertheless, by the time she was seventeen, virginity was but a memory, not necessarily by choice. Yet, for all of this outward confidence, Karen was quite fragile and would remain upset for weeks if she was dumped by the *oke* with whom she was going steady. But then she would recover as if it had never happened and find a new *oke.* Resilient.

'Were you into drugs, Karen?' Sophie asked, as they lay exhausted on their bunkbeds after a day in the wards.
'Sort of. It was impossible not to be. Peer pressure was huge. Like all my mates, I experimented with dagga, but unlike lots of them, I didn't get in too deep. I didn't do Mandrax which a stack of my mates were into. A lot of those kids are completely fucked now, and quite a few have died. I didn't fancy the idea of ending up a low-life with kids around my ankles.'
Karen had higher ambition. She was aspirational. Her mother had instilled in her the notion that if she did not want to spend her life tucking in the corners of sheets in a hotel bedroom or hanging out the *medem's* washing, it was important that she get a proper education. The standard of schooling was at times moderate, at others better than expected. The after-school activities were intensive. She applied herself diligently to both, studying to the best of her ability, doing gymnastics and best of all, playing netball. Pleased with her progress, her headmistress asked her what she intended to do when she left school. She responded, 'Miss, I want to go there by nursing college, but

if I can't get in for thet, maybe I must try to become a teacher.' Nursing was something she had wanted to do since her earliest childhood after she saw the fillim "The Student Nurses" which her friend's dad had got from Blockbusters.

Miss Jantjes had no doubts. 'Karen, you can be whatever you want to be. For sure I will give you a good testimonial, and whatever you want to do, jis go for it my girl. I know you can do it. Jis keep away from drugs.'

To Ms Jantjes' satisfaction and the great pride of her parents, Karen obtained a regulation Matric certificate that would enable her to apply at the nurses' training school for mixed-race women in Somerset West.

Sophie was confused by this information. 'So how come you're here at Groote Schuur and not at Somerset West?'

'Because I can earn a lot more as a nurse in a white hospital. It also offers a lot more opportunities to get jobs elsewhere, maybe even in other countries. I imagined going to foreign countries to help the locals like in the fillim M*A*S*H - wouldn't that have been amazing! I didn't fancy the idea of being a war nurse, though.'

The combined salaries of her parents were about the same as Karen would earn as a nurse of mixed race, but what she could earn were she white, well, that was a prize too far-fetched to contemplate. Nevertheless, think about it she did, and for Karen the thought was mother to the act. And the act was to get herself reclassified as white, whatever the price. As she was to discover, the price was a meeting with Kobus.

# Chapter 4:
## *Sea Point  1958 -1976*

For Sophie Levine the journey had been considerably easier. She had been raised in the middle-class but not unwealthy white suburb of Sea Point, wedged between the Atlantic Ocean and the awe-inspiring mountain with its flat table-like surface. The area bordering the ocean was all high-rise, either hotels or blocks of apartments, many occupied only for three weeks of the year by wealthy white, mostly Jewish holidaymakers from Johannesburg. The area above Main Road was the much sought-after suburb of Fresnaye, the streets named for its Huguenot immigrants who were now only of distant memory. It was in Avenue De Sant that the Levine family lived in a smallish but classy double storey detached house. Smallish by white standards, but by comparison to a redroof in Manenberg, a veritable palace.

Sophie's mother, Hannah, was from a well-to-do German-Jewish family in Frankfurt. In 1937, seeing the rising cloud of Nazism, her family were making plans to leave Germany. The idea was that Hannah would emigrate alone to South Africa and undergo a pre-arranged marriage of convenience to obtain residency. She would then help to bring the other members of her family out one by one and as quickly as possible.

On arrival in Cape Town via Italy, the marriage had taken place and she had been endowed a moderate sum as a wedding gift. She was to use this to assist her family's passage, but tragically they had left it far too late and Herr Hitler would get them before they were able to move out. It would be a long while before Hannah learned of their fate.

CHAPTER 4: SEA POINT 1958 -1976

Despite the overwhelming concern about her family, Hannah marvelled at the beauty of her adopted city and the friendliness of its citizens. She adapted quickly to her new environment. Her English improved quickly, even if with a hint of a German accent that she never lost. She was able to gain employment at a firm manufacturing and selling quality women's garments. The work was dreary; her husband, a much older man, even more so. The marriage was short-lived and unconsummated. Following the annulment, she met, was courted by and married Dr Cyril Levine.

Like most Jewish South Africans, Cyril was born in Lithuania and came to South Africa as a boy with his family in the early thirties. He had studied diligently and graduated as a general medical practitioner at Cape Town University and Groote Schuur – quite an achievement for the son of barely literate but hardworking parents whose home language was Yiddish. They lived initially in a small house below Table Mountain and above the city bowl, and Cyril set up a small practice nearby. Within a few years, he had earned enough to move both home and practice to the more salubrious Fresnaye on the sunnier side of Table Mountain, and they were soon joined by many of his former and now wealthier neighbours.

Their lives were insular, much as it had been in their countries of origin, but unlike in those European *shtetls*, unthreatened. Eventually, Hannah, not really needing to work, gave up fashion to become involved in charitable activities, as had many of her Jewish friends (she only had Jewish friends). Like almost all their neighbouring families, the Levines were strongly pro-Zionist, and extremely charitable to local Jewish causes and the fledgling state of Israel.

Many of their neighbours knew little and cared less about those living in the Cape Flats, unless it concerned their ability to provide services, but Dr Levine never refused when asked to donate for a health centre in

Manenberg, a school in Langa or a sports field in Khayelitcha. He thought the re-zoning of District six inhuman and a stain on the nation's conscience, but realised there was little he could do about it other than to join a medical rota that entailed giving a day a month unpaid to help staff a clinic in Manenberg. Having suffered religious prejudice and the pogroms it produced in Lithuania, racial prejudice was not part of his DNA. His career had been of the utmost decency that brought credit to himself, his profession, his liberal views, and his heritage.

Hannah and Cyril struggled to have a child. Hannah suffered several miscarriages. She was almost forty when the sweetest little girl arrived on planet Earth. An only child, Sophie was indulged by her well-to-do parents, but could never be described as being 'spoiled' – in fact, she viewed with disdain those of her age group who viewed privilege as of right. From her earliest schooldays her parents would include her in all conversations, often about the local community or the state of the country or the new State of Israel.

Sophie would later think back to the time she was only seven years old. She could remember Cyril and Hannah Levine expressing their admiration for their co-religionists' involvement in the African National Congress's struggle for freedom. Nevertheless, her parents were concerned that too much active support would result in the Afrikaans government turning on their significantly smaller Jewish community, a concern shared by most Jewish families in South Africa. This was not without foundation. The ruling Nationalist party was well aware that whereas many of their own people clustered around the lower rungs of the social ladder, Jews appeared to scale these effortlessly - fertile ground for accusations of Jewish domination. Jewish involvement with communism would surely bring retribution. When her parents voiced these thoughts, the little blond seven-year-old became distraught. 'Are we going to be arrested, Mommy?'

'No, my darling, we're going to be fine, don't worry sweetie.'

But Sophie did worry, and would forever continue to be concerned, but not only for herself or her people. The seed had been sown.

At the Jewish school her parents had chosen for her, Sophie was certainly very scholarly but never much interested in sport. Neither popular nor disliked, she did not have many friends, but that was by her own choice, and she was quite happy to be alone in her skin. She went to few parties, and when she did, she quickly became bored. Although unusually blond and described by everyone as pretty, boyfriends were not a big part of her life unless they were able to hold an intelligent conversation. Unfortunately, there were few about who could match her intellect. Rather than spend time with a rugby-mad dullard whose only topic of conversation was whether Western Province could beat the Blue Bulls of Northern Transvaal, she would much prefer to involve herself in an interesting book.

She read voraciously and loved no writer more than John Steinbeck for his humanity. 'Of Mice and Men' really touched her, as did 'The Grapes of Wrath', and it was books such as these that ignited the small socialist flame that was to catch fire later. These books were by no means the only ones: 'Zorba the Greek' by Kazantzakis and Ayn Rand's 'The Fountainhead' alerted her hungry mind to notions of individual freedom. 'Animal Farm' was another, although one that turned her off communism forever - but not from socialism. She believed passionately in a more equitable distribution of wealth irrespective of skin colour. The book that shredded her guts, however, was 'Cry the Beloved Country' by South Africa's own Alan Paton, a social protest against the structures of a society that would later give rise to apartheid.

Sophie, from her earliest age, was anything but cool. She was vibrant with energy and fire. This naturally raised a question: how did a Jewish girl brought up in a capitalist country with every advantage of being white end up having left-wing beliefs, always defending the underdog? Well of course there was the influence of her parents, but as she grew older and into her teens, there were two events that had a seminal influence on Sophie's thinking.

The first was the massacre at far-away Sharpeville, a black township near Johannesburg. Sophie could well recall her parents' horror on learning that sixty unarmed people - many of them women - had been gunned down, most shot in the back by police as they ran. This massacre followed protests about the hated 'passbook', the identification document black people had to carry at all times to define where and when they could or could not travel or work.

Sophie was only too aware of the way dark-skinned people were treated in the country of their and her birth. She would plague her parents with questions such as why whites were allowed to move about freely, whereas dark people could not without carrying a 'pass' or being subject to curfew; why were darker people never seen in the bioscopes and restaurants and on the beaches of Cape Town, except as cleaners? Her parents tried to explain that although they too were bothered greatly, that was the law and to try to change those things was fraught with danger for them individually and for their community. Their words neither frightened nor satisfied Sophie.

The second incident was the D'Oliveira Affair in the late 'sixties. When she was ten, Sophie saw their mixed-race maid Lettie dancing and singing happily in the kitchen. This didn't happen too often.

'Why you so happy today, Lettie?'

CHAPTER 4: SEA POINT 1958 -1976

'No Miss Sophie, we's just heard on the wireless, Basil D'Oliveira going to be coming to South Efrica wiffa English cricket team. We's so excited, Miss Sophie, he's a *Kleurling*, jes like me!' For Lettie, who wouldn't have known a cricket bat from a rolling pin, this was a massive cause for celebration. She hugged Sophie. Sophie had no idea that Basil D'Oliveira was a talented cricketer who, because of his race, had to leave South Africa to play international test cricket, and had represented England with distinction. Anything that made Lettie happy met with Sophie's unquestioned approval, because Lettie had been with the family all of Sophie's life and she loved Lettie as a second mother.

Inevitably, Lettie's joy was short-lived. Two days later, Cyril mentioned at supper that South African Prime Minister Vorster had made it clear that D'Oliveira's inclusion was unacceptable, and the entire tour was to be cancelled. Sophie realised that this news would be upsetting for Lettie. She went to the kitchen where she found Lettie sobbing, and she put her little arm around the woman's heaving shoulders. She would not immediately understand the reasons for Lettie's response, but she would never forget her words: 'It's not bleddy right, Miss Sophie, jes because the man's not white, he can't come to his own fokken land.' Lettie had never used the word 'fokken' in front of her before. She knew it was a bad word and so she realised it was serious.

These events by and large had little effect on the daily lives of the white denizens around her, but they did on Sophie. Why could whites play sport on manicured fields, whereas grass was a luxury unseen on the township grounds that flashed by as they drove along the N2? Why did Lettie call her 'Miss' Sophie, while she would call the older lady simply 'Lettie'? Truth was, few families in white households even knew the surnames of their employees.

When she questioned her parents about all of this, she found their response of 'We try to get her to change, but it's the only way she knows' entirely unsatisfactory. Get her to change? Why didn't they change!

Sophie tended to be of a quiet, introverted disposition until something was said by another pupil or even a teacher that got up her nose; and then, in an icy voice, she would present her well-reasoned contrary viewpoint. She had that ability to make even intelligent people feel that they were not quite as bright as they thought they were, which while admirable was not always endearing or conducive to maintaining friendships. Sophie did not suffer fools easily and took shit from no-one.

In only one respect did Sophie conform to the thinking expected of her. She was intensely proud and very defensive about her love (in a secular kind of way) for the fifteen-year-old state of Israel. She was but nine years old when the small Israeli armed forces (again, the underdog) in a mere six days defeated the combined might of Egypt, Jordan and Syria massed against them. Unsurprisingly, her hero was the Israeli commander with the black eye-patch, Moshe Dayan. From that day, she became as intensely pro-Zionist as her parents and their friends, and immensely proud of Jewish achievement whether in medicine, science, finance, the arts, or warfare.

Residential status in South Africa for Jews, while not overtly threatened, could never provide a feeling of total security. One thing they knew: they were liked neither by the English nor the Afrikaners, nor the Greeks or Portuguese, not because of what they did but who they were - Jewish. An age-old story. For that reason, the very existence of a Jewish state was of paramount importance. When the Germans turned on her forebears, there was nowhere to run. If only Israel had been in existence then...

Sophie enjoyed history more than any other subject, especially modern history. Her teacher was an older man named Mr Meyer Hersch, and it was rumoured that he had been a member of the South African Communist Party before it was outlawed by the government. Mr Hersch, during the course of a talk on the rise of socialism in the UK, paused for a moment and looked at his class of sixteen-year-olds. 'Do we have socialism in South Africa?', he asked. Sophie raised her hand. 'Sir, in this country you can get arrested if you have socialist or communist views.'

'Is that so, Sophie – do you know of any of our people who were arrested or banned for that reason?'

'Yes, there was Bertha Solomon and Helen Joseph, and all the people from the Rivonia Trial, and - '

'How do you know about all this, Sophie?'

'I read a lot. I listen to my parents. I think it's wrong that the ANC is banned.'

Sophie could not fail to hear the comment of one of her classmates: 'Oh, God, she's at it again!'

She turned to the other pupil, who was a terrific cricketer if not generally credited as being a great thinker. 'Yes, I'm at it again, you dumb ostrich, but it's because we refuse to confront what's going on in the townships and choose to live in a bubble of privilege. One day, you prick, that bubble's going to burst.' This was Sophie territory. She had barely got started. Much as he would have liked the discussion to continue, Mr Hersch decided to cool it. 'Yes, well, perhaps we should not be discussing these things in class right now.'

Later, Meyer Hersch spoke quietly to Sophie as the class filed out. 'Be careful, Sophie, take it from me. It's one thing to have opinions, and I respect you for that, but keep them to yourself if you don't want to have problems. Most of the parents of kids at this school believe there is no need to look for trouble, it will find us anyway. You need to understand that although we Jews have white status within the apartheid racial scheme, we are pretty much excluded socially by other white groups. The Afrikaners can be viciously and overtly antisemitic, whereas the English-speaking South Africans practise their brand of prejudice in a more covert way.

'So, we have few illusions about integrating into South African society and have remained relatively isolated from virtually all other national groups, if not always by choice. Instead, we constitute a separate Jewish identity, constructing a rich nexus of schools, youth movements, and welfare institutions. So, take it from me, young lady, tread carefully.'

He was not being unduly cautious. Two parents phoned Dr Levine that evening to complain that his daughter was being a bad influence on their kids and shouldn't be talking politics in class. Cyril of course gave them short shrift.

At a parent–teachers' evening, Cyril and Hannah got involved in conversation with Mr Hersch. They were not surprised when Hersch provided his assessment of their daughter, saying 'She's got a lively and creative mind, as I'm sure you are aware, and not lacking in intellectual energy and stimulation. But you need to be aware as well that she has a feral streak and is not disposed to accepting conventional structures.'

'Oh, believe me, we are!' said Cyril.

Hersch looked at them with obvious concern as he said, 'She does not give way to anyone if she thinks she is right. One or two of the other teachers find her extremely headstrong.'

'Yes, she's always been like that. She was a restless child. Perhaps we were too liberal in her upbringing,' said Hannah.

'And we should all be grateful for that,' responded Mr Hersch. 'She has a strong sense of morality, and I can foresee that she may become politically involved. Perhaps some caution is needed, but I cannot see anyone reining her in.'

He had foresight. It was no surprise to anyone that she was appointed captain of the Debating Society. Because she demolished every opponent from every other school with whom they competed, she was awarded school honours, the first ever to achieve this for debating.

CHAPTER 4: SEA POINT 1958 -1976

Meyer Hersch was arrested later that year. He received a ten-year prison sentence for being a member of the SA Communist Party. Sophie was the only pupil who was upset. She would not know then that three years later the body of her teacher would be handed back to his mourning family after allegedly hanging himself in his cell, although how he came to be in possession of a substantial length of thick rope was never explained at the inquest.

Sophie was constantly in conflict with her teachers, especially those more religious. She totally refused to accept the notion that the Hebrews were God's chosen people, which by definition meant that all the other nations were not. She thought that was the ultimate conceit. Nor could she remotely accept that every word written in the Old Testament was true simply because it could be read in *that* book. Somewhere she had read that the US Library of Congress classified the Bible as 'Non-fiction: Religion' and was the only religious book to get its own subclass. Sophie regarded the bible on the same level as Grimm's Fairy Tales; good stories for kids but definitely not to be taken too seriously.

She aired these views frequently, perhaps too often for her teachers' liking. Such unorthodox opinions did not go down well at a conventionally Jewish school, and there were strongly stated suggestions in the staffroom that she seek education elsewhere. The headmaster, to his credit, would not entertain such notions.

'That girl is extremely bright and I promise you she will bring honour to this school' he argued.

During her matriculation year, events that became known at the Soweto Uprising were taking place a thousand miles to the north. In the cold winter of 1976, a bunch of black school kids in the sprawling black township of Soweto on Johannesburg's doorstep organised a rally in protest against the introduction of Afrikaans, the language of their white oppressors and thus the language of apartheid, as the medium for school instruction. Until then, most classes were held in English and very few in their own Bantu languages. The children accepted English, but lessons in Afrikaans were intolerable. It was estimated that some twenty thousand school pupils took to the streets, and simply refused to return to school until the decision was reversed. When eventually the protests were quelled by the police, nearly two hundred schoolchildren were being mourned by their parents. The photograph of the lifeless ten-year-old Hector Pieterse being carried by Mbusiya Makhubo became iconic and defining of another shameful chapter in the annals of apartheid.

For seventeen-year-old Sophie Levine, it was a pivotal point in her life. She told her parents she wanted to go to Soweto to join the protests. They would hear none of it. 'You've got your matric exams coming up. When you get through that we can talk about protests.'

Sophie raged. 'All you can think about is that the protests shouldn't affect us, like it's not our problem.' That was the moment she realised just how privileged her own upbringing had been by comparison with that of young blacks. She determined that if she was ever able to, she would emulate her hero, the lone-wolf South African Jewish parliamentarian Helen Suzman, in bringing about change. Sophie was later to become very interested and indeed to involve herself in the Jewish contribution to the anti-apartheid movement, but that would be in the future, and things were happening now.

The Jewish community in Cape Town, much like the bigger one in Johannesburg, was insular. It was also highly aspirational. There were not many of Cyril's generation who were professionals, but they were determined that their children should be. So, from their earliest childhood, the kids were shlepped to ballet classes or music lessons or Hebrew school in the afternoons, but this was of secondary importance and only to make them more rounded. It was instilled in their DNA that when they finished school, the boys would study to become doctors, dentists, accountants or lawyers; and if the latter two, these would be the springboard into commerce. It was important that they chose a profession that would bring them security, but also mobility should what happened in Europe befall them too. If you were a doctor or dentist, you could be assured of earning a deservedly good living. But it was also an insurance policy, so that if the Nationalist government, some of whose members had in the past been Nazi sympathisers, turned on them, they could easily move abroad to friendlier countries like England or Australia or the USA or Canada, or of course, Israel.

As for the women, only a few of the most aspirational and intelligent would go on to become doctors or lawyers. It was a very patriarchal society. It was well understood that the men would be the chief breadwinners, so the acquisition of secretarial skills was preferred and encouraged for girls. They usually chose something that involved the arts, or professions like psychotherapy or teaching.

Sophie's head-teacher thought she was ideal material to read for an arts degree at Cape Town University, and then possibly go into teaching, law or even politics. She certainly had the academic ability to do so. Sophie, however, rarely did or said what was expected. When she told the school Principal that she planned to do nursing, he said he was seriously disappointed, because nursing was not what bright Jewish girls did. When asked why she had chosen this vocation, Sophie replied that nursing might not be what bright Jewish girls did but was what her belief system dictated.

Her mother too was disappointed. Her father thought it a massive waste of potential. 'Why don't you follow in my footsteps, Sophie? You can do it, my darling. You would surely make a brilliant doctor, who knows, even a great research scientist. I don't get it, Sophie – the world is your oyster, and all you'll end up doing is taking blood pressures and temperatures at the behest of some authoritarian manager with a quarter of your brains.' But Sophie was nothing if not wilful. All who knew her knew better than trying to talk her out of anything once she had set her mind to follow a particular direction. In any case, earning loads of money was contrary to her every socialist principle.

However, there was a deeper level to Sophie's thinking. Too often she would embarrass her quietly spoken parents, not by what she had said but by being overheated. She knew instinctively that if she were let loose in the free-thinking environment that existed at the University of Cape Town, her over-vigorous brain and motormouth would land her in very deep trouble politically. Mr Hersch's words had not fallen on deaf ears. She was only too well aware that when something really riled her, and many matters did, the off-switch in her brain ceased to function. She would let rip, and later regret.

At nursing college, she would not be in the company of like-minded people and she would be controlled. In fact, it was extremely likely that she would be surrounded by conservative staff whose views were totally the opposite of her own. Well, if she was going to go into politics one day, she needed to understand her opposition at first hand. She also needed to learn self-discipline.

So, after attaining distinctions in biology, maths, history and English, Sophie registered to do nursing at Groote Schuur. All she wanted to do was become the best nurse she could. This was the first step of her journey. She knew greater, more difficult steps awaited her, and these would not be without risk.

# Chapter 5:

## *Groote Schuur 1976*

And so, for Karen Williams nee Willemse and Sophie Levine, their training and time together began. The hours were long, the work demanding, and they pushed themselves and each other. Neither was frivolous, but they laughed a lot. Although Karen had had more men than she had wished force themselves on her in the past, neither was unusually active; the occasional fling with a houseman here or there, nothing of consequence. Matron Gray's words only served to reinforce what they saw as their reason for being there: to serve, to make a difference. Karen would later question whether washing used bedpans made a real difference, but someone had to do it and in general they both took the long view.

Their evenings in were often spent in long discussions about the state of the nation, and here Sophie, given her upbringing, surprised the most with her socialist views. She carried an anti-racist torch that would ignite every time a patient or another nurse dared to make a bigoted remark, but eventually she realised that she was farting against thunder.

They realised that they came from very different worlds with very different perspectives. If one imagined a funnel, then Sophie had come from the wide end, from a culture where the world was her oyster, where anything was possible. Yet, she had chosen to narrow her horizons to the restrictive and restricted world of obeying the orders emanating from senior white women and men wearing white. Hers was a white world.

Karen, on the other hand, had a very different perspective. Coming from a simple background with the intention of broadening her horizons, she would be the one viewing nursing from the narrow end of the funnel. She was determined to make her way up that metaphorical funnel, to achieve a much broader level in life where exciting and interesting choices were available and where she would not be restricted by the limited ambition of those around her. The world was certainly not her oyster, but she saw nursing as a pathway to a better, more comfortable, less dangerous world where she could be respected as a woman and not treated and degraded in the manner of Kobus. She did not feel resentful or bear a grudge against the privileged white community who were dealt the stronger hand of cards at birth, but she was very determined to shuffle the pack in the hope of getting a better deal.

Sophie knew little of Karen's world. Other than the fact that her maid was of mixed race, Sophie had never had much to do with darker people, had never even been into a mixed race or black township even though they were only a (long) bus-ride away. They might just as well have been on another planet. How could she know what it was like to be brought up in a place where just getting through school was a major success rather than a mandatory starting point to higher achievement? But what made Sophie stand apart from her nursing mates was that she *wanted* to know, to experience this other planet. She was intelligent enough to reason that if she could not put herself into other skins and other cultures, she could not complete her exploration of the similarities and differences between them.

After they had been together for nearly three months, Karen felt sufficiently comfortable and safe with Sophie to confide her deepest secret to her: she told Sophie about Kobus. She did not know how Sophie would react, because you could never tell with white South Africans, no matter how liberal they seemed. Sophie simply said, 'I'm not stupid, you know. I knew you were a Kapie from day one. Why do you think I latched on to you? You were an outlier.

But I'm also an outlier, Ka. Nurses' home isn't exactly busting with Jews, is it? At least you're Christian!'

'Well actually I'm not, I'm sort of a bit Muslim, but let's not split hairs.'

'I don't give a bugger what you are, Ka, you're the best friend I could wish for, and I couldn't care less whether you're a Muslim Kapie or anything else.'

Karen, tears in her eyes, simply hugged her. 'Do you think the others know as well, Soph?'

'Well, if they're not blind, probably; but nobody would be dumb enough to say anything to me – they know they'd get their ovaries carved out.'

'With a scalpel?'

'No, dummy, with a kitchen fork! Anyway, who cares? Fuck them all, Ka - just get on with it!'

And get on with it Karen did. She worked hard, harder than any of her counterparts with the exception of Sophie, who, like her, had something to prove. They never complained when they were allocated night duties. They just did what was expected of them, and Matron Gray was content to let them. It was Matron who noticed their caring more than most, not that she would ever have given them the satisfaction of telling them so. Another thing the crusty old bird noticed was that they worked better as a pair than when they were coupled with others. This was an eye-opener for her, because it had always been her experience that buddies should be separated. She was content to allow them to work to their own strengths.

Traditionally, from the time of Florence Nightingale, junior nurses had always taken orders from their seniors, and rarely initiated anything more than routine procedures. Their reasoning and intellectual skills were not fostered or valued – indeed, this was behind Dr Levine's lack of encouragement for Sophie's choice of profession. Sophie was an exception. In Sophie, Matron saw someone highly task-orientated – you saw a problem, you analysed it, you found the solution. Sophie's relationships with both patients and doctors altered perceptibly as she was increasingly seen – and heard – as the first and often the only junior nurse prepared to argue with the doctors. She was only too willing to stick her head above the parapet – the heritage of her liberal upbringing - and there was a minority of both nurses and doctors who thought she needed cutting down to size.

Matron saw leadership potential if other people could get past her being Jewish, but she knew full well that this would be easier said than done. Odd really, considering the disproportionately high percentage of Jewish doctors in the hospital. Even more odd was the fact that Sophie did not seek in any way to ingratiate herself or work more closely with this distinct group of medics. It was abundantly clear to Matron that as far as Sophie was concerned, it mattered little which god one did or did not worship, or whether one's skin was white, black or something in-between. This was a view not always shared by Matron, but she quietly admired Sophie's steadfastness in holding to this tenet.

Karen had a very different agenda. She was entirely unwilling (and for very good reason) to risk mortal injury in being shot down by a group of racially motivated snipers, and there was no shortage of those - doctors, nurses and patients alike. So Karen elected to maintain a low profile – as she put it, to fly between the wallpaper and the wall. The less she was noticed, the less likely she would be to have shit flung at her. She dealt competently with difficult patient issues as well, but there was a softer edge to her than to her roommate. She was a more touchy-feely people-type of person, more sensitive, also that little bit more kind. When there was bad news to be delivered – a death or a relapse - Karen would be your nurse of choice to deliver the message. Karen was the one able to care for people by understanding their personal strengths and motivations, and she learned to enlist other supportive family resources. This needed time, patience and

CHAPTER 5: GROOTE SCHUUR 1976

sensitivity, and Karen possessed those qualities in barrelsful.

Two very strong but different characters; and when you allowed their best talents to meld together, you ended up with the perfect nurse.

The festive season was the time that allocation of duties produced most moans from those who were prevented from celebrating Christmas with their families, but the intrepid two were content not only to be on duty but to work longer shifts. Neither complained when allocated night or weekend duties, and these were some of the reasons that they were able to win grudging respect from their comrades. The one exception was an already qualified, bible-punching young Afrikaans woman named Marie Pienaar who seemed to resent their presence for the exact reason that Matron Gray had singled them out: they were different. And if they were different, they would always be viewed with suspicion. Nurse Pienaar always ensured that they were given the less pleasant jobs. The two were never complimented, no matter how well they did their work.

It had never been their intention to wreak revenge on Marie Pienaar, but a few months later the opportunity arose. They were enjoying their breakfast in the staff canteen, and seated at their table were the radiographer Annie Smith and a Junior Doctor, Paul Rabie, with whom they were on very good terms. The doctor just happened to ask Annie if she could do an x-ray on none other than Miss Pienaar who was complaining of a nasty stomach-ache.

Sophie was not about to miss her cue. 'She gives *me* a royal pain in the guts.'

Karen added her two cents' worth. 'That woman is so uptight! She's always giving Sophie and me the really crap jobs.'

Sophie was quick to follow up. 'And to make it worse, she's a god-pusher, always preaching the word of the Lord.'

Annie Smith, who was herself a bit god-fearing, responded, 'Well, let's not hold that against her. I know she's a bit of a hypo, but getting an x-ray shouldn't be a problem.'

Sophie rubbed her hands together and said 'Listen, you know the date today?'

'Yeah, the first of April.'

'Listen guys, will you go along with it if we play a little April Fools' joke on Marie?' said Sophie somewhat disingenuously.

'Well, depends; what you got in mind, Sophie?' said Dr Rabie.

'This – I want Annie to take an x-ray of me with one of those stray cats that hang about the kitchen lying across my guts.'

'And then?'

'And then you show it to Pienaar.'

'But she'll shit herself!' exclaimed Annie.

'Exactly! So here's my plan: after you've taken her x-ray if there's anything serious you forget the whole prank. But if it's harmless, you show her the cat x-ray and she'll think she's pregnant with a monster child.'

'She'll never believe that', said Karen, 'I'm certain she's still a virgin, she's only ever slept with her bible.'

Annie was perturbed. 'So, what happens if she gets the hump and goes and moans to Matron? Then it's me who's going to be in the doodoo.'

Dr Rabie chortled with laughter. 'Nonono! You know what, she's not a bad sort, and it's time she stopped taking herself so seriously. Annie, you can tell her that I put you up to it. She likes me, we're both Afrikaners, and I think she'll see the funny side of it.'

'I bleddy hope so for your sake, but hey let's go for it!' said Annie. 'If she spots you, I'll tell her the pair of you are assisting me today, developing x-rays and topping up the developing materials. Be prepared to get your hands dirty, ok?'

A few hours later, Marie Pienaar presented herself for her x-ray, unaware that behind the large screen were a doctor and two young women who were struggling to contain themselves. When the x-ray was checked offstage by Dr Rabie and quietly declared to be free of pathology, Annie presented Marie with the cat in her gut. Marie let out a yell of horror – '*Dit kan nie so wees nie!* It can't be!'

There was an eruption of guffaws behind the screen, and the three culprits fell forward in paroxysms of laughter.

Dr Paul Rabie was the first to recover. 'April Fool, Marie! That x-ray is of a cat lying across Sophie's guts!'

To everyone's surprise, Nurse Pienaar too erupted in laughter.

'Wow, that's the best April Fool's joke ever! I was wondering how that bleddy dingus climbed in - that bony thing!! God, you nasty people gave me such a *skrik,* I nearly *kakked* myself!

Paul Rabie did not forget to add, 'The good news is there's bugger-all wrong with you, Marie, your x-ray is clear.'

The good news for all was that the episode broke the ice between the nurse and the two students, and their relationship improved immeasurably.

That evening, Karen sat with her friend as they relived the day's entertainment. They shrieked with laughter all over again until Sophie literally pissed herself. This got Karen going even more - same result. It wasn't all just bedpans.

A few weeks later, Maisie, an elderly English woman was admitted to the wards for investigation of indigestion, vomiting and weight loss. After barium x-rays and gastroscopy, a diagnosis of advanced gastric carcinoma was made but was not disclosed to Maisie as, according to her husband, she was 'very nervous' and had a phobia about cancer. It was obvious to all that she was in God's waiting room, but although dreadfully frail, she never complained or bemoaned her fate, which was a one-way ticket outward bound. For every nurse and doctor who passed by her, she had a smile that spoke of inner contentment and acceptance.

She seemed particularly fond of Karen, and whenever an injection had to be administered or a blood pressure taken, she asked if Karen could be the one to be on hand. Maisie required a lot of physical care and had asked not to be left alone when awake at nights, and it was Karen who was always there at her side, even when she wasn't on duty. She confided to Karen that she was not afraid of dying 'as long as it wasn't cancer' and Karen was not about to spill the morbid details of her condition to this lady of whom she had become particularly fond.

A few days later, when it was realised by everyone, Maisie not least, that she did not have many hours left on this planet, she once more asked for Karen to sit with her. She looked up at the young woman and said 'Thank you for being so kind to me, Nurse Williams'. Then she asked, 'Where do your parents come from? Where do they live?' Without much thought, Karen answered 'District Six, then Mitchell's Plain.' The old woman looked at her and said, 'So you're a Kapie then!' When Karen nodded, the old lady took her hand and said, 'Never mind, darling, you're still a human being!'

Maisie passed away the following day. Karen asked for and was granted permission to attend her funeral, where she was welcomed by the woman's small family and given a beautiful small jewellery box, which was the old lady's dying wish. Not that Karen had much jewellery!

# Chapter 6:

## Taken by the Music Manenberg 1977

'Hey, Ka, whatchyou doing tonight?'
'Going to a jazz concert there by Manenberg Town Hall.'
'Oh...... Who's playing?'
'Dollar Brand. Ag, I mean Abdullah Ibrahim.'
'Who's he?'
She handed Sophie a torn-out page from The Cape Argus:

**Manenberg, Cape Flats: what makes Manenberg tik?**

There are very few famous or for that matter even well-known members of the Cape Coloured community. Yet, Abdullah Ibrahim is one of the world's greatest living jazz pianists, recognised as a prime mover in bringing South African township jazz into mainstream Afro-American music. Many years ago, in the fifties, when he was still Adolph Johannes Brand, he plied his trade in the Coloured townships of the Cape Flats. His grandmother played organ or piano in church, and he grew up influenced by the hymns, gospels and spirituals of church jazz. Not long after, he took the stage name of Dollar Brand, and his band, the Jazz Epistles, were the first non-white South African group to record an LP. That was 1961.

Soon after, Dollar Brand left South Africa for New York, where he became an intimate of John Coltrane and Duke Ellington, bringing recognition of that particular brand (no pun intended!) of South African rhythm that any South African - black, white or in-between - would instantly recognise as Township Jazz. Cape Coloured music. Brand converted to Islam and morphed into Abdullah Ibrahim.

*His most endearing and enduring composition was called "Mannenberg" (with two ns), a thirteen-minute paean to his township origins that has become a jazz icon. It is at once a wistful longing by an exile for his homeland and an uplifting recollection of the beats and rhythms that were part of his everyday life as a young man - sad yet joyous. The tune became an anthem for black South Africans during the Soweto Uprisings in 1976 and is entirely worthy of the great pianist, composer and gentleman who penned it.*

### Richard Simpson

'Mm.... the gig sounds too good to miss. Can I come with you?'

'Don't be focken stupid, Sophie! Have you got a death wish, babe? You're blond, in case you haven't noticed. You know how many blonds there will be in Manenberg tonight? You'll be able to count them on the fingers of no hands! You will stand out like Kobus's dick!'

'I'd really like to go with you – I told you, I've never been into a township.'

'Why am I not surprised? How many whites have? Listen, it's one thing being a *liberaal,* but I'm telling you, don't look for shit - it will find you anyway.'

'So, maybe it's time for me to grow up? I really want to go with you.'

'Sure - if you're determined to commit suicide! But my old man better come as well then. We'll have to pay for his ticket.'

'No problem.'

'I'll call him to meet us at the bus stop.'

'Great, then I can finally get to know him and maybe your mom as well.'

'Alright, Soph, we'll go there for supper, but you should know it's not Sea Point or Claremont.'

'Karen, listen, I understand.'

## CHAPTER 6: TAKEN BY THE MUSIC MANENBERG 1977

'I'd better take bleddy good care of you then tonight, my Sophie. I can't afford to lose my best friend.'

After reading the article once more, Sophie asked 'Who's Richard Simpson?'

'An English journalist, as far as I can tell, but he seems to know his jazz.'

Sophie could not possibly have known that one day she would meet the same English journalist in the most unexpected of circumstances, or that he would have a profound influence on her life.

The concert proved everything they had hoped for, and more. The huge crowd greeted each song with uproarious applause, and "Mannenberg" almost blew the building apart. Not for a moment did Sophie feel unsafe. Later that evening as they returned to Cape Town in the very crowded bus, ignoring the less than sophisticated comments of a few young men *('Hey, les be friends'*), Sophie squashed up against Karen and said, 'I really loved that concert - that guy's fingers can really jive, hey?'

'Ja, he's one of those *okes* who didn't just lie down or take to the bottle.'

'Your parents are just lovely! Your mom's a great cook - the pickled fish was so lekker, absolutely delish!'

'They liked you too, a lot. You were lucky to get home-cooked food. If I was on my own it would have been a tin of Glenryck pilchards. I used to hate pickled fish like my auntie Zena used to make when I was little, but I really enjoyed it tonight, so I guess I'm growing up.'

'I felt very safe with your dad at the concert – they seemed to respect him.'

'Sophie, it was priceless! Those stares from the *okes* when we walked into the town hall.....they couldn't believe a blond chick was *jolling* through our township.'

'Maybe they thought I was an albino.'

Their workdays and often worknights in those first few months were dull and boring. Although some of the work involved theatre-assisting in interesting surgery or obstetrics cases, most of it was rather mundane. Reading blood pressures and temperatures (as predicted by Cyril), feeding the frail, attending the toilet needs of the elderly, cleaning toilets and changing dressings amounted to what was an uninspiring routine. Their friendship lightened Sophie's load. 'Does every task involve human excreta? How long do you think we'll be changing bedpans and wiping backsides before we've earned our stripes?'

Karen nodded. 'It might be a while. I think Matron's got it in for you, Jewgirl'

'Matron is testing me to see if I'll crack, and let me tell you, that isn't going to happen. She must think I'm pretty dumb and maybe she's right. She should know we kugels can't wipe our own arses let alone someone else's,' said Sophie. She laughed at Karen's puzzlement. 'Kugel is a noodle pudding from the Jewish ghettos of Eastern Europe. Sweet or savoury. We use its name to describe spoilt young women whose chief activity is shopping, especially shopping for a husband. What do kugels make for dinner?'

Karen shook her head. 'Dunno.'

'Reservations.'

'You tell really shit jokes.....'

'No, you just don't have a sense of humour, Karen.'

Their days off were spent at the bioscope, as it was called in those days, Sophie preferring films that told of the fight against injustice of whatever hue, and especially oldie westerns like High Noon. Karen opted for more romantic *fillims* like Saturday Night Fever. They were both deeply saddened by the death of Elvis. When there was nothing worthwhile showing, they sought out art galleries, where Karen loved the more traditional art that she had studied for her matric. Sophie's preference was post-modern. Each was, however, quite prepared to accept the other's choices, and they learned much from each other.

## CHAPTER 6: TAKEN BY THE MUSIC MANENBERG 1977

The two young women loved their music and would take every opportunity presented to them to go to the dockland clubs, always in the company of young housemen doctors (because no woman in her right mind would attend such places unaccompanied) to hear artists like Johnny Clegg, son of an English father and Jewish mother from Rhodesia. His group Juluka was unusual in that it comprised both white and black musicians – rather like the keys of a piano, Sophie thought, and particularly admired him for this reason. The band constantly tested and violated the apartheid laws and from time to time they were arrested but never charged. Johnnie became known as The White Zulu, a language he spoke flawlessly, and Juluka's music was rooted in Celtic, Zulu and Jewish influences. But most of all, it was great music to dance to, and dance the student nurses and doctors did, letting out all their accumulated tensions and frustrations. In the early hours of the morning and drenched in perspiration, they would take a cab back to nurses' home, and after a few hours sleep be back in the wards at sparrow's fart.

One night they went in a small party to the Starlite Club, one of the rougher clubs in dockland. Despite its rather decrepit appearance, there was rarely an outbreak of violence at the Starlite, and if there was it would not be due to racial issues. On the contrary, Starlite seemed a microcosm of what could happen if you allowed the races to mix freely. One of the white Afrikaans doctors, Danie, who was there for the first time, and had never mixed with people of other races, set his eyes on a very attractive Kleurling woman, not unlike Karen in appearance. All his previous prejudices vanished in the smoky haze that pervaded the poorly lit dancehall. Dolly seemed equally attracted to him, and it was not long before they were dancing cheek to cheek and sharing passionate kisses as they swayed and sweated to bluesy numbers by the lively jazz band who were resident there.

Danie was looking forward to suggesting a departure to a nearby hotel where he had heard interracial pairs frequently ended up. The hotel, an old but well-maintained building owned by the wife of an ex-policeman, was frequently used for illicit liaisons without risk because those who made best use of it were the ex-officer's colleagues.

After a couple of hours and several beers, Danie excused himself and headed for the toilet. A moment later his new lady followed, ostensibly to the ladies' loo. When Danie returned a couple of minutes later, he was in a state of embarrassed excitement. 'Bleddy hell, guess what happened? I'm standing there, peeing against the wall, when Dolly walks in, walks up next to me, lifts up her skirt and pulls out her cock, I mean his cock. I got such a shock I peed all over my pants! I'm bleddy sopping wet, so I have to go back to res right now!'

The rest of the group nearly wet their own pants with laughter. 'Jeez, Danie, you are so *dom*! Didn't you know that the Starlite is famous for its transvestites?' Just then, Dolly returned, make-up refreshed, and was surprised to see Danie heading out the door to the taxi-rank outside. 'Ag, shame,' she said, 'You can't win 'em all. But tell him Dolly thinks he's bleddy nice and Dolly is always here if he wants her.'

As always, Sophie had the last word: 'He may be a doctor, but he's got a lot to learn – if he ever recovers!'

# Chapter 7:

## *Fresnaye, Sea Point 1976*

A few weeks after the Manenberg gig, Sophie caught Karen's arm. 'Payback time, kiddo…. Helen Suzman is speaking to the Union of Jewish Women next Monday night. Why don't you join me and meet my mom?'

'Cool, babe! Thanks, sounds interesting. It'll be easier for me - I look more Jewish than you. How's it you're so blond? I know it's real!'

'Both my parents are Ashkenazi Jews from Eastern Europe. Quite a few are blond – the odd rape here and there. Maybe we are mixed race as well; some historians think we even have Mongolian blood as Genghis Khan moved westwards. The darker Jews are mostly Sephardis, of Spanish or North African origin, but there's not that many Sephardis in South Africa.'

'Pity I won't meet your father.'

'Actually, you will. My dad knows Helen's husband from medical school, so he's been given special permission to lose his *ballubas* for the night and sit in. And talking of balls, that woman Helen has got big ones! Imagine being the only woman in parliament with all those antisemitic racist Dutchmen! You know what I heard? One of those hairyback MPs asked Helen why she asked so many questions that embarrass South Africa, and she replied: "It's not my questions that embarrass South Africa, it's your answers!" '

Sophie's parents realised that it was unlikely that Karen had been too often, if at all, in a house as opulent as theirs. They felt the shame of being exploiters of another nation - an emotion that few of their neighbours in Fresnaye would ever have entertained. As she entered,

Karen's eyes widened when she saw the pieces of Old Dutch furniture – the *riempie stoel* and stinkwood cabinet placed perfectly below the Pierneef painting. If such a stool existed in Manenberg or Mitchell's, it would have been worn to death by people sitting on it, and the leather strips making up the seat would have been reinforced by bits of rope. But this one was pristine. She said to Sophie, 'I bet no one's arse ever sat on *this* throne!'

The Pierneef was a beaut - 'You know something, Soph, besides when we went to Paternoster one summer, the only holiday I ever had as a child was once when we took the bus to the Little Karoo, and I seen the Swartberge.' She was referring to those dark brooding mountains which the artist depicted so perfectly because they were his own place.

The Levines were privy to Karen's recent history and had debated whether Lettie, who had been with the family since before Sophie was born, should actually serve the food as she normally would. They decided that they should try to be as normal as possible, and if that included having their mixed-race maid serve, then so be it.

Truth was, Lettie was treated kindlier, accorded more respect and paid substantially more than other maids in their social milieu. But then came the flip side: although Lettie had been part of the family for so many years and ate the same food as they, it was never at their table. As socially aware, conscience-driven and morally decent as Hannah and Cyril were, that dividing line was never breached, not even when Lettie was serving a younger Sophie her lunch.

Karen was only too aware, as were the three residents of the curious stares coming from Lettie. But nothing was said. The only concession made by Hannah was not to use the crystal goblets they would normally have set out for the '67 Stellenberg wine.

The polished silver samovar standing on the cabinet had more to do with Cyril's past than Hannah's. Where did

## CHAPTER 7: FRESNAYE, SEA POINT 1976

Sophie say her parents were from? One from Germany, the other, her father's folks, from Lithuania - where exactly was that? Why did Jews live there? Karen would ask these questions over the simple but superb dinner Lettie had prepared of roast brisket and carrot stew, a real treat for Karen.

Karen had asked why they had chosen to come to South Africa.

Cyril explained about the pogroms and the Holocaust, how Lithuanian partisans had only too willingly participated in the mass slaughter of Cyril's relatives.

Hannah continued, 'After the First World War, German-Jews, worried by the rising tide of Nazism, began to leave in numbers, going wherever they could. A few of my relatives had already settled in Cape Town. This worried the SA government, quite a few of whom were admirers of Germany, so they passed a law prohibiting new immigrants unless they were coming to marry someone already there. So my father wrote to a bachelor cousin asking if he would be prepared to marry me, get me citizenship and then annul the marriage. Once I was resident there, I would be allowed to bring out my siblings one by one. The older man agreed to play his role, and everything initially went according to plan. I got my citizenship, we got divorced, which was unfortunate for him because he had actually fallen in love with me. Unfortunately, I did not share his feelings, and not even the fact that he was very wealthy was sufficient reason for me to remain with him. Soon after that, I met Cyril and married for the second time.'

'What about your brothers and sisters? Did they join you?'

'To my everlasting regret, it had all taken too long, and immigration was completely halted. They were all taken by the Nazis and sent to concentration camps. Only one brother survived. But that's not something I want to talk about on such a lovely evening. It's lovely to have you here

– Sophie has spoken so much about you, and only nice things.'

The biggest treat for Karen was not the meal itself but hearing Beethoven's Emperor piano concerto for the first time in her life. No-one she knew played Beethoven in Mitchell's Plain, she mused as she looked at the record sleeve. After dinner, Sophie and Karen walked out onto the veranda, still clutching their wine glasses. Karen looked out and saw the twinkling lights of Sea Point below her, the beaches of Clifton to the left, the backdrop of the Twelve Apostles, and the tip of Lion's Head peeping over the roof above. The sun was setting, and there is no more beautiful place or time to be alive than being part of a Fresnaye summer sunset.

As Karen stood there, she thought wistfully how different Sophie's upbringing must have been from her own. 'I think I'm going to have to marry a Jewish *oke*, Sophie! I'm not used to seeing women treated as equals by men...'

'Then you'll have to convert, Ka, and knowing you, I don't think you'll take kindly to a Rabbi telling you how important it is not to mix meat and dairy foods together, or not to eat bread at Passover or not to *skoff* bacon.'

'OK, I'll cross that bridge when I come to it - first find me a Jewish *oke* who is as gorgeous as your dad!'

'Don't worry, they'll find you! There's nothing a Jewish medical student loves better than a student nurse because he doesn't have to fight so hard for sex. Jewish girls don't surrender their virginity just like that, you know. They have to take us kugels out at least ten times to the best restaurants before we allow them even to touch our tits.'

'So how come you're so different, Sophie?'

'Fuck off, bitch!'

The Sea Point Hall was packed with manicured, expensively-dressed women out in force to meet and listen to someone who actually did what *they* only spoke about – face up to the government. Helen Suzman spoke about the challenges facing South Africa, and the role that Jewish women could play in creating social, if not political, change. She had come from a privileged background, although her parents less so. Her father, like Cyril's, had emigrated from Lithuania and set up a business dealing in hides in Germiston, a small town outside Johannesburg. Then he made his fortune in real estate. They sent their daughter Helen to a convent school (they thought it would be a good experience for a Jewish girl in a gentile world), from where she went on to university and a degree in economics. It was then a short journey into politics, but a very long one through it.

In 1953 Helen was elected to parliament as member of the mainly English-speaking United Party representing Houghton, that most affluent of Johannesburg suburbs where the wealthiest and well-heeled Jewish denizens enjoyed the most comfortable of lives. A few years later, disaffected with the toothless United Party, Helen and eleven other liberal MPs broke away to form the Progressive party; sadly, in the next election in 1961 Helen was the only one of the dozen to be re-elected to parliament in Cape Town.

For six years, she was the only woman MP. The only liberal MP. Against overwhelming odds, she advocated a multiracial and democratic society, her only weapons being knowledge, logic, humour and a waspish tongue. She visited many of the dreary areas to which people of colour had been relocated and was shocked by their squalor. She was one of the few allowed to visit Mandela on Robben Island, and his wife Winnie when she was under house arrest. Suzman's reputation in the wider world was simply too strong for the government to prevent these meetings.

For the next twenty-eight years she would be a constant thorn in the side of the architects of apartheid, and she was ranked abroad as one of the best-known and widely respected South Africans. No one in that Sea Point audience could know that the following year Helen Suzman would be granted the United Nations' Human Rights Award, but all would know why and not one would be surprised.

Karen, who had shown little interest in politics, was visibly moved by Suzman's talk and for the first time really began to understand what was going on in her friend's head beneath the blond curls.

'Wow, Soph, she's quite something! I can see a lot of her in you too. Do you think you will follow in her footsteps? Go into politics?'

'Who knows, Karentjie, but first I have to finish what I started. We have got exams to pass, mountains to climb, so it's time to head back to our little cell.'

# Chapter 8:

## *Toilet duty  1977*

Their training had reached halfway stage – twelve months over, another twelve to go. The unpleasant side was gone (although Matron called the first period character-building) and they were now working in theatre, intensive care, obstetrics and counselling. They would share interesting stories of what went right and what didn't, what emergencies had occurred, stories of the occasional fuck-up made by the younger doctors.

There was one occasion that, while Sophie had been sent to I.C.U., Karen was on duty in the obstetrics ward. She noted the presence of a good-looking young man who seemed to be behaving somewhat strangely. He would spend a few minutes with his wife and new-born son and seemed as excited as any new father could be. But then he would leave them and nip in next door where a young woman had just given birth to a bonny daughter. It didn't take Karen long to realise the second woman was his mistress. This lover-boy obviously believed in duplication. One was good, two was better. The interesting thing was that the wife knew exactly what was happening next door but was not one bit fazed by her husband's promiscuity. Sophie - for whom things were either right or wrong - thought the whole situation untenable. Karen - for whom normal rules didn't always apply - took a more broad-minded view. The two babies were, after all, half-brother and half-sister. If everyone was happy, good luck to them!

They were no longer the juniors. It was expected that they and their colleagues would, to a large degree, have charge of the new batch of trainees and allocate the minor tasks. By and large the system worked well, and Matron thought it beneficial in the development of leadership skills. But it didn't always go smoothly because not all the juniors were as compliant as Sophie and Karen. With junior nurse Vermeulen it didn't go smoothly at all. Vermeulen was the female and much younger equivalent of beloved Kobus - hard-nosed, hard-arsed and built like a tank. In fact, she was stronger than many of the boys at her former school and it was unsurprising that she played rugby with them because few would have had the courage to tell her she couldn't. Quite why she had chosen nursing could be explained by no-one who knew her.

Anyway, one Monday it fell to Karen to delegate the jobs for the week. Karen knew nothing about any of the four juniors who were assigned to her, so she decided to go about it alphabetically, as one does. 'Miss Albert, sterilising duties; Miss Desmond, blood pressures and dressings; Miss Smithson, catering; Miss Vermeulen, bedpans and toilets.'

She heard a rumble from one of them. 'Sorry, Miss Vermeulen, did you say something?'

'Ja, I said you can kiss my arse – I don't take orders from *Kapies*.'

Karen bristled but decided not to take umbrage. 'I understand you don't want the toilet duties, Miss Vermeulen - some jobs are nicer than others, but you'll change round next week, ok?'

'Are you fucken deaf or what? I said I - don't - take - orders - from - Kleurlings.' Vermeulen turned on her heels and walked out. Karen's first instinct was to report the incident to Staff Nurse Pienaar, her immediate superior, but she was still a bit wary of Marie Pienaar. So she went next door and discussed the matter with Sophie. If Karen was bristling, Sophie was incandescent. She positively breathed fire. 'I'll knock her lights out, the bitch! I'll smash her teeth in! Who the fuck does she think she is?!'

## CHAPTER 8: TOILET DUTY 1977

Karen smiled grimly. 'Have you seen her?! I don't think it will be *her* teeth on the floor, so I suggest we do nothing and just let the matter sort itself out.'

Had Karen gone directly to Staff Nurse Pienaar, it might very well have been the scene of a very nasty confrontation, because it was to Pienaar that junior nurse Vermeulen had headed. *'Luister, Juffrou Pienaar, daardie fokken Kleurling se ek moet toilet duty doen!'*

Pienaar looked at her. 'So what's the problem, Vermeulen? Everyone has to be on toilet duty at some point.'

'You don't understand, it's not the toilet duty that I'm pissed off about, it's that Kapie who thinks she can give me orders.'

Now, at this point, you would have expected Marie Pienaar to side with her Afrikaans colleague, but Marie Pienaar had learned some things about kindness and fairness not only from her treasured Bible, but also from the two nurses who had made her carry a cat in her guts. Her eyes narrowed as she responded to the woman in front of her.

'Three things, Vermeulen. One, she's not a Kapie, she's white and has papers to prove it. Two, even if she is a Kleurling, and I don't give a shit one way or the other, she's a bleddy good nurse, one of the best we have. Maybe even the best. Three, if you've got half a brain in your head, which is very doubtful, you will go and apologise to her and tell her you will be so very happy to do the toilets. Or, if you prefer, you can go and discuss the matter with Matron, but I can guarantee that your next action after that will be to find a taxi to take you home. Matron and I both put Williams and Levine through the toughest training we could find for them, including the shit-houses week after week and neither of them complained or refused to work. Matron thinks even more highly of them than I do, and that's saying something. So, Miss Vermuelen-shit-for-brains, you decide and make your choice.'

With that, nurse Pienaar, bible-punching nurse Marie Pienaar who until that moment had never let a profanity slip from her lips, turned away. She actually smiled. After Vermeulen left, Marie said to herself, 'Now I know why people swear – I fucken enjoyed that!'

Vermeulen could not quite bring herself to apologise, but she did go straight back to the ward and ask Karen as sweetly as her trembling lips and clenched teeth could manage where she would find the cleaning cupboard.

# Chapter 9:

## *The English patient*

Both Sophie and Karen were on night duty when they brought John Jameson into the ward from theatre, still unconscious after the emergency removal of his appendix. Karen was the first to have to check the still-comatose patient just before they were due to go off duty for much-deserved sleep. She was more than a little surprised to notice two things. The first was immediately obvious: the man, despite being unshaven, was exceedingly good-looking, a Robert Redford look-alike. She checked his chart, musing to herself all the while.

'Let's see - he had his appendix removed at 9 o'clock. Bugger's still out like a light....... should be coming round in about an hour. Hm, John Frederick Jameson. Frederick?? So old-fashioned. He's too young to be a Frederick, only 30. I don't know any Fredericks, not where I come from anyway; Freddies, ja - we've got lots of Freddies, for sure. He's from Constantia. Rich. Next of kin: wife Regina. Posh. Pity he's married …. he's bleddy cute!'

The second thing she noticed was equally obvious: his shaven penis was semi-erect and seemed to elongate alarmingly as she bent over to check his dressings. 'My god, Sophie, come squizz at this! This guy's got the biggest *piel* I've ever seen! That's a dangerous weapon - he could kill someone!'

'What a way to go!', Sophie chortled. 'But sweetheart, if what they say is true, that's probably a little tiddly sardine for you.'

Karen replied, 'Jealousy will get you nowhere, babe, but I'll tell you what, if he ever offered me the chance, I'd grab it with both hands!'

Sophie giggled. 'You'd need both hands, my girl! Which reminds me, did you ever hear that joke about the cute nurse running down the passage with a syringe in one hand and a big bowl in the other? She's being chased by this very angry male patient clutching his cock - '

Karen interjected, ' - and as she runs past Matron, Matron says "You silly girl, nurse Smidgens, I told you to prick his boil, not to ........." - no, I haven't heard that one, not for at least two weeks!'

'Sarcastic bitch!'

'You should have just said 'Sophie's joke no. 57', and I would have wet my *broekies* laughing!'

'And I thought you were my friend!'

'Enough idle shit talk, Sophie! If Staff Nurse comes in she'll be the hell in. Let's go do some work.'

As they walked from the room, John Jameson opened his eyes very wide and, despite his pain, smiled.

The next day, the two nurses giggled like two schoolgirls throughout breakfast.

When they returned that evening to relieve the exhausted day shift, Karen was first in to check Mr Jameson. Fortunately, Jameson's tumescent penis had subsided to less embarrassing proportions but was still impressive. This of course prompted him to engage the attractive nurse in conversation.

He peered at the badge on her chest. 'I think I have a big problem, nurse Williams. I need relief.'

'That is very evident, Mr Jameson. Is your problem intermittent or constant?'

'What?'

'Does your problem come and go or is it constant?'

'Yes.'

'Yes what?'

'Well, it constantly comes and goes.'

'Very funny, Mr Jameson. It would be better if it went.'

'Maybe you can make it go. It needs the kiss of life, don't you think, Nurse?'

'The kiss of death might be more appropriate.'

'Ok then, perhaps you can just help me to settle it ...'

'When your pretty wife visits you – Regina, isn't it? - perhaps she can oblige.'

'My wife is not the cause of my problem, and definitely not its solution.'

'I am not the solution to your problem either.'

'You are most certainly the cause!'

'I think the anaesthetic from the operation has confused you, Mr Jameson, now be a good boy and go to sleep.'

'"*To sleep: perchance to dream. Ay, there's the rub*" – just a *little* rub, nurse Williams?'

Karen didn't hesitate with her riposte.

'"*For in that sleep of death, what dreams may come when we have shuffled off this mortal coil, must give us pause.*" .... I think you should pause, Mr Jameson...'

'Touche, nurse Williams! You certainly know your Hamlet!'

'Matric setwork. Hamlet and his girlfriend came to a sticky end. I don't like sticky ends.'

'Don't knock it till you've tried it! When I've recovered, I'd like to get together with you.'

'In your dreams, Mr Jameson. *"We are such stuff as dreams are made on, and our little life is rounded with a sleep."* '

'That's not from Hamlet, miss Williams - '

'The Tempest, actually. I acted in that one; played Ariel, the fairy spirit.'

'So you're not just a pretty face.'

'And you won't be one either if you don't go to sleep. Good night Mr Jameson!'

The following day the dressings were changed without alarm bells being rung. Jameson did however manage to make some pleasant small talk before Mrs Regina Jameson imperiously entered, her mere presence sending Karen to the other end of the ward wishing she were a little more elegant. The woman had breeding etched on every inch of her body from her pointed high-heel shoes to her carefully coiffured blond hair.

When Regina left an hour later, Jameson pressed the service button and was neither surprised nor upset when Karen seemed to be the first to answer his frequent bell-rings. That Karen was more inclined to respond to his smooth words than her small blond colleague had not gone unnoticed. He dispensed charm with almost the same enthusiasm as he complained about the dreadful pain he was experiencing in the lower region of his abdomen.

Over the next three days he made Karen laugh whenever she came near him. 'I think my penis has died, nurse Williams, and I'd be ever so grateful if you resuscitate it', whispered John.

Karen quietly responded, 'I think you should ask your beautiful wife the next time she visits you, Mr Jameson', and was surprised when he grimaced as he said, 'She wouldn't want to disturb her lipstick – it takes her an hour to put it on, you know.'

Sophie had noted Regina's disdain for the tall olive-skinned girl whenever Karen appeared on the scene. Regina obviously suspected Karen was of mixed race, but there was far more to it than that. Regina Baker came from prime English stock, Somerset UK to be precise. Her great-grandfather had come out to Kimberley, South Africa, in the late nineteenth century to claim a share of the diamonds so abundant in this mining town. He had found sufficient sparklies to become a member of one of the several large syndicates of English origin that were forming in Kimberley to counter those formed by the Jewish barons from London, Eastern Europe and Germany. Later, moving to Johannesburg, Sir George Baker had been one of the founders of the Johannesburg Polo Club where the upstart

Jews were precluded from membership *(what did they know about riding horses anyway - their only experience with horses was being trampled on during the pogroms).* Unfortunately for Sir George, not all the companies of which he was a shareholder proved rewarding. While many of the original syndicates prospered beyond belief, Baker's fortune had dwindled, largely as a result of later investments in the few gold mines that had failed to deliver.

Regina's grandparents, hardly poverty-stricken but forced to work, had moved to Cape Town and settled in the forests of Constantia. Their son, her father, had gone into merchant banking. This reversed the downward financial trajectory. One of the reasons for this was that working under him was a bright young man named Jameson who showed unusual aptitude for investing client's funds very successfully. Geoffrey Baker felt no qualms about introducing him to his oldest daughter, the only one of three who was not yet married. It was not long before her status changed. Within five years Regina and John Jameson had three daughters of their own, cared for by two full-time maids.

It also did not take long before Regina learned two things about her husband. The first was that his ambition was limitless, matched only by his talent and capacity for hard work. The second was that not all his nights at 'business dinners' were spent as such. She was not the last to find out that he had a penchant for pretty young things in short skirts and of lower station. Especially for typists from Mitchell's. It was not as if he did not desire her – quite the contrary. His libido seemed to be increasing in inverse proportion to her own. Whether her growing disdain for sex - her virtual denial of personal contact with her husband fuelling his desire to seek elsewhere - or whether the thought of him going skin to skin with these women of a social stratum so much lower than her own was just so utterly repulsive, it was impossible to say. Both were probably true. She considered locking him out (and did on the odd occasion) but decided that his rapid rise to a directorship of the merchant bank and eventual maturity would bring him to his senses, and he was bringing home enough money through extraordinary bonuses and share options to maintain her in the lifestyle she felt her not-far-from-royal pedigree deserved.

And now he was winking at this ... this trainee nurse. Yes, she was a beauty, no doubt about that, but only a blind person would not see that there was more than a touch of the tarbrush there.

After Regina and their daughters left, John extended his hand to Karen when she arrived to check his temperature. She ignored it. Unperturbed, he whispered, 'When I can stand up straight – take that any way you like – I'm going to take you out for dinner.'

'Oh, are you now? Forget it! No way, Jose!! Take your pretty wife out for dinner!'

'But what if I prefer you?'

'You got more chance of falling pregnant! I don't mess with married men!'

'Most women would give their back teeth to go out with me – not to mention their front teeth....'

Karen bristled. 'Just what did you mean by that?!' She knew precisely what he meant. It was an urban myth that Kleurling girls in South Africa had their upper front teeth extracted in their teens the better to please their men. The Passion Gap, it was called.

'Nothing, nothing. I just don't take no for an answer. If I want something, I usually get it.'

'Well, Mr Jameson, you are about to have a new experience!'

# Chapter 10:

## *The Newlands Hotel 1977*

The other nurses were being particularly noisy and she could just about hear her name being repeated on the dormitory loudspeaker: 'Karen Williams, call for Karen Williams, line 2....'

'Hey, Karen, howzit, it's John Jameson.'

'I said you mustn't phone me. Why aren't you hearing?'

'I can't get you out of my mind. I think you're beautiful.'

'Don't be ridiculous, man. You've got a lovely wife and three gorgeous daughters.'

'I just want to see you again.'

'Ekshly, I know exactly what you want from me, Mr Jameson, and it isn't to see me. Dream on!'

'No, listen, Karen, please, I'm actually begging you, meet me at the Newlands Hotel tomorrow evening.'

'I said, no way! In any case, I'm working night shift.'

'No you're not, I've checked. Meet me at the Springbok restaurant at the hotel, nice and quiet.'

'Mr Jameson, I said no – I don't need shit. Do you want me to get thrown out of here? If Matron finds out, that's what will happen. Please, don't do this thing.'

'Eight o'clock. Newlands Hotel. I'll be there. And my name is John, okay?'

'Where did you rush off to last night, Ka?'

'I don't want to talk about it!' retorted Karen, but the truth was she very much needed to talk about it. Never had she felt so conflicted. Although John was by no means the first man she had slept with, he was the first married man, and this was uncharted waters. She had taken a dive into a deep pool, and now felt very unsure as to whether she would be able to swim. Sophie was the only person to whom she could turn for a helping hand, but she feared that she would get little understanding or sympathy from her friend.

She was right.

'You were with John Jameson, weren't you?'

'No. I wasn't. I wasn't. I mean ... ag, bugger it, man, I can't lie to you, Sophie.'

'He fucked you, didn't he?'

'Ja, he bleddywell fucked me, ok?! What's it your business anyway?!"

'You're my soulmate, my only mate, Karen, so you are my business. Where did you go? Signal Hill in his big car?'

'You're pissing me off bigtime, Sophie - I'm not a fucken whore. The Newlands.'

'You're off your bloody head!'

'I didn't think it would happen.'

'Oh, you thought he just wanted to look into your big brown eyes and hold hands? Karen, what's out with you? Get real! He's just a spoilt rich playboy, and he's married with little kids - what do you want to get involved with him for?'

'I didn't think it would happen.'

'Then you're even more stupid than you look, *domkop!*'

Karen could barely manage to keep eye contact with her obviously disgusted friend. Sophie, who despite her bluff manner did not lack in kindness, picked up on this and put her arms around the distraught woman. 'Was it worth it at least?'

'Jesus, was it! He was so kind and gentle, you wouldn't believe.'

'That's what worries me – the man is so smooth. And what happens if you get caught? The Immorality Act doesn't play, Karen.'

'You're forgetting I've been reclassified white.'

'So that's OK then?'

CHAPTER 10: THE NEWLANDS HOTEL 1977

'Don't, Sophie, you're supposed to be a liberal but you're making me like a cheap *hoer*.'

'I'm sorry, Karen, you are my best friend here, my best friend anywhere. I love you like a sister. I don't want him to use you and then throw you away, I don't want you to land in the *kak*, babe, and that's where you're heading.'

'Well, it's my problem, ok? Geddit? Now butt out.'

Karen and John met the following week again. And for several weeks after that, at a small apartment that John owned not far from the Newlands Hotel. Sometimes at night, at others in the afternoon. John seemed happy to repeat how much the elegant and classy Regina grated him, although Karen was not always sure that he was being authentic. With each passing occasion, it seemed to Karen, John seemed to be a little less concerned (but certainly not unconcerned) about the act of sex which had begun so frantically that first night at the Newlands, and more and more interested in hearing what to her were trivial stories. Stories about the hospital, her friendship with Sophie, the other nurses and the myriads of illness-bearing patients. For her this was a first - her previous lovers were definitely more focused on areas a metre below her brain.

On one occasion as they were lying together, Karen related a story that was floating around the wards, which she was not sure she believed. 'There's this eighty-something-year-old, very tall guy in Ward 6, he's a bit *deurmekaar*, you know, doolally, and can't care for himself, so one of the nurses was washing his private parts. As she's sponging him, he says to her, "Have you ever seen anything so big?" She doesn't think it's so big at all, but she's humouring him and says, "Only once, this guy in Khayelitcha." And then he says, "My brother says I've got the biggest feet he's ever seen!" '

John's face took on a mischievous grin. 'As a matter of fact, my darling, I've also got a story. Once upon a time, this very unattractive nurse was examining some guy who had just had an operation. She called her mate over and said "This guy's got the biggest cock I've ever seen! Such a dangerous weapon - he could put my eye out!" Which I'm sure you'll agree is not the thing for a god-fearing nurse to be saying. And as for joke number 57......'

'No. omygod, no! You weren't awake, swear you didn't hear me say that! Ohmygod I'm so bleddy embarrassed!'

'And so you should be! I most certainly was awake, why d'you think I had such an erection with you staring at my crown jewels?'

'Jeez, you must have thought I was such a tart.'

'No, but I thought, seeing you were so impressed, I should give you a chance to play real games with my toy soldier.'

'Well, he seems to be standing to attention right now......'

On the first few occasions John used condoms, but as her trust increased he stopped bothering. Most of the time he controlled himself, but every now and then was unable to stop. Did Karen worry about this? Not one iota. Truth was, he filled her every waking thought and probably all her sleeping ones as well. However, when he started speaking about leaving Regina and the three little girls, Karen realised that she had crossed a boundary into territory where she had never been nor would ever fit. *Krill* test passed or not, her home, her family, her upbringing was Mitchell's Plain. Regina's father was chairman of the board of Sun Bank and wore expensive Italian suits; Karen's wore overalls always and dentures occasionally. Regina would have the raw kingklip or yellowtail fish for her dinner parties delivered fresh from Kalk Bay direct to her home in Constantia; Karen's mother would buy tins of pilchards from Pick'n'Pay as she got off the bus in the Plain. This was comparing cut-glass and tin. That was a truth she had to accept. Another: that Mitchell's Plain was even more alien territory for John than the forests of Tokai were for her. Leave Regina? Give up the bank? Move away from his

## CHAPTER 10: THE NEWLANDS HOTEL 1977

three little blonds for a reclassified *meid*? You must be joking! As Sophie said - get real!

The next truth she had to face was that her period was late.

Karen and Sophie had taken a break for coffee in Lower Main Road Observatory, a short walk from the hospital. This was a favourite place of theirs, because more often than not, the new LP by Abdullah Ibrahim would be playing in the background, his intelligent fingers counter-pointing the sometimes joyful, sometimes plaintive sax. On this occasion the mood was anything but joyful.
'What am I going to do, Sophie?'
'How sure are you, Ka?'
'Damn sure; I've missed two periods, I feel sick every morning.....I know I'm pregnant.'
'I thought as much – I'm not blind you know....What does John say?'
'He wasn't exactly thrilled. Says I must have an abortion, and he will be happy to pay for it.'
'Well, exactly as you'd expect, but that's a good next step. At least you can sort out a proper termination with a decent doctor, no Mitchell's Plain backroom job. I'll speak to my father, I'm sure he will advise you whom to see.'
'I don't want your dad involved. I don't want an abortion.'
'Ka, have you lost it completely? The bad news is, you're pregnant. You're nearly a nurse. The two don't go together. Matron will have your guts for garters. What's the good news? You know who the father is - many girls don't. He's got tons of cash.'
'You don't understand, Sophie, he's willing to give me money, but I don't want that from him. Actually, I don't want anything from him.'
'Now think, Karen Willemse Williams: you managed to get yourself reclassified, you're white now. What happens if your baby is more mixed than you?'

'Then I'll go back to Mitchell's.'

'Perhaps you can also go back to Kobus and tell him you want to become un-reclassified - maybe you can get to fuck him again. Karen, I always suspected you were a bit *dom,* but I never realised just how dumb. It's time to un-fuck your brain, kiddo. You are nearly through this training. You have the potential, once you finish, to work in a private white nursing home and earn more in a month than your parents earn together in a year. You have the potential to meet a nice quiet single doctor who will love you for your gentle nature and not for your pussy. I know you love John, but he is not about to give up his easy life to make you a decent woman. Take a little of his money, get done, get qualified, and get on with your life. Don't screw this up now!!'

'Sophie, I don't want an abortion, I want the kid. I love John so much but I'll never get him, and this is the next best.'

'You're insane! Just think for a minute: how are you going to explain to your child why it hasn't got a father? How do you think life will be for your fatherless child? How will you earn a living to support your child if you can't work??'

'I'll work things out, I always have.'

'Work things out, my arse - I'm going to speak to John.'

'Listen very very carefully, Sophie: if you do that, now or ever, I will never speak to you again. This is my problem, I've made my bed, now I must sleep in it.'

'You've spent too much time in bed already, and this is not the time to sleep. What are you going to do, my friend?'

'I have to think about it.'

'Well, think smart not stupid, okay?'

Karen left during the night. No-one saw her go. The next morning, Sophie saw the empty bed and understood. She understood that Karen was determined and strong-willed – Karen had shown this by her determination to get herself reclassified and leave her family at whatever the personal cost. She understood that Karen was fiercely independent. But she also understood that Karen was by far the more sensitive and indeed the more fragile of the two. Beneath it all was a very human soul. It was Karen who would take the loss of a patient more seriously and personally than she. She understood that when it came for them to be tested by life, if either of them was going to buckle, Karen would be first. She understood that Karen had reasoned that it would not be long before Matron Gray realised her condition and would have no compunction whatsoever in dismissing her, and she chose rather to leave on her own terms. And Sophie was intelligent enough to understand that her friend was a proud woman whose genetic make-up did not include seeking or accepting help with matters she could deal with herself.

Yes, the Karen that Sophie knew and loved was indeed a strong and very determined woman. She was strong enough to get through her adolescence in the tough environment of the Plain and come out unscarred. Nor had she been damaged by the indignity of buying her release from Kobus. She had withstood the barbs and taunts of the other nurses and gradually earned their respect and acceptance. She had even overcome Matron's Gray's antipathy. She was determined enough to go ahead with a precarious and ill-considered relationship with a married man. But when the die was cast, this courageous woman had caved in, pulled back - not a little, totally. Pulled back and pulled out.

What Sophie did not understand was why Karen had not shared that final decision with her. Why had Karen chosen to plough her own furrow? Did she not trust Sophie enough? Was she scared that Sophie would continue to pressurise her? Sophie did not understand that Karen's culture had taught her that when the odds were stacked against you, it was more sensible to cut out than to fight a fight you couldn't possibly win; and that when you did cut, you didn't always have to explain the reasons, you just did what had to be done. Yet, Sophie hoped that in the same way that Karen had made her decision to leave home and her family but had later ensured she kept close contact, Karen would also come back to her.

She dressed, went to the ward at seven and waited. Matron Gray stormed in at exactly three minutes past seven, holding a note. 'Explain this, Levine!', she thundered, squinting over her narrow spectacles. Sophie said nothing. Matron waved the note.

'*I hereby tender my resignation with immediate effect. Please accept my apologies. Karen Williams.*'

'What's this all about, hey, Levine?'

Again, Sophie said nothing. Matron turned on her heels and stormed out.

Sophie did not have Karen's parents' phone number, if they had a phone at all. On her first day off, she boarded the bus to Mitchell's Plain, and an hour later was standing at their door.

'Where is she, Mrs Willemse? Please let me speak to her.'

'She is not here – she come beck, tell us what heppened and she jus disappear the next morning. I don' know where she gone, strue's God I don' know. You shouldn't be here, Sophie, it's not safe for you, my husband mus take you beck on the bus. When she come beck, I will tell her she mus phone for you.'

Sophie left with Mrs Willemse's phone number in her bag.

Karen did not phone, but the next day Sophie got a letter.

*My Dearest Soph*

*I'm so sorry that I left so suddenly and never said goodbye. I just couldn't. I could not tell you what I was doing, you would surely have tried to stop me. I could have stuck around getting more and more swollen until I ended*

## CHAPTER 10: THE NEWLANDS HOTEL 1977

*up being thrown out by Matron, and I didn't want to give her that satisfaction.*

*You have been the best friend any person has ever had, but I have to deal with this by myself. Life does not always go as one wants, but I am not unhappy – I want this child. I will be happier if you don't come to look for me again. My parents did not lie to you, they did not know where I was, but now they know. If they ever tell you, they will never see their grandchild.*

*If it's a girl, her name will be Sophie. If a boy, he will be Simon.*

*I love you so much, Sophie. I don't want you to get distracted from your mission. Getting your qualification and doing something worthwhile with it is more important than having to worry about someone with her brains up her arse.*

*Have a good life, my little Jewgirl!*
*Your friend forever,*
*Karen.*

Sophie was not one to give up easily. She bombarded Mrs Willemse with calls, to no avail. Had time permitted Sophie would again have jumped on a bus to Mitchell's Plain, but time did not permit. It was only four months until finals, and Sophie was working overtime both at her studies and in the wards, especially since they were now a nurse short. Much as she cared for Karen, she was not about to blow her own graduation. After that, there would be enough time to find her friend and be on hand through the last stages of pregnancy.

# Chapter 11:

## *Cruel Death of a Courageous Man 1977*

Sophie's graduation ceremony at Groote Schuur in July 1977 was an evening replete with mixed feelings; on the one hand, immense pride at having taken on a system alien to her and conquering it. On the other, an aching void that her comrade-at-arms was not there to share it with her. Her parents were present, perhaps not quite as proud as they might have been had the title of 'Dr' been conferred on her, but proud enough. Dr Levine even recognised a couple of the older sisters he had worked with all those years ago when he himself was a houseman, and they spent the evening sharing pleasant memories.

Sophie mused wistfully how much prouder would Karen's parents have been if their daughter was also stepping up to be congratulated by a beaming Matron, until she realised that they could not have been there at all. Apartheid did not allow for such niceties.

She had decided she would continue on the staff for the immediate future. The change from being a student to becoming a nurse was liberating. She was the one making decisions instead of taking orders. The doctors were more respectful of her and would consult with her. Suddenly she was seeing the human side of Matron Gray, and they got on moderately well. She attempted on several occasions to find Karen, but this proved fruitless. Would she have continued? Almost certainly. But life has a contrary habit of introducing events that derail even the best of intentions, and the event that derailed Sophie was the death of Steve Biko.

## CHAPTER 11: CRUEL DEATH OF A COURAGEOUS MAN 1977

An article entitled *Cruel Death of a Courageous Man* appeared in the Cape Argus written by the British Guardian newspaper correspondent Richard Simpson (he who had written the article on Abdullah Ibrahim). It described how Steve Biko, a black medical student, was first banned, later arrested, and then effectively executed for his beliefs. "Dead in detention - a young man who had founded the Black Consciousness Movement in South Africa; someone devoted to the betterment of his people." It told of Johannesburg's John Vorster Square, one of the symbols of apartheid. One of the most chilling laws passed during John Vorster's leadership was the Terrorism Act which allowed the police to detain indefinitely and in solitary confinement anyone suspected of "terrorism" - defined as anyone who might "endanger the maintenance of law and order". No court could intervene, and no one had access to the detainees. Torture was routinely used. And it was at John Vorster Square that Steve Biko met his death.

Despite her liberal upbringing, Sophie up to this point had never got involved in any form of political activism, had not yet sought opportunities to explore the Helen Suzman option of political protest; but on reading the article, a worm turned in her mind. What she could not have envisaged at the time was that one day soon she would meet Richard Simpson, and that he would play a huge role in her life.

The Students' Council of Cape Town University, with the approval of the Deputy Vice-Chancellor, called for a mass demonstration in honour of Steve Biko, which would also serve as a protest against the actions and atrocities of the South African Police. A similar meeting had been called in Johannesburg. More than four thousand people, mainly white students, attended these rallies, and amongst those in Cape town was nurse Sophie Levine. Her tears for the dead hero turned to unbridled anger as the police who had gathered outside the University Great Hall began to spray teargas at the crowd as they were leaving the hall. Worse, they turned on those protesters nearest to them, beating them again and again with truncheons and *sjamboks*, those nasty leather whips. They did not stop until the Deputy Vice Chancellor forced his way to the front and told the police that if they wanted to continue their beatings, they would have to kill him first. The police commissioner gave the order for the police to withdraw but only if the crowd dispersed immediately. The students, who had never sought confrontation, realised that this was a battle they were never going to win, and noisily left the campus, all the while hurling abuse and insults at the police.

In the midst of the chaos following the spraying of teargas into the crowd, Sophie barely had time to stop and think. She knew she could not walk away. Choking on the toxic fumes, she knelt alongside a broad-shouldered young doctor and started tending the beaten and injured. The doctor introduced himself as David Rousseau. Even in the crush, she noted the gentleness of his tone as he comforted the injured, and his confidence in handling them. He said under his breath, 'Remember the police have spies here. We talk injuries only.'

It was a dreadful day, and Sophie was utterly exhausted when she returned to the hospital. Her tiredness was more than matched by the anger she felt. As she sank into her mattress, she thought about how unnecessary the violence had been; how it would just fuel more anger that would lead to further protests and to more brutality. There had to be another, better way. But her last thoughts as she drifted into sleep were about the kind doctor, David Rousseau.

# Chapter 12:
## *The Good Doctor 1953 -1977*

More than a hundred students, a few quite seriously hurt, were taken to Groote Schuur Hospital. The day after the protest meeting, Sophie and Dr David Rousseau were tending to the beaten and injured. Their eyes met across the large casualty ward. They recognised the anger that they shared. They could barely contain themselves when a couple of khaki-clad policemen strolled into the wards seeking names of the injured. Somewhat surprisingly, it was Matron Gray who told them to get the hell out of her hospital, not because she had sympathy for the protesters, but she cared a lot for her wards and wasn't having dirty boots traipsing about her polished floors.

Later, David approached Sophie and asked if they could meet to discuss what if anything could be done. He was surprised at how quickly Sophie responded.

The following night they sat together in a small cafe near Groote Schuur. Their conversation was not only about the protest meeting and its consequences. David quietly asked, 'What do you make of the Seychelles business?'

Sophie bristled. 'What the hell was Mad Mike Hoare and that bunch of mercenaries doing there trying to get rid of a legitimate socialist government?'

'Well, that's the point, isn't it? The last thing the SA government needs is a possible launch pad on their doorstep for a commie attack on them.'

'So you reckon Mr P W bloody Botha was behind it?'

'I'm damn sure.'

'Well, they sure fucked that one up.'

They laughed. It was obvious where their sympathies lay, and it certainly wasn't with the ruling Nationalist party.

Each was surprised at the origins of the other. He, an Afrikaner protesting against the rule of his own people; she, of an affluent Jewish family. Jews were known to give donations to anti-apartheid charities, even to support liberal protest movements, but not generally to be activists. In fact, with some very prominent exceptions such as Joe Slovo, Denis Goldberg and Albie Sachs, all of whom played a very large role in the ANC struggle, quite the opposite. There were not many who felt as passionately as they did, receiving nothing but scorn from their kin till eventually they learned not to speak. They tended to vote with their feet, and a significant number of Jewish families, fearing for their well-being and seeing no long-term future for their families in South Africa, had emigrated after Sharpeville to England, the USA, Canada, Australia and Israel. Similar activity was on the increase once again. The two spoke for a long while, and when they parted, they promised to meet again and soon. A seed had been sown.

Over the next few weeks, Sophie came to learn a great deal about the kind doctor. 'How come you picked UCT and didn't choose to go to University in Stellenbosch, like most Afrikaners?' asked Sophie.

'I guess I'm not like most.'

'So what makes you different?'

'We need to go back to when I was a child. My father was a god-fearing wine farmer who believed wholeheartedly in the Dutch Reformed Church's teaching that non-whites were always to be subservient to the whites. Every Sunday my two older brothers and I would trek with our dad from our small estate a couple of hours from Franschhoek to our local kerk where the Dominee would never forget to remind us that in the Book of Joshua it was stated that certain people were "hewers of wood and drawers of water." '

If that was what was written in the bible, David said, that was good enough reason for his parents to ensure that

## CHAPTER 12: THE GOOD DOCTOR  1953 -1977

their workers were a race apart. It seemed perfectly natural to David from his earliest days that he could love his Kleurling nanny, Susanna. But little David could also instinctively understand without any conflict why, even though she could wipe his bum and hold his tiny penis and minute little testicles while she cleaned them, or that she could still dress him from nude for play-school at the neighbouring farm, she could never kiss him. It didn't need explanation. That was just the way it was.

'I loved my mother, I loved her smell of brewed coffee and cooking, even if she never did much cooking. There was another Kleurling koek to do that, but Ma was always in the kitchen to see that the koek did it right. One thing the koek never did though was brew my dad's koffie - Ma was the only person to make it for him.

'But you know, Sophie, as much as I loved those smells, I loved Susanna's smell just as much.' Susanna whiffed a little of tobacco, a bit of shoe polish, of the various detergents used to clean the bathroom and to do the washing. This was because in addition to being his nanny, she was also the meid. She tidied all the beds every morning, washed the sheets once a week. She swept the floors, shone the shoes and dusted the ornaments and photos in every room every day. Each Thursday afternoon she was "off", excused from work, and would take the bus into Franschhoek where she would meet up with her buddies from other farms or local homes and have a smoke and some beer and a good laugh before going to the local non-whites bioscope in the evening to catch the latest cowboy fillim. Occasionally, Susanna would slip out with one of her male acquaintances to the park round the corner for a quick *gryp* and even an occasional *naai*.

One Sunday a month her husband would arrive from Cape Town, where he worked as a repairman at Woolworths, and on those days she never left her little room a small way away from the farmstead. She and Jools would make love endlessly until the time came for him to catch his bus back to Cape Town.

'My father Andre treated his workers hard but fair,' said David. 'As long as they did their job, he was happy to pay them their salary every month, even if it was substantially less than he paid his white foreman. If they then took that money and went for a blinder at the local shebeen, well, that did not concern my dad. Some of the neighbouring farmers were known to beat their workers – they took the words of Proverbs chapter something or other very literally.'

He was amazed when Sophie quoted the exact passage to him: ' *"He who spareth the rod hated his son. but he that loveth him correcteth him betimes".* Did your dad beat his blacks?'

'No, but he still considered them as children, to be kept in check – the men were always referred to as "boys", no matter how old they were.' Sophie well knew that black women too were treated as "girls" – no-one ever had a surname - and she found this abhorrent.

It didn't bother Andre too much either that non-white women would have jobs on a farm or in the town while their children were being reared by the grandmother in one of the townships, often many kilometres away. It was rare that a mother, father, children and their grandparents were in the same place at the same time, the singular exception being between Christmas and New Year.

'Very occasionally, my pa would agree to a worker having his wife and child with him for a short period, and I would happily play in the huge garden with the black kid, but I'm ashamed to say I still found it perfectly natural not to invite the child into my parent's home.'

'None of us Jewish kids were any different, David.'

David proved to be an excellent student through primary and high school. He excelled at Maths and Latin, and also at rugby, playing for his all-white team against all the other all-white and mostly Afrikaans-speaking schools

## CHAPTER 12: THE GOOD DOCTOR 1953 -1977

– rugby was the Afrikaners' national sport, whereas the soft English played soccer. When David was fifteen, however, an event occurred which shook his foundations to the core.

'Susanna suddenly took ill with a violent pain in her guts. My parents had gone off to Stellenbosch to buy provisions for the farm, my two older brothers were on a rugby tour, and it was left to me to find medical attention for the stricken woman. I phoned the doctor in Franschhoek to say that there was an emergency and he told me he would drive out urgently to attend to me. I said to him, *"Nee, Dr Conradie, die probleem is nie met my nie, dit is met Susanna, die meid.'* Dr Conradie bluntly told me that if it was not I who had the problem, then I had to find someone else, as he only did house-calls for whites. If the maid needed treatment, I needed to phone the non-white hospital just outside Franschhoek and get them to send an ambulance. So I rang. After a long, long wait I was told that there would be a delay of about four hours before an ambulance could be sent.

'By this time, Susanna was throwing up quite violently and was in severe pain. My dad returned an hour later, and to his credit did not waste a moment – he bundled Susanna onto the back seat, me in front, and drove furiously to the non-white hospital some thirty kilometres away. We carried the now unconscious woman into the hospital and waited with her in emergency for another hour. Trying to get a doctor's attention was futile – there were just too few and too busy. By the time they got to Susanna, she was gone.'

The woman who had brought up Andre's three sons and who had worked for his family for twenty-three years was no more.

Sophie put her arm around his shoulder, and he took her hand. The sadness they shared was palpable. She could only think that she would have reacted in exactly the same way had the trusted and beloved servant been her own Lettie, Mrs Lettie Somebody who was still with her parents.

'My dad was visibly upset, but just shook his head. That was the way of things – it was God's will.'

David, though, was utterly distraught, no less than he would have been had his mother Marie been lying dead in front of him. For him, that was a reset moment, a turning point in his life. Every thought of following in his father's footsteps was instantly jettisoned. He made two decisions there and then: the first that he would become a doctor, and the second that the doctor he would become would be compassionate to *all* races. So, when he matriculated eighteen months later, he chose to go to Cape Town to study medicine rather than to the racially segregated Stellenbosch, a decision that did not please his father, and David ended up in the wards of Groote Schuur.

Like that of Susanna all those years before, Steve Biko's death would profoundly affect him and lead him together with Sophie to a path of action he could never have foreseen when he was a child on the farm near Franschhoek.

# Chapter 13:

## *Protest 1978 -1982*

Both Sophie and David were extra-cautious because it was known that some of the most vocal and active of the protesters were in fact police spies. Over the next months, however, they learned to trust each other, and to share their dreams of a more just and equitable society based on social and academic freedom, not on skin colour. They realised that active protest was futile and would only earn them jail sentences or worse. Instead, they became involved in local activities. They wrote articles in the Cape newspapers, they lobbied Cape Town's business leaders, they organised small but effective strikes at factories.

On one of their sorties, they travelled out along the airport highway to meet a medical colleague, Dr Neil Aggett. Neil had graduated at UCT medical school the year before David, and although they had had contact, their shared liberal values were not developed because, after graduation, Neil moved to a hospital not far from Johannesburg. Later, Neil became involved in the Black Trade Union Movement that had recently been active in the Cape. On this particular day, he had organised a workers' strike in Langa, one of the poorest of the black townships, teeming with crime and seething with anger. David was interested in seeing how Neil went about his business and learned that he did it with surgical precision. After the short march was over, the workers dispersed and Neil, David and Sophie chatted at what passed for a cafe. Sophie saw the same qualities of commitment in Neil that she had witnessed in David and realised that both were prepared to put their lives on the line for their beliefs.

A few months after the Biko demonstration, Sophie got a message to attend Matron Gray in her office. There was little doubt in her mind what this was about, or what the likely outcome would be.

'What the hell are you up to, nurse Levine?'

'What do you mean, Matron?' Sophie knew exactly what Matron meant.

'Do you remember when you enrolled for your training, you were asked to sign an undertaking on pain of dismissal that you would not become involved in any political activities?'

'Ja, Matron, I remember that very clearly.'

'So please explain why you are organising strikes in the townships with a group of commie doctors?'

'Somebody's got to do it, Matron.'

'Well listen carefully, Levine, that somebody is not going to be one of my nurses, okay? I have every right to sack you on the spot, but you've been a very good worker, so I'm going to let you off with a very strong warning. Cut it out, d'you hear me!'

'Yes, Matron, I hear you, thank you Matron.'

Was Sophie upset by this interview? Was she angry? Neither. The following morning, she went back to Matron Gray's office and handed her a simple hand-written note.

*Dear Matron Gray,*

*I'm very grateful to you for allowing me to train under you and fulfil my ambition of becoming a nurse. I respect you for upholding your principles, even if I don't respect the principles themselves. I do believe you have made a better person of me, but I'm no longer prepared to lick your arse. Some things have to be done, and it is not for you to stop me. The twenty-first century is not far off, so It's time you moved into the twentieth.*

*I will not give you the pleasure of dismissing me. Therefore, please accept my resignation from your staff with immediate effect.*

CHAPTER 13: PROTEST 1978-1982

*Please convey my regards and deepest respect to my colleagues.*
*Sincerely,*
*Sophie Levine.*

Matron Gray was speechless and could only gawp over her *pince-nez* as Sophie walked away.

Her resignation was immediately followed by that of Dr David Rousseau. Now they were free, if freedom can exist in a police state, to pursue their dangerous agenda. David introduced Sophie to a colleague of Reverend Ambrose Reeves, Bishop of Johannesburg, who had got involved in putting to use the money from the International Defence and Aid Fund that had been donated by European benefactors. This fund, first started at the time of the Treason Trial by Canon Collins of St Paul's Cathedral, London, was secretively funnelled through to South Africa to pay the legal fees of those on trial for treason, as well as for many other political prisoners. Without this cash resource, many more protestors and freedom fighters (or terrorists, if you took the government view) would have gone to the gallows, not least Nelson Mandela. The IDAF had been able to pay the generously reduced but still substantial fees of the best advocates in the country. Sophie was far too young to get directly involved at the time and could not have known that not much later she would.

Sophie and David were becoming increasingly involved in SHAWCO, which was a student health and welfare organisation run by the University of Cape Town. SHAWCO grew to become an essential part of care for the elderly and disabled in the townships, as well as assisting in youth development. By the time that Sophie and David got involved, the Manenberg Centre was just being started, and David especially was devoting much of his time to its development. The Centre was to provide a medical clinic, as well as facilities for the visual and performing arts alongside a sports project. Manenberg, of course, held a special place in Sophie's heart. For different reasons, neither would be there to see its opening.

Their involvement with the Manenberg Centre was a sharp reminder to Sophie of her friend's back story. With aching heart, she often wondered how Karen was getting on, but nobody she spoke to knew. Her phone calls to Karen's parents always produced the same response: 'We think she ok, but we don't know where she living. We shall say for her to telephone you.' Karen never did. Sophie's calls eventually ceased because bigger battles were there to be fought.

By this time Sophie and David were living together, an unusual relationship in the morally conservative South Africa of the early eighties. Much good it did them. They were both so busy in their respective activities, more often than not clandestine and at different and remote hospitals. When they were together, which was rare, their time was spent planning campaigns rather than enjoying each other's bodies. Nevertheless, their love for each other grew, and with it fear of what consequences their actions might bring in the future.

This was not unfounded.

Sophie realised that she had embarked in a direction that was by no means predictable. More predictable, she thought, was the likelihood that, if not already so, her activities would come to the attention of the Security Police. She was not wrong. On several occasions they had been taken into custody for questioning. They were never arrested, probably because the government was wary of admitting that one of their own, a doctor no less, was against their grand vision of apartheid. *Why did it always seem to be doctors who were the troublemakers?* Nevertheless, David was regularly questioned and occasionally beaten, although never severely enough to cause him to change his position. They did however impound his passport.

In truth, both had gotten off very lightly. In the scheme of things, they were thought to be relatively small fish. Were they considered any bigger, they would probably have been arrested, detained without trial, and transported to Johannesburg. On the way they would have been put in the rear of a steel-lined police van with a loose spare wheel that would have knocked them around rather badly without a hand being laid on them. Once in Johannesburg, they would have been taken to the headquarters of BOSS, the Bureau of State Security, where electric shocks, nail-pulling and other delights would have been inflicted on them. And if they were really big fish, it was not unknown to accidentally hang oneself, or to "fall ten storeys out of a window after slipping on a bar of soap while showering".

It was not surprising that the government and its law enforcers were so paranoid about activists. Hardly a week went by when *Unkonto I Sizwe,* the military arm of the ANC, did not explode a bomb or attack a military or police target. This type of action achieved very little in the short term for *Unkonto*, but their activities were just the excuse the government and its state-controlled Afrikaans newspapers needed to cast the ANC in the role of *die swart gevaar*, the black danger - aided and abetted by the movement which white South Africa feared most: communism. Nelson Mandela, *Unkonto I Sizwe's* internationally known founder, had by now been in prison on Robben Island for fifteen years, but the snake had developed new heads, and it suited the government very nicely indeed to stoke the fears the whites had of being slaughtered in their sleep by marauding black mobs spurred on by the spirit of Karl Marx.

As a consequence, it became increasingly difficult for David and Sophie to continue to protest openly. They were being given little choice but to operate underground, a place where they did not want to be. And then their colleague and friend Neil Aggett was taken by the police - and the police did not play.

Just as Steve Biko's death had been a defining moment for Sophie and David, so at that time was that of Dr Neil Aggett, whose trade union activities were to cost him his life at the age of 28 early in 1982. Not long after the Langa protests, Neil and his girlfriend, Liz Floyd, who was also a doctor and an anti-apartheid activist, were seized by the security police in November 1981. They were held in solitary confinement at Security Police Headquarters. They never saw each other again.

Liz was haunted by hearing Neil being tortured in an adjoining office in Johannesburg's notorious John Vorster Square police station. A team of policemen regularly covered his head with a wet towel. They tied the towel so tightly that Neil struggled to breathe. He did not know if they planned to suffocate or electrocute him to death. The shocks made him scream compulsively as electricity lit up his body in flaring sheets of pain.

Seventy days later, Neil Aggett was found hanged in his cell. The police said he had committed suicide, but his inquest revealed that he had been tortured. Aggett made an affidavit 14 hours before his arrest that on previous occasions he had been assaulted, blindfolded, and given electric shocks. For the first time in a South African court of law, former detainees gave evidence of torture. A witness, Mr Ngwenya, told the court, "He was entering the storeroom where our belongings were kept. He appeared not to be walking normally. He was walking wide legged, and I suspect something was wrong with his private parts."

Incredibly, Magistrate Kotze ruled that the death was not brought about by any act or omission on the part of the police. Dr Aggett was the first white to die in detention. Many people of colour had preceded him, and many more were to follow.

CHAPTER 13: PROTEST 1978 -1982

Fearing, not without reason, that the net was closing around them as well, Sophie and David made plans to leave South Africa for the chillier but much safer climate of England. There they could campaign openly without fear of arrest and torture, as Peter Hain, a student who was later to become a Labour MP, was doing so successfully. Over the last few months, they had built up a dossier of people or groups that might provide a network of support, a few in Europe, most in England. Sophie could leave legitimately, and would depart first, but because David's passport had been confiscated, he would follow a few weeks later using a forged passport and taking the traditional escape route through Swaziland.

She kissed David farewell at the airport.

As the flight departed, Sophie was a cauldron of emotions. On the one hand, she felt desperately sad that she was running from a fight where others with more courage had remained, regardless of the consequences. The sadness was tempered by the thought that by going to the UK, she and David could probably do more valuable work than they could achieve on the ground in SA. She was concerned that he was not with her, but as she waved farewell to him, she felt confident that his resourcefulness meant it would not be long before they were together again. She was sadly mistaken.

It was the last time she would see him because he was involved in an accident as he passed Khayelitsha township. His front tyre burst. His car left the road, hit a pylon and exploded. There was not much left to bury. This time the Security Police had done their job efficiently.

# Chapter 14:

*London* 1982

Completely unaware of what had happened, it was Sophie's good fortune to arrive in London during a late summer when the parks were resplendent in their beauty and the days were still long. She found temporary digs, as all South Africans and Antipodeans did in those days, in Earls Court. After a couple of days of sightseeing, she set about looking for a hospital job and accommodation nearby. Neither proved difficult, as the agency she approached was well up to the task. Within a week, she had moved into a small apartment in Highgate, north London, and began work as a nurse at the nearby large but creakingly old and quite depressing Whittington Hospital.

A minor problem she experienced initially was in understanding the multitude of accents that were directed at her. She could get by if they spoke slowly and enunciated their words clearly, but most did neither. Then she realised that they were probably having the same difficulty with her! In South Africa she thought she spoke perfectly normally. Here, in England, her guttural sounds sounded foreign, almost barbaric. Such irony!

Then the telegram from her father arrived, one of the last to be delivered in the UK before telegrams were replaced by tele-messages. Cyril had read about an accident on the M2 where an Afrikaans doctor had been killed. Although the newspapers had not blatantly stated it, there were rumours that David Rousseau had been a political activist. Not being entirely unaware of his daughter's clandestine activities, if not the full extent of them, he decided it would be safer not to phone her, as his

## CHAPTER 14: LONDON 1982

line might well have been tapped, but to use the quickest possible postal service. Despite the somewhat veiled but extremely sympathetic message, Sophie realised immediately that David had been brutally murdered.

She retched but nothing came. The tears did not come. Just numbness. Numb in her body and her mind. Then she reeled and sank to the floor. One of the other nurses ran to her, and all she could remember saying was, 'Those bastards killed him...'

The days passed, lonely days, filled with cruel hours. She had not realised just how much she loved the kind doctor. Now, she was alone. Alone, a stranger in a foreign land. Her colleagues tried to understand, but from where could understanding come? The only emotion Sophie was conscious of was blind rage. Oh, how she needed Karen to pacify her, to comfort her – but Karen was she knew not where. Later, when some degree of feeling returned, she felt utterly broken. The pain she felt with each breath was a barbed knife cutting into her chest, her guts, eviscerating her. She considered which the best way would be to kill herself. Overdose? Under a tube-train? But as her senses gradually resumed, she thought that the outcome of this course of action would be to hand the Security Police the very victory they had sought to achieve. The elimination of opposition to the state regime would be acceptable by any means.

No! She would find a way to ennoble David's sacrifice. She would find a way of helping to bring the oppressors down, however long it took. It was only by following this train of thought that she managed to stay alive, to continue working - and the mere pressure of work helped her through those terrible grim days, made worse by the onset of winter - dull, grey, dispiriting.

Everyone she knew in Cape Town who had ever been to Britain had always said that the most difficult thing to get used to was the dull weather in winter, when the days were short. Sophie found that she was spending all day indoors anyway, so even if the weather deteriorated it would be unlikely to affect her too much. What she did find however was that she was missing little things, mainly food items. She had never ever given thought, when living 'at home', to how much she appreciated having a rusk in the late afternoon with her tea, nor had she realised what a peculiarly South African custom this was. She was bemused when she went into a supermarket or deli and asked for rusks, and someone handed her a packet marked 'Farley's Baby Rusks'. They in turn were left perplexed when Sophie tried to describe Ouma [granny] muesli rusks. She was talking about this to a colleague who had spent time in London; she literally jumped with excitement when the colleague mentioned a deli in Belsize Park, a few stops up the Northern line, where the Mozambican owner sold not only Ouma rusks – muesli, wholewheat, or plain buttermilk – but Simba crisps, Provita, Peppermint Crisps, Five Roses tea and, best of all, real proper biltong! So, every couple of weeks Sophie would walk up through Regent's Park and get her supply, her fix as she called it.

The days passed slowly. Sad days. Boring days. Meaningless days. She found working at the Whittington much less of a challenge than Groote Schuur, where the work ethic was somehow more immediate, and if there was a job to be done, you did it, you did not delay it simply because it was 'not urgent.' The variety of illnesses was also less than she had experienced back home, where on a daily basis she would have come across diseases and sicknesses that were not to be found in any textbook.

What pleased her greatly, however, was that one's skin colour was simply not an issue. She liked the diversity of both the patients and the staff – she was routinely encountering doctors, nurses and patients from every conceivable country, but predominantly from the West Indies and the Indian subcontinent. Thinking about South

## CHAPTER 14: LONDON 1982

Africa, which she did often, she saw more clearly than ever the impossibility of living meaningfully under apartheid.

Some weeks later an airmail letter arrived bearing a South African stamp. It was from Karen. Sophie ripped open the envelope.

*My Darling Sophie*

*Where do I begin? Do I apologise for running without confiding in you? for saying that I never wanted to see you again? for behaving like a total arsehole? It probably won't help, but I am deeply sorry, my darling friend. I keep asking myself why I behaved that way, and the only answer that I can give is to plead temporary insanity due to hopelessly fucked-up hormones and emotional distress. If one day you experience the torment I was going through, and I sincerely hope you won't, perhaps you might get to understand a bit. I was an emotional wreck, I wasn't sleeping, and I felt so wretchedly guilty and ashamed of myself. If I'd had the guts, I probably would have topped myself.*

*I'm very glad I didn't, though, because I now have a beautiful little boy, a sweet, coppery little fellow who as promised was named Simon. I tried to find you at the hospital to let you know and was informed that you had left suddenly without explanation (we now have that in common!). I simply did not know where to get hold of you, so I phoned your mother. She explained your sudden disappearance and your flight to London. She told me you are now working at the Whittington (have I spelled that correctly?) and also told me about your friend's terrible "accident." Bastards!!! May they rot in hell!*

*We had Simon's christening a few weeks ago. I wanted to write to you to be part of the ceremony, if only in spirit. I so much wanted you to do me the honour of being godmother and attending the ceremony which was at a small church in Observatory. The ceremony was a simple one, and afterwards the small group (no nurses!) came round to my little flat nearby in Obz. How I missed you! My proud parents had prepared a simple but delicious meal that included pickled fish and bobotie followed by creamy melktert. You would have smaaked it!*

*Sophie, I have to tell you that, whereas a while ago you were 100% my best friend, that no longer applies – our friendship is now diluted. Your place at the top of the pecking order has been stolen by this little boy I now hold in my arms, sucking his fingers and toes. That's him sucking, not me, although he loves it when I do! Little boys are just like men!*

*I chat almost daily with my mom. She's feeling pretty lonely these days because my dad spends so much time on the booze. We talk about our old friends, the gossip from Manenberg and Mitchell's and the news of where and who the gangs are shooting.*

*Your mother told me that it was not safe for you to be communicating with anyone in this country (the security police have eyes everywhere) so I am not expecting a response. Sophie, I know that we have to continue in the state of apartness (what a disgusting word!) but I know in my heart that no matter the distance, we will always remain close to each other. If we don't catch up in Cape Town, Simon and I will have to come to London.*

*I hope that happens soon. I miss you so much.*
*All my love,*
*Karen.*

Despite knowing full well that meeting up with her friend would definitely not happen soon, the letter lightened Sophie's dark mood. Karen had not mentioned John in her letter, so Sophie concluded he was most likely out of the picture, probably permanently. Oh how innocent and gullible her friend had been, so utterly beguiled by the smoothest of operators – arsehole!

## CHAPTER 14: LONDON 1982

Karen's letter put her in a quandary. Of course she wanted to respond, to offer her congratulations, to tell Karen where her activities had led her. But Sophie remembered Helen Suzman recounting how the Department of National Security had tampered with her mail, withdrawing it from the mailbox she was using down the road. She knew there was no effort they would spare to incriminate those suspected of aiding and abetting communist revolution, and by definition therefore betraying their country. In anything related to the security of the ultra-paranoid country of her birth, communication with anyone was fraught with risk for all parties. Sophie realised she should do nothing that would place herself on the Special Squad's radar. She knew it would be foolish to discuss her clandestine activities with Karen lest her friend be contaminated and acquire more knowledge than was good for her. Sophie did not wish to make her friend an 'accessory after the fact'.

Karen of course would be upset, but Sophie was not going to take any risks, especially now that Karen had responsibility for another little human being. She would later do it anyway, but held back for the time being. Eventually she sent Karen a short note, simply saying she was feeling alright but would not be writing for a while. She did not sign it nor post it locally.

The winter passed into spring. Another summer, this time very wet. Winter again. She was wrong about the weather not getting to her. It wasn't the main cause of her distemper, but it certainly added to it.

Sophie had been promoted to staff-nurse and was having to deal with a group of underlings who were more concerned with reducing work hours and increasing earnings than healing. Even this responsibility was unable to ignite the woodenness that Sophie felt within herself. She rarely went out, and when she did it was always alone and mostly to theatre or cinema. This stimulated her for a few hours but by the time she returned to her small apartment the numbness would have returned. Not by any stretch of the imagination could Sophie be said to have enjoyed her first two years abroad. but the one thing she knew with certainty was she could not return to South Africa while the existing government was in power.

Karen had often thought of writing again to Sophie, especially during Simon's early days, but she knew that her soul-sister was living in exile. Reluctantly, she decided she did not wish to make it easier for the security police to track Sophie down and cause trouble. So, with the passage of time those thoughts receded, and she thought maybe the best thing was to stick to her determination not to be dependent on anyone, and let the old relationship, however much it had meant to her, just be laid to rest.

Then, a letter, as unexpected as it was welcome, arrived from Sophie. After months had passed, Sophie had decided that it was indeed time to respond to her friend - to hell with risks, and damn the bastards!

*Greetings, Karen*

*Howzit my darling, and howzit with the little one? He must be two already, and I've missed all of it! I'm really sorry that I have not written all this this time. Just a teeny bit paranoid that those evil shits are out to get me as well.*

*You seem so happy, and I am so pleased that you did not take my advice to get yourself sorted. Sometimes (you will probably say at all times) I can be hard-arsed, but I so much wanted you to see the nursing course through. Now, as I re-read your letter, I realise that there is a more important purpose in life, and that is life itself. You have created a new one, and my wish for both of you is that you will be blessed with health, happiness and that Simon will have a better sense of humour than you!*

## CHAPTER 14: LONDON 1982

On the other hand - on the other hand there are four fingers and a thumb - that's a joke, Karen, number 97 – on the other hand, never have I needed your presence as much as I do right now. As you are aware, I received some very bad news, and have been battling to come to terms with it. My heart has become a lump of ice.

I am dedicated to my work, because if I wasn't, I'd spend my time thinking, and thinking is something I don't want to be doing. The hospital was around when Disraeli was a kid, it really creaks. I realise how lucky we were to train at GS. We dealt with diseases there that aren't even in the textbooks here.

The West Indian and Asian nurses are lovely, but so laid back! To my amazement and occasional amusement, I have found I have become a strict disciplinarian. I cannot tolerate incompetence and substandard idleness. I'm not too popular with the nurses and cannot say I have made many friends. No, change that to ANY friends. I never realised how obsessive/compulsive I am - Matron Gray incarnate! With hindsight, I suppose I should have had more respect for the wise old bird. Unfortunately, the matron here is the polar opposite of our good lady, a really wishy-washy liberal type, so somebody has to take control. She's terrified of me!

My sex-life is non-existent - I'm suffering from disuse atrophy! The doctors don't interest me - too much shoptalk, boring as stale dog droppings. There are one or two that under different circumstances I might have considered suitable to relieve the atrophy problem, but if I am honest with myself, the mere thought of fucking another man is puke-inducing. I have rightly become known as The Iceberg, and it bothers me bugger all.

I am tempted to tear up this letter. It's such a load of self-sorrow. But hey, if I can't share that with you, then with whom? As I read it, I realise what a misery-guts I have become, but maybe the mere act of writing to you might bring about positive change. No, it will! I feel better *already! It starts now – today is the first day of the rest of my life.*

*So let me tell you about something happy that happened today. I was supervising in obstetrics with a lovely little midwife (no, you should know which way I swing, not that I am swinging at all these days). Our patient was a Jewish woman from nearby Stamford Hill, which has a large Hassidic community. They don't believe in birth control, in fact the opposite – the only purpose of having sex is to increase the Jewish population to replace those lost in the Holocaust, and Sara was about to have her tenth child! Imagine that, Karen, she is only a couple years older than I am, and I will probably never have kids. Doing nothing for my nation – how sad is that?! Anyway, she gave birth to a gorgeous little girl. It was my pleasant duty to go out and inform the family that they had another daughter and sister. The whole bunch had come to the hospital in their mini-bus, and when they heard the news, they all burst out singing and dancing in the passage. Now here's the interesting thing. The oldest daughter was here last year giving birth to a little girl who will be older than her newly arrived aunt.*

*And on that happy note, it's time to end, go to the mirror and SMILE.*

*All my love,*
*The (about to thaw?) Iceberg.*
*PS If you do want to write, address it to Jenny Ward (she's someone at the hospital that I can really trust) and post it from a post box not too near your home.*

Still paranoid about being detected, she gave the letter to one of the nurses who was about to leave on holiday to post from Portugal. Another letter was soon dispatched from Observatory Cape Town to Archway London.

*My Darling Jenny,*

## CHAPTER 14: LONDON 1982

*It was so good to hear from you at last, and that you are trying to get over the lousy hand life has dealt you. Keep going, babe!*

*On this side of the world, I must tell you that I am living with a man. His name is Simon, he's small, but very wise. He doesn't give me grief, and I love him to bits. Soon he will be starting school, and if he is half as smart as I think he is, I think he will get on just fine. I have no other man in my life and am very happy to keep it that way.*

*I've got a job, working with a really kind, accommodating dentist in Claremont. He's one of your tribe. He pays me well and appreciates my use of the skills you and I learned together. The good news is there isn't a bedpan in sight!*

*My folks are very helpful in caring for Simon. They've both more or less retired. I couldn't work without their help. My old man is hitting the bottle more than ever, but he adores Simon, and the feelings are mutual.*

*I am probably the happiest I have ever been and have no regrets about anything or anyone. The only thing that could improve it would be being able to see your fierce face instead of picturing it. I'm sure that will happen very soon.*

*Till then, my darling!*

*Yours as ever,*

*Karen.*

*ps the photo I've enclosed is of guess who ......*

Sophie, easily reduced to tears, wept once more with joy. How wonderful that her friend sounded so happy, and as for the photograph..... there was this handsome child. You could tell he was Karen's son, but there were clear signs that his father, the handsome philandering banker, had contributed generously to the gene pool. And standing next to Simon, the woman whose memory had sustained Sophie through those dark years; the woman who was as beautiful as ever she had been; the woman who despite all odds being stacked against her seemed at peace with the world and with herself.

She did not delay with her reply.

*Hi Babe,*

*I know I said we shouldn't communicate, but you know what, babe, I miss you so much. Hardly a day goes by when I don't think about you and your little Simon. To tell the truth, time has ceased to have meaning for me.*

*You cannot believe the joy that I felt when I received your letter. My Karen - thriving!! You are amazing! When I think of how I had feared for you, when I think of how I begged you to get a termination, how pleased am I that you were strong enough to believe in yourself! Your Simon is indeed a handsome young man, and I hope he will not be much older when we finally get to meet.*

*My story is rather different. It has not been an easy journey, but it has been one of personal growth. I am no longer the person who loved clubbing at the Starlite, or who played games with nurse Pienaar's x-ray. Nobody here understands my jokes, so I've finally given up telling them. It's not that the British are unable to laugh – some of the tv shows are very funny – it's just a different culture. I do not laugh much these days, haven't since those fascists murdered my David. (If you are reading this, you bastards, your time will come sooner than you think.)*

*But from adversity comes strength, and I am stronger and more determined than ever that his death will not be that of just another dissident. I wish I could tell you more, but that will have to wait. Suffice it to say that you will not believe what I have got involved in, what strange things I do!*

*It took me a long time to get to like London, but I've got over the weather and the insularity of the people, and rejoice in its tolerance and liberal spirit. There's more racism here than you would believe, but it's not the central*

CHAPTER 14: LONDON 1982

*part of their lives. People just get on with things. The hospitals and transport services wouldn't exist if not for immigrants from the West Indies and India and Pakistan. Indian food is what I have grown to love, and although completely different to your mother's cooking, I think about her every time I go into the New Delhi Tandoori or the Karachi. I hope your parents are well – please give them my fondest regards.*

*TV and theatre are wonderful – I love the political discussions where people can state their opinion without getting beaten up or arrested – and there's a political satire called "Yes Minister" featuring Nigel Hawthorne. I can't begin to imagine a show that mocked Mr Fucking Botha!*

*I now consider England home, but know that I have another home to return to when the time is right. May that soon.*

*Take care my darling and may your cup of happiness overflow.*

*Your friend forever,*
*Sophie.*

Then Richard Simpson came into her life, the same Richard Simpson who had written so eloquently on Abdullah Ibrahim and the demise of the medical student Steve Biko.

# Chapter 15:

## *Richard Simpson 1984*

In the early eighties, Richard Simpson was a political reporter living in London. He enjoyed working at the Guardian, which was considered the foremost of English intellectual broadsheet left-wing newspapers. He was typical of his profession, unassuming but determined to reveal truth in all its colours. Having come from a lower middle-class background lacking in privilege but with an excess of socialist principles, he had been determined from his earliest days to fight (metaphorically) for those principles. He loved football, and would happily have become a sports journalist, but sport was for pleasure. Social change was the quest that drove him. By his prolific reading he had become worldly in every way. Initially, he had not strayed far from his birthplace in Crouch End in north London, but eventually he was assigned to travel abroad to any place where inequality reared its head - which meant he travelled a lot.

He was by nature a pacifist, eschewing the use of a sword but with the capacity to cut an opponent to shreds either with his tongue or the written word. He had an easy way with words, and his articles always brought a modicum of clarity to the most complex of situations.

The seventies were heady times for those who had voted Tory Edward Heath out of power and replaced him with Harold Wilson of the Labour Party. Unfortunately, the legacy of the miner's strike had cut deep into the nation's psyche, and not even a Labour government dared to award inflation-busting salary increases to the members of the trades union who had voted them into power. This of course went down very badly with ambulance drivers,

## CHAPTER 15: RICHARD SIMPSON 1984

underground train workers, the police, teachers, and not least the nurses. The situation that had begun in the seventies had still not been remedied in the eighties.

Difficulty had arisen about remuneration at some NHS hospitals in North London, and Richard was assigned to interview the leader of the local nurses' union who was threatening to call her members out on strike if they weren't to be adequately compensated for working overtime. He had a great deal of sympathy for their cause. Just the previous week he had written a strongly worded article berating Margaret Thatcher and her team for not being more sympathetic to the nurses of Great Britain. Richard described the nurses as a seriously overworked, grossly underpaid and extremely dedicated group of highly skilled professionals. So, unsurprisingly, Richard was welcomed most warmly by the nurses' spokesperson, Staff Nurse Sophie Levine.

He knew a little about Ms Levine: she was an expatriate South African who had arrived in London three years previously. She had apparently left Cape Town in something of a hurry. He had been made aware that Sophie's left-wing activities at Groote Schuur Hospital were under intense scrutiny by the South African Security Police Special Branch, that notorious squad that had been involved in the detention (and too often with the deaths) of political protesters. There had also been talk that her life partner, a doctor who was to have joined her, had died in mysterious circumstances.

It had not taken Sophie long to observe the apathy that seemed to characterise the nurses' union meetings; everyone saying something needed to be done but few willing to do it. Sophie, by contrast, was. Richard quickly realised that this forthright, outspoken woman he was interviewing was someone quite extraordinary. Sophie and Richard struck up an immediate rapport, which led to an invitation for him to join her for tea in the nurses' staff room.

There, the highly articulate little firebrand with her thick South African accent made her case with a series of soundbites that rolled off the printing presses of the Guardian the next day to the general acclaim of Richard's colleagues, in particular his editor. Richard phoned Ms Levine that evening to thank her for being so cooperative and ended the conversation by asking her to join him for dinner the following night at a cheap and cheerful bistro near the Whittington Hospital.

He got there a few minutes early and was already a glass of chianti ahead of Sophie when she arrived. She accepted a glass of the inexpensive wine, and he refilled his own. The atmosphere at Mama Gina's made it easy to relax, and the gnocchi slid down as easily as the wine. The gentle saxophone jazz music of a Fausto Pipetti cassette provided a not-too-intrusive background to the conversation, and they spoke easily. Although she was able to talk calmly about the loss of David, her anger towards the South African police in general and the Minister of Police in particular was intense. She did not allow this to put her into a bad mood but said she would only return to South Africa when Nelson Mandela became the leader of the country, never doubting for a moment that this would happen.

She told him about her days of nursing at Groote Schuur, also about her friend who had become white. And then disappeared. They had recently begun to correspond. Sophie felt certain they would meet again.

It did not take Richard long to realise he had found a woman much like the *canoli* they had just had for dessert – firm on the outside but a soft, sweet heart. The three hours Sophie and Richard spent together passed quickly, and it was she who said they should meet again soon. They shook hands before she boarded the bus back to the Whittington, and her genuinely warm smile left him in no doubt whatsoever that this was a woman with whom he

## CHAPTER 15: RICHARD SIMPSON 1984

could easily spend the rest of his life. And Sophie had similar feelings.

The nurses' grievances largely having been met, Sophie returned to her routine, the only difference being that she allowed a few minutes extra each morning to read Richard's column in the Guardian. The hospital seemed to be gradually moving into the 20$^{th}$ century; new computer technologies were emerging that facilitated record-keeping and storage. This was not of much interest to the nation, certainly not as much as the goings-on at a certain ranch in Dallas, where the dastardly deeds of JR Ewing were keeping the nation enthralled. One who was not enthralled was Richard, who found the decadence of Southfork nauseating.

After the newspapers had sated on the marriage of Prince Charles to Diana, they were turning their attention to the Falklands. While virtually the entire country thought the invasion by the Argentines unjustified, Richard's was a lone voice for their cause on historical grounds. This was partly because he simply couldn't bear Margaret Thatcher, and it irked him that her popularity increased so greatly after the invasion was repulsed. Sophie shared these feelings.

*

*My Dearest Karen*

*Reading about your love for the little chap and the joy of motherhood lifted me, but made me question myself deeply. Why throughout my life have I always chosen the most difficult route, the biggest challenge? Why do I always have something to prove? What's so wrong with ordinary? I remember your words to me that day I expressed interest in going to Abdullah Ibrahim's gig. You advised me not to look for problems, but I am only too well aware that I have, for that is my way. I can only conclude that you are by far the happier and more content.*

*The good news is, things are beginning to change.*

*I am in a strong relationship with a really interesting man – his name is Richard. He's English, about ten years older than me, and smokes a pipe (but not too often). Can you believe that?! I go nuts when somebody smokes a cigarette, but somehow his pipe doesn't seem to worry me. Maybe I'm mellowing with age, or maybe it's the wine-soaked tobacco he uses that gives off such a nice aroma! He is gentle, measured (most of the time) and intelligent (all the time). I find what's going on in his head even more interesting than what's going on in his trousers, and you've not heard me say that about many men!*

*He is kindly–looking, and that's because he is kind. I'm lucky to have known three gentle men: my dad, David and now Richard. He is my totally reliable core, the antidote to my excesses.*

*He cares about other people and he cares about me. Richard writes for a newspaper. I don't want to state what his political inclination is, but I can tell you what it's definitely not – it's not hard right. Richard is a campaigner and was very helpful in getting us nurses a pay rise. We nurses still get paid shit considering the work we do and the long hours, but our lot has improved a little.*

*He is teaching me to listen to other people's views and not be such a hothead. I've learned that works much better in the UK, not like in SA where everyone is always telling everyone else what they should or shouldn't be doing. He's always reminding me that I've got two ears but only one mouth for good reason.*

*We work on a lot of projects together, none of which it would be wise to write about. Have I become paranoid? Well, I wouldn't be if the bastards didn't keep hounding me! Sorry, joke....*

*I have grown to love London. Theatre is amazing – there's an actor from Cape Town by the name of Anthony Sher (one of my tribe, and he's gay!) who is really highly*

## CHAPTER 15: RICHARD SIMPSON 1984

*regarded. I remember how you used to love Shakespeare and I'm beginning to as well.*

*Richard and I go walking on weekends on Hampstead Heath, which is like walking on Table Mountain without the mountain - lots of beautiful trees and bushes, rolling hills and great views of the City. The Heath is my refuge, my place of calm, my sanity restorer. It's walking distance from the little apartment where I live (there's nothing flash about Richard), and every spare hour I have is spent there.*

*Anyway, enough gabbling. So listen, if you want to write, please feel free to do so, c/o Jenny Ward, and send photos if you can.*

*Send my very best love to your parents.*
*Love you, babe!*
*Your soul sister xxxxx*

*PS You might not remember, but it was Richard who wrote that article about Dollar Brand / Abdullah Ibrahim that got me to insist on going to that gig in Manenberg, the first time I met your parents. How's that for closing the circle?!*

Richard was able to persuade Sophie that she should broaden her interests away from local nursing problems and direct her energy towards the more general health issues of the late eighties. AIDS and drugs were becoming a growing social problem. They both ran ongoing campaigns, he from the viewpoint that the only way to deal with the drugs issue was to decriminalise drug possession and usage completely. Sophie was more concerned about dealing with its effects. She would thunder on about the need for adequate treatment facilities, at that time more or less absent within the NHS. She started writing articles for different magazines and even (with a bit of leverage from Richard) for the Guardian. Both participated in the occasional late-night tv discussion, and their faces became recognisable to the intelligentsia.

So much for her low-profile cover, but no threats seemed forthcoming.

As had happened with David, she had grown to love this quiet man, and it was only a matter of time before she moved into Richard's small but comfortable apartment near Archway, North London. Conveniently, the flat was within walking distance of the Whittington. Their relationship was easy, fuelled by their common interests in politics, the arts and world music. One thing Sophie did not share was Richard's passionate love of football in general and Tottenham Hotspur in particular. Like all Spurs supporters, he learned to accept their lack of achievement and just enjoy the fluidity of their passing, none better at the art than the Argentinian, Ossie Ardiles who had had to leave Spurs during the Falklands War (another reason for loathing Thatcher!)

Richard never missed a Spurs home game, and for that matter, few away matches. Despite her antipathy to football, Sophie would try to arrange her schedule so that she could accompany him when Spurs were playing away, and although she found his moods determined by Spurs' success or otherwise, she was getting to see some interesting and often beautiful parts of the country, none more so than the Derbyshire Dales near Sheffield where they would cycle for miles.

When Spurs were playing at home, Saturdays were a Richard-free day. If Spurs won, Richard would head for the White Cockerel pub with his mates to celebrate, and if they lost, they would head for the same pub to commiserate. When she wasn't on duty, Sophie attended a yoga class run by a Russian émigré in nearby Highgate. Later, she would take in an art-house French or Italian movie or a matinee play in the West End. The only thing that could make her forego these pleasures was the need to meet a publication deadline, but being who she was, this was a rare occurrence.

CHAPTER 15: RICHARD SIMPSON 1984

Sundays, whatever the weather, were for walks together on Hampstead Heath and Kenwood, lunch in a bistro, and a gallery in the afternoon. Sophie so enjoyed the freedom of movement and thought, without having to peer over her shoulder or fear a knock on the door. She slowly began to feel more and more at home, to forget the sunshine, beaches and mountains of Cape Town. Although those aspects of her former life were fading, she did not, could not forget the good doctor. But her life was to be lived now: she was with Richard, in London, and it was not long before she was the proud possessor of a British passport.

For some time now, Sophie had been attending talks by expatriate South Africans who spoke of the political struggles that were going on in their homeland and the work they were doing abroad to facilitate this. She knew that these talks would sometimes be attended by members of the same Special Branch that had murdered David, and that they would surreptitiously be taking photographs, so she never attended without a broad scarf that covered her blond curly hair and lower face.

One of many she attended was delivered by a far more famous expatriate, Harold Wolpe, by then a sociology lecturer at the University of Essex. In 1963, Wolpe had been imprisoned after the Treason Trial but somehow escaped with three co-conspirators. The 'somehow' had involved bribing a not very bright prison guard, and for the price of a Studebaker Lark (at that time a highly desired car) had fled to England. Sophie was impressed by Wolpe's erudite mind. Also in the audience was an attractive woman, who Sophie later learned was Wolpe's wife AnnMarie who had played a large part in his escape. Like Sophie, she too had been forced to leave South Africa in great haste.

It was not difficult to spot the three undercover agents in the audience – they were the only people wearing ties!

She knew that, like everyone else there, she had been photographed, and hoped they would have fun trying to nail her.

Sophie had also met the eminent writer Nadine Gordimer, who was born in Springs, a mining town outside Johannesburg. Her father, a watch-maker, was an immigrant from Lithuania as were most of his ilk, and her mother was from an assimilated Jewish family in London. While at university in Johannesburg, Nadine joined the ANC. The arrest of her best friend in 1960 and the massacre at Sharpeville spurred Gordimer's entry into the anti-apartheid movement.

Thereafter, she quickly became active in South African politics. During his trial, she helped Mandela edit his famous speech, "I Am Prepared to Die", delivered from the defendant's dock. When Mandela was released from prison in 1990, Nadine Gordimer was one of the first people he wanted to see. Literary recognition for her accomplishments was to culminate with the Nobel Prize for Literature in 1991.

Inspired by these individuals, Sophie decided that the time had come for her to get her backside out of neutral and start operating actively. It was time to exact payment for David's death. It was time to give her life meaning. She knew she could do it, whatever the cost.

The final kick in her butt was when she heard how what had begun as a peaceful demonstration in Langa, a black township in the Eastern Cape, had resulted in the deaths of several people who were gunned down by the police. At their mass funeral, which happened to coincide with the 25th anniversary of Sharpeville, twenty more people were murdered. When Molly Blackburn, a member of the Black Sash (a protest group assisting the victims of apartheid) attempted to instigate an inquiry into the Langa massacre, she too met with an unfortunate car accident that cost her life. Not for the first time, Sophie felt enraged and vengeful.

## CHAPTER 15: RICHARD SIMPSON 1984

By this time, Sophie had completely lost her enthusiasm for the day-to-day mini-dramas of the wards; she decided to resign, but continued to be involved in nurses' politics. She was also involved in other, more serious, activities, but felt she needed a break to refuel her energy, and she suggested to Richard that they travel to Berlin to meet her uncle.

# Chapter 16:
## Obz *1985*

Observatory, or Obz as it was colloquially known in the eighties, was one of those suburban areas of Cape Town which could be best described as 'poor white'. If you wanted to understand how racial mixing was possible in South Africa, then the place to go was Obz, where people neither noticed nor cared if others were the same or different. The area was so diverse. The people who came in were down-at-heel Afrikaners, 're-classifieds' and Kleurlinge (or *'klonkies', as they were condescendingly called*). The individual rooms of Obz's small single-storey houses were ideal for landlords to let out (if at a pittance) to these poorer people, and the houses were becoming crowded. If the residents worked at all, it would be in menial jobs in the nearby city centre of Cape Town, or, if they were lucky, at the Lion Match factory just off Lower Main Road in Obz itself. Some others were able to get jobs as cleaners or in supermarkets, but unemployment was high.

Observatory was a depressing place by day, characterised by the perpetually drunk or stoned human detritus that hung out on the pavements awaiting an opportunity to cadge a free cigarette or bum a drink. Best of all from their perspective, they would relieve more affluent passers-by of their purses or wallets as they walked through the narrow streets, and use the proceeds for drugging up. The violence that was so characteristic of other cities like Johannesburg up north was not generally required; just showing a knife or gun would suffice for the better-off to agree to a quick redistribution of wealth. Unlike their black Josie counterparts, the Obs residents just

## CHAPTER 16: OBZ 1985

couldn't be bothered with violence. Well, why shoot the *oke* if your victim was happy to support the purchase of some shit-hot *DP dagga.* Durban Poison cannabis was really *bakgat*, the best. That stuffed wallet would also fund a bottle or two of Kommando, a raw brown liquid that rejoiced in being labelled as brandy.

At night, Obz was a very different place. Lots of *oere,* turncoat Kleurling policemen, were around to take care of the wealthy young white male students who attended the nearby University of Cape Town or were in the process of becoming doctors at Groote Schuur up the road. These young bucks knew that for the price of a beer they could hear great Cape jazz played by mixed-race musicians. For the price of an extra meal they would enjoy the illicit thrill of *naaing* a *Kapie.* To *naai,* by the way, means 'to sow', and if they were unlucky enough to get caught 'sowing' a Kleurling woman, a few rands would usually suffice to ensure that the law enforcement officer enforced very little law.

Karen and the little but rapidly growing Simon lived in Obz. She had found a small apartment in a decent large building that had once been a factory making shoulder pads for the dresses that were fashionable in wealthy Claremont, a short bus-ride down Main Road. She was fortunate that she had been able to find steady employment as a dental nurse in Claremont at a very up-market private practice, where her previous training as a nurse stood her in very good stead as she assisted Dr Errol Joffe. Dr Errol was a young Jewish dentist born in Muizenberg, that little village a few kilometres down the road from Obz. Because of its bracing sea air, Muizenberg was much beloved by the Lithuanian-born Jewish holidaymakers from Johannesburg who flocked to the two Kosher hotels every December. For a few weeks of the year, Muizies was a hive of social activity, for the rest, a sleepy seaside village much loved by the surfing fraternity.

Dr Errol was kind, paid her well, and never sought to take advantage of her, which was more than she could say about many of his patients. The women treated her a little sniffily, and the men lusted after her body like dogs seeking a bitch on heat. On more occasions than she cared to remember, the 'why-don't-we-meet-after-work' question followed the moment Dr Errol stepped out of the surgery to check an x-ray or speak to another patient. Not once did she respond positively, if only because she needed to get back to her Simon, who was now nearly five. She did not want to get bitten again by a married white man, no thank you.

The arrangement with her parents was working well. Karen would drop the little boy at his 'for whites only' play-school on her way to work. She had chosen this simply because it offered better facilities. Her mother, Magda, would collect Simon at lunchtime on her way back from her cleaning job at the Cape Sun Hotel where she did the early shift. Unfortunately, Karen had to tell the school principal that it would be her maid, not her mother, who would collect the child; because, unlike Karen, Magda was not white and therefore could not be Simon's grandmother but could easily be Karen's maid. Magda would feed Simon and take him to the park to play with the other white kids while she chatted to the other nannies.

Magda had lots in common with them, not least the fact that not a single upper front tooth was to be seen on any one of them. It was rumoured that this was so because the *Kapie okies* (and indeed also the white men) got better blow jobs if the teeth did not get in the way, but this was probably *kakpraat* – bullshit. The truth was that her fellow Kapies just found the look sexy in women, and it became a rite of passage. Karen found this ironic, because she had a full complement of stunning white teeth - straight as any white person would wish to have, no orthodontics needed for her! Her job was to help Dr Errol's patients keep theirs.

## CHAPTER 16: OBZ 1985

As for the men, losing those upper front teeth was part of the gang culture, especially if you could say you lost them in a fight or they got knocked out by the police when the *oere* raided their shebeens and confiscated their home-brewed liquor, unless of course you settled them some rands and some decent dagga.

By the time Karen got home to Obz, Simon would be bathed. A simple supper would have been cooked by Magda. Her dad Kallie would arrive, change out of his janitor's overalls, and enjoy a *dop* or two of Kommando brandy. They would enjoy an hour of each other's company, Simon would get three goodnight kisses and be put into his small bed on the side of Karen's slightly larger one, and Magda and Kallie would head off to the bus-stop for the half-hour ride to Mitchell's Plain (much quicker than their incoming morning journey).

On weekends, if the weather was good, they would all prepare a picnic and head off to Muizenberg, not a great distance from Mitchell's. There, they set up an umbrella on the 'Coloureds only' beach to the left of the 'whites only' beach on the other side of the little stream, the *vlei*. The beach for blacks was still further along. Karen remembered the time when, as a child, she and a few of the kids from Mitchell's decided to go swimming at St James, just beyond Muizenberg. St. James was a posh white area that had a natural rock-pool filled with seawater. When this small group of dark kids descended on the pool and had the cheek to actually enter the water, the locals were in uproar. It did not take long before a squad-car arrived and four policemen set about the kids, lashing them with their *sjambokke,* those painful leather thongs. Almost as bad was the tongue-lashing Karen received from Magda when she tried to explain the wheals on her arms and legs. They did not try that stunt again.

But all seemed at peace now. Simon loved to run to the edge of the sea or play in the shallow waters of the *vlei* as the little stream entered the sea, safe as could be. There was no possibility whatsoever that Karen would be seen by a white friend (she had had few of those anyway besides Sophie, whom by now she had not seen for some years), or by any of Dr Errol's patients - that lot went to the posher beaches on the Sea Point side of Table Mountain. It was only in summer that the whites-only beach filled up, and that was with Jewish families that had been driving the thousand-mile journey from Johannesburg for years and years because they valued the *luft* - and bracing the air was, especially in the afternoons when the winds came up. Karen could easily have walked across the *vlei* and be chatted up by the Jewboys, but all they would be interested in was what was concealed by the part of her bikini that was south of her navel. She needed that like a hole in the head. No, her life was simple and uncomplicated, and she intended to keep it that way. And if she ever felt like sex, her hand was a perfectly adequate lover and she would find herself thinking of John Jameson.

Karen decided it was time to write once again to Sophie, and hoped fervently that she was still at the same address. A letter was duly sent, addressed to Jenny Ward at the Whittington. Fortunately, Jenny was one of the few originals who was still working there, and she knew to whom it should be passed.

*Howzit Babe,*

*I hope all is good and that you are enjoying London living. Are you still so bolshy? I hope you are not up to your neck in crap, although I would not be surprised if you were.*

*This photo I've included was taken by my dad at a park in Mitchell's, and it's probably just as well that he's the one who's not in it because he's pissed most of the time. I'm surprised he managed to hold the camera steady. Still, he's very good with Simon, who fortunately looks more like his father than his mother. I'm sure you will agree that he is divine! He is now five and is the absolute reason I have for*

## CHAPTER 16: OBZ 1985

*being alive. My mom takes care of him when I am at work, and she is undoubtedly the best carer in history.*

*I was so pleased to hear that you are living with a newspaper reporter (you were always a bit weird in your tastes) and that you have found a smart, caring guy who seems to love you for what you are and not just for your gorgeous body. I hope you're not ruining your relationship with too many crap jokes! I must say I can't picture you lying in bed with a guy who's smoking a pipe as he caresses you, but each to his own.... no, seriously, my babe, you deserve everything that he can give you, and even more important, that you can give yourself.*

*What about me? I earn enough as a dental nurse at Dr Errol to be able to support the four of us. My salary is supported by the lavish tips I get from the white male patients who think that is a passport to the treasure that lies inside my broekies. Fat chance! What is with these white okes that they find us girls so desirable?! Don't their wives and girlfriends like sex, or is it the adventure of crossing the colour bar? That it's still unlawful and therefore has a spirit of danger attached? It sickens me to my gut that everything is about colour in this fucked-up country. South Africa is still the same racist state, but we just get on with it.*

*Quite interesting really, how my life has progressed. When I was growing up, I thought that if I could be classified white, my whole life would change. Well, it did, up to a point. First, it enabled me to get into training at Groote Schuur, but that went tits up when I fell for John. But now that I've got Simon, my life could not be more Coloured than it is .... and you know what? I couldn't be happier.*

*I hope you like the photo.*
*I still love you so much, more than ever. Take care.*

Simon was a lovely kid, happy as a dog with two tails, and why not? He adored his mother, and his grandparents not less. He looked so much like Karen, tall for his age, light-skinned, and only a whisper of *krille* in sight (only later did he begin to question why his oupa and ouma had a lot more *krille*). He didn't need a father, because Kallie was there, and he had not one but two mothers - *'Sweet, man, lekker'*, as Kallie would say.

Simon really was thriving. When he got to his 'white' primary school, he slotted in easily. All from poorer homes, many somewhat mixed-race, all decent kids by any standards. After school he played football with the boys in the park, and because he was an ace striker, he was usually first to be picked. But it was in the classroom that he really shone. Although Karen was by no means unintelligent, young Simon had obviously inherited his uncanny talent to manipulate figures from his real father. There was no arithmetic or mathematical problem that was beyond his ability to resolve.

What of his ability in linguistics? Zulu and Xhosa and seven other Bantu languages were spoken by ten times as many people as those whose home language was English or Afrikaans, yet those of European origin were the official languages in apartheid South Africa. Rather than one or other being preferred as was the case in most other schools, Observatory Primary School was dual medium. That is to say, lessons were conducted in both of the official languages, and Simon was more than competent at both. Simon, whose mother spoke English and whose grandparents spoke Afrikaans, outshone all his buddies. He read books way beyond those prescribed for his age, and his teachers suggested putting him up a year. Karen sensibly refused. Unsurprisingly, she felt immensely proud of him, and was saddened only by her parents being unable to attend the school annual prize-giving to see their Simon scoop the laurels. Of course, she wished Sophie had been there too.

# Chapter 17:

## *Sophie goes to Berlin 1985*

Neither of them having had many days off since meeting, Richard reacted positively to Sophie's suggestion that they celebrate their second anniversary of being an item by going for three days to East Germany to meet, for the first time, her mother's younger brother. Solly Stein and his wife Masha lived in East Berlin. Sophie, after much effort, managed to obtain a visa. This was far more difficult than she had imagined - at the time South Africans, even those with British passports, were deemed undesirable tourists in all Communist countries. Eventually, a short-term visa was attained, and they took off for Tegel airport.

When Sophie and Richard arrived in West Berlin, they were much impressed by the vibrancy of the city, especially the Kurfurstendam with its restaurants and sex shops, not to mention the Berlin Philharmonic. The next day they took a bus through Checkpoint Charlie into the East part of the divided city and were immediately struck by the drab grey monolithic blocks of apartments and the lack of neon of any kind. Dull just didn't begin to express it, but they weren't there for the scenery, and their meetings with Solly and Masha were a joy. From them they learned the story of Hannah's family about which Hannah was unable to speak because her mind had blocked it out.

At the time of Hitler's rise to power, the Stein family had been in Berlin for close on a century and were relatively prosperous merchants. They were assimilated German-Jews, proud not only of their country's rich culture but the contributions made by its Jewish citizens to German literature, philosophy, medicine and science. To say that they were shocked when Hitler and his henchmen turned against them is grossly to understate the case. Most were in denial - it can't happen, the good Germans won't let it! Others saw the writing on the wall.

Solly explained to Sophie that there were those who got out as quickly as they could to Argentina, Uruguay, Cuba, South Africa, anywhere they had family. Others, like the Steins, moved more slowly. 'We decided that your mother would be the first to go out to South Africa. We hoped she would become involved in the family's fashion business in Cape Town, and that once she was established, the rest of us would follow.'

The rest of the family were not so lucky.

On infamous *Kristalnacht* the Stein family business in Berlin was burnt to the ground. Not long after, Hannah's parents, three brothers and two sisters were rounded up and eventually sent to Auschwitz. The lives of all except the youngest, Solly, ended in the gas chambers. Sophie, listening with a mixture of horror and awe, asked Solly, 'How did you manage to survive?'

'Well, I was young, strong and willing to carry out whatever menial tasks were thrown at me. If there wasn't food to eat, I did without, eating sawdust just to fill my belly. By convincing myself I was no better than an animal, I managed to survive like one. I did not lose my mind because I no longer believed I had one.'

Sophie wept silently.

Unbelievably, Solly survived in the camps for six years, and during that time the only support system he had was from members of the German-Jewish Communist party, one of whom was Masha, a girl-woman two years younger than he. Most of the group perished, but she too eked out an existence until both were liberated by incoming American forces. They were offered a new life in America by the International Jewish Agency and set off by ship immediately after their registry-office marriage.

On arrival in New York, they were met by the IJA and provided with a single small room in the Bronx that had no hot water. There was no heating either, but after Auschwitz the lack of those amenities did not bother them. They were provided with food rations, sent to evening classes to learn English, and given temporary jobs as assistants in a bakery. Once this terminated, they were pretty much left to their own devices to find further employment. They survived the next two years by doing piecemeal work – life was tough, but they were alive and together.

Two years after they arrived, there was another arrival, a little boy who gurgled contentedly when he wasn't asleep. He was no problem, but now the single small room and lack of heating, education and work was. So, when a letter arrived from their surviving Communist party friends suggesting they return to East Germany where they would be given decent housing with heating, jobs, and proper education, they decided after initial hesitation to go back.

How could they do this, Sophie asked. The short answer? The one thing they had learned in Auschwitz was pragmatism. If East Berlin could give them what New York could not and if it was a place where they would not be judged by their accents, then so it would be.

Three years after their return, Solly emerged with a degree in economics and Masha with a teaching diploma. He went on to become a college professor, she headmistress of a secondary school, and their son a scientist.

Sophie was simply in awe that two people who had suffered so much be so forgiving, so worldly and so warm. 'How were you able to live in the country that had sought to destroy your people and brutally killed six million of them?' asked Richard, who had been left utterly numbed by a horror he had only considered in the abstract before. Solly's response to this question that he had been asked so many times was simple: 'Amazing as it might seem, we managed to forget our past simply because it was too painful to remember it.'

As the years went by, Solly was able, through the International Jewish Agency, to establish contact with his sister Hannah in South Africa and keep in regular contact by letter. However, because of South Africa's paranoid anti-communist policies and East Germany's isolationism, they were not able to meet. Not until many years later.

Masha's eyesight was failing, and Solly's health was a problem, but neither of them was deterred from enjoying every minute of their lives. The one blight was their son, by now married. As with so many offspring of Holocaust survivors, Karl was a moody individual, and it was not long before his marriage foundered - but not before the arrival of a lovely little girl, Jesse, who became Solly's reason for wishing to live to a ripe old age (which he did). When she completed school, Jesse became not only an accomplished artist but a guide at the magnificent and only just completed Holocaust Museum in Berlin designed by Daniel Liebeskind. It was only when Sophie stood in the memorial garden of the Museum that the enormity of the Holocaust hit her and she wailed uncontrollably, and Richard, who had no direct link with the events of the war, wept with her.

# Chapter 18:

## *The Defence and Aid Fund 1985 - 1990*

Before she fled from South Africa, Sophie had been involved in meeting clergymen and lawyers involved in putting to use the money clandestinely received from the International Defence & Aid Fund. Those generous donations from different European sources had saved the lives of many fighting the system in South Africa. The IDAF had been able to pay the fees of some of the best advocates in the country. Nelson Mandela and his co-conspirators had reason to be very grateful to have these resources available. So, when she accepted that for the foreseeable future her destiny lay in London, and now that she was no longer a nurse, she knew exactly whom to contact. He was a solicitor by the name of Robert Kramer who had offices near Piccadilly Circus.

Robert, like her, was the only offspring of a wealthy Jewish family that had run a huge business wholesaling electric goods in Johannesburg. After the infamous events at Sharpeville and fearing for their future, his parents had sold up and left for London when Robert was only a child. Robert was a courageous and admirable man, a brilliant solicitor who was prepared to put his career in jeopardy to support individuals in a country he barely knew. His parents were not activists, but Robbie certainly was, and hardly a week went by when he did not go across to St James's Church near Piccadilly Circus. He would kneel down and say his prayers and rise clutching an envelope stuffed with Swedish krona or Dutch guilders or another European currency that had been left under the cushion. His job was then to make these notes 'kosher' and ensure that the funds were transported safely to his legal colleagues in South Africa to be put to good use. Robbie Kramer was not the mastermind of the clandestine collection scheme – he was just one of several agents who worked with a mystical kingpin, a certain 'Mr X', who aside from his somewhat melodramatic soubriquet was another lawyer in the City. His real name, William (Bill) Frankel, was never mentioned until many years later when his identity was revealed.

Sophie met with Robbie, and before long another Jewish South African was kneeling in a London church or making occasional trips to the continent to look for and vet new contacts who would support the Defence & Aid Fund. This became a significant activity in her life as well as actively supporting Peter Hain's Anti-Apartheid in Sport movement that played such an important role in breaking down the rule of the white Afrikaner regime in South Africa. As with her clandestine activities with David in Cape Town, such involvements were fraught with risk. Although Sophie was one of those whose parents had prefaced every action with the words 'be careful', she set aside her earlier caution. she was now in high-risk territory. She was aware that letter-bombs had injured and on occasion killed others. Although her eyes constantly scanned her surroundings, Sophie never saw anything that might warn her that others were watching, but even in England one could never be too careful.

Richard supported her every inch of this journey, even if she was now spending more time with Robbie than with him. He never thought for a moment that this was for any other reason than fighting for the cause in which they both so passionately believed. His Guardian column was benefitting as well from the bits of information that she considered safe to share with him, and he had furthered his reputation as a fearless proponent of just causes.

As if this was not sufficient to put herself in potential peril, Sophie, at Robbie's suggestion, began to attend meetings of the neo-Nazi National Front. She frequently went to meetings and marches in the East End of London and Luton, protesting about the support for those immigrant Bengalis whose presence in the UK the NF were trying to curtail. Sophie, being blond, looked not at all Semitic and fitted in perfectly. It was assumed by the not always brilliant ultra-right-wing group that she, being a white South African, had to be a card-carrying member of the ruling white authorities in her home country. They were particularly welcoming to her because the founder of the NF, Arthur Chesterton, had been born near Johannesburg in Krugersdorp, a stronghold of apartheid, and had emigrated to England to spread the gospel of racism. They assumed she felt the same way as they did about the ever-increasing presence of foreigners, especially dark-skinned foreigners, and most especially the Bengalis who had taken over Tower Hamlets and were now aiming to extend their presence.

They did not examine her credentials with any care and accepted without question that her name had morphed into Marie De Klerk. She rarely missed a meeting and impressed her cronies when she appeared at marches with placards bearing the highly intelligent slogans of *'Wogs Out!! Fuckoff back to Paki.'* and *'England For Whites!'* There were frequent clashes with anti-fascist groups from which Sophie managed to maintain a safe but respectable distance – she had had her fair share of being whacked in Cape Town where at least she had marched with and not against the group she supported.

Most of her colleagues-at-arms assumed that she was keeping her distance to avoid getting her pretty face redecorated, which was okay with them because more than one skinhead got turned on by Sophie's presence, hoping to get a screw later. Therefore, they were willing to make allowances - what she lacked in physical contact with the oppo, she more than made up for in vocal sloganeering.

Within a short time, she succeeded in gaining their confidence, and was invited to attend the meetings of the more senior echelons of the NF. There she was made privy to the nefarious plans and plots of the leadership, who being mostly male were only too happy to have an attractive Aryan woman to provide some glamour. She listened as they espoused their views that blacks were biologically inferior to whites. The NF was strong on anti-miscegenation and had nothing but scorn for white women who allowed themselves to be defiled by black men. To them, mixed-race people were an abomination. They would question Sophie on the niceties of the Immorality Act in South Africa and how her colleagues back home stopped black guys fucking white girls.

Another NF bugbear was that Jewish finance was controlling the world, and that the Holocaust was an invention so they could steal a homeland from the Arabs. Sophie saw a certain irony in this: who did they hate more, Jews or Arabs? And there was something else that she found ironic: here she was, a spy amongst these hardened right-wingers, the very type of people who had infiltrated the socialist meetings in Cape Town. The wheel had surely turned full circle!

Never for a moment did they suspect that she was feeding information to Robbie, who would ensure that important information about plans to disrupt anti-apartheid meetings was passed on to people who mattered.

It would be far more interesting for someone to write how this process got Sophie into serious difficulties, but so adept was she that no-one ever suspected her of being anything other than the committed white supremacist conspirator she had ostensibly become. Her activities had to come to an end sometime, and they did for the most prosaic and pathetic of reasons: one the senior skinheads had taken a big shine to her, and when she rebuffed his clumsy advances, he turned against her and became physically threatening. Knowing full well that if he began to

CHAPTER 18: THE DEFENCE AND AID FUND 1985 - 1990

suspect her veracity, she would end up as dogmeat, so she decided to call it a day. Nevertheless, the whole experience had given Sophie a modicum of self-respect, an emotion she was not always sure she deserved.

As time went by, Sophie thought often about her friend in Cape Town. How was Karen doing? Had she found a special someone to replace John? How old was Simon now, five? Was he at school yet? She thought frequently of David too – how she wished he could have been there alongside her. And then she thought, if he had been there alongside her, how would her relationship with Richard have panned out? Would he have been just another spoke in her wheel of protest? So many questions, but Sophie was a do-er, a woman whose head was ruled by her heart, and her heart was set on making her world, wherever it happened to be, a better place.

Midway through the eighties, the first signs of a thaw in the South African government's policy emerged when it was announced that the Prime Minister, the arch-conservative P W Botha, would be making a very significant speech. Rumour had it that P W Botha's namesake, the moderate Pik Botha, had helped the Prime Minister to draft a speech to announce momentous changes. Expectations ran high that a turning point had been reached, but Sophie could not quite believe it, and as so often before, her feelings proved prescient. In the event, following pressure from the diehards in his government, the Prime Minister did use the phrase "today we have crossed the Rubicon", but removed what was supposed to precede it, namely the government's intention to dismantle apartheid and release Mandela. The effect of the speech on the world, and on many South Africans, not least Sophie, was that of a bucket of iced water in the face. She knew that her homecoming was still a long way away.

# Chapter 19:
## *Karen  1982 - 1999*

During the years that Sophie was so involved in attempting to rectify the iniquities and inequalities of her country from six thousand miles away, Karen's life by comparison had ambled along on a smooth and stable pathway. During this whole period she worked diligently at the dental surgery, where after a few years she was promoted to become receptionist and eventually practice manager. The practice was growing, and many of the new patients were people of colour who these days seemed far more interested in preserving and maintaining their incisors in pristine shape than losing them. To cope with the increased demand, Dr Errol had taken on an Associate, a new Stellenbosch graduate, Dr Stoffel, and a new dental nurse, Sara. Karen could not but be aware that Stoffel needed mothering, but she had religiously managed to keep any involvement with a man safely in the distance, and she wasn't about to mess on her own doorstep. Still, Stoffel was lively and fun, and he and Sara really brought some much-needed new life to the practice.

Karen started to attend sculpture classes with a local art teacher and began to incorporate disused products such as fractured and discarded instruments from the surgery into her abstract sculptures. She also found use for the unused last remnants of dental impression materials - she would squeeze pastes from their tubes, mix, and allow to set in exotic colours and sculptural shapes to become parts of her figures. She had appreciated that, even though small, a simple tooth had a beautiful shape, and she brought these forms into her abstract work, much to the delight of Celeste, her mentor, who saw in her an original

## CHAPTER 19: KAREN 1982 - 1999

and refreshing talent. Celeste encouraged Karen to extend these into larger sculptures, and there was even talk about an exhibition, but just being involved was enough for Karen. She was entirely self-contained and did not require external validation.

She and her little family would take two weeks' vacation every year at the same little hotel near Paternoster, some three hours by bus from their home. Paternoster was a quiet little village up the north coast comprised entirely of small homes owned by fishermen of mixed race. There were no shops, no bioscope, only one hotel, no restaurants, but it was a safe little haven. It was later to become much sought after by wealthy white Capetonians who wanted a weekend pied-a-terre, but at the time it was a place simply to relax and walk the abundant sand dunes and enjoy the daily sea catch, simply grilled on a hot coal fire. Karen would often go onto the dunes to practise the simple yoga techniques she had picked up from a guru in Obz, and this was a welcome antidote to the stresses of work, such as they were.

For the rest of the time Obz was her home. Karen's life could not have been more routine, but she was very content. By this time also, she had put all thoughts of ever seeing Sophie again out of her mind; given that during this entire period Sophie was living in exile in England, it seemed that this was a fair assumption to make.

Karen's main concern was that it was already the mid-nineties and Simon was now seventeen (seventeen years in which she had not seen Sophie). It was time for his matriculation exams, but he seemed far more interested in sport than study. He was now established as one of his school's better rugby players and an occasionally brilliant cricketer. He had even been noted as a potential provincial player in both sports. She needn't have worried. Simon managed to achieve a first-class pass almost without breaking sweat, and notched distinctions in English, maths and science.

When Simon was awarded a scholarship to study at UCT, she was elated beyond description. This was a stunning achievement for a mixed-race boy, for that was how she thought of him and by the same token had reverted to thinking about herself; the irony being that, by this time even if she was classified white, it was completely irrelevant to Karen.

*17th January 1996.*
*Dearest Sophie,*

*I hope all is well with you, my lovely one.*
*Well babe, the turn of the century is approaching, and we now have a black President. For us, things in this country are slowly – still very slowly – beginning to change. Coloured people are now getting decent jobs and being paid decently in the civil services and places like the post office, but unemployment is still high.*
*As these photos testify, I am now the proud mother of a three-distinction matriculant! Yes, my Simon cracked top A grades in English, science and maths and Bs in history, geography and Afrikaans (yes, it is still compulsory to be bilingual in the two white languages). His graduation ceremony at his school in Obz was undoubtedly the proudest moment of my life, but can you believe it, my parents weren't there to witness it. They felt they would be an embarrassment to Simon and to me, never mind that the only reason I slipped through the net was thanks to that mega-dickhead Kobus!*
*I asked, begged, pleaded with them to accompany us, but they are still stuck in their old world of apartheid. Maybe they do have a point - although the laws have changed, old attitudes and prejudices still persist. So it goes, Pussycat, so it goes.*
*Simon has been awarded a scholarship to study science at Cape Town University and his headmaster thinks*

he could excel. At least it's a liberal uni, so he's not likely to have a problem because of his skin colour which is a couple of shades darker than the others will be, but that won't bother Simon. They will love his extremely quick feet bursting down the wing on the rugby field, and Mr Fielding, his sports coach, is sure he will make it straight into the first team.

I continue to work at Dr Errol - quite routine, but I like it that way. The new associate dentist is a handsome young Afrikaner, really lovely guy. He needs mothering and is panting to give me shots, but no way that's going to happen! This job is too important to me to put at risk by crapping on my own doorstep. In any case, I've forgotten what it's like to have a man inside me and that bothers me niks – absolutely nothing.

Are you still with your pipe-smoking Richard? I wish you hadn't mentioned that to me - It does rather cloud the image! Your mother says you haven't been arrested yet, so I guess you're safe. You may not be aware how proud your mother is of her daughter, but says she doesn't hear from you too often, and even if she did it still wouldn't be often enough. Now I'm beginning to believe what you told me about Jewish mothers!

She tells me your father is still working and still going out to Manenberg every month. What special people your parents are! I've arranged to visit them soon, and I can't wait to see them and your beautiful home. I will be taking Simon with me. He is barely aware that another world exists on the other side of the mountain, a world I knew briefly, a world where lives a father he knows nothing about; a father who is head of a big bank, is always in the newspapers, who has no idea that he has a son of whom he would be so very proud...

Take care and stay safe!!
Your Karen.

# Chapter 20:

## *The end of Thatcher 1990*

Sophie and Richard had taken a slightly larger flat together in Gospel Oak, at the poorer end of Hampstead Heath but still close enough to enjoy the Heath as their garden. Most days of the week, regardless of season, they would walk through the rambling and hilly ancient woodlands, past the three bathing ponds where they occasionally had a swim. They would enjoy the London panorama from Parliament Hill, and finish with coffee at the adjoining stately home, Kenwood House. Sophie could honestly say that those days were the happiest of her time in England, and they were joined if not by marriage vows, then certainly by an intense desire to see the end of Thatcher, whom they loathed with equal passion.

The eighties had changed Britain. It had seen the fall of the unions and the rise of the City following the 'Big Bang' deregulation of financial strictures. It had been party to the rise of middle-class drug culture, and it had seen the rise in popularity of Margaret Thatcher. Ever since the battle of the Falklands and her other momentous victory, the subjugation of the miners' unions, Maggie Thatcher had assumed iconic status with a large element of the British public but was just as passionately abhorred by a minority that included Richard. What made them react to her with even greater vehemence was her support for the Butcher of Chile, its former President, General Augusto Pinochet. That Thatcher could have offered a home and respite to a tyrant who was personally responsible for the disappearance and death of thousands upon thousands of decent, earnest young students opposed to his brutal totalitarian regime was utterly unacceptable to Richard,

## CHAPTER 20: THE END OF THATCHER 1990

and ridding his country of her was therefore a cause to be pursued to the end.

The nineties dawned in England with the realisation that the Thatcher party was over, and the hangover had begun. Small businesses that had over-extended themselves began to go to the wall, and the High Street lights which had burned so brightly in the eighties were beginning to dim.

Imagine their joy when Margaret Thatcher knew that even though she was adored by a majority of the population of Britain, she could no longer count on the unbridled support and blind faith of her Tory acolytes in Parliament, and the crowning point came just three months later. Margaret Thatcher resigned. She eventually stood in front of No.10 Downing Street saying her goodbyes, to be replaced by the anodyne but thoroughly likeable Tory, John Major. Even though Sophie and Richard were ardent Labour supporters, this was like winning the pools.

The event that Sophie knew was inevitable and for which she had prayed for so long had finally been announced: the ANC was to be unbanned, and Nelson Mandela was to be released. Their cup of joy was overflowing. This was massively exciting but with it came uncertainty. Would those in exile remain proscribed and unable to return, or would they be given safe passage? Sophie was unsure whether the unbanning of the ANC meant there would be carte blanche for the many political exiles to return, but she had to believe it would. It turned out the only thing that was clear was a total lack of clarity. The South African government remained silent, but, ever the optimist, Sophie believed they could at least begin preparing their plans to return to the country of her birth.

Then came the announcement that Nelson Mandela was to be released on the 11th of February 1990. Sophie wept like a baby when she watched as the television camera showing him leaving prison and beginning, in his own words, 'the long walk to freedom'. So did Richard. It seemed finally that reality was ready to meet hope.

This was momentous news, but as it turned out, it was not the only big news. Just a few months later, Iraq invaded Kuwait and the Gulf War began. This of course angered Sophie, but at that stage it was something that was happening somewhere else and not the dominant issue in her life. To the Guardian and their reporter Richard, however, this was an event that overshadowed everything, and Richard was not about to rush off to Cape Town.

The new year dawned with other exciting developments. Europe ended sanctions against South Africa. South Africa's President, Mr F W De Klerk, he who had thwarted the Rubicon speech, announced that the laws of apartheid were to be repealed. The constitution for the new South Africa was unveiled, its chief architect being one Arthur Chaskalson whose talk had inspired Sophie ten years before. Sophie hardy dared to believe that this could be happening. She was euphoric, but euphoria too often leads to disappointment, for yet again, things were happening elsewhere.

The fragmented Yugoslavian Republic was erupting. Serbian guns began pounding Sarajevo in Bosnia, and the city had become besieged, hungry and very dangerous. An area ripe for Richard to investigate and report. So, more activity for Richard, more delays. By this time, Sophie had been in exile for fourteen years. She began to fear that her return would always be superseded by other events in this turbulent, constantly changing world. She began to experience doubts. Did it really make sense to want to go back? England had become her home, she had acquired British citizenship. What purpose would she serve back home? Did South Africa indeed need more whites, even enlightened ones?

In 1994, the first free elections were held in South Africa, resulting in an overwhelming victory for the ANC. Sophie could barely control her happiness when Mandela was inaugurated as President at that bastion of apartheid, Pretoria. The die was cast – she could finally return. It was only a question of time before they would leave for Cape Town. Once there, her overwhelming priority and most joyful task and would be to re-unite with Karen.

She should have known that the enemy of fulfilment is great expectation.

# Chapter 21:
## Simon  1996 - 2001

At the time that Mandela was getting down to the serious business of ridding the country of the iniquities and inequalities of apartheid, Simon had turned 18. By dint of his scholastic and sports abilities he had been awarded a scholarship to the University of Cape Town to study science. Given his background and the total absence of a real father, this was an astonishing achievement. Karen was as proud a mother as could be. She had settled easily into life as a house-owner in Obz, which was an acceptable environment for Simon to study and within easy reach of UCT, and there was no man to create difficulties for her. Her parents visited regularly now that the mania of race segregation was being weeded out of the lawn of society. She had little to do with her neighbours anyway and cared less what they thought.

Simon performed reasonably well in the first couple of years of his studies, although without setting UCT alight. He was however a very well-balanced young man, enjoying his studies a lot but sport even more. He was a regular first-team selection for the under-twenties 'Ikeys' rugby team and, being fleet of foot, was tipped to make the senior squad before too long. Most of all he was enjoying his social life and was a regular visitor to the same Obz Cafe frequented by his mother over the past fifteen years, but hardly ever at the same time.

Unfortunately, life does not always behave as kindly as it should, and Karen should have known better than to expect it to.

## CHAPTER 21: SIMON 1996 - 2001

Simon had gotten into a relationship with Lucy, a well-bred young UCT arts student of English extraction, to the utter displeasure of her parents who resented his easily visible mixed-race origins. That these negative feelings should have been consigned to the dustbin of recent history cut no ice with them. They bristled when he was occasionally brought to their home, and under no circumstance would they countenance him spending a night there (even if in a spare bedroom, of which there were several). This did not prevent Lucy and Simon developing a very strong relationship, and eventually sleeping together at a friend's house when the owners were abroad.

When their daughter became pregnant, the parents forced Lucy to have an abortion and to break off her relationship with Simon. Lucy, surprisingly, acquiesced totally. Even more surprising, she recovered from this traumatic experience quite quickly and got on with her studies. Simon, on the other hand, took it all very badly. He found it very difficult to concentrate on course work, and started smoking dagga – heavily. The reasons for this are difficult to comprehend and might have been partly genetic in origin (Kallie being addicted to alcohol, and Simon's unnamed father to sex) and partly social, but whatever they were, Karen was perturbed. Simon assured her it was 'recreational', and, seeing that every UCT student was smoking dagga anyway, his new habit should not have given her or anyone else cause for concern.

When his studies fell by the wayside and it was noticed that he was missing more lectures than he attended, he was threatened with sending down. He did not wait for this to happen and decided to drop out, a decision which caused Karen more grief than anything she had experienced in her life. She could not begin to understand the reasons why he took the loss of his child and the breakup with Lucy so badly, so she blamed herself for not taking a stronger stand, and for the first time deeply regretted that Simon did not have a father to keep him in line.

She thought it best to have it out with Simon, although she wasn't holding her breath that it would have any effect. 'You know, Simon, for all those years since leaving Groote Schuur, I have put you first, before any other consideration. You are and always have been my reason for living, and what you are doing is breaking me. Don't you realise your entire future is about to go up in smoke?'

'Butt out, Ma, it's my life, ok?'

She tried to reason with him. It helped nought. She changed tack. 'I beg you to go back and finish your course. Your degree and every reward that will bring is only eight months away.' *Niks*. Nothing. He was immovable. He listened, then thrust his own knife into her heart.

'You did pretty much the same thing, didn't you, Ma? Why did you skedaddle from Groote Schuur when the going got tough? I didn't ask you to have me, did I? You had a choice. You could have done the same as Lucy and we wouldn't be having this conversation.'

She retorted that at least she hadn't resorted to drugs, and of course he walked out of the room. This made her feel even worse and wish she hadn't broached the subject. He was doubly right – it was his life, and she too had cut and run.

Simon easily found work in a meat-packing factory to earn money for a ticket to India. He headed for Goa, where he sniffed coke, shot heroin, and even took LSD tablets. He could not honestly say that he spent a single day there without introducing some substance into his body. He did not work as such, but managed to provide food and drugs for himself by doing the one thing he was capable of, pimping himself out to older women who had come there for no other purpose than sexual gratification and were prepared to pay for it.

CHAPTER 21: SIMON 1996 - 2001

He remained in India for 18 months, spending most of his time on the beaches of Kerala in a drug-induced haze. When he returned to Cape Town in 1997, he was addicted to cannabis and also indulging regularly in coke. Karen was shocked by his appearance – he had become as thin as a pipe-cleaner and had a perpetually glazed, vacant expression. She felt she had no choice but to take him in, hoping that good sense would prevail. Of course, it did not.

Simon was hooked, and, to fund his needs, he stole from Karen, her parents, and local shopkeepers. This got to the point where Karen was simply at the end of her tether, and, unable to take any more, she kicked Simon out.

Simon was literally on his own. He went back to the meat-packing factory, but, being zonked out of his mind almost all the time, did not last long there. He somehow managed to keep his mind clear enough to survive a brief interview and get a job as a waiter, but of course this too was extremely short-lived. He continued his life as a petty criminal, stealing cash and jewellery from the older women he slept with, and being as good-looking as he was, there was no shortage of those.

Eventually, as his needs grew, he became a street pusher, selling on anything he could access from other drug dealers. When he couldn't find a woman's bed, he slept rough. He became part of the increasingly large community of dropouts in neighbouring Salt River until he was arrested in mid-1998 when he was caught in possession of a handbag he had 'accidentally borrowed.' No, the judge didn't believe it either. Simon was sentenced to four months in Pollsmoor prison, a gang-infested hell-hole ironically located in the forests of Cape Town's most beautiful suburb, Constantia.

If you were brought up in Manenberg, Pollsmoor would have been less of a culture shock than it was for someone who had spent two years at UCT. If you are a pretty boy, as Simon was, being inside a Cape Town prison with its intense gang culture has something of an inevitability about it – you will become the *meisie,* the 'little girl-friend', of one of the gang leaders. This had nothing to do with homosexuality and everything to do with sexual gratification by whatever means available. Given that prisoners did not have individual cells but were herded into pens with as many as fifteen others, it was not difficult for the cell leader to satisfy himself whenever he so desired. Then, when the next pretty *meisie* came in, the current *meisie* would be handed down. Simon was no exception and, after the leader had had enough of him, he was gang-raped by the lower echelon of *Group Sewe-en-twintig*, 'Gang 27'. Although an extremely unpleasant and painful experience, two good things did happen.

The first was that, incredibly, he did not acquire HIV.

The second was that his rear-end experience brought Simon to his senses, and just when you would have expected him to turn even more to substances that would make his environment less hellish, he totally switched off from drugs. This was all the more remarkable because it is a fact that in Cape Town prisons, drugs are even more freely available than on the street. The warders colluded with the gang leaders because it kept the prisoners relatively quiet and therefore easier to control. A far more pertinent reason however was that if the warders did not cooperate, they would be taken out - permanently - by a new prisoner. Any newcomer who wanted to join one of the gangs could only prove his worth to the leader of the gang by accepting the leader's order to kill someone who had offended him. And there was no surer way for a warder to sign his own death warrant than to attempt to stop the flow of narcotics into Pollsmoor. If Simon had spent any longer than four months in prison, he would inevitably have been given the choice: kill or be killed.

Throughout his period of incarceration, Karen visited him each week, but he expressed nothing of his daily

CHAPTER 21: SIMON 1996 - 2001

experiences. Karen nevertheless found his plight heartbreaking, blaming herself for having thrown him onto the streets. When Simon was released, she felt she had no choice but to allow him back into the home, on condition that he put every effort into getting a job.

This proved much easier said than done. Despite his best efforts, Simon was unable to find employment. Who after all would give work to a young man who obviously had at least a modicum of non-white blood, whose only cv entry was an educational experience in the state *tronk*? His two years at university counted for nothing. But he was still clean of drugs, well-behaved and inoffensive, and Karen felt comfortable in resuming what passed for a social life.

She was enjoying her work, and whatever she did, she did well. Besides her skilful ability to be her employer's second pair of hands and then his mouthpiece, she had the remarkable ability to make his patients feel completely at ease. She had a good memory and was always able to recall what they had discussed on a previous occasion or where they had recently been on a holiday. In short, she made them feel human, which is always a nice thing to feel when you are undergoing what was often an unpleasant experience. Whether it was a soft hand on a stiffening arm or a quiet word when they were obviously stressing, Karen was as good a dental nurse as she would have been a medical one had she still been at the big hospital up the road.

Karen had recently celebrated her fortieth in the quietest way she could manage, sharing a bottle of champagne with her parents and Simon. They say life begins at forty, and as far as Karen was concerned, that would be a fine thing. Then Karen met Philip.

# Chapter 22:

## *Philip  2001 - 2005*

In the late nineties, Obz was showing encouraging signs of regeneration. Yes, there were still some drunks on the street, but there was also a steady influx of foreign students who were, by and large, law-abiding. Many were medical students and junior doctors from Groote Schuur just up the road. The small but attractive cottages formerly occupied by poorer mixed-race families were being bought up and the former owners were using this new-found wealth to buy bigger properties further out, letting out rooms and becoming landlords. Their former homes in Obz were being tarted up and the suburb was becoming increasingly gentrified. Property prices were rising. The shops in Lower Main Road were gradually taken over, zhuzhed up and upgraded. Trendy restaurants, coffee shops and quality second-hand record and book shops were becoming increasingly popular with those who did not wish to pay the prices of the more affluent surrounding suburbs.

The Obz Cafe has long been a favourite of the local population, and on the few occasions that Karen ever went out, it was a place much to her liking. The music was good, on occasions even brilliant, mostly recorded but occasionally live. The bread used for toasties or sarnies was best baked-down-the-road 'healthy' wholegrain that provided the wrapping for scrumptious salads of yellowtail tuna or rare smoked beef. Their cheesecake and carrot cakes were legendary. The food was simple but well-prepared and, most important from her perspective, cheap. Not that she wasn't earning a decent living at Dr Errol's, but she was having to support the still jobless Simon. When

## CHAPTER 22: PHILIP 2001 - 2005

she did appear at the Cafe, she would sit quietly reading at a table. The books she read were by writers such as James Mitchener or Margaret Atwood, well written and informative, and her favourites were 'The Color Purple' by Alice Walker, and Toni Morrison's 'Beloved', stories with which she felt great affinity.

Although now forty, she still attracted men like bees to a honey pot; however, the local men soon realised that they were not going to get much from her, and eventually let her be.

Philip Case was a different story. He lived in a recently renovated three-bedroom house in leafy Claremont two suburbs away, and was one of those well-to-do early-middle-aged men whose wives had sensibly informed that drinking excessively was not conducive to a stable relationship, and he had been given the heave-ho. The fact that the demands of these same women might have been the reason that these men took to drink in the first place did not seem to enter into the equation, but often the men found themselves cast out. They found that in places like Obz, single women were usually available who would cost them substantially less than their Claremont counterparts, and, as far as the women were concerned, the proceeds would be used to satisfy the next day's retail therapy or recreational nasal inhalants.

One Thursday night Philip sat down at the Obz Cafe. He was taking his drying-out seriously and ordered a hamburger and fruit juice at exactly the moment that Karen walked up to purchase coffee and cheesecake, which she intended to nurse (no pun intended) for the next hour. Philip studied her carefully without staring too hard, thereby avoiding offence to Karen. Nor did he approach her immediately, waiting rather to bide his time, which came when she walked up to the bar for a second time to get a beer. He asked her quietly what time the Cafe closed, and when she said that it remained open till late, contact had inoffensively been made.

'May I join you?' said Philip. Karen's brain instructed her mouth to say 'No thanks', as it always did, except that the instruction got distorted and came out instead as 'Ja, if you want to'. She frowned at her mouth and said 'What the hell d'you think you're doing?!' and her mouth responded 'What the hell indeed, he seems harmless enough'.

And so it began.

Philip was not so crude as to try and bed her that evening, nor even the next week, but when he pitched up there for a third time, this dark, broodingly beautiful woman was quite agreeable to meeting a couple of days later for dinner after work. For the first time in years, Karen thought she might actually enjoy a man's company without feeling that all he was after was her body.

The restaurant chosen by Philip was L'Equipe, a quiet place where the live music by a classical string quartet reminded Karen of her evening with Sophie's parents. The food was French in style and sumptuous in taste, and the wine was the best that Meerlust could provide.

'The staff seem to know you pretty well, Philip.'

'I guess they should – I've been coming here for years,' responded this easy-going man. 'Once upon a day, the restaurant got into cash-flow difficulties and was about to go tits up. Was I going to allow my favourite eatery go to the wall? No way. So I loaned them enough to recover, and deferred repayment. The police were called in to check out the front-of-house manager. The bugger had been quietly drawing small amounts of cash every evening for years, but all he can spend it on now is drugs in Pollsmoor. They've tightened up, restructured. Service and profit have improved and they have repaid my loan. I will be a guest here for as long as they and I survive, whichever comes sooner.'

Philip's chat-up was innocuous and non-invasive. The bottle of Meerlust went down smoothly, although Philip conscientiously did not as much as taste the rich red claret. 'I used to have a problem with alcohol. It was my best

## CHAPTER 22: PHILIP 2001 - 2005

friend, the only thing that would stop me remembering my ex. You don't want to know the details. Anyway, a spell in rehab, and I've been dry for two years now.'

Magda had been more than happy to spend the evening caring for her only grandchild and sleep over, so Karen for once was not under pressure to hurry home. Without having to worry about Simon, Karen ended up back at Philip's small but delightful designer house, and not only spent the night there but enjoyed sex for the first time in many years. Their lovemaking was passionate but not frantic. With her last thought being that it had been worth the wait, Karen eventually sank into blissful sleep.

Why had Karen taken this step, twenty-odd years after her short-lived affair with John, and despite having turned down countless others through work? Simple. The tall, well-built Philip had a winning smile, which frequently lit up his very pleasant face. He was not an in-your-face, I've-done-this, I-do-that type. Yes, he was nearly fifty, but was slim and athletic looking. Yes, he was divorced and had two grown-up children who had moved to live in Australia with their mother, but this bothered Karen not at all. He did not seem to ask much of her and treated her with kindness and respect. Even when she told him of her Kobus experience, he seemed not to care. In short, he was easy-going, casual and fun. And great in bed.

After several evenings together, Philip suggested that it might make sense for him to get to know Simon as well. Karen was hesitant. 'I'm apprehensive, Philip. There's simply no predicting how Simon will react. He's a young man who is still a child.' Philip put his arm round her shoulder and comforted her. 'Pick your moment, Karen, and hope for the best.' Realising she had little choice, Karen waited until a rare moment when Simon appeared relaxed, although she was well aware that this could change in an instant.

'Simon, I've met this guy and he seems rather pleasant. He's very kind to me and he's quite keen to meet you. I've told him you don't always like new people, but he's promised to respect that you are number one in my life.' To her pleasant surprise, Simon actually smiled. 'Hey, that's ok Ma, if you like him, he must be a nice guy. I'm sure it will be fine.'

Karen whispered quietly to herself, 'From your mouth to God's ear.'

How did Simon take to this new factor in their lives? Surprisingly well, actually. From the first time they met for a walk on Muizenberg beach, Philip's undemanding nature seemed to resonate easily with the highly-strung wire that was the new post-India Simon. Part of the reason Simon was so highly strung was that he had managed to stay drug-free for over a year but had far from shaken off the effects of the process of withdrawal. However, his developing relationship with the older man was a stabilising factor, and Karen was intensely grateful for it.

It turned out that Philip was a very wealthy man; he had had a successful equipment-leasing company which he sold a couple of years before for lots. After the relationship with Karen had been going along smoothly for a year, he suggested that she and Simon leave Obz and move into a small but very neat apartment that he owned in Newlands, between Obz and Claremont. He, Philip, would continue to live in Claremont but was very happy to support them, see Karen three or four times a week and spend time with Simon as well. For Karen this was, if nothing else, convenient workwise, and she hoped that Simon would be better able to seek a job, possibly as a waiter in one of the numerous boutique restaurants that were springing up all over these shishi suburbs.

Unfortunately, every silver lining has a dark cloud. Philip was being savaged by outrageous demands from his former spouse, still in Australia. The problem was the exchange rate, and although Philip had lots of South African rands, they did not translate into lots of Australian

## CHAPTER 22: PHILIP 2001 - 2005

dollars - and his two daughters and former wife required lots of Australian dollars. Philip had no choice but to sell the Newlands apartment and to move Karen and Simon into his personal house in Claremont.

Dark clouds seem to attract other dark clouds, and very soon Karen found she had not just one but two. Six months after they moved to Claremont, the still-jobless Simon, whose self-esteem was at nought above zero, started drugging again. The problem was that whilst Simon was prepared to accept the presence of Philip a few times a week, seeing him all the time was another matter altogether. He was becoming increasingly resentful that he was no longer the sole focus of his mother's attention. Karen was his, and this interloper was staking a claim for her body - this did not bother Simon - but also for her time, and Simon was unwilling to put up with that state of affairs.

Simon renewed his love affair with dagga. He soon moved on to coke, then crack cocaine and *Tik,* methamphetamine. He disliked crack, preferring to snort white powder up his nostrils, a habit he could ill afford. Induced paranoia was one of the side effects of the inordinately large quantity of substances that he was abusing, and Simon was becoming increasingly paranoid, especially as far as Karen was concerned.

If this was the only problem, they might have been able to deal with it and sort it out *(yeah, pull the other one.)* But it wasn't. Philip, as Karen was well aware, had a disability similar to that afflicting Simon, the only difference being the orifice through which it entered. When the going gets tough, the tough get going, and the place where Philip went was The Three Bells. Although he had been abstinent for two years, he started hitting the bottle again for the same reason he had hit it on former occasions - to drown out thoughts of his former wife.

If Simon was less than happy to have Philip around, Philip soon found Simon's presence utterly unbearable. Had Simon been at work all day, it might not have been so intolerable, but he wasn't, so Philip increasingly sought refuge at The Three Bells, where more than one seasoned stalwart benefited from his always open wallet. They were not alone. Simon also benefited substantially from the same source, but not by invitation. It was only a matter of time before he started stealing again, and the person from whom he stole most was the inebriated Philip, until Philip realised why his wallet was always almost empty first thing in the morning.

People who abuse alcohol share a common characteristic - physical aggression. So, the moment Karen left for Dr Errol's surgery, Philip would wade into the bigger Simon, and Simon gave as good as he got. Their fights were extremely physical and one or the other or both would emerge with newfound facial decoration. Karen was aware, albeit less than fully, of what was going on while she was at work. By the time she returned, Simon would be holed up in his room watching one of his Star Wars tapes and Philip would be asleep in his room until woken for dinner.

It was not Karen's job generally to prepare dinner. That task fell to Mrs Fatima Roelofse, who was turning out to be Karen's third dark cloud. Fatima had worked for Philip and his former wife and growing family as cook and housemaid for nigh on twenty years and she was still angry that the previous *medem* had abandoned her and her *maasta*. She could not understand why anyone would leave Philip, who by comparison with her useless layabout husband was a veritable saint. So, when Karen came into the picture, Karen whom she knew with absolute certainty was no more white than she was, Fatima was never going to be happy. But she was shrewd, born of years of fighting for her turf, no matter how small a patch it might be. She would find subtle ways to let Philip know not only how useless in the home Karen was, how badly she cooked (when she cooked), how much she wasted on groceries, but also drop little hints on Karen's provenance. It mattered little to Philip. Karen had already told him of her

## CHAPTER 22: PHILIP 2001 - 2005

humble origins, and for the rest he was too drunk to care. At least in the beginning.

Things went from bad to worse. Unable to afford cocaine now that Philip's wallet was no longer lying around, Simon had begun to smoke large amounts of easily available and relatively cheap industrial cannabis known in other countries as skunk, far more toxic than anyone imagined. Across the country, cannabis farms were springing up in houses, garages, gardens and warehouses, and each harvest was made up of different strains, some more toxic than others. The more THC the industrial blends contained, the more likely the skunk would be to induce psychosis, and Simon was becoming increasingly paranoid. On the rare occasions he left the house, he was certain that everyone was watching him, even from passing cars. Every sound had sinister connotations: a ticking clock, birdsong, rain on the windows, especially police sirens.

Then, the voices in his head - unfriendly voices, critical voices, angry. They made him feel he was being crowded out of his own skull. He was sure (not without reason) that Philip was crowding him out of the house. There wasn't space in his delusional brain for his thoughts *and* Philip. Had he gone to a psychiatrist (the furthest thing from his already overcrowded mind) he would have been diagnosed as psychotic, and his way of dealing with his psychosis was to smoke even more skunk, believing it would cure his symptoms.

Philip too was drinking increasingly heavily and had become physically abusive not just to Simon but to Karen as well, which would enrage Simon and lead to the most horrendous violent encounters. Karen would beg them to stop, but each continued to self-medicate. She felt she was being squeezed by a nutcracker, between Simon on the left and Philip on the right. She despised herself for allowing herself to be abused, for not taking Simon and heading clear of this madness but unfortunately her fear of an unpredictable future over-trumped her pressing need to move on.

Always in the mistaken belief that by showing him warmth he would behave more tolerably, Karen did not stop Philip from coming to her room. Once begun, the sex they had was animal-like in its ferocity. However, it all got too much to bear. She was set on leaving the house with Simon and returning to Obz, when Philip, pissed as the proverbial newt, one night entered her room and entered Karen. She tried to push him off, then succumbed. She heard his yell, different to that of his usual climax. She heard him gasp, saw his hand clutch his left breast, and felt him fall forward onto her.

Fortune had finally shone its face on Karen, although she did not immediately realise it.

The autopsy showed that Philip had had a massive coronary thrombosis, and this heart attack had killed him instantly. At the time, Karen was sure that not only had her violent benefactor died, but with him the sanctuary of the lovely Claremont home. What would happen to them now? Philip's family in Australia, who saw Karen as a gold-digger from the wrong side of the colour bar, demanded that she and Simon vacate immediately and give possession to the rightful owners, Philip's family.

However, Philip had left a will with his attorney, and to Karen's utter amazement she learned that Philip, despite his monstrous rages and his antipathy towards Simon, had still found the kindness to leave the house to Karen. Despite this, Philip's family did their best to have the will overturned and Karen and Simon legally evicted on the grounds that Philip was an alcoholic at the time of making the will, but the lawyer who had drafted his will was an old friend of Philip who disliked the former wife and had long had the hots for Karen. He therefore attested to Philip's sobriety, and the family were unable to overturn its terms.

CHAPTER 22: PHILIP 2001 - 2005

Fortunately, also, Philip had not forgotten his long-term servant, and the cash gift Fatimah received was enough for her to accept Karen's suggestion that a friendly parting of the ways would be in the best interests of all.

And then, another unexpected windfall. Six months after Karen inherited the house, Karen received a letter from the late Philip's attorney. The tidy insurance policy he had taken out - with her as the sole beneficiary - had finally been paid up, and would she care to give them a call to arrange handover.

Half the battle seemed won – apparent financial security. The other half – Simon - was to prove much more difficult to resolve, and as Karen would learn, the money left by Philip would only go so far.

Karen had no fixed plan for the future, but one thing she felt strongly about was that she did not wish to share this chapter of her life as it now stood with Sophie and she simply stopped communicating with her soul-sister.

# Chapter 23:

## Sophie's return  1996 - 2005

Despite Sophie's resolve to return to South Africa as soon as the African National Congress led by Nelson Mandela came into power in 1994, it was nearly two years before Sophie and Richard returned to her motherland to pledge their support to the ANC. The events that were creating history in other parts of the world had ensured that Richard was required elsewhere, not least in newly recognised and devastated Bosnia Herzegovina.

During that lull, Sophie began to experience severe misgivings. She had no friends worthy of the name except for Karen, but would she be able to locate her erstwhile colleague? She knew it would not be easy. Would she be welcomed back by her own community, or would she be seen by her family's friends as an outcast, a traitor who had literally gone to the dark side?

What of her beliefs? She was no longer an active operative – there was no longer a reason to be one. Would her return be valued by the ANC to whose cause she had wed herself and lost the good doctor? Did the ANC even need or want returning whites, or would there be reverse apartheid? Sophie had this awful feeling that she had become irrelevant. Time would provide the answers to all those nagging questions, but the worry remained.

Their opportunity came a few months Later. Richard arrived home in a rare state of high excitement.

'Nailed it, Sophie! They've offered me the job I wanted for so long. Guardian are allowing me to become senior political reporter for the Cape Argus while continuing to write for them as their Southern African correspondent. Couldn't be better!'

CHAPTER 23: SOPHIE'S RETURN  1996 - 2005

Needless to say, Sophie's elation outmatched his. She had already negotiated a position with the Health Council of South Africa as an adviser and consultant. They decided it would be best that Sophie fly on by herself initially, and Richard would follow at the earliest opportunity. Again, angst. Stress in her life for the past couple of years had dropped dramatically, yet once more she was seeking change. How would she feel about leaving this city that had become her home? Despite the rain, the grey skies and the overcrowded tube trains, she had grown to love this sprawling multi-cultural city for its arts, its culture but most of all for its tolerance.

Her return to South Africa proved much smoother than she had envisaged. Sophie had envisioned being questioned on arrival at Jan Smuts Airport (as it was still known then). She was surprised when a young black woman greeted her in Xhosa with a *"Wamkelekile! yiba nosuku olumnandi* - welcome, have a good day!" No questioned asked. No interrogation. She was just another foreigner with a British passport. She indeed hoped she would have a good day, and many more after that!

From Johannesburg she flew to Cape Town to be greeted joyfully by her parents who were now in their eighties. Although she realised they would have aged, their appearance was a reality check on the time they had endured apart. Sophie spent her entire first month with them and experienced the strange sensation of being in a place entirely familiar to her where nothing had changed except her. Not quite true - there was a black government and a black President in Parliament just up the road. There was a ghostly feeling of disconnection. Oft-times she felt a stranger in her own land but eventually she was able to adjust.

Then Richard arrived, and that too had a feeling of unreality. The man with whom she had lived for more than a decade had to be introduced to her parents! Unsurprisingly, each quickly accepted the other without reservation although the parents were constantly having to explain aspects of their Jewish life about which Richard knew very little.

The one pleasant surprise, for them if not for the country, was the relatively low cost of living – the South African rand had devalued by two-thirds compared to the pound during the time she had been away, and Richard was earning British Sterling. This enabled them to buy a beautiful apartment in scenic but windy Camps Bay, close to the parents' home in Fresnaye, that was three times the size of their small flat in north London. Best of all was the view of Camps Bay beach in front and of the glorious Twelve Apostles mountains behind.

The hardest part for Sophie? Dealing with the feelings that she bore for Dr David Rousseau that had not evaporated and became acute back on home turf. She realised that however much she loved Richard, it was a love that he would have to share. Richard, being the sensitive and sensible man he was, took this in his stride and simply got on with his work, while Sophie fruitlessly tried to establish exactly who rather than what had caused David's death fourteen years before.

Richard drew her attention to an article in the Cape Argus. A certain Eugene de Kock had just been sentenced to two life imprisonment terms (with an extra 212 years thrown in for good measure just in case) for murder and kidnapping. De Kock was the commander of a death squad in the eighties known as C10. His numerous victims had all been "enemies of the State", the sort of activist that David Rousseau had been, although he was not listed as one of the victims. Sophie experienced a grim sense of satisfaction that at last the tide was beginning to turn.

Eventually she realised that she was expending emotional energy that could be put to better use. She knew that the twin causes for which she was going to fight - AIDS and drug abuse, often intertwined - would be those that

CHAPTER 23: SOPHIE'S RETURN 1996 - 2005

not only David would have respected, but issues that could bring Richard's journalistic skills into the mix. As time passed, they were both concerned about the lack of effort of the ANC government in respect of AIDS. Sophie took on the cause of trying to get anti-retroviral drugs for AIDS victims while Richard returned briefly to England to set up a charity to fund the anti-retrovirals.

During all this time, Sophie had tried to trace Karen, who by now had sold the Claremont house to put an end to the nagging Aussies and had moved several times, always renting. Karen's parents too had moved, so finding them proved equally difficult for Sophie - Williams and Willemse were not uncommon names, and tracing Karen was proving an impossible task. Inevitably, as Sophie became more and more immersed in her work, the search for Karen took less and less priority, till it took none at all.

The new century dawned without drama. Legal discrimination along racial lines in South Africa had theoretically ended with the demise of apartheid, but classifying individuals according to their race was still being used by the ANC government for monitoring economic changes. Yes, wherever possible, whites were being replaced in jobs by blacks and people of mixed race, but it was a slow process. The legacy of apartheid still loomed large and the need for huge imbalances to be redressed remained a priority. Sophie, desperately needing something to divert her mind from the constant battle against the problems besetting her homeland, decided to broach the subject with Richard. 'O great guru who has wisdom of all things, what shall I do to take my mind off drugs and bugs?'
'How about tennis?'
'Are you mad?! You know what I think of sport.'
'Well then, I suppose gym's out the question too.'
Her look was withering. 'Whatever made me think you were all-knowing....'

'Seriously, Sophie, do what you've always been good at. Work on a project, but one that's for your own interest, and for once not all about others. Like, write a book, or do some painting, or even a correspondence course in astrophysics.'

'Aha! Much food for thought there, o wise one.'

What Sophie decided to do was to involve herself in part–time study for a Master's degree with the University of Cape Town. She needed a subject that was both important and personal to her. She decided it would be interesting to look at the contribution made by her co-religionists to the anti-apartheid cause. Given that the Jewish population of South Africa was only about 2.5% of the white population and 0.2% of the total population, Jewish involvement had been disproportionately large. Jews in substantial numbers were conspicuously present in literally every aspect of the anti-Apartheid struggle — political, military, legal, cultural. It might prove to be a worthy theme for a thesis, and the more thought she gave, the more energised she became. Just one more reason to be grateful to have Richard's presence in her life.

The first thing to be done was to find a tutor who would supervise her project. She settled on a part-time UCT lecturer, Linda Sedley, several years older than Sophie, who had had grim first-hand experience of The Struggle. Linda had been an activist and been operative when Sophie was at Groote Schuur. Like so many of the brave women of that era, she had endured house arrest and ongoing harassment in the years that Sophie was abroad. Linda had personally met many of the people Sophie wished to research, and she was more than happy to share her stories and memories.

'Those were heady days, Sophie, and many whites with nothing personal to gain and a great deal to lose took huge risks to help the ANC cause. Members of your community, in particular the women, figured in the protest movements in high numbers. You're probably aware that at the Treason Trial in 1956, half of the 23 whites arraigned were Jews, including six Jewish women - relatively, a very high proportion. They made a very significant contribution to the ANC eventually coming to power. From my own experience I well remember many of the people involved who put their very lives at risk for what they perceived to be a greater cause.'

Linda reflected for a few moments, reliving memories, many painful. After a brief pause, Linda continued, 'In his autobiography *Long Walk to Freedom* I can recall Nelson Mandela commenting, *"I have found Jews to be more broad-minded than most whites on the issues of race and politics, perhaps because they themselves have historically been victims of prejudice."* In fact, among whites it was Jews who would offer Mandela the greatest support and encouragement; those who first offered him employment when few white firms would hire a black, those who hid him when he was forced to go underground; those who, as lawyers, defended him at trial; those who, as journalists, supported the anti-apartheid cause.'

To Sophie, this was perplexing. 'So, Linda, given what you've just said, I don't understand why the support the ANC received from their Jewish comrades has been forgotten so quickly. It's like it's been airbrushed out of their history. I don't understand why, now, there's such an alarming level of hostility in the ANC to the State of Israel and by association to Jews as a group. It really rankles.'

Linda ruminated for a moment. 'The reasons could be both complex and simple, Sophie. There's been an increase in the number of black South Africans converting to Islam, particularly among the women and the youth. Remember, blacks *and* Indians were the victims of apartheid, so it's not unnatural that they should gravitate to one another. The acceptance of Islam has become part of a radical rejection of a society based on Christian principles seen as having been responsible for establishing and promoting the

Apartheid doctrine through the Dutch Reformed Church in South Africa. I don't have to tell you that the influence of radical ideas is very evident among South African Muslims. Branches of the Nation of Islam are already established in South Africa, and their firebrand leader Louis Farrakhan paid a visit to South Africa and was received by President Nelson Mandela. As you can imagine, Farrakhan's sharp critique of Jewish people and whites in general did not lend him favour with the Jewish press.'

Linda continued, 'At a more prosaic level, the ANC rank and file are mostly black and overwhelmingly poor; the Jews are white and perceived to be rich, ergo ... nevertheless, it's worth exploring. One thing you need to be aware of, if you are not already, is that some of the people you will be writing about have dissociated themselves from their origins, and no longer considered themselves part of the faith.'

'You know, Linda, I came to realise this while I was in London. A small but influential number of left-wing Jewish intellectuals are virulently anti-Israel. I'll certainly look out for it in my research... My big question is, though, will you consider working with me?'

'I'd be honoured to supervise your thesis, and I can certainly connect you with relevant individuals and groups; but be aware, you will encounter a lot of hostility. By the way, have you ever been to Liliesleaf Farm? It's a museum now, and you'll find a lot of useful information there.'

Sophie left in a state of high excitement. She really felt buoyed that her chosen theme was considered by a survivor of The Struggle to be worthy of exploration. So, when the opportunity arose soon thereafter for Richard to interview the curator of the newly created museum in Rivonia, Sophie did not hesitate to accompany him. The trip might just help to make sense of many of the issues and doubts that had sprung up in her mind, issues that brought into question the validity of her return to South Africa.

## CHAPTER 23: SOPHIE'S RETURN 1996 - 2005

They flew from Cape Town to Johannesburg and were only mildly surprised to find every cabin crew member either black or Coloured. By contrast, the pilots were both white. The more things changed, the more they remained the same ...

The drive from the airport in the rented Mazda took them past the ramshackle dwellings of Alexandra Township, little different from those poverty-stricken townships on the outskirts of Cape Town, and continued into the opulence of white Sandton with its elegant homes, manicured gardens and abundant foliage. The contrast could not have been more stark. When they arrived at Liliesleaf, they were struck by how peaceful and green it all looked; a far cry from the purpose it had once served. In those days, Liliesleaf Farm had been a cauldron of clandestine protest in the remote countryside, now it was a museum in the centre of a residential suburb on the outskirts of Johannesburg.

The first sign that greeted them bore the inscription *"LIBERATION: we invite you to walk the Liberation Path - a snapshot of the struggle for freedom from white minority rule."* The walk proved stimulating. In this small museum could be found virtually the whole history of *Umkhonto We Sizwe*, the armed wing of the ANC.

In 1961, Liliesleaf had been purchased by Arthur Goldreich and Harold Wolpe, two of the names on Sophie's list. It was to function as headquarters for the underground SA Communist Party and a safe house for political refugees such as Nelson Mandela. Mandela had needed a safe place from which to operate and had lived there under an assumed name, ostensibly employed as a caretaker farmer. He was captured the following year in Natal, shortly after his return to South Africa on completing military training in Morocco. He was sentenced to five years imprisonment for leaving the country illegally.

On 11 July 1963, a dry-cleaner's van drove through the gates at Liliesleaf. No pressed suits inside, no freshly laundered shirts. Just dozens of armed security policemen acting on a tip-off to arrest one of the ANC's high command, Walter Sisulu, who was hiding out at this farm. How the police came by the information that he was there remains a mystery to this day. A mole? An informant? Had he been followed? Whichever. To their delight, they found not just Sisulu but a cadre of *uMkonto we Sizwe* personnel who were plotting guerrilla action even as the police smashed in the doors. The security police had hit the jackpot.

A total of nineteen were arrested, including five whites, all Jewish. The police found a number of documents during the raid that had been naively hidden in a coal bunker, each incriminating Mandela. As a result, he was charged and brought to trial with the others. Call it bad luck or ill judgment, this was to have been the final group meeting in the farmhouse in any event, as the activists had already decided to move to another safe location. And final meeting it proved to be, there or anywhere else. The heart of *uMkonto weSizwe* had been ripped out.

On the wall of the museum was a copy of The Rivonia Review: *"State Says Rivonia was the HQ For Civil War."*

At the so-called Rivonia Trial in Pretoria, the eight-man Defence team was made up of two Afrikaners, a Greek, and five Jewish lawyers. It was advocate Harold Hanson who made the final plea in mitigation, and so powerful was it that the 17 were spared the gallows and sentenced instead to life imprisonment on Robben Island. They would spend many years there but would live to be released, to see the end of the system that had so downgraded their lives, and to see Nelson Mandela become President.

Lilliesleaf Farm was proving to be everything that Linda had foretold – a veritable treasure-trove of information. As Sophie ambled through the exhibits, she was particularly struck by the words of one of the Indian trialists, Ahmed Kathrada: *"During my stay in Europe, I visited the Auschwitz concentration camp in Poland which left a strong and lasting impression on my mind. It forcefully demonstrated the effects of racism and made me more convinced than ever of the need to eradicate the power of racial supremacy which has grown to alarming proportions in my own country."*

Sophie remarked to Richard, 'Remember when we visited the Jewish Museum in Berlin? This so echoes my feelings then.'

With sadness in his voice, Richard's responded 'Indeed. I remember well the revulsion I felt when I realised what could happen when a nation becomes poisoned by racial prejudice. I found exactly the same in Kosovo.'

As they walked though yet another room filled with homages to those who had been prepared to risk their lives, Richard's attention was drawn to the stories of those who had *not* been on trial because they had been fortunate enough to do a runner and were in exile, or had escaped from prison. In the article which followed their visit, Richard wrote:

*"These included Albie Sachs, Harold Wolpe and Joe Slovo. In 1982, Slovo was to lose his wife, Ruth First, a journalist, academic, anti-apartheid activist and member of the South African Communist Party. While in exile in Mozambique, she was brutally murdered by a letter bomb sent by South African government agents. Her funeral in Maputo was attended by presidents, members of parliament and envoys from 34 countries.*

*"Now fast-forward some thirty years from the infamous Rivonia Trial. In South Africa's first multi-racial elections in 1994, Joe Slovo was elected to parliament. He was rewarded with the post of Minister for Housing, and his memory is still venerated by older ANC members.*

*"In 1963, Arthur Chaskalson was part of the Mandela defence team in the Rivonia Trial. Thirty years later, Chaskalson became the first president of South Africa's new Constitutional Court and later its Chief Justice. He*

*acted as a key advisor on the creation of the new Constitution of South Africa. The Court's first major decision was the abolition of the death penalty."*

Sophie had met Arthur on a couple of occasions when he had spoken at legal gatherings in London and she had been impressed by his erudite mind.

These brave people would all be recognised in Sophie's thesis. Before leaving Liliesleaf, she purchased a copy of a book by Harold Wolpe's wife AnneMarie that recounted the story of Wolpe's escape, and as she delved into the book, Sophie empathised fully with this woman's story of a life in exile. Sophie thought for a brief moment about the possibility of writing her own memoirs but decided that her studies and thesis were more than enough to occupy her mind for the immediate future.

Sophie pondered about the people she wished to include in her thesis. What about the eminent writer Nadine Gordimer, whose books Sophie has found so stimulating? Nadine, who had advised Mandela on his famous 1964 defence speech at the trial which led to his conviction for life, was also active in AIDS causes. Sophie felt that this woman would be well worthy of inclusion in the development of her study.

Another was Helen Joseph. At the Treason Trial eleven years before the Rvonia Trial she was inaccurately listed as one of six Jewish women defendants (born in Eastbourne, Sussex, she had married a Jewish dentist), and she had written a dramatic account of the four-year trial. Although all were acquitted, she was the first person to be placed under house arrest, this at the age of 57. She survived several shooting and bombing attempts by secret service operatives, and her ban was eventually lifted 23 years later. A large hospital in Johannesburg now bears her name.

The most legendary of all was Helen Suzman. No thesis could exclude Suzman's contribution. In a parliamentary career that spanned forty years, she was in the forefront of

## CHAPTER 23: SOPHIE'S RETURN 1996 - 2005

the fight for the human rights of the downtrodden under apartheid. She made it her mission to see that Mandela and other political prisoners received the best treatment possible from a legal and penal system structured to humiliate and degrade black prisoners. Sophie remembered the time she attended the talk by Helen in Sea Point, and this made her think of Karen.

Yes indeed, there was much to be investigated and many to be written about, and Sophie was determined to do it. When she discussed her proposal with Richard, she could not hide her admiration for the martyrs. 'Wow, they were an amazing bunch, utterly dedicated to their cause. They didn't have to get involved, they chose to.'

Richard pointed out that her own contribution had made a difference too. Sophie was not fully convinced. 'I know I was involved, but by comparison, I did very little. Nobody would ever have thought me worthy enough to be eliminated.'

'Don't belittle yourself, Sophie, you just did your dangerous job so well that it ceased to be dangerous. But if you are not satisfied and want a letter of recognition, it can be arranged ...'

Sophie flung a book at him. 'Cynical dickhead!'

# Chapter 24:

## *The Prisoner 2005*

Simon Williams was unemployed and unemployable. He was totally dependent on dagga and skunk. He would be lighting up around ten times every day, and as a consequence did not *get* stoned, he simply *was* stoned – all the time. People who are stoned do not tend to be quick on their feet. Simon wasn't on his feet at all. Where he was, at all times, was on his bed in his room, playing with his increasingly large collection of Star Wars toys and figures and watching the expanding series of Star War movies. Life for Simon had become total identification with the adventures of Luke Skywalker, Han Solo, Obi Ben Kanobi, and most of all with the prince of darkness, Darth Vader. Indeed, it was the latter with whom Simon was developing a growing affinity.

His speech had become slower, more often than not rambling, and he could take two minutes to complete a sentence. His previously trim figure began to balloon due to lack of exercise combined with the increased appetite that cannabis gave him. The condition of his teeth and gums began to deteriorate, not just from the heavy smoking but also from increased (mainly sugary) food intake; and as his teeth turned yellow, so his skin turned grey. His eyes would appear glazed most of the time except when he got angry, and the reasons why he would erupt were neither easily predictable nor preventable.

Why did Karen tolerate this? Simple. It had become the path of least resistance. On a previous occasion she had kicked him out and he had ended up getting raped in prison. Was she going to allow that to happen again? Absolutely not. What were her alternatives?

## CHAPTER 24: THE PRISONER 2005

One was to try to find treatment for Simon within the state hospital system. Unfortunately, smoking dagga is a normal recreational activity for many South Africans. Really, what do you do when you pitch up at a state hospital and tell them you are dependent on dagga, and the doctor says, 'So?' ; and you say, 'It's blowing my brain', and the doctor says 'So?' If, on the other hand, you were at a private white hospital and you attended and said 'I still suck my thumb', they would call in two psychiatrists and three social workers and monitor you day and night lest you were a potential suicide.

So, what then? One alternative was to see a doctor privately. Unfortunately, in South Africa, the only people who can afford to go private are high money earners (usually whites) and those on insurance schemes sponsored by their place of work. The insurance scheme provided for Karen by the kindly Dr Errol was valuable, but had limits on every type of claim, and Simon's annual allocation would be used up by February. She certainly wasn't keen to dip into her savings any more than she absolutely had to, and regrettably she was having to. The proceeds of her legacy were fast disappearing in a haze of ash, and it was neither her haze nor her ash. Her earnings were good, but not that good, and in any case, who wanted to spend one's entire savings on trying to prevent Simon from sending stuff up in smoke or snorting it up his nose?

Karen came to a decision. The only thing that she could do to limit the possibility of him carrying out his threat of killing himself and/or someone else was to keep him locked up at home. 'Let's do a deal, Simon. Either I'm going to throw you out again and not give a fuck what happens to you, or we make a pact. I will allow you to remain here. and you will be allowed to smoke 'clean' dagga, but only if you agree to give up stronger drugs.'

'Like what, Ma?'

'You need to cut out coke, skunk and *tik*. They're doing your head in. Do you think you can do it? Are your prepared to do a deal? I have my doubts.'

'Let me think about it, Ma.'

'There's nothing to think about, Simon. You can either agree or you can bugger off right now.'

Simon, managed to push aside the fug from his mind, or what passed for a mind, and realised Karen wasn't joking. 'Ok, I don't want to end up in Pollsmoor again. But there is something that I want. A dog.'

Karen decided that for once Simon had actually come up with a good idea. A pet, something to care for, would be good for Simon, and she allowed him to go to the SPCA and pick out a castaway. Strangely, he selected the mangiest looking of the entire bunch, one that was also somewhat old in dog-years. He named the dog Skywalker – no surprise there. Skywalker was allowed into Simon's room where, being old and incontinent, he frequently peed on the floor. This didn't seem to bother Simon, and he and Skywalker became inseparable.

The end result of all of this was that Simon had become a prisoner of his own making within his own room in his own home. His only company was Karen, Skywalker, and his Star Wars dolls. Unfortunately, the damage had already been done, caused not only by the earlier skunk and *tik* but by the various medications on which he was also now hooked. This chemical cocktail had rendered him psychotic. His dreams became focused on repelling attacks from Stormtroopers and the assorted creatures that populated outer space. Sometimes he would be victorious, on other occasions he would be captured and have to fight his way back. The dreams could be vivid, and this created violent thoughts in his mind when awake. He was becoming increasingly aggressive. He regularly threatened to injure someone, in particular the ex-soldier who lived upstairs who was trying to kill Simon's dog – or so Simon believed.

## CHAPTER 24: THE PRISONER 2005

But somehow or other the pact held, and the threats remained threats.

One morning, Karen had just made a coffee for herself and had picked up the novel she had started the day before. She was enjoying it – this American Paul Auster wrote really well, she thought. Simon came shambling into the lounge. He started speaking, very slowly, almost rambling; it was obvious to Karen that he was very confused, even by his own standards. As he shuffled into the room, Simon mumbled, 'They came again last night, Ma ...'

Karen looked up calmly, still holding her book. 'How many this time, Simon?'

'Four Sith Troopers and two bounty hunters ... six of them from the Dark Side.'

Karen put down her book and frowned. 'Wow, even more than last time! Did they take anything?'

'No, much worse. They were trying to screw up the ... the ... the hardwiring in my brain. I don't want them to control my brain but if they get the password they can do it.'

'Did you and Skywalker fight them off?'

'Yeah, the Force was with us. Skywalker was brilliant!! I got lucky this time, but we've got to do something ... we've got to move, Ma ...'

'Moving won't change anything, Simon.'

'Ma, I don't think you realise how serious this is!'

Karen remained entirely unfazed by this conversation, because it wasn't the first time they had been there. She decided to change tack. 'Simon, I've got a present for you!'

Simon's attitude changed immediately - he really was like a child again. 'What is it, Ma?'

She handed him a flat parcel. 'Here, open it.'

Simon took out a framed certificate – he read the inscription in a slow, faltering voice, like the child to which he had regressed:

*'This certificate is presented to Mr Simon Williams in recognition of going for one full year without skunk and tik – a brilliant achievement!*

*From his ever-loving mother and friend, Karen.'*

Simon began to cry softly and went to hug Karen. 'Ma, I couldn't have done it without you! You should get a certificate as well!'

Karen beamed. 'We make a pretty good team, don't we, Simon? Maybe next year it will say *In recognition of going a whole year without dagga*.'

'I am really going to try, Ma, but smoking a joint does help me when I get agitated - like now.'

'Dagga is bad shit, Simon, and it's doing your head in. What's bugging you, anyway?'

'The same as what's always worrying me - that dog-poisoning retard upstairs – he keeps threatening to kill Skywalker.'

Looking upwards towards the neighbour's apartment and shaking his fist, he shouted: 'You are messing with The Force, you ugly bastard!! You are trying to destroy my dog, but I will destroy *you*!'

Karen groaned but said nothing. She thought about the cul-de-sac her life had become, and because she was unable to turn time backwards, she was stuck where she was. There was no way out ...

# Chapter 25:

## *Simon Loses It 2005*

Not long after this episode, Skywalker died. Skywalker had died, according to the vet, of old age. Simon of course did not believe the vet - he blamed the neighbour for the old dog's death. He knew for certain that the ex-soldier had poisoned his dog. This paranoia about the ex-soldier was driving Karen demented.

'Ma, I'm gonna have to take him out – permanently. I'm gonna have to put an axe between his ears. I must, before he poisons me too.'

She felt herself becoming really angry. 'Shut the fuck up, Simon!! What's brought this on now?!'

Simon looked at her venomously. 'My room smells of poisoned dog piss.'

Karen responded in a sarcastic tone, which, with the way Simon was these days, wasn't a good idea, 'Funny how the smell of dog piss never bothered you while Skywalker ran around here!'

Simon shook his finger at Karen. 'You don't believe me, Ma – you never do! You always take his part.'

'I'm not taking his part, but he's a lot more scared of you than you are of him!'

Simon started to pace the room again.

Karen was sure that he had not taken his medication. 'Have you taken your stabilisers, Simon?'

'No, where are they?'

'Where they always are, above the fridge in the blue ashtray.'

Simon picked up the tablets, threw them into his mouth, and downed them without water. Karen observed this and was concerned, because she was sure that Simon's excessive smoking was dehydrating him. Simon on the other hand was totally unconcerned. 'Tap water makes me feel nauseous - fizzy water is OK.'

'Too much fizzy water's not good for your kidneys. In any case, we haven't got any. I need to get down to the supermarket. Perhaps I'll go a bit later.'

'No, Ma, please don't go out – I start to panic when you're not around. I'm really petrified you won't come back - like the other day, you were gone for ages.'

'I was at work.'

'Why won't you quit ?'

Karen was becoming exasperated - children are supposed to grow into adults and become more intelligent, but the very opposite was happening; this over-age child was regressing. She had already been forced to cut down to working part-time. She could not restrain herself from saying, 'Sure, Simon, I'll just phone Errol and tell him that I don't need my salary which I'm using to fund your drugs and food, and they'll just arrive anyway courtesy Pick'n'Pay.'

Karen quickly regretted this outburst because she could see Simon beginning to seethe with rage.

'Don't patronise me, Ma! You know it's not a good idea to wind me up!' He grabbed the framed certificate and threatened to throw it at Karen. She put up her arms in protection; he let it fall onto the settee.

Karen got up and turned away, moving towards the iron gate, never for a moment taking her eye off Simon. She saw him lunge towards her. She tried to get behind the gate - too late. He jammed his foot in the gap. As he grabbed her throat, she tried to kick him, but missed. Simon, now in a frenzy, punched her in the face. He pushed her to the ground, falling on top of her. 'Get off me, Simon!' Karen was panicking – she could barely breathe. She flailed about, trying to push him off, but he was strong and gripped her throat again. Gasping for breath, she begged him to let go, but to no avail. The pressure on her throat

## CHAPTER 25: SIMON LOSES IT  2005

continued. Then Karen managed to get a hand free and grabbed his testicles, squeezing as hard as she could. Simon let out an agonised yell. His hands dropped from her throat, releasing her.

As she lay there gasping for breath, Simon's hands clung to his wounded and very painful nether regions. Finally, Karen regained enough breath to scream at her son, 'Fuck you, Simon, you nearly killed me!'

'I'm sorry Ma, I'm really sorry - I shouldn't have grabbed you. It's the damn drugs!'

'You're the one abusing the damn drugs, why can't you see that?'

'They make me schizophrenic ... the doctor said so ... I lose control ...' Simon burst into tears and sat sobbing for what seemed a long while.

'That's the second time this week. It used to occur occasionally, but it is now happening too often for my liking. Enough, Simon ... I've had enough.' Karen was feeling the impotence she had experienced on so many occasions during the past five years. 'Oh, we'll sort this out later – I need to clean up. Now go to your room!'

'Sorry. I'm really sorry ... ' Simon shambled off to his room, still sobbing.

Karen sighed heavily, shook her head, and turned towards the kitchenette where she made an ice pack that she applied to her face. Coming back into the lounge, she poured herself a brandy. 'How did I let my life get so fucked up?'

Fucked up it was, and matters were definitely not improving.

# Chapter 26:

## *The TV Debate 2005*

Simon was resting in his room. Karen was in the lounge, bored out of her mind. She picked up the latest *SA Mail & Guardian*, and there on page 6 was an article that caught her eye. It was about a guy named Jeremy Acton who had founded The Dagga Party of South Africa as a political party. It seemed that this former pig farmer smoked eight joints a day *(child's play, thought Karen, my son does more than that!).* Acton described how he had used dagga medicinally to cure a cancerous lesion on his nose. What caught Karen's eye was the sub-note: *"Tonight, the SABC is presenting a discussion on whether cannabis should be legalised."* Tonight was now.

Karen didn't think the discussion would be worth watching. What did these talking heads really know? The closest they would have come to skunk was in a textbook. Anyway, she switched on the tv. Two women were being interviewed – and she was shocked to recognise one of them.

'My god, its Sophie!'

She turned up the volume.

Louise, the younger of the two women on screen, was animated, determined to drive home her message. 'We don't want a nanny state! The Legalise Cannabis Alliance believes it is our people's right to choose dagga as a recreational drug if that's what they wish to do, the same as they smoke tobacco or drink alcohol.'

Sophie Levine replied with equal passion: 'I don't think it's that simple, Jenny!'

## CHAPTER 26: THE TV DEBATE 2005

Jenny Wilson, the tv host, turned to Sophie: 'Sophie, from your experience as a former nurse, what's your take on the campaign to legalise dagga?'

'You know, the dagga that the hippie generation used was always thought to be relatively harmless. Unfortunately, it has evolved into skunk. Skunk is twenty-five times more potent, toxic, and addictive than hippie grass, and it's causing brain damage that we're only now becoming aware of, and - '

Louise, with all the passion of youth, interjected. 'That's their choice! If you treat people like adults, they make adult decisions!'

Sophie responded in measured tones, 'Even if one has the right to behave like an idiot, it does not necessarily make it a good idea. The fact that more and more people are using skunk is an issue for politicians to deal with. What I'm interested in right now is how we deal with the effects. It may be an individual with the addiction, but it's the entire family who suffers the consequences. We have to provide support not just for the family member who abuses the drug but for the rest of the family as well.'

Louise tried to interject once more, but Jenny stopped her. Sophie continued: 'We must provide training for doctors to deal with drug abuse. We need to tackle the problem of prisoners who become addicts while in prison. But most of all we must change the conditions in this society of disadvantaged people that lead to its uncontrolled use in the first instance.'

Jenny, looking at the clock, prepared to bring the discussion to an end. 'As you say, no simple solutions, but we must leave it there. It's been an interesting chat, and our thanks to Louise Smit from the Legalise Cannabis Alliance and also to Sophie Levine, chairperson of the Campaign for Drug Therapy'.

As the credits rolled, an announcement followed verbally and on screen: *'If you have a story that you want to share with Sophie, she can be reached at Sophie@SATV.co.za/drugabuse.'*

Karen grabbed a pen and paper and noted the information. Speaking to herself, she almost cried. 'Sophie, I'd give anything to see you again!' And then the reality of her situation sank home. 'No, it's been too long, it's not going to happen.' She tore the note in half. 'I can't let her see me like this!' She grimaced, once more asking herself how she had allowed her life to become such a comprehensive mess.

She reached for the two pieces of paper she had just binned, sellotaped them together, and put them in a drawer. It would be a while before she would go back to that drawer, remove the paper, and finally write to Sophie.

# Chapter 27:

## *The Darkside Doctor  2005*

Simon's attacks and beating up of Karen were happening with increasing regularity, and more often than not some part of Karen's body was bruised and raw. It was pointless thinking about getting him into private therapy – his record of absconding within hours was total. Getting him into a state hospital was an option that offered security, until she remembered what had happened when he was in prison, and she wasn't about to set her Simon up for a repeat. She decided to call one of the medically trained therapists whom Simon had consulted some time back. Dr Prinsloo had not managed to achieve the desired outcome of getting Simon dry but seemed the best of the bunch. When he seemed willing to make house calls, she felt cautiously optimistic.

And so Dr George Prinsloo began to make his weekly visits to Karen's house to give Simon an injection of pethidine which would sedate him just enough to last till his next visit. Strangely, the doctor seemed to be charging very little for his services and did not actually take money from her – just kept saying, 'No no don't worry, Karen, we'll sort it out sometime.'

Unfortunately for Karen, she was about to discover that, like many of the men she had encountered in her life, Dr George Prinsloo was a charlatan who eventually made demands for payment that were far in excess of his stated fees. His purpose became clear – Dr Prinsloo wanted her body, and threatened that if she did not make herself available, he would have Simon committed to a state institution. So, caught between a rock and a hard place, Sophie chose the rock. She informed Prinsloo that she was going to complain to the Medical Council. This proved sufficient, and the rock did not require further application. They never saw him again, but with his absence, Simon's violence returned.

Simon's drug needs were increasing, her cash resources were diminishing. Worse, she was finding it increasingly difficult to continue working for Dr Errol. When she did go out, she returned to be attacked and beaten by the son whom, in spite of everything, she loved. So, to her deep regret and that of Dr Errol and so many of his patients, she gave up her job. What now?

As she mindlessly paged through a glossy local magazine she had picked up at the supermarket, an article caught her eye. *'Secret Life of a Pole Dancer.'* The author was a young mixed-race woman who by day worked as a secretary and plied her night-time trade at a club in the city. The photo of the attractive woman could have been of Karen herself - tall, slim, graceful, with looks that could halt traffic; muscular in a very feminine way. Karen remembered that she too had once been fit, had been admired by the guys in her school and by the doctors, and later by the men in the Obs Cafe. Now what was she? Soft. Slightly overweight. Unfit. When was the last time she had done any serious exercise, any at all?

Yet here was this dancer woman - stripped off save for a skimpy bikini. Her neon 6-inch heels and the shiny pole were mere accessories. But what caught Karen's attention most was the glow, the look on the woman's face. There was a woman totally at ease with herself. That photo spoke of someone who was seriously enjoying what she was doing at that moment. Karen began to imagine the woman's life by day. How was she occupied? Hid behind a computer screen at work? At an estate agency? corporate office? And by night? It wasn't difficult to observe that what she was doing was bringing pleasure to herself - apparent by the sense of fulfillment the dancer exuded - and to the leering, white-collared corporate businessmen dressed to the nines in the background. She looked confident, probably felt sexy, unfazed. She was living, really living, the double life. Karen pictured the dancer twisting and turning and landing gracefully with a split - that seemed a far cry from her own lot: a silent woman in the lounge of an apartment, a silent woman whose sole mission in life was to keep her son off the streets. Did the dancer have such a son?

And there, at the bottom of the article, was an ad for pole-dancing classes in Long Street, the beating heart of Cape Town, and a free late-evening introductory class was on offer. Karen's first thought was to ignore it. Dancing in public? You must be joking! However, night classes were a possibility because Simon blotted out very early, never waking till morning – his variety of pills saw to that. This might just be the opportunity to get out of her home, out of this prison. She had no thoughts of anything beyond that. Karen looked at herself in the mirror, and what she saw was an attractive woman who, despite showing a few small wrinkles and the first tiny signs of a few hairs turning white, had lost none of her beauty and little of her stunning figure. Could she do this? Yes! And as had happened on that previous occasion, the thought became mother to the act.

Tucked above a row of shops and restaurants, the studio wasn't easy to spot - no signboards, no indication of the place. However, Karen knew to look out for a particular building in the area. The building looked innocent enough. Just a climb up the stairs, and there it was. Behind its brass gates was another flight of stairs, covered in a plush red carpet and illuminated by the soft lights above. The walls were draped with velvet, and the air beyond those gates brought a hint of sensuality and intrigue. This was the place. Karen had arrived early. She wondered whether she might be the only person responding to the ad. Then, in walked her instructor.

She introduced herself as Candy, short for Candice, and Karen was instantly in awe of her. Candy was one of the most gorgeous women she had ever met in her life. Candy opened the conversation. 'I'm expecting a few others to come along, but it's good that you're nice and early. We can have a bit of a chat before we start. What brings you in tonight, Karen?'

Karen hesitated but then let flow. 'I'm a carer for my son. He has problems. Drugs. The only time I can get out is when he's asleep. I spend almost all my time at home, I'm unfit and getting overweight. I used to be a happy, confident person, but that seems to have disappeared. So when I read that article about Sarie Pieterse, and saw your offer at a time I can get away, I thought maybe this is an opportunity to bring myself back to life.'

'Well, I'm very happy to see you here. Perhaps we can make this a new beginning for you. I'm not suggesting that you will become a dancer in the club, although there's absolutely no reason why not – there's plenty men who would prefer the company of an older woman. But I do think that it's a great opportunity for you to get fit and have fun while you're doing it. I want you to understand this: I am forty-five years old. Most probably an age similar to yours. Most of my friends are not like me and some look fifteen years older, but I set out on a different course. I want to remain young. I want you to do the same. The training will be tough but fun. Our girls come to training for different reasons: to get fit, to learn new skills, or to work in a club. And if it's the last one, they have to be prepared to show off their bodies, and I mean nearly *kaalgat* – almost nothing on. In order to truly master this course, the first thing you got to believe in that is you're still beautiful and sexy, which, looking at you, my darling, should not be difficult.'

Much as she appreciated the sentiments Candy had just expressed, Karen felt anything but sexy. Just then, four other women arrived, and Karen immediately saw she

## CHAPTER 27: THE DARKSIDE DOCTOR 2005

was easily the oldest of the novices. Tough to swallow – where had the years gone? But she also realised, age notwithstanding, she was the best looking of the bunch. This was reassuring. She'd come to give it a go and give it a go she would.

Ten minutes later, Karen was dressed in one of the black bikinis and three-inch heels that Candy had provided for the five aspirants. Three-inch heels! Karen had never worn anything with heels. As the surrounding mirrors glared at her within the studios, she felt self-conscious as all hell. All she could hear was the voice in her head and imagine the sound of their sniggering voices: 'Look at her tummy. Look at her thighs. Look how silly she looks.' She wanted to shrink and disappear. She felt anything but confident as she draped her long legs round the pole and held on to it as she hung her head back. Then she saw a different picture in the mirror. Her hair was loose, she wore a bold, red lipstick – a striking difference compared to the woman who had arrived wearing mules, a tracksuit and no makeup.

All self-consciousness simply evaporated, together with all thoughts of Simon. She thought about what Candy had said to her – "You are a beautiful woman" – and knew she was. Karen so enjoyed that first class that without hesitation she signed up for six more, and then another six. This was the outlet of tension she had been seeking. She was the keenest member of the studio. The one thing she did not do was join the other trainees for a post-session drink - she would hasten back to Simon. At no time did she feel shamed in any way, but nor did she feel inclined or ready to appear in public. Weeks of training turned into months, the flabby muscles became taut, the eyes became brighter, her confidence soared. Even Simon noticed it. but Karen did not share her secret.

However, even as she became more adept and confident, the nagging thought always gnawed at her mind - pole-dancing in a nightclub is not often done for the exercise alone. As Candy had said, it involves not only women who offer themselves to be ogled, but spectators who are then encouraged to part with their money as the dancers encourage them to drink and dance. Was Karen ready to turn her passion into her occupation? She had regained her self-confidence and with a bit of a shove from Candy would be ready to go public. As far as going nearly *kaalgat,* well, that was a decision for the future.

And then, on a quiet night, she took the plunge. Soon the whispering mirrors turned to cheering crowds as Karen spun across the pole, flipping upside down and landing gracefully on heels that could strike through a heart. After the dance, she found herself quite comfortable sitting with a middle-aged man ordering champagne, and then retiring to a private cubicle for a five-minute shadow dance that involved removal of her bikini but no touching.

The pole-dancers' cardinal rule was, you could titillate the clients, but you didn't accept the offer of the men who danced with you to sleep with them as well. Well, that was in theory. Her colleagues were doing precisely that. The men were quite willing to pay handsomely for the privilege, and the club would allow it as long as the dancers saw them after hours and paid a percentage of their fees to the club. For Karen that was a step too far. Yet, despite the seediness of her new activity, Karen's sense of self-worth escalated dramatically.

As time went by, Karen was only too well aware that one big thing was still missing from her life. Companionship. There was no Sophie, no John, no Philip, not even Dr Errol. Just Simon. When she worked at Errol's practice, at least she had input from other humans, whether they were staff or patients or visiting reps. Now? Zip.

She had grown to love Candice, but Candice's first and only love was her business. The other women working at the club were pleasant, but she had little in common with

## CHAPTER 27: THE DARKSIDE DOCTOR  2005

them. When she was feeling strong, she could manage quite well without the company of others, but the sheer weight of Simon was bogging her down, not to mention that she was desperately short of money.

The realisation dawned on her that what these club attendees wanted most, as she did, was company. The men were generally frustrated white professionals and suits whose wives 'didn't understand them' and who liked the idea of a close encounter with someone, especially a someone who was obviously at least part Kapie.

So Karen decided to break out.

She found no difficulty in getting clients. She would take them to a nearby well-appointed apartment block, one of which was furnished but unoccupied, that she rented by the hour from the mixed-race janitor who was happy to have the undeclared revenue this brought in. Most of the men were happy just to chat and would reward her with cash, but for those who wanted a fuck, well she would simply not be available. She was, however, quite prepared to give them a jolly good sighting of herself and allow the men to pleasure themselves, and this seemed to be acceptable to most.

She began to ask questions of her own morality, but justified her actions with the notion that the additional income was essential to support Simon. As a secondary factor, she rationalised, she was bringing a little bit of pleasure to the lives of men who were patently bereft and lonely within their boring lives and pitiful marriages.

On a few occasions, the client 'in therapy' would turn nasty, but a loud shout would bring her friend Piet the janitor rushing into the room. Piet was an elderly but sturdy man, who, unbeknown to Karen, had set up a mini-window through which he could observe all Karen's activities. Of all the women who used his apartment, he liked her body the best, her small but pert breasts, her trimmed but still full bush. He liked the way she whispered gently to her man that he was her best. Piet's right hand never went underused, and if there was any truth in the old cliche, he would surely have gone blind within a month.

By now Karen's parents were no longer working, having been given a modest stipend by their former employers that was just about enough to keep them in food and Kallie in drink. He would spend a few hours and then eventually all day at the White Feather, a grandiose name for the seedy shebeen down the road in Mitchell's where they still lived. They visited Karen from time to time, and even offered to move in so she could return to work at Dr Errol, but she had been replaced and that was no longer an option. In any case she was now totally wrapped up in her dual life, her protective role with Simon by day (not to mention the 'victim' status she had taken on), and her new-found night-time occupation.

# Chapter 28:

## Mr John Jameson  1979 - 2005

During all these years, how had Karen's erstwhile lover and Simon's real-life father fared? Hmm. How often had she asked herself that question? The trajectory of his life had continued pretty much on the same path it had been forging when he first appeared in Karen's life. An increasingly ambitious and successful private banker, a failure in marriage. A serial philanderer, especially with pretty young ladies of colour. On the credit side he was a devoted father to his daughters, a generous benefactor to numerous charities and good causes, and an armchair politician determined to rid the country initially of the racist white Nationalist government, and later the increasingly corrupt ANC.

Had he ever really loved the aristocratic Regina? If he was truthful to himself, he would probably say he had not. However, the marriage had provided a solid stepping-stone to getting himself onto and up the ladder of promotion. Wealth creation, societal upgrading and self-fulfilment had unerringly followed. Now he was at the top of the ladder and at the top of his game.

His father-in-law got on amazingly well with John, appreciating him more and more for his business acumen and ability to charm clients into investing large amounts of capital with the private bank that had risen to be the largest and most influential in the Cape. Within a few years, he had become his father-in-law's natural successor at Sun Bank, and because of this, Regina had for many years tolerated John's indiscretions and dalliances. As far as she was concerned, he had fulfilled his evolutionary imperative and produced three lovely daughters who were her absolute joy. The three girls had gone on to study at American universities, returned and found careers and partners within an acceptable social milieu.

John had obviated the necessity for her to pursue anything other than charitable work and improving her bridge and tennis; her status amongst her peers had risen in direct proportion to her husband's elevation. Sex was not that important to her, and on the few occasions that it was, her tennis coach was not uncompliant, and it helped to pass a rainy afternoon. Strangely, the only person who was not that fond of her was her father, who saw her for what she was: a social climber, and a gold-digger to boot.

Eventually, after twenty-five years of a marital ship foundering on the rocks and slowly sinking, it keeled over when one of John's affairs became embarrassingly public and widely publicised. John, still handsome and of good physique, had got involved with a beautiful young tv actress of Indian extraction, got her pregnant and aborted, and paid through his nose for the privilege. Because of the high profile of the young starlet, the press had a field day. This proved one insult too many for Regina. It was one thing her husband spending afternoons fucking pretty secretaries in his secret pad that she knew all about, another thing altogether to be cuckolded in public. And with an Indian woman! So, she had given him the bullet. However, because of the prevailing morality of the day, John's reputation had actually risen and he had even gained the unexpressed approval of her father.

John experienced no difficulty whatsoever in his return to being single, and few weeks went by without his photo appearing on an inner page of a newspaper or magazine with an attractive woman on one or other arm, flying off to or returning from somewhere exotic. It was therefore hardly surprising that Karen Williams became aware of his peccadillos, because she was an avid reader of these periodicals. However, she was intelligent enough to realise that, even if she still carried a candle for him, and even if he had left her with a gift that had become a poisoned chalice, he was her past and not her present, and she was glad of that. She should not have been so naive.

*

Karen reached breaking point. She had been whacked about by her son for the umpteenth time. She needed help, and the only person who could possibly provide it was her oldest and dearest friend. She went to the drawer of her desk.

*My Darling Sophie,*
*It's been so long since we were last in touch. I hope you are well.*
*Saw you a while back on tv. I have wanted to contact you on so many occasions, but just could not bring myself to act. Now, here I go, doing just that! You looked amazing, still dishing out shit to the incompetent and unintelligent. Nothing new there! I am so proud of you, and so ashamed of myself. I just need someone I can talk to and unburden myself, someone who won't sit in judgment, who will listen to me without wanting to fuck me.*
*You remember the Karen who shared your life in those happy days at Groote Schuur? Well, she is no more. What she is today is a fucked-up mother of a drug-addicted son, prisoners in their own home. Unfortunately, Simon's brain is probably less developed now than when he was ten years old – as you well know,* tik doesn't play *– and he is completely paranoid. He thinks the neighbour is trying to kill him. This applies to any neighbour, all neighbours, and he forces me to change apartments more often than most men change underpants. I'm dead scared that, if I don't give in to him, he'll end up killing someone, and that someone could easily be me. Come to think of it, perhaps I am the one who is paranoid! I know you have been working with people such as myself.*

*Why are men such pathetic creatures? I have yet to meet one whose brain is more than a support system for his dick. I have yet to meet one who isn't dependent on drink or drugs or sex, or a combination of all three. One who doesn't talk with his fists.*

*I had not intended to sound so pathetically wretched, but if I can't tell you what I have become, whom can I tell?*

*My address is at the top of this letter. It's been a long time since we've been in touch, and I will fully understand if you are too busy to respond. One way or another, I will battle through, I always have.*

*You are still the person who means so much to me. You are still my beautiful Sophie with the crap jokes. You are still my best friend, my only friend and will always be.*

*With all my love,*
*Your broken mate,*
*Ka.*

No sooner had Karen posted the e-letter than regret set in. Why had she written such a pathetic letter, so full of self-pity and self-sorrow? She would be amazed if Sophie wanted anything to do with her after all these years. Why would she? Surely Sophie had much bigger battles to fight.

# Chapter 29:

## *Old Friends Meet Again  2005*

Sophie arrived at the rented Claremont home that, remembering Karen's past, was far prettier than she had expected. She pressed the bell, the door opened, and thirty years of life shrunk to nothing as the two women looked at each other, then hugged, then cried as they swayed. Eventually the tears stopped, and Sophie took Karen's hand. 'Ohmygod, Karen, you are as beautiful as ever!! How are you?!'

'I'm good, I missed you so much! Jeez, Soph, you've hardly changed!'

'I wish!' Sophie snorted - since last seeing her friend, Sophie had lost a man she loved and more recently, a father. How good it felt to be with someone so familiar, so alive, whatever the obstacles in her way. For Karen, looking away from Sophie's knowing eyes, she noted the blonde hair darkening with age, the gentle creases at the side of her mouth. Nevertheless, it was still like a door opening and letting in the sun.

Suddenly, Sophie started to giggle. 'You know what I suddenly thought of?'

Karen, quick as she could get the words out, said 'Well, if it's not one of your amazingly awful jokes, it must be that time we switched the x-rays on that bible-punching *doos* of a nurse Marie Pienaar when she had that bad bellyache.'

'Exactly!!'

They both erupted, and continued to reminisce, reminding themselves of events, matron, silly jokes. 'Well, as it happens,' said Sophie, 'I've got a really good one for you: did you hear about the nurse who died and went to hell? It took her two weeks to realise she wasn't at work!'

For once, Karen actually laughed. God, it was good to be together again. It was as if everything that had happened over this long gap had been put in a balloon and let loose to fly away.

As Karen made coffee, Sophie's words stumbled over themselves in their hurry to be heard. 'I thought I'd never fall in love again, but Richard blew in like the wind, and I gave up nursing and we threw ourselves into changing the world. Nothing ambitious! Richard spends every spare minute writing, article after article, and I'm going to meetings and getting angry; when he's watching football, I'm putting together speeches on x, y, z.... I can't wait for you to meet him, Ka.'

''Sophie, this is quite difficult for me. Let me meet you first, Let's just catch up a bit. There's so much you don't know about my life right now, and so much I wish I didn't know. I need to tell you about Simon because what you will see now is what he's become, a twenty-nine-year-old little boy who's had a really hard struggle these past few years.'

Sophie put her arm round Karen's shoulder. 'It's ok, Ka, it's ok my babe , I'm here ..... when you're ready you'll tell me the whole story.'

'How's your mom?' asked Sophie. 'She worked in a hotel, didn't she?'

'At that time she did, and she switched to doing very early shifts so she could take care of Simon. After he retired, my dad became child minder as well, a pretty good father substitute until he took to drink. Then he started doing a lot of good work for The White Feather.'

'That's a pity - is he ok?'

'Sort of ... being a janitor kept him fit, and most of the time he copes with the brandy, but I'd hate to see his liver.'

'How's your mom dealing with it?'

'She's probably relieved that he's not trying to naai her all the time.' They laughed.

## CHAPTER 29: OLD FRIENDS MEET AGAIN  2005

'But enough about me, what about your folks, Sophie? Are they still in Fresnaye? I remember, they had such a beautiful home there. Your dad was such a kind man.'

Sophie said quietly, 'Cyril died about five years ago just after his 75th birthday. Prostate cancer.'

'I'm so sorry to hear that. His death must have been very tough on you and your mother. I so admired her and your dad. Will I ever forget that *riempie stoel*, that Pierneef painting. The *Emperor* is still my favourite piece of music. How often do you get to see her?'

'About twice a month. She's let the house and now lives in a retirement village in Hout Bay, and she introduces me as her not-so-Jewish daughter.'

'What happened to you after I left? Did you complete your training?'

'Yes, I stuck it out to the end. Then I met David Rousseau.' She told the story of her brief life with David, but Sophie's activities were so far removed from Karen's mundane existence that Karen was unable to relate in any way at all.

A little while later, as they sat in the lounge, Sophie said 'Tell me what's happened since you left Groote Schuur.'

A long pause, and then, like a waterfall flowing, she poured out the story of Simon - his schooling, the university debacle, the drugging.

'Oh, my Sophie, it's bad, really bad! It's killing both of us.'

'I get it - I work with druggies, you know.'

'Ja, I know – when I saw you on Question Time, what you said about the whole family suffering the effects of addiction, that really reached out to me. I wanted to speak to you, but I couldn't; I wanted to write and something held me back ...' - the tears fell once more, this time not of joy.

'Well, you did, and I'm really glad you did! Where is Simon now?'

'In his room. He hardly comes out, and when he does, more often than not he rips into me.'

Karen put her hand to her face, feeling the lump where Simon had punched her two days before. She smiled in an embarrassed way but said nothing.

'It's that bad, hey, Ka?'

'It's that bad! My life has not been easy recently, Soph- how's that for English understatement - Simon could do with a strong man to calm him right now but there's no chance of that happening.'

'Wouldn't you consider contacting John?'

'Why would I want to do that now?'

'To tell him that the kid he brought into the world is giving his mother a very difficult time.'

'No way! What's past is past. Remember, he wanted me to have an abortion. Simon's my son, not his.'

'Why are you so against speaking to him?'

'So much water has flowed under the bridge since then. I cannot, no, I *will* not go back. He's an international playboy, and look at what I've become.'

Sophie's cell phone rang – she paused, then answered. '... they lost? Fuck! Better not come round then if you're going to be unpleasant.'

Karen interrupted. 'No, let him - I want to meet your guy, and he may as well hear the whole sad saga from me as second hand from you.'

Talking to Richard, Sophie teased, 'Karen wants to meet you, I can't think why.'

# Chapter 30:

## *Names Become Faces  2005*

Richard was in a foul mood when he arrived at Karen's home, and in truth would rather have gone for a couple of single malts at The Albatross. He thought of his old mates doing the same at a pub near White Hart Lane and felt very nostalgic. Then he realised he was becoming something of a curmudgeon, and this was probably the moment to be doing something about it. It wouldn't be fair on Sophie for Karen's first impression of him tobe in a bad light. Karen however welcomed him warmly, and he immediately became aware of the reasons Sophie had wanted to invest so much time and energy in the woman's life. That the woman was beautiful was beyond dispute, but Richard could also feel the impact of a kind and caring person. He could sense why a profession such as nursing would have been as logical a choice for Karen as it had been for his Sophie, if for very different reasons.

He sat back as, unconcerned by a male presence, she related her story about the three men in her life: John Jameson, Philip Case, and Simon Williams.

'As soon as Simon started school, I got a part-time job as a dental nurse at a practice where they didn't just extract your teeth. Private. Very posh. The job's very routine, but you know something, guys, at the end of the day nursing is nursing whether you do it in a ward or a dental surgery. The patients are shit-scared and would much rather be somewhere else, and you have to make them feel that it's all going to be ok.'

Richard, who since his schooldays had never loved going to his NHS dentist – everyone there was always in a hurry – could sense immediately how this woman could put one at ease.

Sophie could feel Richard's own tensions lessen – never an easy process when Spurs lost!

He asked Karen, 'What's it like working three feet away from the same person all day long? The only dentists I knew were always stressed, and the atmosphere would make me feel tense.'

'Yeah, I understand what you mean. Still, Dr Errol is quite a special guy. He's cool. None of your Matron Gray attitude that makes you feel like shark-shit all the time.'

Ever sceptical, Richard said 'One reads stories that when you work so closely with someone, it often ends in an affair.'

Karen burst out laughing. 'No chance, not with this guy! You wouldn't notice Errol if he was the only other person in a lift. But his patients worship him, and so do his wife and kids. So do I. No need for me to change that! On the other hand, I got a lot of "can we meet sometime after work" from the Claremont married men who were obviously tired of eating white chicken at home and fancied a taste of chocolate for dessert.'

Sophie tried to ignore the somewhat pejorative description of women of European stock. White chicken?!

'Did you give them sweeties, Ka?'

'I'm *dom*, but not that dumb, Sophie. Once was enough, thank you very much!'

'Did you never want a serious relationship?'

'I was having a serious relationship - with my Simon. No, I led a very quiet life, but I did get involved with a local battered women's home. All the girls there were victims of male violence. Some of those women were gay and had been raped by guys whose sole purpose was to show how misguided their thinking was that another woman could possibly be better than a real man with a proper dick. And as for those who did have boyfriends or husbands .... their *okes* were testosterone junkies. When I wasn't taking care of Simon, I was glad to be able to make lives a little easier for those fragile women. I guess my nurse's training wasn't entirely wasted....'

'That's really impressive,' said Richard.

'And the stupid thing was, I didn't realise how close I was to becoming part of the statistics when I was with Philip just before he died. He really used to *bedonner* the hell out of me when he got plastered or when Simon got up his nose.' Karen then related in detail her dysfunctional relationship with Philip Case, how it had started off with such promise before becoming blighted by his return to alcohol. She gave a wan smile, but it was obvious to her visitors that she was not far from tears.

Then it was time to talk about Simon. She described Simon's happy upbringing and how it had all changed when he got to university.

'Why did he take it so hard?'

'I can't explain it, but it was probably the first time Simon had ever really loved someone besides me and his grandparents. That was the first sign he had ever shown of having a more sensitive nature, but it really rocked him. He's definitely my son! Anyway, he started drugging, and it quickly became worse. His grades were suffering. He was warned by the UCT authorities that his scholarship would be withdrawn, and he saved them the trouble by dropping out. Well, like mother like son. I was upset, sure, but who was I, the great nursing drop-out, to sit in judgment of my Simon?'

'You're being very hard on yourself, Karen. You aren't the only nurse to get pregnant nor the only mother of a child on drugs.'

'Yes, well, fine, that's quite easy for you to say but it doesn't make me feel any better.'

'You're right - how *would* I know? I'm sorry, my darling, I should be more sensitive to your feelings.'

Richard asked what Simon did after he dropped out.

'Worked for a few months as a supermarket packer or whatever other odd-job he could find to earn a few bucks and then headed off to India. India was exactly what he was looking for at that time. No wonder so many kids go there when they finish their army training. He experimented with every drug that he could shove up his nose or in his arm or up his arse. He eventually returned, and I could barely recognise him. Thinner than a pipe cleaner, eyes as blank as a dead cat.'

'Typical junkie look,' said Sophie - how many times had she encountered this!

Karen described how he began to steal from her, from her folks, from local shops; how he took her credit cards, sold her most treasured possessions, meagre as they were. Then Karen started getting demands from dealers threatening her and her parents with injury if she didn't settle his debts. Reluctantly she paid up, but eventually she just couldn't take any more and locked him out. 'This of course drove him into bigger theft and eventually to street-dealing, and he ended up being sent to Pollsmoor for four months for peddling low-grade crack. and also for minor theft. And of course he was gang-raped in prison. And of course I blamed myself.'

'Not wanting to get too personal, but did he end up with HIV?' inquired Sophie.

'Amazingly not, and he was bleddy damn lucky not to. He behaved for a few months when he came out, stopped drugging for a while and really tried to get a job, but nobody wanted to know and then it began all over again. Like he's got a death wish. I couldn't throw him out, so I have to support him.'

Richard, ever the realist, said softly, 'You're not supporting him, Karen, you're carrying him. Can you not see you've become a willing colluder? You think that you can prevent life's crap falling on Simon by letting it fall on you instead, by being available 24/7 to be dumped on? That's all an illusion. *You* cannot cure him, and unless you start some serious tough love and get him take responsibility for his own actions, he hasn't got a snowball's chance in hell of sorting himself out.'

'I know... I know. I told you, I'm not dumb. But what's my alternative? Kick him out again? How long do you think a darker-skinned kid can be on the streets before the police pick him up? So I keep him here. Our relationship is close, much too close, and it's terribly destructive. We're at each other's throats all the time – well, he's literally at mine! If I can run faster than Simon, I lock that gate over there to stop him physically attacking me when he gets psychotic. This has happened on quite a few occasions, and the attacks are getting more frequent, I don't always manage to get the gate locked in time, and he beats the living shit out of me.'

'He really needs treatment before he kills you - or himself – or both!'

Karen's reply was laced with sarcasm. 'Treatment! He's had it all! That cupboard is full of every medication you can think of and a lot that you can't. They're not helping, they've made him worse.'

'Yup, when you mix street drugs and medication, the cocktail is explosive,' said Sophie softly, feeling the pain of her traumatised friend. She put her arm around Karen and hugged her. Here was the living embodiment of the point she had made to the *Freedom to Choose* lady – addicts rarely suffer alone.

Lifting her hands to her face, Karen said 'I keep thinking ... if I could buy time ... if I could find the right help for him. It's just so bloody difficult on my own – the boy needs a father ...'

As was his way, Richard had sat quietly listening, but now raised his voice: 'He's got one, Karen. John is immensely wealthy and powerful, and I'm sure that if he was made aware he would give his assistance without hesitation.'

Karen sighed. 'I don't think I could face speaking to John again, let alone meeting him. We can't just pick up where we left off. He's a bigtime playboy, I've seen his photos. No, what's past is past. I've made my choice and I have to go it alone.'

'Can you manage Simon alone?'

'It's getting more and more difficult. We are totally dependent on one another. He is my reason for living, and regrettably I am his means.'

Sophie spoke up: 'You're playing with fire, you know. I'm not sure if it was reported in the SA papers but there was a terrible story recently about an English guy of 22 who had been doing pot since the age of 13 who hacked his girlfriend to death at an English private school where her father was a master. The guy was a top university student suffering from crack-induced paranoid schizophrenia. He is now in Broadmoor psychiatric prison and will probably be there for life.'

'But that's just my point, Sophie - I'm terrified that if I let Simon loose he will do the same thing. He hardly ever leaves the house. Damage limitation is the best I can achieve right now: by allowing him to harm me, he is less likely to harm someone else. So, I agreed to keep him supplied with dagga, provided he went off the very hard stuff, cocaine, skunk, tik, whatever.'

She continued, 'I had to give up my dental nursing job. I can only leave the house when he's asleep and can't stay out during the day for longer than a couple of hours, otherwise he smashes me up. I had to get him seen privately but this bastard doctor who pumped him with pethidine was more interested in screwing me than helping Simon.'

Karen then related how she had turned to pole-dancing, and how the dancing had led to, if not sleeping with clients, at least entertaining them for money. 'It didn't bother me at first, but it's not a nice thing to know I'm selling myself.'

## CHAPTER 30: NAMES BECOME FACES 2005

Sophie shook her head. 'You're far from that, Karen. You're just doing the best you can. Aren't you scared of getting beaten up? I can just see Dianne Keaton getting pulverised by that psychopath in *Looking for Mr Goodbar*'.

Karen cringed and said ruefully, 'No, I do the pulverising! Some of these guys literally beg for a good spanking, which I am sort of happy to deliver. They are tired of being honest accountants and law-abiding citizens who always do what their wives tell them. You wouldn't believe it, but the one thing that they all want is to be naughty and then be punished for it. I'm like their psychoanalyst, their mother-confessor. Most the time they don't even want sex. I could do a nice side trade on telephone sex, but I go stir crazy if I can't get out of this flat. Just seeing a different building is such a win! Do you know, I haven't had a single day away on my own for ten years!'

As Sophie continued to console her, Richard couldn't resist chiming in, 'John could organise a fantastic holiday for you.'

'You keep pushing, Richard. The last time he saw me, I was almost a nurse. Now I'm a fucking pole-dancer, for God's sake, practically a hooker! How would he be if that hit Business Day?'

Richard smiled ruefully. 'If I've got anything to do with it, the Cape Argus is going to get there first!'

# Chapter 31:

## *A Lesson in Star Wars 2005*

Just then they heard music wafting through the interleading doorway. Simon had obviously awoken but there was no sign of him, so Karen decided to take a chance, and, opening the gate, led Sophie and Richard through to his room.

As Richard and Sophie entered, they could not help but see it was a shrine, covered wall to wall with Star Wars miscellany. The thought suddenly struck Sophie that this affinity for Star Wars had literally been written in the stars – the first Star Wars movie had been released exactly at the time of Simon's birth. One of Richard's favourite soundtracks, *All About My Mother*, resonated softly through the room. Richard loved cinema, and Almodovar was right up there with his favourite directors. He grinned. He saw an opportunity opening up that he was not about to let slip. 'Hmmm. That's one of my favourite albums.'

Simon just sat there with a blank expression, but after a few moments, in a slow slurred voice decided to test Richard. 'Oh yeah? What do you think of the last track?'

'The one by Ishmael Lo? Brilliant! Since I came to live in SA, I've enjoyed listening to African music, and he's one of the best.'

Something penetrated the haze that was Simon's mind. He asked: 'Who are you into?'

'The usual musicians from Senegal and Mali - Youssou N'Dour, Baba Maal, Salif Keita - but I recently got a Zimbabwean album by Tuku that I play all the time.'

Simon was beginning to get interested. 'Do you guys ever go to gigs?'

'Sophie's too busy, but I go when I can. I saw Tuku in Mitchell's Plain a few weeks ago – knocked my socks off! Sellout crowd. I think I was the only white person there, I must have stuck out like a polar bear! Sophie said I was lucky to get back at all, let alone in one piece!'

Sophie nudged Karen as she remembered her own experience in Manenberg all those years ago.

'You've got big ones, Richard,' said Karen. 'That was taking your life in your hands!'

'Not at all, I often go into Mitchells to interview someone or other or to research a story - never had a minute's trouble or ever felt threatened.'

Sensing another opening, Richard said to Simon: 'Maybe we can get to go to a gig together sometime?'

'Wow, that would be amazing! Unfortunately, I'm a prisoner here. My Ma does not allow me out, in case I meet some nasty coke dealer from Nigeria and frazzle what's left of my brain.'

Richard could sense the frustration Karen would be experiencing, living with this manboy. He was finding it difficult to keep his annoyance in check. 'Hold on chum, it's not your mother who is imprisoning you, it's you who is keeping Karen locked up.'

'Ok, I guess I can't argue with that ...... I panic when Ma goes out. I start yelling, and the fat fucking bastard upstairs starts yelling at me to shut up. He's called the police several times and tried to get me arrested.'

Karen, barely able to contain herself, intervened. 'Actually, the neighbour is not fat, to my knowledge never fucks, and unlike you isn't a bastard. He's a sixty-eight-year-old ex-soldier who could probably beat the shit out of you with one hand. Actually, that's quite funny - he only has one hand, the other got shot off in Caprivi. He swears he has never phoned the police, although he has every right to do so because you can be an obnoxious git when the drugs take you.'

'Why do you always take his side, Ma? You say kind things about him, but I know 100% he poisoned Skywalker.'

Karen snorted. 'He would have had every right to poison your dog. Skywalker was a mean little runt, but the vet said he died of old age.'

Sophie sensed it was time to get away from that issue, so she got Simon involved in a whole discussion about the moral themes running through Star Wars. This set Simon wafting on about the forces of good and evil, but after realising this could go on for days, Sophie cut it short. 'This space stuff's all a bit other-worldly. How do you feel about your world?'

'If you want my honest opinion, I think that life's a pool of shit, and I'm in at the deep end.'

'So wouldn't it make sense to stand in the shallow end?'

'Sure it would. Do you really think I wouldn't like to be normal, whatever normal is? Never mind the fucking shallow end, I want out of this pool.'

Sophie was cynical. 'Is that really so? You made the choice to go there. You choose to be there. So, the only person who can get you out is *you*, Simon. You need proper medical assistance.'

Simon was becoming agitated. With shoulders shaking, he addressed Sophie: 'You were and probably still are Karen's best friend, and that is the only reason you have been allowed to enter this holy of holies. But let me tell you, lady, with all due respect, you know jackshit. The main achievement of all universities since the eleventh century has been to produce wankers of every hue, tone and colour. Doctors are the biggest wankers of all, and in this royal pantheon of jerkoffs, king wanker is Dr fucking Dark Side who pumped me full of pethidine so that he could screw my mother.'

Sophie retorted, 'He pumped you full of pethidine so that you would stop beating up your mother!'

## CHAPTER 31: A LESSON IN STAR WARS 2005

Richard was now hearing one of his pet bugbears. He waded in. 'I get what you're saying, Simon. Most medics make their living by treating us as if we were nothing more than chemical formulae, and they regard addicts as formulae gone wrong. Find the right drug to balance the wrong one, and all will be well.'

Simon shot back, 'What about becoming addicted to the *right* drug as well? Do you think I'm not as hooked on pethidine, valium, ritalin and twenty others that I could mention, as I am on weed?'

Looking at him kindly, Richard said: 'I have to agree with you. Chemical imbalances as a cause of medical illness is a conspiracy set up by the whole pharmaceutical industry. If you don't have a full set of chemicals, just find the missing ones. If you have the wrong chemicals, blot out the deviants.'

Simon nodded. The corner of his mouth lifted slightly in grim pursuit of a smile. He was beginning to appreciate this man, if still cynical of his motives. 'Most of the people who are trying to sort us out are middle-class, middle-aged, financially secure social-worker types who have got nothing better to do with their time. They know diddly-squat about what's happening because they've never been there. How much do you know, Sophie, how much do you understand? Have you ever even smoked a joint? Can you tell coke from crack?'

Sophie reflected. 'Actually, I do know. Don't forget, I was your age once too, and very partial to weed, but it's been a long while. Never did LSD though. Did you?'

'Sure! Nearly flew off the top of the Krishna temple in Bangalore. Got the t-shirt, babe.'

Richard gave him a filthy look. 'Don't you dare "babe" Sophie! She is probably the person more than any other in South Africa who has worked with druggies like you and empowered them to reclaim their own lives. And if you really want to reclaim yours, and I think you do, you had better start by being less of a smart-ass!'

Karen began to see a punch-up looming, but to her amazement Simon smiled and said 'Ok, I apologize. You both seem genuinely decent guys, and I really shouldn't diss you. Specially you, Richard, 'cos I want to go to live gigs again and I suspect I would be allowed to go with you.'

Richard was now getting quite annoyed. 'Not much chance of that - I don't hang out with women-beaters.'

Simon started to lunge at Richard, but then pulled back.

Richard realised he had made a bad move. 'I'm sorry, I shouldn't have said that.'

Sophie decided to defuse the escalating situation. 'Here's a suggestion, Simon: if you can cut down the cannabis and stop attacking Karen, then you get to go and see Star Wars at the Imax and a few gigs as well - and your mom gets free time to spend with me. How does that sound?'

Simon ignored her and picked up one of his Star Wars figures.

Sophie realised it was time to exit. Speaking quietly, she said 'OK, we've got to go. If you like my idea, give us a shout, ok?'

Simon humphed, 'Don't hold your breath!'

As they were driving back, they could not but be aware of the larger than usual cloud covering Table Mountain, its famous 'tablecloth'. It all seemed so peaceful, especially by comparison with the tempestuous hour they had just spent with a clearly troubled young man.

'I feel so sorry for Karen. It's quite heart-breaking seeing her now compared to the vibrant girl I knew.'

'I can see why you care so much about Karen. Unfortunately, I'm not sure there is a solution to that kid's problems.'

Sophie had to agree.

# Chapter 32:

## *The cat is unbagged  2006*

It was very soon after that the cat was let out of the bag. Or, to mix one's metaphors, the elephant in the room was let loose. Karen's father returned from The White Feather one Sunday evening in a particularly advanced state of inebriation. Totally pissed - *poegaai*. Magda was talking to Karen, and Kallie went through to Simon's room, feeling very angry about some undefined thing that was irritating his anal sphincter. For whatever reason, he attributed the cause of this irritation to Simon's biological father, whose name had been lurking in his subconscious for years. So when Simon raised the question, as he had done many times before, as to who his father might be, he felt obliged to tell Simon the answer that Karen had all those years refused to divulge to Simon: he informed Simon that his father's name was one John Jameson and that John was a rich Cape Town banker. He even mentioned the name of the bank.

Surprisingly, Simon did not initially see this as terribly exciting, because, like Kallie but for different reasons, he was spaced out. But as indifference gave way to something resembling clarity, he saw an opportunity to connect with his father, and decided to contact John.

*

John Jameson, immaculately attired as always – pinstripe suit, starched white shirt, paisley tie and matching pocket square, shoes shone so you could see your face - was sitting at his desk when a light on his intercom flickered.

'What's up, Judith?'

John was rather proud of his ability to make excellent secretarial choices, even if they did change rather more frequently than was conducive to efficiency. Judith, who was no exception, normally did not take or pass on unsolicited calls or visits from strangers, but on this particular occasion she was in a particularly jovial mood and one could probably guess why. In the dulcet tones Judith knew turned him on, she whispered, 'There's a nice young man in my office asking to see you.'

John too was feeling in the most benign of moods. A gentle knock on the door followed. 'Do come in, old chap!'

A rather nervous and uncertain Simon entered. This was not the sort of place where he was used to hanging out. John was surprised at Judith's description of the ashen, unkempt fellow in front of him, who was anything but nice. His obviously well-worn track suit that reeked of some noxious substance was certainly not the type of suit that normally passed through John's door, and it was probably the first time that trainers had ever trod on his Siamese carpet. Nevertheless, difficult as it was in this case, John had learned not to judge a book by its cover, and who knew what fortune this man might have inherited that might soon be passing through his fingers?

'Hallo, my good fellow, I'm John Jameson,' he said, oleaginous as an oil slick.

'Good afternoon sir.'

'Oh, do call me John. Take a pew,' John said, motioning to the luxurious leather chair in front of his desk. *(Where did this English affectation come from? Regina?)* 'How can I be of help?'

Simon sat uneasily, and, speaking very slowly in a monotone voice said, 'My name's Simon - Simon Williams.'

'Jolly good to meet you, Simon – travelled far?'

'Claremont.'

'Nice area! Here on business?'

'No, most businessmen are wankers.'

## CHAPTER 32: THE CAT IS UNBAGGED 2006

How did Judith let this fellow in, thought John. 'What an insightful fellow you are, Mr Williams! Given that obviously well-considered viewpoint, what brings you to see me? Have you come to learn some new techniques, a strong forearm pull or a good wrist twist?'

Simon was unaware of the sarcasm. 'I'm looking for my father.'

A cry for help for anything that didn't involve money was unusual to someone of John's status, but he tried to sound at least a bit sympathetic. 'Why, is he missing?'

'He's never been around.'

'So why are you looking for him now?'

'I need his help. He owes it to me. I'm his son.'

'What's his name?'

'I believe it's John Jameson.'

'John Jam- ' John leapt up. 'What's your bloody game, Williams? Do you think you're the first person claiming to be spawned by me? Just because I've been around the block a bit, you buggers think you can put the screws on me? I'll have the police in here quicker than you can pick your dirty little nose, you young thug! Don't get funny with me! Get out!!'

'I'm not trying to be funny. My mother's name is Karen Williams. She was a nurse at Groote Schuur Hospital in 1977.'

John sat down as if he had been struck with a heavy blunt object. '1977. That's when I had my appendix out. A nurse ... at Groote Schuur... Karen Williams ...'

'She's my mother. I was born in 1978. Her father got drunk last month and told me you're my father.'

'Her father told you? He says you're my father, ag I mean I'm your father?'

'Ja, that's what grandpa said.'

'I find it hard to believe that you are Karen's son. Karen was so gentle! I really liked her – she disappeared – very suddenly. Where's she now?'

'Asleep. At home.'

'Can I speak to her? Can I see her?'

'No way!! She'd kill me if she knew I was here. She isn't even aware that I know you're my father.'

'Allegedly!'

John sat gazing into space and, talking to himself more than to Simon, muttered 'I ... I liked her so much. I thought she loved me too.'

'So you are my father?'

John was startled. 'No. Perhaps. I don't know. We'll have to do some tests. Does she have another man?'

'No, it's just the two of us at home.'

'Is she still a nurse?'

'She quit nursing when she got pregnant with me. She can't work during the day.'

'So how does she earn money?'

'She has a night job. She has to pay for my dagga, I can't do without it.'

'Well, I can't give you any - I don't deal in drugs. I'm head of a bank, not a damn narcotics ring.'

'I don't want drugs, I want a father.'

'I find it hard to believe that you are her son.'

'I'm sorry I don't meet your specifications.'

'Well, you have not exactly presented yourself in a way that has me bursting with pride.'

'If you don't like me, that's OK, I'm sorry I bothered you. I wish I could tell my Ma I met you - I don't like keeping things from her – but I'm not going to, I don't need to upset her. She is my closest friend. Better than that bitch at university. Or her murdering racist parents.'

'You went to university? I find that hard to believe!!'

Simon told John that he had been at UCT.

'Oh really? I was also there – I studied politics and business.'

'I was doing science. Dropped out because I was doing drugs as well.'

'Didn't Karen stop you?'

'No-one can halt the Force', said Simon emphatically.

John snorted. 'The force? What force?'

'The Force in Star Wars.'

John raised his hands to his head. 'I can't believe what I'm hearing! What's Star Wars got to do with this?'

'Everyone has to choose between The Force for good and the Dark Side.'

'Now I've got to worry about the Dark Side too? What are they, a football team from Nigeria? You know, I think you've completely lost the plot!'

John was beginning to find this conversation tedious. He could see a train-crash looming: in his mind, the spectre of blackmail reared its ugly head. He envisioned a situation where Simon, this hideous character whom he had allegedly spawned, would begin to put the screws on him for ever-increasing sums of money. He foresaw a situation where he would have to pay up and set himself up for the next pay-round; and if he did not, everything he valued - his career, his position as CEO at the bank, his Rolls Royce, his golf friends, his father-in-law and best friend, his political aspirations – all of it would be up shit creek. Paddleless.

'Look, don't try this stunt again. I wasn't born yesterday. Please, just go. You must promise never to contact me again, do you understand?'

Simon stood. 'May the Force be with you!'

As the younger man shambled through the door, John found himself repeating sarcastically: 'May the force be with you! *May the force be with you*? Fucking bloody hell.'

Fortunately for him, John heard no more from Simon, for Simon returned home to resume his relentless relationship with the noxious weed. Nor did Simon mention to Karen his foray to meet his father. He had liked John about as much as John had taken to him. He had no intention of developing the relationship, and if he wasn't going to see the unpleasant man again, what was the point of upsetting his mother? At least now he could stop nagging to be informed. He had gone, he had seen, and he wasn't one bit impressed. If that was what a father was like, he wished he hadn't bothered so much.

# Chapter 33:

## *The Press Club Luncheon 2006*

Life has a habit of toying with those who endure it. In what seemed most of us would say was a bizarre coincidence, the final piece of the jigsaw was about to be put in place by the least likely person of all, Richard.

Sophie and Richard had entered a swank harbour building, she very simply but elegantly dressed, he in a well-used sports jacket, tie, and grey trousers. Richard was well used to attending the monthly talks organised by the South African Press Club. The topics were always current and interesting, and the lunches, prepared by a former chef from the Cape's premier restaurant, La Colombe, never disappointed. The superb wines, each time from a different Stellenbosch or Franschhoek vineyard, made even the occasional tedious talk an agreeable experience.

Sophie had only been there on one previous occasion. Albie Sachs was the speaker then, another of her tribe, a man who, after joining the ANC a long time before, had lost an arm and very nearly an eye in an explosion while in exile. Sophie wondered how he was able to speak of his experiences as dispassionately as he seemed to be doing, but she guessed that one thing all of these exiles had in abundance, herself included, was emotional control.

On this occasion, Sophie had been reluctant to accompany Richard because the topic of the speech was *"The Cost of AIDS to South Africa".* Nobody knew better than Sophie what the cost was, and she didn't feel in the mood for sitting through another predictable lecture by someone who on the balance of probabilities knew less than she did. Nevertheless, Richard had been insistent. The speaker, Professor Seymour L Cohen, was an eminent physician and researcher on sabbatical from Ann Arbor, Michigan. He had spent his time at Groote Schuur well, and pulled no punches as he excoriated the policies and misguided philosophy of President Thabo Mbeki in respect of HIV. In spite of her earlier misgivings, she found the talk insightful and educational.

After the talk, they were privileged to be seated at the same table as the eminent speaker, Sophie to the left of the Professor. Their rapport was immediate, so much so that she barely noticed the tall, slim man with salt-and-pepper hair sitting a few places away on her left, who was staring intently at her throughout the meal. If she paid much attention to him at all, his face was vaguely familiar, but she could not place it. However, when Professor Cohen left the table after promising to e-mail her, she saw the greying man advancing towards them. He reached her and in a soft voice said, 'Hello Sophie, you may not recall, but we met many years ago, when you and a lovely nurse named Karen tended me so considerately at Groote Schuur Hospital.'

Sophie almost keeled over. ''Omygod, I thought you looked familiar. You're fucking John Jameson!!!'

John smiled sweetly, 'So they keep telling me!'

When she regained her composure Sophie said, 'Sorry, pardon my rudeness. This is my partner, Richard Simpson.'

John's tone became ingratiating. 'Richard and I have crossed paths before as well. I read your column regularly, Richard, and although you're very dismissive of my banking colleagues and me, I do respect your writing.'

Richard didn't respond.

Glancing at Sophie, John oozed, 'You were kindness personified; more than a bit bolshie, but over-all the essence of a caring nurse.'

'And you were in pain, but that didn't stop you from being an outrageous flirt!'

Richard suddenly joined in. 'There are many husbands who would not be concerned if you were only flirtatious,

CHAPTER 33: THE PRESS CLUB LUNCHEON 2006

Jameson, but you've got a reputation for being the greatest Lothario in the Cape since Cecil Rhodes!'

'I would have enjoyed being with just a quarter of the women with whom my name has been linked.'

'I wouldn't be surprised if you had,' said Sophie. 'I must say, if you hadn't been so arrogant, even I might have been responsive to you. You certainly charmed my friend Karen - I couldn't keep her away from your bedside!'

'Hmmm, there's more truth in your words than you realise.... I don't know whether you were aware of it, but Karen and I had a rather torrid affair.'

'I was only too well aware, probably the only person who was. What were you thinking, John? She had no chance. Fucking hell!!!'

'No, I was fucking Karen, actually - and then she suddenly disappeared....'

'And her nursing career with her!'

'I didn't expect that.'

'What *did* you expect?'

John did not attempt to respond. What he did say quietly was, 'You know something, Karen was probably the only woman I have ever truly loved.' He looked at Sophie – were those tears in his eyes? 'Did she keep contact with you, Sophie?'

Sophie, as briefly as she could, described their meetings with Karen and Simon, at the end of which John commented, 'Simon came to see me a month ago. He was drugged out, so it was a massive shock for me to learn that I was the father of a ghastly dopehead. To be perfectly frank, I'm not too keen on seeing Simon ever again, but I would dearly love to see Karen. Will you let me have that address?'

'I wish I could, but she's very resistant to raking over old coals.'

'I understand. Nevertheless, if you put in a good word, she might re-consider. In return, I can assure you of my unqualified support for your anti-drugs campaign, which could be very helpful to Simon.'

Sophie looked at him and said, 'Let's keep in touch.'

Richard grimaced.

As they walked into their apartment an hour later, Sophie suddenly whacked Richard across the shoulder. 'You set it up! You knew John would be there, didn't you? Swine!'

'Who, *moi*?'

Richard had been called to London for an editorial meeting and, unusually, Sophie had a little time on her hands. She decided to call John.

'Hi John – Sophie Levine. I've been having some thoughts ...'

The following day they met at John's office on the upper floor of the modern high-rise building in the Cape Town CBD that was literally an eye-opener for Sophie. She tried to imagine what it must have been like for Simon. The panoramic view to the left of his desk showing Table Mountain covered by the famous tablecloth cloud was matched by that on the right of the Victoria & Albert Waterfront (*one could safely assume that none of this had been noticed or appreciated by Simon, but that's living in a haze for you*). Sophie outlined her thoughts point by point and then summed up. 'I see it this way: Karen and Simon are in a lose–lose situation. We have eased it to a limited extent, but the boy needs private therapy in a secure environment.'

'You mean somewhere like the Lansdale. I know it only too well.'

'There's no way that Karen can afford the Lansdale.'

'Yes, but I can. Look, Sophie, I'll be honest, I can't stand the sight of that boy, but I'll give whatever's required to help Karen.'

'And to help your son, whether you like him or not. I was hoping you'd be agreeable to offering Karen financial

## CHAPTER 33: THE PRESS CLUB LUNCHEON 2006

assistance, but she won't accept it if she knows it's come from you.'

'So get around it, Sophie, make up a story that you've managed to get him accepted for a medical trial. Tell them it's from some big drug company who have had success in the past. That's not inconceivable, you know.'

'Brilliant, John! That just might work! And if it does, we can tell the truth later.'

'Let's worry about later later.'

On his return, Richard expressed his misgivings about whether the venture would turn out to be successful. His main concern was that he did not believe that either Simon or Karen had the desire to break their dependence on each other. Nevertheless, his personal antipathy to John notwithstanding, he too offered his unqualified support.

# Chapter 34:

## *Nervous Expectations  2006*

The proposition was mooted, and to everyone's surprise was given the green light by Karen. Things moved quickly. Karen and Simon were collected from their home by private taxi. Simon was dropped off in the beautiful grounds of the Lansdale Clinic in Stellenbosch, an hour from Cape Town. Karen was driven to Molenvliet, a wine-farm nearby where a stunning cottage with mountain and vineyard views had been reserved for her to do little more than walk, swim and read or take the shuttle into Stellenbosch. Such a vacation would have been fantastic for anyone, but for Karen it was an experience beyond belief. Never in her whole life could she have imagined being in a setting of such complete serenity and utter beauty, and some mysterious benefactor was footing the bill.

Karen, who was not inherently stupid and had a pretty strong idea who the benefactor was, was not of a mind to reject a release from their prison as long as it did not entail meeting John. She loved the restful days, and found the staff extremely friendly, but the evenings tended to be somewhat boring, so she saw little reason not to revert to her part-time occupation; on a few of those nights she took the shuttle into nearby Stellenbosch, spent an hour or two in the bar of a luxury hotel and was transported to her cottage in a BMW or Merc by a lonely Stellenbosch man whose wife did not understand him.

For Simon, therapy with a group of highly skilled professionals and counsellors as forced withdrawal ran its course was difficult but ultimately effective. The nurses were caring and attentive, the doctors pleasant and

## CHAPTER 34: NERVOUS EXPECTATIONS  2006

reassuring, and as far as Simon could tell, not a single wanker in sight. After initial resistance, Simon began to relax, to think more clearly, to eat good food heartily. He almost began to enjoy the company of others drying out there. He joined in the group meetings and discussions without rancour, and was gradually shedding his paranoic fear of being attacked. He swam, sunbathed and ran in the gardens. He was more active during those four weeks than he had been in the ten preceding years, and it felt good.

A month later, the same driver collected Karen, then Simon. She was surprised at how much weight he had lost, how his pallor had disappeared and how calm he seemed to be. He greeted her warmly, and for the first time in as long as she could remember, Karen felt happy.

Richard and Sophie arrived at Karen's at about 6pm, Sophie finely dressed, he in denims and a casual shirt. Not a particularly unusual Saturday night for them, but for Karen and Simon a momentous occasion; momentous because for the first time in recent memory, Karen and Simon were about to leave their apartment together to go out for the evening. Karen, like her friend, was immaculate, wearing raised heels for the first time in ages not for work. Simon was dressed far more casually, still wearing a track suit but one that had been washed and pressed. They would be heading for the Victoria and Albert Waterfront. The women had booked a new seafood restaurant. Karen and Sophie would be returning to the area that was once so much part of their time together at nurses' home, the place where the Starlite Club had once been their favourite haunt but was now just a memory. It, and all the other dives in the area, had been razed and replaced by a massive upmarket retail, entertainment and restaurant complex.

The men would be heading to the nearby Convention Centre a short distance away to see the local superstar Jimmy Dudhlu perform before a sell-out crowd. Simon was visibly shaking with excitement – he was about to attend a gig for the first time in his life.

As the two women settled at their table after their aperitif, Karen looked totally overwhelmed.
'I cannot believe you worked this, Wonderwoman!'
Sophie gazed at her friend, who stood out in a room full of beautiful, well-groomed women. 'I must admit that when I made that suggestion to Simon, I wouldn't have been the least bit surprised if he had told me to go and screw myself. When you phoned me to say that he was up for the challenge, I couldn't believe it.'
'Believe me, Soph, I had my doubts too, bigtime. But you know what, he really liked you guys, and the thought of going to see Jimmy Dudhlu was irresistible. So, he managed to smoke a bit less, a lot less actually, and hold himself in check every time he thought of whacking me. I'm really grateful to the two of you.'
'Well, it was mainly Richard.'
'You've found a good man, Sophie, and I'm happy for you.'
Sophie couldn't help but think what might have been for both of them, but this was not an evening to feel sad.
As the waitron set down their main courses, Sophie looked at her favourite seafood dish – baby kingklip on the bone – the one local fish above all she had missed in London. She glanced around and observed that a decent number of people in the restaurant were not white, something that would not have been possible before her hasty departure. She hoped to herself that Dr David Rousseau might be observing this somewhere and smiling, By the time the two old friends had finished their bottle of chilled Chenin Blanc, they were giggling happily.
When the men returned, Simon was ecstatic. 'Ma, that was the best evening of my life!!! The gig was awesome, and Jimmy did a whole lot of new stuff. And Ma, the back-

## CHAPTER 34: NERVOUS EXPECTATIONS  2006

up band – holy shit, you can't believe how brilliant they were! Richard, you are legend!'

After their meal, they walked along the docks, licking Italian ice-cream cones, seeing Table Mountain lit up in the distance and enjoying the balmy evening.

Two weeks passed with no sign of relapse or aggression from Simon. Sophie invited Karen and Simon to spend an evening at their apartment in Camps Bay, that luxurious but windy suburb much beloved of British tourists. They avoided all talk of what the future might bring, instead enjoying Richard's cooking and the view of Lion's Head and the Atlantic Ocean. Karen could not avoid comparing this to her simple apartment and thinking how life might have panned out had she made different decisions, but did not dwell on it. She and Sophie were just happy to be together. The evening passed well enough, and both guests seemed relaxed and at ease with each other as well as their hosts. Had a corner been turned?

After they left, Sophie embraced Richard. 'That was such a good evening, darling. You've been amazing!'

A few days later, Sophie phoned Karen to invite her and Simon to come for another dinner. Although she did not mention it to Karen initially, it was Sophie's intention to throw caution to the winds and invite John as well. Could this be the beginning of better things?

# Chapter 35:

## *A Night to Remember 2007*

It was a cool but crisp evening at Richard and Sophie's apartment in windy Camps Bay. Richard for once looked well-geared in a polo-neck shirt and cords. He was enjoying a beer on the terrace as he listened to some gentle jazz guitar music. Sophie, beautifully but simply dressed, joined Richard. He handed her a glass of chilled white wine.

Richard sipped his dark ale – old habits die hard. They chatted through the events of the day. Sophie congratulated Richard not only on preparing the dinner but having managed to do a reasonable job in clearing the kitchen as he worked. She could just hear the dishwasher doing the first load of pots. 'The lamb smells delicious! You really are learning to use our local spices. I can smell the cinnamon and coriander from here.'

Richard took her hand. 'I have to say, I'm rather amazed. That Simon actually committed to going into the Lansdale was unexpected - that he remained there for the full month without drama was beyond belief – and they're on their way here! John should also be here soon.'

Sophie sipped her wine. '*Ongelooflik,* as they say in Afrikaans – unbelievable! That took me by surprise as well. When I asked Karen if there was just an itsy-bitsy chance that John might be allowed to join us for this evening's celebration, I didn't think there was a snowball's chance in hell that she would respond positively. In fact, she almost seemed thrilled!'

'You done good! By the way, you look rather pretty, young lady!'

## CHAPTER 35: A NIGHT TO REMEMBER  2007

'Thank you, kind sir! The pretty young lady would like a refill.'

'I think you may need it tonight, Sophie.'

'What do you mean?'

'Well, I don't want to sound like a pooper, but I don't feel quite as optimistic about the evening's outcome as you do. You're a Gemini - do you remember the theme song of all Geminis?'

'Of course I do, you remind me often enough: *Roses are red, violets are blue, I'm schizophrenic, and so am I.*'

'Well, in Simon's case, it's *and so am I, and so am I, and so am I*. Anything is possible with that kid, and it just depends which one of him, or more to the point, which few of him turn up.'

Sophie shrugged. 'He seemed a different person when they were last here. Why don't we just chill and take it as it comes?'

'Well, think about it, Sophie. Karen and Simon have had a very fraught relationship, but at the same time it's very complete and self-serving for both. They are co-dependent on each other, even though it's been a no-win game for both. Each was quite comfortable about blaming the other for creating their losing position, but neither had the courage to deal with the nasty real world out there and try to win the game. They had developed this symbiotic relationship where each considered the other as being the jailer, but neither was willing to walk out of the prison unless they were being shoved - and it's you who did the shoving.'

Sophie was not quite sure whether the feeling welling in her chest was anger or concern or a combination of both. Was Richard about to fuck things up? She controlled herself, took a deep breath. 'I think *shoving* is a bit OTT, Richard. I never put pressure on either of them. I simply offered them the possibility of making a different choice.'

'Somebody said there's nothing that concentrates the mind so wonderfully as a lack of choice. By giving them one, you are offering them a possibly better world, but at this moment a world of uncertainty, and they might well choose to go back to their miserable but very predictable zone of discomfort.'

'Don't you feel they've committed to moving forward?'

Richard shrugged. 'OK, let's assume all goes well, Simon continues to recover and returns to the outside world - what is he going to do there? He's nearly thirty, a university dropout, no cv besides a criminal record ... do you think they will be queuing up to offer him a job? No, he will return back to his nest, and mother hen Karen will welcome him back because her life will have become meaningless without him. And there they will remain until Simon either kills himself or kills her or kills them both.'

It was Sophie's turn to shrug. She was beginning to feel really uncomfortable. 'Lighten up, Jeremiah - you are a prophet of doom. I hope it won't come to that. Anyway, we've given it our best shot.'

'Maybe yes, maybe no, maybe ... But it's become a mission for you, Sophie, and it's beginning to affect our own relationship.'

This was what Sophie had instinctively feared. Nothing came without a cost. She tried to defuse the growing tension. 'I'm sorry, Richard, I realise I have become quite obsessive about this whole thing; it's the way I am. But you've also been totally involved, my darling.'

'True, but I'm not sure I want to continue to be if this doesn't work.'

'I am sure *I* do.'

'Why?'

'Karen is my friend.'

'So am I.'

'This is not about you, Richard.'

'True, but it isn't about you either.'

'So what do you suggest I do?'

'It doesn't really matter what you do, Sophie.'

'The only thing I can't do is nothing.'

## CHAPTER 35: A NIGHT TO REMEMBER 2007

'Doing nothing is actually better than doing the wrong thing.'

'Do you think I'm doing the wrong thing?'

'Well, perhaps it isn't a matter of right and wrong, but about whether we are expending a lot of energy doing something that has little possibility of creating lasting change.'

'Do you think that they are not capable of change?'

Richard frowned. 'How many psychiatrists does it take to change a lightbulb?'

'That's an old joke, but I'll play. One, but only if the light-bulb really wants to be changed. Yes?'

'Yes.'

'So which one of them is the lightbulb?'

'They both are, Sophie, and neither can work without the other. At the moment they are both alight, but they are flickering.'

'Don't you think they want to be changed, Richard?'

'No, I don't really think so.'

'Is it important?'

'Is what important? that they don't want to be changed?'

'No, is it important what you think? It is apparent to me that you are neither a psychiatrist nor an electrician.'

'It is equally apparent to me that what you are doing is like trying to catch lightning in a bottle, and I don't want you to get your fingers burnt in the process.'

'You know, Richard, one of the best things that has happened to me of late is my renewed friendship with Karen. You know how much she means to me, and I've put a lot of effort into trying to get them out of their little rut. I am not going to stop now. I really believe that Karen wants him to recover and lead a normal life.'

'Does Simon want that too?'

'He sounded really together when I spoke to him this morning, and I don't want you to show any negativity, because he'll pick it up immediately.'

Richard gave her a wry smile. 'Don't worry, sweetheart, you've invested so much energy into making this thing happen, no way am I going to screw up anything. I shall just be my usual calm unflappable self and make them all feel uncommonly welcome.'

Sophie leaned over to kiss his forehead.

The doorbell tolled.

# Chapter 36:

## *The Reunion*

John entered the room. He was wearing a smart dark suit, a starched white shirt and an immaculately knotted red paisley tie. Shoes polished to the nines. He handed Sophie a beautiful bunch of white roses. The attached note had just one word on it: 'Thanks.' For Richard, a bottle of Johnnie Walker Blue Label, which he was only too happy to open immediately. He filled two tumblers, and they clinked glasses as John surveyed the view below him with the lights of Camps Bay twinkling on the ocean as the sun set. Richard could not but be aware of the reason women were ready to make themselves available to Jameson – the man oozed class, wealth, charm and sophistication.

Sophie smiled. 'I'm really pleased you're here tonight, John.'

'As am I, Sophie. A toast to both of you! Cheers!!'

Richard looked at their empty glasses and refilled without hesitation. This was a night to forget old hostilities. 'I have to say, John, you've done a decent thing. Footing the bill for the Lansdale and Karen's holiday was extremely generous. I know how much they appreciated it.'

'Please don't make too much of the money aspect. I'm not short of it, and given that my legitimate kids are behaving like little bastards, I may as well spend some of it on the real bastard who now seems to be behaving like a decent kid.'

'I'm not sure we should take that for granted. We visited him a couple of times since that first encounter, and if there's one thing we've got to know about him, it's that his mood shifts in less time than it takes to light a joint. He can slide seamlessly from one personality to another. Most of the time he seems to be quite a gentle soul, but he can go from charming to vicious and back again without changing gears.'

John responded, 'Well, then, it may turn out to be an interesting evening.'

He wasn't wrong.

The doorbell rang once again. Karen was tidily dressed and her eyes were sparkling. Simon, although casually attired, looked neat. They greeted Sophie and Richard warmly. 'Howzit, Richard?' asked Simon, and Richard, shaking his hand warmly, replied. 'As annoying as any pimple on the nation's backside can be!'

Karen and Simon moved through onto the terrace. Suddenly the air filled with tension. John was very cool to Simon, but not as cool as Karen was towards John. She had last been in his company thirty years before. She was filled with trepidation. How would she feel? Her heart was pounding. She barely had the courage to face him.

Richard tried to break the ice. 'I'm sure you remember John.'

Karen, with not so much as a look at John, shot back, 'There's no way I could forget John!'

'How good it is to see you again, Karen.' John moved toward her. She moved away just enough for him not to touch her. John transferred his gaze to Simon. 'I am ...er... thrilled to see you too, Simon.'

Simon nodded, but nothing more than that. Sophie, sensing the escalating tension, forced a glass of wine into Karen's trembling hand and engaged Simon - she picked up a large book from the coffee table and casually handed the book to him.

Simon was taken by surprise. 'Hey, what's this?'

Sophie beamed, 'It's a state-of-the-art Encyclopedia of Star Wars, including all the characters from the latest

## CHAPTER 36: THE REUNION

series. That's your reward for staying the course at Lansdale.'

'Wow, wowwowwowwowwow, it's the 30$^{th}$ anniversary edition! Sophie, I love you!!!'

'Well don't just stare at the cover! Open the bloody thing!'

Simon became engrossed in his new book and allowed Sophie to shepherd him out of the room. Richard shuffled off to the kitchen.

Karen moved to the other side of room, and a few seconds later, John followed. A minute or two of embarrassed silence ensued. John smiled: 'Do you plan not to talk to me ever again?'

'No, just not for the next thirty years!'

She too finally smiled and offered her hand. John took her hand in his and she allowed him to hold it for a few seconds before withdrawing it.

'It's been a long time, Karen.'

Karen finally looked at this man she had thought about so often. 'I was dreading this, but it's good to see you.'

John whispered, 'I honestly missed you.'

'I think it was a hit rather than a miss – right in the bullseye!'

'I wish I had done something earlier.'

'You had a wife and kids.'

John looked wistful. 'That's true, but you could have had me.'

'I had Simon instead!'

Just at that moment, Simon and Sophie came back into the room. Simon looked at Karen and John, who surreptitiously drifted apart. Simon frowned.

Richard joined them, carrying two glasses of red wine. He immediately picked up on Simon's changing mood and tried to distract him. 'How's it all going, Simon?'

'Pretty good thanks.'

'I too have a pleasant surprise for you, Simon. I've got us two tickets to see Baba Maal in three weeks' time.'

'Wicked! Oh wow, Baba fucking Maal! That's amazing! Thanks so much, Richard.'

As John moved towards the centre of the room, Simon turned to John. 'I must also thank you for what you have done, er ...er... It would seem very odd to me to call you Dad or Sir, so with your permission can I just address you as John?'

'Of course, Simon....it's going to take a while for us to get used to each other, but tonight is a great starting point not only for our relationship, but also for your mother and me to get to know each other again.'

Simon frowned again. His mood changed immediately. 'Yeah? Well, let's not rush things, John, one step at a time, eh?'

Karen responded, 'Don't worry, Simon, I'm not about to desert you. John and I have both changed a great deal over the years, and I've got very used to living alone with you as my bodyguard.'

Simon shot back, 'Great, well let's just keep it that way, ok?' He smiled again. 'Sorry everyone, I guess I'm feeling very anxious about the immediate future. Mom thinks I am paranoid, but I know I'm not ... if only they'd leave me alone!' He laughed, as did Richard and Sophie, but Karen just shook her head.

Sophie decided it was time to be the host again. 'This seems a good time to have some nosh.'

Simon retorted, 'Sophie, that's disgusting! Do you know what nosh means?'

'Of course I do, Simon! It's the Yiddish word for food!'

Simon looked bemused. 'I don't do Yiddish, but in my circles, nosh means oral sex.'

'That's definitely not what I had in mind right now. What I do have in mind is eating delicious cheese and spinach tartlets which Richard has in the oven, so please excuse me while I go and get them onto a platter. Richard, do some more drinks, will you?'

## CHAPTER 36: THE REUNION

Sophie and Richard moved off. Simon picked up the Star Wars encyclopedia again, and as he became engrossed in it, Karen and John drifted slowly towards each other. Their hands touched briefly, but unfortunately this did not go unnoticed by Simon. He slammed the book down, and they hurriedly separated.

Sophie returned carrying a plate of little tarts and offered them around. Richard returned with drinks. he asked: 'Is anyone feeling chilly? I can light the fire - the logs are prepared.'

Karen, who was completely used to rooms that were never warmed, responded that she was fine. As they sat down at the table for the sizzling spiced lamb, the smell of which brought back memories of Auntie Zita's *bobotie*, Karen asked Sophie how her campaign was progressing.

'Much better now that John's got involved. We are pressurising the hospitals, doctors and nurses to get their act together.'

Simon decided to enter the conversation. 'About time, too! I don't mind nurses too much, although some of them can be fascist bitches. Talk about you like you're not even there. But if you want my opinion which I'm sure you don't, but have it anyway, the doctors are a bunch of prime slimebags. I've yet to meet a doctor who doesn't have his own personal agenda, mainly getting a leg over with the nurses. As far as I can see, their patients' real needs come very secondary.'

'That's quite a cynical view' observed Richard.

'They are one and all A-grade charlatans, and more of them are on dope than any of you will ever know.'

John joined in. 'You may well be right, Simon. They're highly stressed. Nevertheless, most doctors are still motivated by a desire to heal. To be of service.'

Simon, sarcastic as only he could be when the mood took him, retorted, 'Just like bankers, I suppose. Now there's a bunch of noshers!'

John ignored the barb and said to him, 'What about the Lansdale? You seemed to benefit hugely from being there.'

Simon erupted. 'Fuck the Lansdale!'

John still did not rise to the bait. 'What's the alternative? If the state health service is not properly organised, it will simply grind on, get older and less able to cope with the demand of those who cannot afford to go private.'

Richard asked Simon what he would do to change things.

Simon's response was measured and chillingly angry. 'For starters, either change the subject or get out of this flat as quickly as I can. This atmosphere of patronising do-goodyness is suffocating me. You all behave like mechanical robots, a bunch of R2-D2s, following your simplistic belief-systems and useless rules. Much better to be like Chewbacca or Han Solo, take life as it presents itself.' His shoulders shook with anger. 'What I need to do right now is to get back to my home.'

John, who had absolutely no idea how to manage someone else's anger, suggested Simon should take a deep breath. Simon did not want to take a deep breath. All his antipathy to John came tumbling out. 'I don't want to be your Eliza Dolittle, and you, my dear... father... are sure as hell not my 'Enery 'Iggins. You think all you have to do is make it possible for me to live in your normal world, and then I and my mother will be free? Yeah, free as the other robots! Truth is, my rehab means less than bugger-all to you - you just need me to be off Karen's back. You're only in on this because you've never forgotten how great my ma is in bed - allegedly!'

Richard was getting annoyed as well. 'That is so unfair, Simon! Nobody in this room is interested in anything other than your well-being. You'd got yourself into a very dark place and been there for a very long time, which I suppose was your choice, but you were also keeping Karen there, which was certainly not what she wanted.'

## CHAPTER 36: THE REUNION

Sophie added, 'John has been very helpful in creating an opportunity for you to climb out of your deep hole.'

Karen had tried not to get involved but blurted out: 'And you are turning on him because you think he will be fucking me before the night is out!'

'Well, won't he?'

'If he does, and it's extremely unlikely, he will be the first man in a long time who won't be leaving money on the side table, money that paid for your dope. You want to leave, leave. But if you do, you will not have me there to wipe your arse for you ever again. Been there, done it, getting off this train – you want to ride, ride on your own.'

'Well said, Mother dear, it's about time you stood up to me. I was wondering how long it would take you to wise up. You should have thrown me out long ago and got on with your life. But you know what? You needed me just as much as I needed you, maybe even more. I saved you the trouble of having to face your own demons.'

Karen, realising where this was going, pleaded, 'You are so right, Simon, but it's enough now for both of us – we've got to break this cycle, we've got to move on - we can do it, the two of us can do it.'

Only Karen could have envisaged what followed. Simon went berserk. He lost it completely and started smashing lamps and ornaments and everything else in reach. Plates of food flew around the table. His fury was terrifying. Sophie had often heard Karen speak of his uncontrolled rage, but this was the first time she had witnessed it in action and her first thought was that Karen was lucky to be alive. But it was John who moved first to stop him, grabbing his shoulders. Unfortunately, as unfit as Simon was, John was even more so, and he could not restrain the wild bull. Simon lurched forward, picked up a log and brought it crashing onto John's head. Everyone screamed, but no one louder than Simon: 'Fuck you, dear father ... dear vader ... Darth Vader...fuck you all!'

John sank slowly to the carpet with blood streaming from his scalp. The carpet began to redden. Simon nonchalantly threw the log down and walked out of the room. Sophie rushed to John, Richard to the phone to call for an ambulance. Karen ran after Simon as he strode out of the apartment. As they reached the street, she bundled him into a minicab waiting for another party, telling the driver if he did not leave immediatlely with them, she would kill him. He had the sense not to argue, and on arrival at home twenty minutes later, Karen shoved Simon through the interleading door and locked the gate.

# Chapter 37:

## *The Aftermath*

The scene when the para-medics arrived was one of utter devastation and carnage; a semi-conscious moaning man lying on the carpet, blood oozing from a gash in his head that appeared to have punctured his very soul; the hand clutching his head purple with congealed blood; the white carpet littered with broken dishes and food and ornaments surrounding a scarlet patch that was forming a halo around the moaning man's head. A woman was cradling the prostrate man, her dress covered in blood. A man was holding his own unbloodied head and saying nothing.

An oxygen mask placed in position, injections to prevent infection and to alleviate shock, an assurance that he was likely to recover from the wound, and they were gone.

Sophie looked at Richard. 'If you dare say I told you so, we'll need another ambulance!'

Richard, as was his way, said nothing, and as was his way put his arm around Sophie's heaving shoulders and led her to the bedroom. Neither slept much. A phone call to the nearby Somerset Hospital informed that the recently admitted man was now conscious and saying very little but would be likely to recover. Nevertheless, they would be keeping him under observation in the hospital for at least three days.

As she lay on her bed, utterly shattered, Karen reflected on the events of the evening, one that started with so much promise and finished an unmitigated disaster. Although Sophie and Richard had engineered the get-together with the best of intentions, how much better would it have been just to let sleeping dogs lie. Yet for all of that, she was grateful that she had been able to close the circle of a relationship that she had endured all her adult life. She replayed the electricity she had experienced of seeing John again. Simon was quite correct in his perception that they could not wait to touch each other once more, but he could not fully know how all those years apart had not dimmed the urge she felt to have him inside her again. Now she knew with absolute certainty that it would be the last time she would ever see John, the man who had for so long literally been her dream lover. For all she knew, he might be in hospital, or even dead, and she did not have the courage to make the call to find out.

She thought about the effort that Sophie and Richard had put in to reverse Simon from his one-way path to self-destruction. Could she ever face them again? The flames of shame that seared her heart would not easily be extinguished, and she knew that, at least for the time being, she would avoid all contact.

And what of Simon? She was sure that it would not be long before Simon returned to his drugs and Star Wars dolls, and they would resume their mind-numbingly dull relationship in the prisons they had created for each other. As events turned out, once again she would be proved to be inaccurate in her assessment of the way the universe worked, because, despite her worst forebodings that Simon would return to the *status quo ante* and that the normal business of jailer/prisoner co-dependency would be resumed, this turned out not to be the case.

Simon, with what passed for a brain, actually felt rather good after clobbering his father. He had waited for nigh on thirty years to discover his father's identity, but when the connection was made, there could have only been one outcome as far as Simon was concerned. Just as it was Luke Skywalker's destiny to kill his evil father Darth Vader, so it was Simon's to eliminate John, and he thought he had

## CHAPTER 37: THE AFTERMATH

made a pretty good fist of it. Strangely, he did not feel the need to celebrate his achievement with a freshly rolled joint of dagga. Maybe some good had come from this whole recent experience. Maybe he really had dried out this time...

What of John? He spent a couple of days in hospital, had twenty stitches and a lot of confusion for the next few days. Several press reporters hovering like vultures in the reception area had been refused permission to speak to him but were informed that he had had an accidental fall and was making satisfactory progress. Fortunately, John did not suffer organ damage, or not to anyone's knowledge anyway, but later had difficulty in getting his clients to believe he had slipped in the shower. When one was a womaniser and philanderer on the Jameson scale, such an injury could only have been caused by an irate husband, and John was content to leave it at that. After the first couple of phone calls to the hospital and a fleeting visit, Sophie and Richard stayed shy of him. He, by the same token, made no effort to contact them.

Despite Sophie's many attempts to get in touch, Karen steadfastly refused to answer calls. She could have gone to Karen's flat, but Sophie was intelligent and sensitive enough to sense the shame Karen would be feeling, and made the decision not to push it, not for a while anyway. By the time she decided to have another go, Karen and Simon had moved once again, were once more elusive, and eventually Sophie stopped trying.

# Chapter 38:

## *Politics 2008 - 2010*

The first ten years of ANC rule exceeded all expectations. There had been no outbreak of inter-racial war as feared by many whites, Mandela seemingly having engineered harmony in the rainbow nation. South Africa was back in the sporting fold, and with Mandela's support had even won the rugby World Cup. Schools were becoming integrated. A Black middle class was slowly beginning to emerge. People of colour were taking over the civil service formerly dominated by Afrikaners, and a small number were even becoming very wealthy.

But early in 2008, as they sat down to watch the news, Sophie started fidgeting. The reports, as it did so often in those days, seemed to concentrate mostly on stories related to President Thabo Mbeki's incomprehensible resistance to the well-established belief that AIDS/HIV was caused by virus transmission.

'I simply cannot believe', she muttered to Richard, 'that Mbeki thinks HIV is nothing more than a legacy of the poverty created by apartheid. It just doesn't make sense – is the AIDS epidemic in the USA also a legacy of apartheid?' She was fuming. How arrogant was the President!

'You're very restless, Sophie.'

'*You* bloody should be as well', she snapped back. 'This isn't what David and I fought for all those years ago, and it's definitely not what you and I awaited the past 15 years. It is not why I became a member of the ANC. Mbeki's such a well-educated man, so intelligent about most matters, yet when it comes to HIV, he and his moronic Minister of Health seem to believe the witchdoctors and *sangomas* rather than orthodox medical research. He's in the pocket of a tiny group of dissident scientists. They're saying, you want to cure AIDS, eat vegetables!'

'Well, why don't you do something that will really have an impact where it counts?'

'Like?'

'Like standing for Parliament.'

'Are you serious, Richard? Are you saying "as well as" writing my thesis and busting my gut campaigning, or "instead of" ? I only work 14 hours a day at present, so I should have lots of time.'

'No, seriously, Mbeki considers you an irritating but distant critic right now, so you need to get where he can actually hear your voice. I don't think there's much chance that you will influence him to change his mind, but at least the outside world will hear you and put more pressure on him to allow the use of anti-retrovirals.'

'But the ANC will never let me stand in the next election.'

'So resign from the ANC, join the Democratic Alliance who will welcome you with open arms.'

'They're still basically a white party - I'd be seen as just another rich white fossil.'

'Then join Inktatha – you've always respected Chief Buthelezi.'

'True ... I've met him on several occasions, and he is extremely personable and very charming. But, as you are well aware, his tribal Zulu loyalties over national unity led to a virtual civil war in Kwa-Zulu. He's got a lot of blood on his hands!'

'Even so, it's all calm now. You'd be the first Jewish white woman to be an MP for a black party, so you'd be in a unique position to sound your views. Why don't you send an e-mail to him and see how he responds?'

Although Sophie was nothing if not headstrong, she always gave serious consideration to Richard's considered and measured opinions. Three days later an e-mail was pinged to Chief Gatsha Buthelezi. To her great surprise he responded virtually immediately, suggesting she stand as MP for a Cape constituency that was seriously disenchanted with the ANC because it had failed to provide housing as promised.

Six months later, Sophie took her seat in the beautiful parliament buildings in Gardens, Cape Town, and a new chapter in her life began.

Her days became ones of intense involvement, unlike many of the ANC who seemed to be in the beautiful parliamentary building for no other purpose than the perks they afforded: parties, free aeroplane travel, chauffeur-driven cars (usually elegant Mercedes). During that time, Sophie thought of Karen not very frequently. Eventually, her conscience began to stab rather than simply prick, and Sophie eventually decided to call Karen. Karen was delighted. Despite Sophie's huge and unending workload and the fact that for the first time she would miss a parliamentary session, she decided to take a morning off to meet Karen and invited her friend to meet outside the historic Parliament building. She led Karen through the security check, and they made their way to the MPs' coffee shop. Karen couldn't help noticing that Sophie's blond hair and pale skin placed her in a distinct minority, and she remembered that similar incident all those years ago in Manenberg at the Abdulla Ibrahim gig. Sophie was hardly aware that for her friend just to be able to leave home for a few hours was a gift, and the visit to parliament merely the icing on the cake.

It did not take long for Sophie to become a real irritant to the ANC, and she began to clash regularly with President Mbeki not just on HIV but over his continued support for President Robert Mugabe of Zimbabwe, despite evidence of Mugabe's use of political violence in his suppression of the opposition movement. Mismanagement of Zimbabwe's economic policies had resulted in uncontrolled

CHAPTER 38: POLITICS 2008 - 2010

hyperinflation of the economy and increased poverty for the broader population while the government fat-cat strongmen became ever richer and more repressive. Sophie began to receive threatening letters and messages addressed to "The Blond Jewish Bitch". This was not what Mandela had fought for and was prepared to give his life for. Nevertheless, she never missed a session, and because she had developed a powerful health blog, it was no surprise when she was appointed opposition Health Spokesperson.

Sophie continued to campaign with unflagging energy for a programme to use anti-retroviral medicines to prevent HIV transmission from mother to child, and she worked closely with AIDS activists in the provision of free condoms. Her efforts were not going unrewarded, because international drug companies, stung by the relentless pressure, were now offering free or cheap anti-retroviral drugs to South Africa. But still the Health Ministry remained unmoving.

Sophie stood to address Parliament. 'Madam Speaker,' she began, and was immediately jeered by ANC MPs. 'Madam Speaker, it is my regrettable duty to inform this House that South Africa, with less than 1% of the world's population, accounts for 17% of the global burden of HIV infection. The New York Times has reported that an estimated 365,000 people have perished in South Africa due to President Thabo Mbeki's AIDS denialism.' The jeering reached a crescendo. Sophie continued, barely able to hear her own voice: 'More than two million children have been orphaned due to the epidemic.' Sophie yelled, but no one heard, or if they did, they did not care. She remembered the title of the great writer Alan Paton's heart-rending book, *Cry, the Beloved Country,* and within herself Sophie shed bitter tears. She had expected the struggle to be difficult, but this was like climbing a mountain wearing lead boots that were tied together.

That night, she expressed her frustration to the ever-patient Richard. 'I don't think I can carry on much longer. It's like Sisyphus rolling his rock up the steep hill! I've never felt so frustrated!'

'Hang in there, darling. They may not be listening to you in parliament, but the big pharmaceuticals sure as hell are, and prices of ARVs have dropped massively, and it's thanks to you.'

Sophie could only shake her head, and then her whole body shook as the tears came flooding out. If Richard knew only one thing, he knew Sophie was not a quitter, and she would not give up her fight.

# Chapter 39:

## *Skoppensboer 2010*

Over the next few months, Simon seemed to manage holding on to the new, improved, cleaner-than-clean version of himself, as if the assault on his father had never happened. It was if, with that single blow to John's head, the addictions, the dependencies, the assaults on Karen, the friendship of Sophie and Richard, the hateful father, and most of all the feelings of paranoia had all been bundled up, locked in a trunk and dropped into the sea. He was not by any stretch of the imagine a complete human being – no one with half a brain could be – but he stopped clinging to Karen and allowed her to go out for periods during the day on her own, as long as she did not stay out for *too* long.

Karen thought to herself how amazing it was that it took that act of violence to convince Simon that he had to take responsibility for his actions. It was as if he had smashed his own skull with that log. Since that evening, she had stuck to her word and had not been spending all her days with Simon, and she managed to find the occasional locum job, so he had to finally learn to deal with his shit by himself. Wasn't there the risk that he'd start drugging heavily again? Well, this was a possibility. He did have the occasional joint, but nowhere near the earlier levels, and he seemed to be managing quite well. He was now as close to being clean as he was ever likely to be.

He was no longer dependent on his different cocktails of medications either, and he seemed to be able to take care of himself when Karen wasn't there. Sadly, there was never a chance that he might find work, but he managed to do some basic cooking, managed to keep himself clean.

Karen saw the irony, thinking 'He has no choice, and he seems to be doing very nicely indeed!' They owed a big debt of gratitude to Richard for making them aware how dependent they had become on one another, and how destructive that had been for both. Now just get on with the business of living.

On one afternoon, a fateful one as it would turn out, Karen has gone out, ostensibly to do some essential shopping. Simon was in his room. He was busy tidying his Star Wars figures sitting on his chest-of-drawers. A Baba Maal album was playing. Still one of Simon's favourites, he was humming through a slower tune when his cell phone rang. He turned down the music and answered the call.

'Hi Mum, how's it going? Yeah, I'm fine.'

'What're you up to?'

'Just re-arranging "The Return of the Jedi" characters and listening to Baba Maal. ...Yeah, don't worry, I'm quite enjoying the veggies you left in the freezer - the lasagne was delicious.' Simon paused for a moment and then resumed the conversation. 'I might go out later to the SPCA, I'm thinking of getting a new dog ... No, I won't buy fucking drugs! No, on second thoughts, maybe I should mug a few grannies for their purses, buy some skunk. ... You've got to trust me, Ma. ... Ok, see you later, Ma. Who knows there might be a new Skywalker to greet you! Thanks for phoning, love you, Bye!'

Simon switched off his cellphone, paused for a few moments and lit a joint - for no particular reason other than he felt like enjoying Baba Maal's music all the more. As the slower tune finished, a much faster tune with heavy drum rhythms followed. Simon turned the music up very loudly and started dancing to the rhythms, holding and inhaling on the joint. He turned the volume to max. Somewhere in the fug, he heard a voice coming from the apartment upstairs.

## CHAPTER 39: SKOPPENSBOER 2010

*'Turn the bleddy music down! I'm trying to get some rest!'*

Simon either didn't hear, and if he did, he certainly didn't care; he carried on dancing, trance-like.

*'Hey, I said turn the bleddy music down, or I'll bleddy do it for you!'*

Simon just carried on rocking from one foot to the other, oblivious to everything but the pulsating rhythms. There was a loud banging on the ceiling. Simon heard the banging and stopped dancing. The music pulsed on, driving through the walls and the ceiling.

*'You're driving me focken mad with your bleddy native music. I'm coming down to turn the focken thing off!'*

For some peculiar reason, not having heard anything before besides Baba Maal, Simon heard this.

He paused for a while, looked around, sorted through a pile of his Star Wars stuff and finally picked up a heavy-looking light-sabre. This was no plastic imitation, this was a serious item, Simon's most treasured possession. This was the steel light-sabre Karen had bought him for his twenty-fifth birthday. He banged it against the edge of the cupboard, listened to the noise it created, smiled happily and walked slowly to the door. He opened the door, leaving it open and quietly made his way upstairs.

The sounds of an altercation punctuated by intermittent swearing drifted through the building, culminating in a resounding *thwack*.

Baba Maal played on, oblivious to everything. The music alternated from plaintive folk songs to pulsating rhythms. No one was dancing.

Five minutes later, Simon re-entered his apartment. He no longer held the light-sabre. He paused for a few moments, noticed the blood on his hands and shirt. He walked to his cupboard, taking out a whole batch of bottles, and slowly poured the contents onto the cupboard work-surface, and carefully stirred them. Leaving them there, he turned and exited once more, returning a few moments later with a jug of water and a glass. He poured water into the glass and slowly swallowed the tablets, one by one, the whole process taking several minutes. He went to his tv, selected "The Return of The Jedi", set it to video play and returned to lie on his bed. The dialogue of the film slowly became softer and softer, and the film slowly went more and more out of focus until finally the screen turned black.

Karen returned not too late from a profitable night out, heard no sounds from Simon's room, and went to sleep. When she woke at 9am, she still heard no noise, so she went to Simon's room where he was still lying on his bed but not breathing. On his bedside table were dozens of medication bottles, all empty.

He was thirty-one years old.

She screamed, and ran upstairs to the neighbour's flat, and then the real horror struck. The door of his flat was open, and, surrounded by a dry pool of blood and many flies, the poor man lay in his entrance hall. Next to him was the light-sabre, Simon's most treasured possession, which he had used to bludgeon the poor man to death. Next to the light-sabre was a single playing card: the jack of spades. Karen knew exactly what this signified - Simon's favourite poem was an Afrikaans one by Eugene Marais called '*Skoppensboer*' - the Jack of Spades - the Grim Reaper. Darth Vader had struck again.

She sat on the stairs for a very long time. Eventually the tears stopped. She had feared this for so long. If you fear something, she had read somewhere, you make it more likely that it will happen. Did she make this happen? Why didn't Simon kill her, why did this poor man have to die? Sophie had warned her, why didn't she listen? Why did he turn out the way he did? She was to blame she was to blame she was to blame. And now what, look for some more pills? How will you carry on, you don't deserve to live.

The tears began again. She doesn't remember picking up her phone, doesn't remember anything. Just utter

## CHAPTER 39: SKOPPENSBOER 2010

despair. She would remember later and the tears would begin again, but they wouldn't make him young again, wouldn't bring him back, they wouldn't bring the neighbour back, they wouldn't bring John back, or Sophie back ...

After the police had taken a statement and removed both bodies, she was left with the task of arranging two funerals. At the crematorium, she was the only person in the room when first the older man and then Simon was dispatched to a galaxy far, far away, and sorrowful Karen was left to carry her guilt for having brought him into the world. Two of the most misunderstood emotions are shame and guilt, and after Simon's death Karen was overwhelmed by both. At no time did she attempt to inform John that his son was dead.

Nor did she contact Sophie. Because Sophie's name and face appeared so frequently on tv, Karen knew exactly what her friend was about, and what her friend was about were big issues. On the odd occasion that Karen felt tempted, she held back because she knew that Sophie did not need the added complications of her, Karen's, own life when there were bigger problems to be dealt with. In any case, she was quite used to living on her own and, to tell the truth, had reached the age where she simply did not need anyone else. She simply got on with her own totally predictable life.

Simon was gone, her parents too, John was history for the second time, and as far as Karen was concerned that was how it would remain. John was now president of his late father-in-law's bank and would be for a short while longer. Then she would read that John's Mercedes had been intercepted at a traffic light by four gun-wielding thugs and he had been shot to death - an event that was taken to be just one more hijack and burglary. In fact, he had been unceremoniously executed, the work of hitmen employed by an irate supermarket magnate whose wife John had been fucking. The local newspapers had a field day, and several errant women and their equally errant husbands were severely embarrassed. All things considered, as far as John was concerned, Karen had probably got off lucky, but if it were possible to feel even more sad, she did. This time, no tears – just aching sadness. Sadness that etched her brain till she couldn't think of anything but his face, his body, his soldier at attention. For the second time, her heart felt as if a dagger had been plunged into it. How she wished it had.

She listened to the telephone message from Sophie to tell her of the funeral arrangements but did not return the call. Then the tears came once more. Never was she more alone, helpless, hopeless. Would she never contact Sophie again? That was never her thought. She knew she would, but being a fatalist, she would wait for the propitious time.

It did not take long for Karen to realise that remaining in the apartment of death was not an option, and she needed to do something that would keep her sufficiently busy so that her mind was not constantly filled with remorse, guilt, regret and a hundred other negative emotions. So she headed for Groote Schuur Hospital.

# Chapter 40:

## *Unfinished Business  2010*

A greater challenge was about to face Sophie. She had met Archbishop Tutu on several occasions, and he had expressed his thanks for her fight against drugs and AIDS. Nevertheless, she was taken completely by surprise when her phone rang and she heard Desmond Tutu's unmistakable voice addressing her. He got straight to the point.

'Sophie, you are well aware that I have been actively involved with the Truth and Reconciliation Commission, where many hundreds of people have come forward to confess their activities and wrongdoings during apartheid in exchange for immunity from prosecution.'

Sophie felt a chill hand clasp her heart. 'Are you about to tell me that the person....' She could not complete the sentence.

'Yes, Sophie. His name is Sergeant Frikkie van Zyl and he is to appear before the Commission next week. He has confessed to cutting through the tyre of Dr Rousseau's car and causing the accident. He will say that he was merely the knife - the hand was the security police. They all say that, but that's the way it is and it's probably true. Anyway, I invite you to be present and testify should you wish to do so.'

Sophie felt as if she had been hit with a baseball bat and could only stammer: 'D'you know, I've waited thirty years to find, to face this man. To look into his eyes and say, do you know what you did, do you know what kind of life you destroyed?'

'It's not an easy thing to do, to confront your dear friend's killer, but it will be cathartic and will help to bring about closure and healing of a long-festering wound.'

A week later, Richard accompanied Sophie to the hearing. Tutu met them and explained that he advocated traditional African jurisprudence in the spirit of *ubuntu*, an approach to life that emphasizes generosity of spirit. Tutu had proposed that the TRC adopt a threefold approach: the first being confession, with those responsible for human rights abuses fully disclosing their activities, the second being forgiveness in the form of a legal amnesty from prosecution, and the third being restitution, with the perpetrators making amends to their victims.

Tutu had to deal with its various inter-personal problems, with much suspicion between those on its board who had been anti-apartheid activists and those who had supported the apartheid system. Not only the security police but the ANC's image was tarnished by the revelations that some of its activists had engaged in torture, attacks on civilians, and other human rights abuses. This was made worse by insinuations that the ANC, to protect its own, did not want these cases pursued. In their police chief's words: 'If you go after the apartheid generals, then you open the door to cases against us,' and that was not acceptable. So, to the ANC, the solution was to try to stop all cases.

Former sergeant Frikkie Van Zyl was, as Sophie remarked to Richard, a *nebbish.* A nobody. He was no more capable of making the decision to slash the tyre than he was of refusing to do so, or to understand that what he had done was wrong. This did not of course prevent him from saying he was sorry for what he had done, for he had at least sufficient grey cells in what purported to be his brain to realise that if he did not, his chance of amnesty would vanish.

Sophie steeled herself as she took the witness box to read the statement she had prepared.

## CHAPTER 40: UNFINISHED BUSINESS  2010

'Mr Van Zyl, if you were any more intelligent and could understand what you have destroyed, I might have had great difficulty in bringing myself to forgive you. What you destroyed was a member of your own tribe who was kinder than you; who brought health to the poor; who cared that there were poor people who were poor just because their skins were dark; a man who was smarter than you and those who gave you orders. By cutting his tyre, you destroyed a man who had the potential to become a leader of this country. The world is a poorer place for his absence, but it will not be for yours when your time comes. Do I want to see you spend the rest of your life behind bars? Until today, my answer would undoubtedly have been yes. Now that I have seen you, I no longer wish that. I forgive you, Mr Van Zyl, but suggest that when you walk out of here, you will at least remember that you are not better than those you have persecuted all your life. Dr David Rousseau is dead, but his memory lives. It is all I have left. You have your thirty pieces of silver.'

After they thanked Bishop Tutu and left the proceedings, she clung to Richard as she said, 'I finally understand how the Holocaust happened.'

# Chapter 41:

## *Further Unfinished Business 2010*

There had been many changes at Groote Schuur Hospital since Karen was the first woman of colour to attempt to become a nurse there. Now, most of the student nurses were non-white and most of the patients were non-white. The surgery where Professor Christian Barnard had performed the world's first heart transplant had been turned into a museum, even a shrine.

For the second time in her life, Karen Williams nee Willemse stood in front of a Matron. Matron Gray was the late Matron Gray, and had been replaced by Matron Meintjies, born in Mitchell's Plain. Karen felt a pang as she thought that, if things had panned out differently, it might have been her sitting there. Ms Meintjies asked her to be seated. *'Wat kan ons vir jou doen, Juffrou?'*

'I don't know if you can do anything for me, Matron, but I'll never forgive myself if I don't ask. It's like this. Thirty-two years ago, I had almost completed my nurse's training at this hospital and had to leave hurriedly because I was pregnant. Anyway, my son died a few months ago, I now have no living relatives, and I want to complete my training.'

Matron Meintjies stared at Karen in disbelief - she was utterly flabbergasted. 'Are you serious, *Juffrou* Williams? You are older than I am! Do you realise that most women have retired from nursing at your age to look after their grandchildren, and you want to begin again?'

'No, not quite begin again, I can do the basic stuff like injections and blood pressure and sterile dressings and assist at operations and work in intensive care and so on, so I'd like a credit for that. Obviously, I don't know new technology and techniques, but I can learn. I'm also a qualified dental nurse. I'm not looking to be paid, but it would mean a great deal to me to get my nurse's badge.'

'Well, I have to say we've never ever had a request like this before, and it is extremely unlikely – *extremely* unlikely, I must emphasise – that we agree to take you on. I can't see that we could possibly accommodate you here at Groote Schuur. I can however ask the Board of Governors if they would allow you a special dispensation to train at one of our branch hospitals like Athlone or Manenberg.'

'Does that mean I wouldn't graduate here at Groote Schuur?'

'All nurses affiliated to our greater hospital group graduate here. Why's that so important to you?'

'Unfinished business, Matron.'

Matron Meintjies viewed the older woman with compassion. 'Well, I'll see what I can do, but I make no promises.'

Ms Meintjies put Karen's bizarre request to the governing board. Eyebrows were raised, questions asked. One of the senior members of the Board, one of the few whites in the room, did not raise her eyebrows but burst out laughing.

'What's tickling you, Staff Nurse Pienaar?'

Marie Pienaar related the story of how her x-rays had been switched all those years ago, of how she thought she had accidently swallowed a cat. By the time she had finished, the whole Board was giggling. Then she told them of how Karen, by her dedication, had changed her white woman's perception of colour. Two weeks later, Karen got a letter informing her that she would be accepted as a student to work at Manenberg Hospital and would be required to complete one year only of full-time training. She would be required to commence in a month's time. She would be paid at senior trainee level and there would be no promise of employment after graduation, although the possibility existed.

Did Karen inform Sophie of her unlikely return to nursing? No.

Karen relinquished her lease and reported for duty at a small but hopelessly overcrowded hospital that had not even existed when she had lived there previously. On the credit side, all the equipment that had not been stolen was relatively new. Unfortunately, there was not much left, as theft was a huge problem, especially goods that were made of recyclable metal. Many of the patients were victims of drunken brawls or stab wounds in robberies or gang fights, and although Karen worked her butt off, she felt elated. She owed none of her time to anyone else. She was hugely admired by the junior nurses and respected by the doctors. In the year that she spent at Manenberg, she was not the Mother Superior but was certainly the Mother Confessor to whom many of the trainees came for advice, not always on surgical matters. After she had been there for a few months, she found that even the matron would seek her opinion from time to time. Ms Meintjies occasionally came over to Manenberg for meetings, and never failed to inquire how the senior lady was getting on.

Karen spent most of the year in theatre or in the intensive care unit. She also spent time in the dental unit where her dental experience was invaluable in decision-making and dealing with emergencies. One the busiest clinics at the little hospital was that which was involved in alleviating dental pain, mainly for children. Unfortunately, the unit was not equipped to carry out repairs and simple fillings, so the only other option was extractions, and this was usually done under sedation or anaesthesia. The clinic was operational only on a Monday afternoon when a rota of visiting dentists came in to provide voluntary service. During the year that Karen was there, the scheduled dentists, mostly new graduates, came to rely heavily on her expertise, and the efficiency of the unit increased three-fold. This having been said, the unit was not without its dramas, and never more so than when one of the junior nurses was asked to set out a tray for sedation. On that particular day, the dentist was delayed by a road accident and arrived a little late. Already a bit flustered, he failed to check the drugs on the sedation tray. The first patient was an extremely nervous young girl who required extraction of a very decayed molar.

Karen was the senior nurse on supervisory duty, and she walked in as the dentist was about to administer what he believed was the sedation drug but in fact was its antidote, the drug that was supposed to be given afterwards to reverse the sedative. She glanced down at the tray and immediately saw the error that had been made by the junior nurse (not entirely her fault as the boxes were of a similar colour) and was about to be compounded by the surgeon. She quietly and quickly drew the dentist's attention to the mixed-up drug, which, had it been administered would have driven the already nervous girl hysterical without the means to reverse it. This would then have had to be reported as a 'serious incident' to the head of the hospital, who in turn would have had to report it to the Health Council with dreadful consequences for both the dentist and junior nurse. Both had cause to be extremely grateful for Karen's experienced and vigilant eye.

The intensity of activity helped enormously in taking her mind off Simon and his manner of death. Occasionally she would go out to the Dr David Rousseau SHAWCO Health Complex teeming with patients with drug issues. She thought that this might be a good reason to get in touch once more with Sophie, who had no idea of its existence, let alone that it had been so named, but Karen was not yet ready for this.

It was not that unusual to see a pregnant trainee or nurse moving around the wards – how times had changed! Matron Gray would be turning in her grave, thought Karen on more than one occasion. The level of discipline was lower, but Karen felt certain that the students were a whole lot happier. From her own perspective, the second time round was significantly easier and far more interesting. Using a computer for any purpose whatsoever was virtually unheard of in the late 70s, yet they were now being used to record, store and transmit data, and to assist with diagnoses. Brave new world!

She did not socialise much with the other nurses, preferring to spend her spare time catching up on sleep. For the rest, she was content to go to a cinema on her own, for by now there were several in Manenberg. Karen managed to locate a few old friends still living in what were by now dilapidated bungalows, and sharing a meal with them was as much social contact as she required. One of these was the daughter of Auntie Zena, who had long since departed to the great deli in the sky. Karen found in Eva an understanding and sympathetic ear, not least because Eva's second son had gone the same route with the same outcome as Simon.

On a few occasions, of an evening she would hop the bus and travel back to Obz. By this time, the Obz Cafe had become the haunt of distinctly middle-class white medical students, of whom Karen had more than enough in the wards. So she would head for a place round the corner called Tagore's, a really viby live jazz cafe. On one occasion, the patrons were enchanted by the mellifluous voice of one Bea Benjamin, a talented lady of colour who all those years ago had been married to Abdulla Ibrahim. Ms Bea had also been living in exile in New York for many years where she had sung with Duke Ellington but had finally come back to her home in Cape Town. Karen was deeply saddened when a couple of days later, she learned that Ms Bea had passed away the day after that gig. Karen was pleased that she did not have the same effect on Abdulla Ibrahim, thus avoiding the world being deprived of the music of her people.

## CHAPTER 41: FURTHER UNFINISHED BUSINESS  2010

As her graduation day approached, she decided that it was time to get over the shame she had felt for so long after Simon had done his best to open John's skull. She sent an invitation to her old friend by post and followed this up with an e-mail. Simple, no? No. Nothing in the new South Africa was simple. Sophie had changed her e-mail address. The surface mail letter was languishing in some sub-post office back room and probably still is because no-one in their right mind really expected delivery – the new crop of untrained postmen could not be bothered to deliver to luxurious white suburbs. Karen did not reason that this was the cause. Had she done, she would surely have tried to phone, but where emotions are involved the mind does not always act rationally. She simply thought that Sophie, having given her all to rehabilitate Simon, had decided that the game was not worth the candle and quite understandably wanted nothing more to do with her. That was her assumption, and in the words of a popular aphorism, 'to ASSUME is to make an ASS of U & ME'. What she failed to realise was that had Sophie but known, she would have smashed the gates of heaven and hell to be there.

Consequently, on the second important occasion of her life, and for the second time in her life, Karen would not receive a response from Sophie. *So gaan dit* - so it goes. On a hot December's night Karen gathered with a large bunch of graduands in the big hall at Groote Schuur. The air of excitement was palpable, the din overwhelming. How her parents would have loved this, but they were no more and she was alone.

Then just as the ceremony was about to begin, she saw a woman striding towards her, a woman whom, had she encountered her in the Gobi Desert she would instantly have recognised, a small woman with blond curly hair and a determined stride. Sophie reached her and took her hand, and Karen saw the joy on her face and the tears in her eyes. Karen could barely control herself but she heard her named being called to come forward to be given her nurse's cap, badge and epaulettes, and she held back her own tears. Matron Meintjies waited till the tall woman stood next to her and started to speak. The din hushed.

Karen was given a warm commendation by Matron Meintjies who praised her tenacity and dedication. She spoke of the challenges that Karen had faced, and how she had overcome them. And then, somewhat cryptically, she said she hoped that the unfinished business had now been completed. Indeed it had, and there was Sophie to witness it. Karen was justifiably proud, and her pride increased tenfold because Sophie was able to share her joy.

When the presentation to Karen was over, she was rather surprised to see another woman step forward, whom she also recognised instantly: Sister Marie Pienaar, she who had made it her business to inform Sophie of the impending graduation. Pienaar, Karen and Sophie shared a wild dance of joy, whooping and jumping up and down. 'Congratulations, Nurse Williams, I wish you God Almighty's blessings', said Pienaar. Some things just never changed.

The surprises of the evening had not yet ceased. The next person to approach her resembled a boiled egg in an egg-cup, but she had no idea who it was. Tweedledum, or maybe Tweedledee? The egg stepped forward and said '*Veels geluk*, Nurse Williams, lots of luck. I am very happy for you.' If Karen did not immediately recognise the egg, the voice was one she would have picked out from the deepest echelons of time. 'Kobus van den Berg! What the fuck hell are you doing here, and where's your hair and your moustache and your big belly gone?'

Sophie answered the first question: 'I invited him. Being who I am, I thought that seeing it was Kobus who set you on your path, even if wasn't in the nicest way, it would close the circle nicely if he were here to see you complete your journey.' Sophie had traced Kobus through a contact - after all, it was not that difficult to locate a

## CHAPTER 41: FURTHER UNFINISHED BUSINESS 2010

former Director of Reclassification. Although much had changed in his life, Kobus was only too glad of the opportunity to salve his conscience.

Kobus said 'You may not believe this, Miss Williams, but I have to say I felt very ashamed for the things I were doing. So when my job were no longer necessary, I went to see my Dominee and confessed how I was taking advantage of youse women. He told me if I didn't want to go to hell, I must repent. So I joined his group of sinners, I shave my hair, and I fast. I no longer have a job but I have peace and love and god in my heart, and now I am here to beg your forgiveness.'

'Bullshit, Kobus, you were just a product of your fokken misguided nation. I cannot ever forget how you treated me, but I suppose on this night above all others I must forgive.' Karen, ever pragmatic, thought this was not a night for retribution. 'At least you showed good taste. Anyway, you gave me the best story I have ever had to tell, and I must have repeated what happened to at least a thousand people. You're legend, Kobus!!'

The white egg turned red with embarrassment, and Karen almost put her arm around him but decided that was a bridge too far. So when he said 'I must go now,' she acknowledged the role he had played in her life. 'Thank you, Kobus, I wouldn't have been here tonight without your help, even though you had an evil way of giving it.'

Sister Pienaar departed. So now it was just the two of them, and Karen finally unburdened herself of the sad saga of Simon's death. It was heart-rending, but Sophie could completely understand why Karen had been unable to call her at that time. 'I get it, girl, but you know what, tonight's a happy night, so let's just get pissed and enjoy it.' And they did. They sat at Tagore's until 2am, grooving with the mellow music and with each other, and then took their respective taxis, one to Manenberg, the other to Camps Bay, promising to catch up again soon.

Karen would spend a couple of years more at Manenberg, but she was finding the workload increasingly demanding, which of course made keeping regular contact with Sophie difficult. Karen would absolutely not hear of her friend coming out to Manenberg. It was not a safe place for pretty blond women to be spending their spare time, especially at night. They did meet occasionally on weekends in Obz or at the Waterfront, but in reality their worlds were as far apart as they had been in the past. When Karen received a call from Dr Errol to say that once more he needed her assistance, she felt she had achieved her objective and had paid her dues, and was happy to return to Claremont to live and work. Claremont was certainly a more genteel environment than Manenberg, which was becoming increasingly lawless. She said her goodbyes to Eva, promising to return to visit and inviting Eva to come and visit her, but the promise remained mostly an intention and rarely an act.

Karen also went to say goodbye to a new neighbour, an Englishman who had come to live in Manenberg to act as a missionary. Peter's home was always filled with young men trying to work out their problems with words rather than knives. Karen had nothing but respect for this young white foreigner and sympathy for the uphill struggle he faced, because she knew better than most how difficult it was to shake off the drug barons and their weapons of violence and death.

# Chapter 42:

## *Mr X  2015*

Karen hoped that her move back to Claremont would facilitate spending more time with Sophie, but of course Sophie was now busy on her own agenda, and Sophie's agenda was to pin the AIDS-denying president of South Africa to the wall. This meant she was busier than ever, and the casualty was Karen whom, despite the best intentions, she now rarely had time to think about, let alone try to meet. On the few occasions when they did arrange to have a fleeting coffee or grab a sandwich, Sophie more often than not cancelled at the last minute because she had to attend some important discussion or meeting or to vote. Karen did understand and accepted the situation fully.

This of course made Sophie experience her own guilt for the lack of support she was providing for her friend. Was it more important to act for the greater rather than the individual good? This had always been Sophie's credo, but there came a point where she realised that she was failing the individual, so she felt she had to do something about it. She decided to take a morning off to meet Karen. and invited her friend to meet outside the historic parliament building. She led Karen through the security check and they made their way to the MPs' coffee shop. They sat in on a debate, which by sheer coincidence was about the rising rate of crime on the Cape Flats. Karen listened attentively – she could have told these people in their suits and smart frocks a thing or two about life there! After the debate, they had lunch in the MPs' dining room, a relic of the days of the British Empire when this building had been constructed. Karen was gobsmacked – the parliament building and the whole parliamentary process were a universe away from her humble experiences of Manenberg. She left in awe of her feisty friend, but at least fully understanding why Sophie's time was so limited. And for Sophie there was still the business of anti-retrovirals to be resolved.

Finally, finally, towards the end of his stint, Thabo Mbeki and his Minister of Un-Health relented and agreed to the use of ARVs and for the third time in her life, Sophie's tears were of happiness unbound. The provision of ARV treatment resulted in 100,000 fewer Aids-related deaths in 2010 than in 2005 and Sophie could justifiably feel she had more than played her part.

One day, as Sophie was preparing a parliamentary report, an item on a website that she had been researching caught her eye: *Newsmaker – William Frankel: The courageous life of 'Mr X'.* She read that Bill Frankel, a south African-born London lawyer, was at the centre of a highly secretive web in the UK, the International Defence & Aid Fund, which distributed some £100-million for the defence of anti-apartheid activists in political trials in South Africa during the height of the apartheid era. Sophie was not surprised to learn that he had been awarded not just the OBE by Her Majesty's Government but the Vice-Chancellor's silver medal at the University of Cape Town.

The award ceremony in Cape Town was the first occasion on which Frankel – known only as Mr X in IDAF circles for nearly three decades – had broken his silence in his acceptance speech and told the incredible story in his own words. Frankel said his identity was known by very few within IDAF, and not even his immediate family or his legal partners were aware of his double life. The cherry on the top was when the President of South Africa conferred on Bill the Order of Luthuli Silver Medal, describing Bill's "excellent services" with the Defence and Aid Fund in the liberation struggle against apartheid.

## CHAPTER 42: MR X 2015

Sophie's eyes widened when she read this paragraph. She had been totally unaware of the real identity of the lawyer who had run the show in those exciting days in London, but hoped one day to meet him in person should she ever return there. From her own perspective, it was not just being Mr X's agent's agent, but infiltrating the National Front and obtaining and passing the information so useful to Richard and Robbie that had thrilled her. Exciting days they were, but that was then, and this was now; and it was now, 2017, that its President was pillaging her long-suffering country.

# Chapter 43:

## State Capture  2017

Richard handed an article he was writing to Sophie to proof-read.

**Mail & Guardian, Cape Town & Guardian UK:**
**Richard Simpson Reviews the Reign & Fall of Jacob Zuma**

"Jacob Zuma, like Thabo Mbeki before him, had been hand-picked by Mandela to accede to power not only as reward for his activities in The Struggle, but also because the always fair-minded Mandela felt that having had two Xhosa Presidents, it was now time for a Zulu. Unfortunately for his beloved country, he chose the wrong Zulu.

Jacob Zuma, a man of very humble origins who was barely literate, came to power in 2009 with the support of a left-wing coalition of trades unions, the Communist Party, the ANC Women's League and Youth League. Questions about his business dealings came to the fore, but the 783 corruption charges against him relating to an arms deal were soon swept aside on procedural grounds.

During his term of office, it became increasingly obvious that Zuma had developed an unnaturally close relationship with three Indian émigré brothers, the Guptas, who had been sent to South Africa by their far-sighted father to increase the family fortunes. So it began.

Zuma and his patrons, the Guptas, became so closely entwined that they were collectively referred to as the "Zuptas". They are alleged to have colluded to place cronies in key positions to take control of whole branches of the state, thus keeping Zuma in power and out of prison.

## CHAPTER 43: STATE CAPTURE 2017

*On the advice of the Guptas, government ministers were sacked and replaced with Zuma puppets or members of his family. This amounted to 'state capture'. The new Minister of Justice was happy to wash away the charges of corruption against Zuma. The new Chief of Criminal Investigation was happy not to re-open the cases. To add insult to injury, the special investigators from the fraud division known as the Hawks, who were appointed to investigate the alleged corruption, turned out to be in the pay of the Zuptas as well!*

*Other stooges or members of Zuma's family were placed in charge of government-run utilities such as Eskom (electricity), transport, arms manufacture, and the uranium and coalmine industries, the latter of whose largest customer was Eskom, which purchased their coal at inflated prices.*

*The Zuptas not only seized control of the country's wealth but also of its media, as the government systematically took over state radio, tv and several newspapers, placing its own stooges in control and ensuring a 'yes sir' media controlled from the top. It was Zimbabwe all over again.'*

Sophie felt utterly sickened as she read Richard's erudite words. Was it for this that David Rousseau had paid with his life? Steve Biko? Neil Aggett? Chris Hani? The countless others who had been part of The Struggle? Surely it was not for this that she herself had spent more than ten years in exile, put herself at risk and was probably only alive today because she hadn't risked enough. She had sat in Parliament and been forced to listen to Zuma and his cronies as they systematically put in place the mechanisms to steal, not just from the wealthy, but from the poorest of the poor, from their own supporters, the people of the towns and villages throughout the country. She and others in the opposition parties raised their voices, but to no avail. No one was listening, least of all those from whom most was being taken. Basic services were being eroded. Nothing was being invested in renewing the infrastructure of ailing nationalised institutions and utilities that had been systematically stripped of their assets.

Her South Africa was going the way of many other African countries, and none more so than neighbouring Zimbabwe, run by corrupt politicians, fat-cat scoundrels who cared for nothing but self–enrichment and the more the better. It was not so much that their noses were in the trough, they had become the trough. Being an ANC member of parliament wasn't an obligation to work for the betterment of the people they served, it was a key to endless parties, German limos, first-class flights and accounts in Dubai, and they were doing this shamelessly. To make matters worse, although Zuma's tenure as President was due to terminate, he was understood to favour his ex-wife to succeed him both as leader of the ANC and as President in order to retain his control and to avoid prosecution for still pending criminal charges. Retribution, however, was not far away.

As Richard later wrote in the Mail & Guardian:

*The fall of Jacob Zuma had been slow-burning. Charges of corruption were eroding the ground beneath him, the noose of renting out the government to his business friends tightening around his neck with every arrest of a crony. The tsunami of support had disappeared, leaving in its stead a puddle of stagnant water.*

*Then he was gone.*

*Now the Gupta brothers and Duduzane Zuma, one of Jacob's sons, are on the run, probably safely ensconced in that laundromat of international financing, Dubai, where it is alleged that they have squirrelled away 30 billion rand. That is more than £2 billion. Or $2.5 billion. Handed to them on a plate by the people of South Africa courtesy of Zuma's loyal ANC chieftains who had sold themselves to* *their puppet-master for small reward by comparison - what irony!*

Fortunately for the country, in December 2017, Mrs Zuma was narrowly defeated by Cyril Ramaphosa in the election for the ANC Presidency. "Fortunately" is a relative word.

# Chapter 44:

## Sophie's Choice 2018

On Valentine's Day 2018, Sophie reached her 60th birthday. Normally this, coupled with Zuma's exit would occasion celebration, but she felt little joy – her dream of a democratic non-racial Rainbow Nation upholding the principles and standards of her idol, Madiba Nelson Mandela, had been reduced to rubble by his successors - first by the AIDS denialist Thabo Mbeki, then through corrupt State Capture by the despicable Zuma and his Gupta cronies. Would the new, much more likeable and hopefully less corrupt President Ramaphosa have the courage and the political constituency to ensure that Zuma would spend the rest of his life in prison? Very unlikely, thought Sophie. Given that half the ANC were still loyal to Zuma, his successor Ramaphosa, much as he despised Zuma, had no desire to split the ANC down the middle. Not only was Ramaphosa proving for the most part insipid, from Sophie's viewpoint, he was allowing rampant antisemitism.

And now Julius Malema was demanding compulsory confiscation of all farmlands held by white farmers, in spite of similar action reducing Zimbabwe - the onetime breadbasket of Africa - to a basket case. These were not idle threats, and it was becoming quite commonplace to read of yet another Afrikaans farmer who had been murdered defending his property.

Nor had the gang-wars diminished on the Cape Flats, where too many children were still growing up fatherless and in poverty. The situation had worsened considerably and there had been a surge in the murder rate as many of the newer gangs like the Junky Funky Kids defended their

## CHAPTER 44: SOPHIE'S CHOICE 2018

drug and gun rackets turf. A former police colonel had stolen over 2000 guns from police storage to sell to these gangs. The auguries were not good.

All these issues needed redressing, but Sophie realised that she had carried her fight as far as she could, and it was up to others to pick up her baton. She decided to step down from her parliamentary seat and bow out of politics, and to devote her time to completing her master's dissertation, on which she had been working on and off (more off than on!) for the past eight years. She was given a standing ovation led by President Ramaphosa, who reminded everyone there of David and Sophie's activities in the early eighties, and of her later unending fight to bring AIDS and drug abuse under control.

Finally, finally, Sophie completed her dissertation, which had morphed from a master's project to a full-blown PhD thesis, and submitted it to her supervisor. It had taken her far longer than she had anticipated (a PhD thesis always did), but she, like Edith Piaf, had no regrets. She was looking forward to spending much more time with Richard and connecting with Karen once again.

Unfortunately, Sophie was about to endure much greater personal tragedy. Her beloved Richard suffered a crippling stroke. After ten days in a coma, he left her forever. She was bereft. How she had loved that quiet man, never ceasing to be amazed by his eloquent way with the written word. Given good health she would probably live another 30 years, another half a lifetime, most likely on her own.

More in hope than anticipation, she sent an e-mail to Karen telling her what happened and giving the funeral details. She received no response, and as Karen had done before her graduation, assumed that the constant breaking of arrangements had got Karen so pissed off that she couldn't be bothered. Why oh why do humans have so little faith in their friends? Why do they always blame themselves?

Sophie had expected the funeral to be a relatively low-key affair, but the event was attended by over two hundred people. She knew Richard had been highly respected, but the small chapel was filled to the rafters with friends, news colleagues, and not least by politicians from across the political divide. It suddenly struck her that they were there not only to respect Richard but to honour her as well, but, much as she appreciated the acts of homage, the company she wanted most was not there.

Then, like the whisper of a breeze, she felt a presence move quietly up to her side. She did not have to look to know it was a tall, still beautiful woman. Although Karen rarely left home these days except to go to work, she had asked Dr Errol for the afternoon off and made her way to the cemetery chapel and pushed her way through till she reached Sophie's side. Never had Sophie been so pleased to have her friend next to her. Karen held her hand through the moving eulogy delivered by the editor of the Mail & Guardian. He paid tribute to a man who had always fought bigotry, prejudice and corruption. Karen did not leave Sophie's side till the last well-wisher left the chapel, till there was just the two of them. And only then did Sophie's tears flow, and this time they flowed sorrowfully.

This was payback time for Karen. Over the next few weeks, she rarely left Sophie's side in the evenings and on weekends. Sophie had a strange realisation: in all the years she had known Karen, they had only really spent a tenth of them in each other's company. She discussed this with Karen, who also had a very interesting lightbulb moment: a best friend is not someone you chat to every day or see every month, it's whom you love unconditionally, regardless of your time apart.

# Chapter 45:

*Bali 2019*

Eventually, Sophie realised that mourning had to end, and that life had to be lived.

'Hey, Karen, enough of the sad stuff. I think the time has come for us to get off our arses and do some travelling.'

'Deffo up for it, babe, I've got stacks of leave due to me, and d'you what, I'm more than sixty and I've never ever been out of the Cape.'

Well, now's the time, kiddo, let's get some brochures and get the effen'ell out of here.'

With no one else to support, both realised that they had earned and saved enough to start taking the holidays that circumstances had always denied them. Karen had many weeks of leave due to her, and Dr Errol as always was pleased to oblige. He had by now got quite used to this woman's comings and goings.

Karen was correct in saying she had never been abroad, she had never even left Cape Town except for the Swartberge and Paternoster. She had never been on an aeroplane nor on a ship. And now here she was, suggesting to her friend that they take a flight to a place somewhere far away and join a cruise. Sophie of course thought this was a wonderful idea, and the two headed to a travel agent at the Waterfront to discuss possibilities.

They decided to fly to Bali. The flight was a long one, necessitating a stop in Hong Kong, a city so big and crowded and buzzy that it made Cape Town look like Sleepy Hollow. After a day of sight-seeing and market-shopping that left Karen gobsmacked and breathless, they caught their connection to Ubud.

After a few days of being pampered by the delightful Balinese in a wonderful seaside resort, they boarded a beautiful clipper ship with a hundred other middle-aged people to voyage under sail around the islands. Most of the actual sailing took place in the early evening and through the night, and each departure was heralded by the theme music by Vangelis from that wonderful film 'Chariots of Fire' being blasted through the ship's speakers as the ship's crew hoisted the sails. On one occasion, as the sun was setting, Karen scaled a rope ladder on the tallest mast all the way up to the crows' nest where the view of sea and horizon was little better than on the deck but the sense of achievement was huge. Sophie, being Sophie, had no desire to indulge in such frivolities, but it was she who sat at the right hand of the ship's Captain at dinner, although it was Karen who thought the Captain's cabin very elegant indeed.

When they were not at sail, the passengers' days were spent snorkelling in crystal-clear water and barbecuing on small beaches in palm-covered coves, and the two women were feeling for the first time what it was like to be somewhere for themselves. The highlight was a stop at a small island to view the Komodo dragons – giant prehistoric scale-covered lizards up to three metres long. They were informed that being bitten by one of these creatures invariably proved fatal, and the fact that all that protected them from such a fate was a long stick with a forked tip in the hand of a single guide was not entirely comforting. They did however make it safely back to the Star Clipper for dinner and a night on deck sharing drinks with some very interesting fellow passengers and dancing to the one-man orchestra that was Luigi Santorini as he played and sang his vast repertoire of songs old and new on his electric keyboard.

There was one individual who dominated the dance floor and, despite being in his mid-seventies and the oldest passenger on board, he was tireless and inspiring. He

## CHAPTER 45: BALI 2019

would salsa, cha-cha, rumba and rock'n'roll for three hours without a stop and encouraged many others who would not otherwise have stepped onto the dance floor to do just that. The two women, both fit, joined in whenever they could, and when there were no men to dance with, danced with each other.

Karen persuaded Sophie that they had both paid their dues, much, much more than their dues, and it was indeed time to dance. You don't stop dancing when you grow old, she told Sophie, you grow old when you stop dancing. It was time to grow younger, and a new life was about to happen.

# Chapter 46:

## *Salt River – the Shelter 2019*

On their return, Karen decided that it was time to give notice of resignation to Dr Errol, not for the first time but definitely for the last, and that proved the catalyst for Errol to sell the practice to his associate, Dr Stoffel Smit.

Sophie had taken over Richard's mantle and busied herself writing for the Guardian while Karen found the time to create sculptures and thought that perhaps she might be ready to exhibit, then decided against it - travelling was too much fun! The Komodo trip proved to be the first of several to exotic destinations they had read about – the Patagonian fjords on a cruise liner; Petra and Wadi Ram in Jordan by Land Rover, both so ancient and interesting; Jerusalem and Tel Aviv on a minibus, each place more interesting than the last. This was Sophie's very first trip to Israel, the ancient land that was so dear to her – she loved everything about it, but it was the energy of its people and the ability to live each day as if it was their last that most astonished her.

However, for people such as the two sisters, as they now regarded themselves, hobbies, writing and travel could only provide temporary respite from what life expected of them, what Matron Gray all those years ago had drilled into their psyche – they were there to serve.

'Karen, remember you told me that you had got involved with a local battered women's shelter – does it still function?'

'I'm not sure, but I think it folded due to lack of funds. In fact, I'm sure it doesn't exist any longer.'

'Well, how's about we resurrect it, and combine it with a centre for drug rehab advice?'

'Great idea, Sophie, but there's just one tiny little problem with your suggestion.'

'Wozzat?'

'How are we going to fund it?'

'Simple, babe, we are going to use a slice of my inheritance that's lying around in a building society doing very little. I don't intend to pay for the shelter ad infinitum, we just need the start-up costs, and once it's up and running we can get the province to support it.'

'What happens if they don't?'

'They will, because I know the right people. Do you remember what Helen Suzman said, nothing ever grew by doing nothing.'

'Except weeds and Kobus's dick.'

'Karen, have you always been a smart-arse? I'm serious about this.'

'Ok, I'm up for it if you are.'

Obz having become too middle-class and expensive for such activities, the search for a property in Salt River began. Neighbouring Salt River, closer to the docks, like District 6, always had a poor working-class population of mostly non-white people serving the garment industry factories. Somehow it had survived the apartheid Group Areas Act but did not survive the import of cheaper foreign textiles and clothing, and although never salubrious, had become very run down. The drug barons and gangs had found this fertile territory, and violence was never far away. To counter this, a vigilante group named PAGAD [People Against Gangsterism And Drugs] had been formed whose modus operandi was to burn down the homes of drug dealers, often with the criminals still inside, and had itself come to be proscribed as a terror organisation. Unfortunately, as was so often the case, it was the women who suffered most. Beatings of women by their drugging, unemployed men were commonplace, and there was no shortage of women in crisis.

Four months later, the doors of the sanctuary opened to their first guest. Then to another. Then to lots of others. Sophie invited Ms Selina Ncube, a progressive black member of the provincial council to come around and observe their project. Selina was another who for years had worked to bring the ANC into government and then become thoroughly disillusioned by the snouts in the trough. She had left the party and had found her way into the Democratic Alliance. She was a respected figure in one of the few provinces in South Africa that was not ANC-controlled. Selina, who knew and respected Sophie through her time at the Cape parliament, was massively impressed by Karen's commitment and energy. Selina thought the project very worthy and promised to ensure that the necessary funds would be raised on a regular basis. Karen would be in charge of the day-to-day running of the sanctuary, and Sophie's job was to ensure they were adequately staffed and never ran out of funds.

It proved to be very labour intensive, but neither of them had ever shirked hard work, despite Matron Gray's initial reservations all those years ago. The two 'sisters' ran the project for a couple of years, sadly having to watch it grow in number and size. When they felt their mission had been accomplished, they decided to hand it over to Ms Ncube, who had kept her promise and who was only too happy to be handed the reins and given the responsibility.

# Chapter 47:

## *Farewell 2020*

There was one more event to be heralded. Sophie's mother Hannah was about to celebrate her 100th birthday, and although the dear old lady was frail, she was in full control of all her faculties. Sophie, together with the other senior citizens at her retirement home that had now grown into a small village, decided that a large party should be held. There was to be a special surprise of which only Sophie was aware: she had arranged for first-class tickets to be sent to Solly and Masha to fly to Cape Town from Berlin.

They were met at the airport by Sophie. With the exception of Masha's failing eyesight, both were in very good health. Hannah of course was not present because their visit was to be a complete surprise. 'I really did not think we would ever see you again, Sophie, and definitely not in South Africa. The flight was wonderful, so much *shnaps* and delicious *happschen* - we were treated like royalty', beamed Solly. Masha simply clutched Sophie and smothered her in kisses as the tears streamed down her cheeks, soon to be mingled with Sophie's own. As with everyone arriving at Cape Town airport, the drive into the city in the sight of the poverty-ridden townships they passed was a kick in the groin. This did not last, as they were taken to the luxurious Mount Nelson Hotel, one of Cape Town's most enduring and treasured institutions, for the evening. As they sat on the veranda enjoying a glass of wine, Masha looked up at Table Mountain towering above them enveloped by the cloud that was its tablecloth, and said 'I heard it was beautiful, and even with my poor eyesight, I can see why.'

They would not be presented to their sister until the very moment that Sophie would call on them to propose the toast to Hannah, Sophie's only concern being that the shock of seeing them should not cause a premature end to the party. Fortunately, it didn't, and the smile that lit Hannah's craggy face when her brother and sister-in-law walked into the room was like the sun rising over Table Mountain. It had been forty years since they last set eyes on one another. Sophie had asked Solly to prepare a speech, and despite English not being his first language, he delivered the goods with intense passion. Hannah took each by the hand and hung on to every word of Solly's oration, which was not only about the ability of families to endure, but also of the faith they had that their people would do so as well. Sophie reflected wistfully that she would not be contributing to this ongoing eternal story but felt no regrets that she had not added to the population of planet Earth.

During the time Solly and Masha spent with Hannah, they and Sophie never left her side, reminiscing joyfully about their earliest days and remembering with sadness those who had perished. How Sophie loved these two intelligent people who had lived through the worst of the twentieth century without rancour or anger!

Three days before their scheduled departure, Solly had cause to deliver a second oration, this time at Hannah's funeral. Their sister, Sophie's mother, had passed away peacefully in her sleep ten days after her centennial celebration, a quiet end to a quiet life. She had outlived Cyril by a quarter of a century, twenty-five years that had seen the promise and excitement of the Mandela rainbow nation being decimated by AIDS and State Capture. Nevertheless, her last ten days were amongst the happiest of her life, spent with the three people she treasured most. Solly and Masha did not weep as they said their goodbyes first to Hannah, and then to Sophie at the airport - they were far too inured and accepting of life's vicissitudes for

## CHAPTER 47: FAREWELL 2020

that, but expressed their gratitude for having been able to share the two important events that had occurred during their short stay. They also extracted a promise from Sophie that she would fly to Berlin to celebrate their big birthdays in three years' time. This was a promise Sophie was only too happy to make.

The two women orphans decided it was time to move into Hannah's former home in Fresnaye. The house had been rented out for years but was now vacant because the tenants had decided to emigrate to London where their son was a successful stockbroker. The building had been well cared for, the riempie stoel and the Pierneef were restored to their former positions, and memories found their way out of every crevice where they had been waiting patiently for the propitious moment to emerge. This seemed as a good a place as any for them to enjoy their golden years – together as always, even when they were apart. Except that it didn't turn out that way.

# Chapter 48:

## *The Plague 2020*

For several years, diverse groups of professional people – politicians, epidemiologists, mathematicians, medical practitioners – had heard rumours that the world was at great risk of a super-virus that, if and when it happened, would annihilate great swathes of population everywhere. Sophie had certainly heard these doomsday prognostications when she was deputy Minister of Health, but she was only too well aware that the ANC government was far less interested in what might happen in future than in what *was* happening now. What they were interested in now was plundering whatever funds they could lay their hands on from every department they controlled, which was pretty much everything. For several years already, hospitals had become chronically underfunded. Doctors, unions and management fought over scarce resources, and it was mostly those who were at the point of delivery who came short while administrators thrived. One senior doctor described the situation as "an epic failure of a deeply corrupt system", while another spoke of "institutional burn-out ... a sense of chronic exploitation, the department of health essentially bankrupt, and a system on its knees with no strategic management".

And that was *before* Covid-19 struck.

Paradoxically, the first cases to be reported were in affluent white areas and seemed to have been brought in from America by small groups of people returning from holiday. The large mass of the black and mixed-race population seemed unaffected at first, and this of course led the government to say it was a "white disease". The firebrand maverick leader of the Economic Freedom Fighters went even further and said it was a "rich Jew

## CHAPTER 48: THE PLAGUE 2020

disease." The numbers however were few, and to his credit, President Ramaphosa reacted quickly, and the country went into total lockdown. Unfortunately for the people of colour, lockdown meant being locked into their poverty-stricken townships where there was chronic overcrowding, lack of food supply and a total cut-off from work opportunity. The supermarkets and shops dried up. People were starving. The none-too-bright Minister of Health banned the sale of cigarettes because Covid affected the lungs, and this led to a thriving underground market economy. Large groups of people congregated at protest meetings where social distancing was an impossibility, so the disease spread to the masses and became rife. As was the case with AIDS, there was chronic under-reporting, so the situation did not seem nearly as bad as it really was.

Karen and Sophie, on the other hand, although also in lockdown were relatively unaffected. Yes, they were told not to leave their home, but when home was Fresnaye and not Manenberg, that was hardly a hardship. Nevertheless, being who they were, they viewed the tragedy playing out twenty kilometres away with growing concern. It took an exclusive, weeks-long BBC investigation inside filthy hospitals in South Africa to expose an extraordinary array of systemic failures resulting in exhausted doctors and nurses being overwhelmed with Covid-19 patients and a health service near collapse. That investigation was the tipping point for Karen. What was she doing sipping wine on a balcony watching beautiful sunsets when there was stuff to be done? As was always her way, the thought became the action.

'Sophie, I can't just sit and watch this – I'm going to go back to Manenberg to see what I can do to help.'

'I damn well think you should, but you are not going alone. I'm joining you.'

'I don't think that a good idea. Remember what I said when you wanted to go listen to Abdullah Ibrahim?'

'Of course I remember. You said I'd count the number of white girls there on the finger of one finger.'

'Exactly. Same applies now.'

'Exactly. I went with you then and I'm coming with you now. I'm the nurse, remember?'

'Think, Soph. You've always cared about the underdog, always been prepared to put yourself at risk for others less fortunate than you. But you know what, it was mostly from a distance. Let's be clear my Sophie, working in Manenberg is nothing you've ever experienced in your life. Deffo not a place for white girls with clean hands.'

'Listen carefully, Karen. You go, I go. I put up with three years of crap at Groote Schuur, I never once complained. I will do what I have to now, and I won't complain this time either. It's time for me to broaden my horizons, live how the other half lives.'

'So how come you waited so long?'

'Cut the sermon, let's go pack.'

The two women decided that travelling between Fresnaye and Manenberg was not an option, so their first act was to rent a small apartment near the hospital. Not that they really needed this, because there was little time for rest. Nothing could have prepared them for what was to follow.

As a doctor (one of only two infectious disease specialists in a province with a population of about seven million) informed them, 'The hospital has been without a permanent chief executive officer or management team for a year and a half, after the last team was sacked for alleged corruption. We were working with a skeleton staff even before Covid-19 and now we're down another 30%. Covid has opened up all the chronic cracks in the system. Services are crumbling under the strain, and it's creating a lot of conflict.'

Karen and Sophie were well aware that patients had been literally fighting for beds and many were sleeping under newspapers. Medicines and oxygen were in short supply. What they were unprepared for was the uncaring and damaging actions of South Africa's powerful unions during the crisis – they had been extremely active in bringing their people out. Laundry workers, cleaning staff, porters and some nurses had gone on strike. The sudden union-backed closure of smaller clinics in particular pushed more patients towards the city's big hospital, quickly overloading the facility. As the doctor said, 'Any sense of altruism or duty has gone. It went a long time ago. Each time one staff member tests positive, all staff down tools.'

When key staff began to strike or fall sick with coronavirus, nurses were forced to act as cleaners; surgeons were washing their own hospital laundry and there were alarming reports of unborn babies dying in overcrowded and understaffed maternity wards. There was a total lack of personal protective equipment, oxygen shortage, a severe shortage of ambulances, no ventilation.

The township was beset by fear and sense of a deepening crisis. Physical, mental and emotional fatigue became the currency everywhere. Departments were turning on each other and using Covid-19 as an opportunity to air every grievance that ever happened, and everything was blamed on the legacy of apartheid.

Nevertheless, the two women were not there to change union policy. They were there to add two pairs of hands to a dreadfully overstretched staff. Was this appreciated by the staff? In Karen's case, totally. Her reputation acquired during training went before her, her experience and wisdom provided a degree of leadership that was sadly lacking, and her indefatigable energy assumed legendary status.

For Sophie, a very different experience. The word soon got around that she was Jewish, and the Jewish population of Cape Town were being blamed for the whole coronavirus pandemic in the Cape. The reason for this began with a rumour that a couple of families who had attended a bar mitzvah in New York had imported the disease on their return. When a lie is told often enough, it gains traction. The fact that Sophie was working every bit as hard as her adopted sister made no difference. She was a problem and was seen as the cause of the escalation in cases.

After they had been there for a month, one of the doctors came to Karen to say that it was unwise for Sophie to remain there – the rumours of impending action against her were rife. Sophie needed to get out, and quickly.

'We're leaving, Sophie.'

'Why "*we*"?'

'If they don't want you, they don't get me either.'

'Listen, Karen, if I could put up with those corrupt self-serving politicians, I can get through this too.'

'I didn't want you here to begin with, but you insisted. Do you remember all those years ago when you told me to think smart not stupid and to un-fuck my brain? Well, this is payback time. We are both doing a good job here, but in the grand scheme of things, it makes bugger-all difference. The nurses will be overworked with or without us. Some will die. Patients will die here with or without us. This Covid thing is bigger than us, so it's time to get the fuck out of here.'

They returned to Fresnaye. The luxury, the cleanliness, the lack of bustle, it all felt completely surreal and almost indecent. Three days later, first Karen and then Sophie began to show symptoms. Because it was obvious that they had contracted the virus while still at Manenberg, this lessened the guilt and regret they felt they felt about the circumstances of their leaving. They hadn't deserted the Titanic, they had been thrown off, and their only objective, their only duty was only to survive. They made the decision that they would not seek medical help, because it would avail them nothing but it would put a doctor at risk. They would quarantine and wait. They would recover, or they would not. That simple. Russian roulette. Sophie was the

## CHAPTER 48: THE PLAGUE 2020

one who seemed to get symptoms mildly, suffering from mild temperature, awful but short-lived headaches and extreme tiredness. All this lasted for no more than a week.

Karen, on the other hand, was hit full on. For a week she hovered on the brink of death, at times barely able to breathe. But Karen had fought terrible battles in the past and survived, and she survived this one. Her soul sister was at her side at every moment; Sophie wasn't going to let Karen escape from her a second time. Karen gradually stopped the wretched coughing and gasping for air, and slowly began to regain her strength. It took several weeks before she managed to walk without assistance, but as the days grew longer and the sunshine increased, so she strengthened.

'Phew, I was worried about you, babe.'

'Well, lucky it was me and not you, seeing that I'm so much stronger than you, white girl.'

Sophie just smiled happily.

She should not have.

As had happened twice before, first with David, most recently with Richard, *Skoppensboer* decided to contact Sophie. Just when Karen seemed to have regained her strength, just when she seemed to have recovered, just when she began to plan her long-delayed sculpture exhibition, Karen developed extreme tiredness, dizziness, loss of appetite together with loss of taste, but worst of all problems with memory and concentration. Her brain literally seemed to be encased in thick fog. Their doctor voiced the opinion that Karen was still suffering symptoms of what was coming to be known as 'long Covid'.

*Skoppensboer* was biding his time, but three weeks later he called and left his card. The Jack of Spades. The Grim Reaper would wait no longer.

The funeral was a quiet affair. Dr Errol and all his staff were there. No one else. John was gone. It was time to let sleeping dogs lie and let the dead lie in peace. Even though they had spent less than a tenth of their lives together,

Karen seemed to have always been there and Sophie knew her friend, her sister, would never leave her. From now on, though, just a bricolage of memories. Sophie thought of Kobus and Abdullah Ibrahim, how different they were as human beings; she remembered Magda's pickled fish; she even thought of John's erect penis. She remembered Matron and Marie Pienaar and the cat. Most of all, she had in her mind a tall slender girl who had been proud of how she had shown her *broekies* but not gone commando to the boys at school during netball; she who had a beautiful, chiselled face, the face of a courageous, fearless, selfless battler whose life was about her son until it wasn't.

# Chapter 49:

## *Paying the Piper  2024*

When Cyril Ramaphosa became President, there was great hope that with his proven competency in big business he would turn things around, that the economy would pick up, that priority would be given to rebuilding the decayed electricity supply system, that the rot of Zuma would be stemmed.

It didn't happen.

The biggest disappointments come when expectation is greatest. By 2024, the still popular Zuma was threatening a comeback and his presence hung like the sword of Damocles. Ramaphosa proved gutless, scared to do anything lest it cause the ANC to split down the middle. So, corruption continued, the electricity supplies dwindled and power outages got longer and water shortages followed. The country spiralled slowly downwards along its own inertia and the poor remained poor and it was worsening.

The ANC looked for a bail-out and they looked north and east but not west – Russia, China, Iran, united in their hatred of The Great Satan America, all saw the strategic benefit of investing in South Africa, but the price that the African country would have to pay would be huge. When Ramaphosa announced that South Africa would be taking Israel to the World Court in support of Gaza, it was not through any altruistic motives. They needed a scapegoat, so they blamed the much-dwindled 50,000 immigrant population from the pogroms of Russia for everything that went wrong: *they* had enslaved the 50 million other citizens, *they* were running Cape Town and the Democratic Alliance, *they* were the new apartheid and *they* had to be punished.

A World Anti-Apartheid Conference led by Ramaphosa was held in Johannesburg that had as its agenda the elimination of the scourge of Zionism and enforcing divestment from any business that supported it. It was the down-payment for financial bailings-out rendered by the wealthy Arab states. The piper had to be paid.

As Sophie observed this unfolding of mass hatred, she thought back to her mother's brother and his wife and what they had gone through in Germany; she thought about how David Rousseau had been sacrificed; about her time in England, her work with the Defence and Aid Fund. She thought about Groote Schuur and Manenberg. She thought about how Nelson Mandela's vision of a happy Rainbow Nation had proved just so much pie in the sky. She thought about how her friend had to be turned white to achieve a better life, and Sophie's heart broke.

# Chapter 50:

## *Colour Me White*

Sophie was now 65 years old, and despite feeling utterly bereft, realised that if she spent her days moping, she would sink as surely as her friend had sunk. For many years, she had got by with the presence of her friend in her head only. It was time to do it again. For Sophie, life had to continue. All that she could do now would be to learn from the lessons of her past difficult days, so that each next day would be a new beginning. There was nothing she could do other than that which she had done all her life - find a cause to which she could give her all. She would have to re-invent herself.

*

Two years later, the play *Colour Me White* based on a book of the same name was performed first at the Baxter Theatre in Cape Town then at the Edinburgh Festival to great acclaim. The play went on to be performed at the Almeida Theatre in London, winning accolades and opprobrium in equal measure. Her critics were fierce: how dare a rich white woman write about a young woman of colour who had to sell her body to pass as white? What would the author have known about drug culture in a poor mixed-race community? How dare she use the word "Coloured"? The liberal left, the woke generation, the Black Lives Matter movement were livid: this was outrageous cultural appropriation and should never have been allowed. The more the critics raged, the more theatre goers flocked to see the mixed-race actress from Cape Town give a searing performance that earned her a Bafta award, followed by a Tony when it transferred to Broadway. The young man who played her drug-addled son was similarly commended.

The author of the play, however, steadfastly refused all public appearances and suggestions of awards. *Colour Me White,* after all, was not about the author. It was a story that had been written many years before in the most difficult of times.

# *Acknowledgements*

With my grateful thanks to:

My wife Adrianne who was subjected to many redings and re-readings, for her positive suggestions;

Shyama Pereira, my first editor, who pushed me further, so much further than I ever intended to go (my first draft was 1/3 of what you have just read).

Felix Hodcroft, my present editor, who assisted in the structuring and gave me licence to express myself. Felix has been an endless source of encouragement.

Robin Carlisle Democratic Alliance MP; tireless fighter for democracy and fairness

Pam Carlisle, who inspired this story

Dr Ruth Rabinowitz, Inkatha MP

Bill Frankel, 'Mr X', lawyer and philanthropist

Dr Lothar Fulde and Prof Cyril Meyerowitz for their support

Natasha Esbach for giving me different perspectives.

I began writing this story 17 years ago and it grew and grew and grew.

## About the Author

Ed Bonner was born and educated in Johannesburg, South Africa, where he graduated as a specialist prosthodontist in dentistry. He has lived in London for many years. He is an expert witness in medico-legal cases and has given evidence in court and at tribunals on many occasions. This combined with his extensive experiences in South Africa form the backbone of his first published story, **Trouble Will Find You.**

His second novel, **A Bad Investment,** is a story about a property developer and a gold-digger whose lives intersect.

The third story, **Open Wide,** is autobiographical but written as a novel about his always interesting professional career and includes many medico-legal and clinical stories that, were they not true, would be unimaginable.

**Director, Transformed** is the humorous story of a former film director of erotica prevented from working by a crippling contract and struggling to regain his profession. It is only when he meets a surgeon battling to fund a new hospital in rural India that he re-finds a purpose in life and love.

**A Rhapsody of Composers:** In this collection of stories behind the stories that affected the lives of great composers from Bach to Bernstein, Ed Bonner has sought answers to these questions in an always fascinating and often light-hearted manner.

All have been published and are available on Amazon & Kindle.

ABOUT THE AUTHOR

**Trouble Will Find You**

The fall of a talented facial surgeon is at the heart of 'Trouble Will Find You.'

Dr Nick Simpson from Ballarat Australia is awarded a scholarship to study at University College London. His prodigious skill with a scalpel leads him to become chief surgeon at a prestigious hospital in Leeds. He and his solicitor wife are much admired. He is at the top of his game. Inexplicably, Nick goes through a crisis of self-doubt. He becomes addicted to an unnecessary medication, begins to forge prescriptions, and his career is almost ended by his disdain of ethical conduct. His life begins to spiral downwards. He has to appear before a medical tribunal where he is brought down by a vindictive female colleague and gets suspended from practising in the UK. However, he is allowed to work abroad and decides to seek a position in South Africa.

Dr Simpson attempts to resurrect himself and his career at a remote hospital in rural South Africa where he meets interesting people and experiences life in Africa with all its warts and beauty – snakes, witchdoctors, vultures, river rafting and exploding arteries. He develops a relationship with a young widow and her family who give him hope. Will he find redemption?

**Some Amazon / Kindle Reviews of Trouble Will Find You:**

What's most brilliant about this novel are the things that come, unfiltered, from writer Ed Bonner's brain and pen. It's a pacily-written, exciting and moving saga about fall and redemption. The characters are fascinating and resonant. You will learn much about advanced medical practice - and malpractice; about the tragedy of post-apartheid South Africa. And you won't be bored; not for a moment.

*I loved the surgical detail - obviously the author knows his stuff!*
*I look forward to more stories from this talented writer.*

This is an engaging book made very interesting given the author's deep and personal medical and legal knowledge .Written in a fast but nuanced pace, I quickly became absorbed in the charismatic protagonist's life and found it difficult to put the book down.

*Imbued with the author's own rich life experiences, one travels alongside, learning about medicine, the law, unknown territories and colourful people, rejoicing in their highs, shattered by their lows, expecting the worst, but hoping for the best. A well-rounded story, this is a book I would highly recommend.*

Ed Bonner is a storyteller par excellence. His deep understanding of the medico-legal world and of South Africa provides a context and a setting for Nick, the protagonist, to experience the fragility of career and the beauty of deeper self-understanding and of relationships. This is a book worth reading.

*An absorbing story of how determination and character overcome troubles of many types which confront a man of special talents but lacking in real world common sense. The author's descriptions of events, adventures, political and legal matters are so alive they provoke the reader to contemplate them as if they were the victims.*

## A Bad Investment

Jeremy Lawson, even as a child, was unattractive. Rejected by young Shelley, he resolved never to put himself in a position again where he could be hurt by anyone. He didn't need women - or friends for that matter. He just needed to be smart, and was. A lone wolf forging his own path, he would become an extremely wealthy property dealer - but not necessarily kind to those who crossed him.

Then Chloe Jenkins entered his world – with intent. A beautiful if avaricious young woman, she decided that middle-aged Jeremy was fair game to be separated from some of his wealth. Her lover, Karl Janssens, a failed footballer and cybercrime criminal with a prison record, was far more ambitious. He wanted all of it. He wasn't worried about the Nigerians…

So the game began.

ABOUT THE AUTHOR

**Open Wide**

The phone buzzes. A voice says, "Does your expert do murder?"

I suppress a snigger: "Not intentionally, as far as I am aware. No definitely not. Well, not to my knowledge, although some of his patients may say differently. To whom do I speak?"

"This is Winchester Crown Court - we've got a murder trial and we need an expert witness for the defence."

The tale of Freddie the Knife Killer is one of over 3000 unusual, even surreal medico-legal cases experienced by Dr Ed Bonner involving murder trials, medico-legal hearings, visits to prisons; cases concerning sex-workers and female genital mutilation; business schemes involving nefarious Russians and an extremely dumb Duke. He has a myriad of anecdotes about his colleagues, nurses and patients, none weirder than the certifiably insane psychiatrist, all related with humour and pathos by his long-serving manager.

**A Rhapsody of Composers**

Why?

Why did Elgar decide to sail to a city deep in the Amazon Jungle where there more mosquitos than people?

Why did Bach fight a duel? Did he really attack another musician? Did he write *A Whiter Shade of Pale?*

Why did Ravel compose a symphony only for the left hand? Why did Camille Saint-Saens not speak to his wife for 45 years?

Why was Mahler's most serious music rooted in his childhood experiences?

Why was Wagner considered a rabid anti-Semite as well as a genius?

Which composers were brought low by syphilis? Why did the composer of possibly the most popular opera of all time think it was a failure?

Why was Richard Strauss considered a Nazi sympathiser?

In this collection of stories behind the stories that affected the lives of great composers from Bach to Bernstein, Ed Bonner has sought answers to these questions in an always fascinating and often light-hearted manner.

**Director, Transformed**

You are 60 with a successful career directing erotica. What do you do when your uber-smooth agent says erotica is not what it used to be and you're dead meat, past it? His pompous lawyer has got you over a barrel with a duff contract, so you fight. In court. You attend a life-transformation seminar and meet a tempestuous Brazilian. Then you meet the surgeon who needs money to build a village hospital in India. You are good at getting money. Will this be the opportunity you are both seeking? Will your once ever-loving wife support you, or are her interests elsewhere? The story of Evan Planer's determination to prove he is not a has-been is narrated as a heart-warming, rumbustious and humorous journey from Hampstead to Bandrakut in India. You will enjoy the journey.

Printed in Great Britain
by Amazon